DUMBARTON OAKS
MEDIEVAL LIBRARY

Jan M. Ziolkowski, General Editor

THE HISTORY OF THE

KINGS OF BRITAIN

DOML 57

The History of the Kings of Britain

The First Variant Version

Edited and Translated by

DAVID W. BURCHMORE

DUMBARTON OAKS
MEDIEVAL LIBRARY

HARVARD UNIVERSITY PRESS
CAMBRIDGE, MASSACHUSETTS
LONDON, ENGLAND
2019

Copyright © 2019 by the President and Fellows of Harvard College
ALL RIGHTS RESERVED
Printed in the United States of America

First printing

Library of Congress Cataloging-in-Publication Data
Names: Geoffrey, of Monmouth, Bishop of St. Asaph, 1100?–1154. |
    Burchmore, David W., editor, translator. | Geoffrey, of Monmouth,
    Bishop of St. Asaph, 1100?–1154. Historia regum Britanniae. | Geoffrey,
    of Monmouth, Bishop of St. Asaph, 1100?–1154. Historia regum
    Britanniae. English. (Burchmore)
Title: The history of the kings of Britain : the first variant version / edited
    and translated by David W. Burchmore.
Other titles: Dumbarton Oaks medieval library ; 57.
Description: Cambridge, Massachusetts : Harvard University Press, 2019. |
Series: Dumbarton Oaks medieval library ; 57 | Includes bibliographical
    references and index. | Text in Latin with English translation on facing
    pages ; introduction and notes in English.
Identifiers: LCCN 2019007468 | ISBN 9780674241367 (alk. paper)
Subjects: LCSH: Geoffrey, of Monmouth, Bishop of St. Asaph, 1100?–
    1154. Historia regum Britanniae. | Britons—History—Sources—Early
    works to 1800. | Great Britain—History—To 1066 —Sources—Early
    works to 1800. | Great Britain—Kings and rulers—Early works to
    1800.
Classification: LCC DA141 .G46 2019 | DDC 942.01—dc23
LC record available at https://lccn.loc.gov/2019007468

Contents

CONTENTS

Introduction

TWO VERSIONS OF THE *HISTORY*

Geoffrey of Monmouth's *History of the Kings of Britain* was among the most widely read and lastingly influential books written in England during the middle ages. The standard, or "Vulgate," text of Geoffrey's work survives in nearly two hundred manuscripts from the twelfth through the fifteenth centuries, even more copies than survive of Bede. Roughly a quarter of the work is devoted to the life of King Arthur, which stands at the head of all subsequent accounts of Arthur's career in the chronicle tradition. A host of figures prominent in Arthurian romance, from the works of Chrétien de Troyes through Malory's *Morte d'Arthur* and Tennyson's *Idylls of the King,* first come to life in the pages of Geoffrey's work—names such as Merlin, Guinevere, Mordred, Bedivere, Kay, Yvain, and Gawain. It was the ultimate source of the stories dramatized by Shakespeare in *Cymbeline* and *King Lear.* More than this, it invented a sweeping account of the legendary history of the Britons that covers nearly two thousand years, from their arrival in Britain with the Trojan refugee Brutus through their final loss of sovereignty to the Saxons after the death of their last king, Cadwallader.

All of this Geoffrey claimed to have found in a "very old book in the British tongue" that was given to him by Archdeacon Walter of Oxford. Geoffrey's work, which he called simply the *Gesta Britonum* ("Deeds of the Britons"), presented a deliberate challenge to those written by the leading historians of his day, William of Malmesbury's *Gesta Regum Anglorum* ("Deeds of the English Kings") and Henry of Huntingdon's *Historia Anglorum* ("History of the English").[1] For them (as for all other writers from Bede through John of Worcester) the history of Britain began with the Romans, and dominion over the island passed to the Saxons soon after the arrival of Hengist and Horsa in 449.[2] In the half-playful, half-serious epilogue to his book, Geoffrey orders William and Henry to remain silent about the kings of the Britons, since they do not have the book that Walter brought over from Brittany.[3]

The text translated here for the first time is commonly known as the "First Variant Version" of Geoffrey's work. All of the surviving manuscripts refer to it simply as the *Historia Britonum* ("History of the Britons"). The Variant's chapter numbers, given in this volume in square brackets, were adapted from those used in Faral's edition of the Vulgate, and where the two versions differ, some numbers may be skipped or out of order. The Variant does not contain Geoffrey's prologue and dedication (opening instead with the description of Britain in chapter 5), his introduction to the Prophecies of Merlin in Book 7, or his address to Robert of Gloucester at the beginning of Book 11. In place of Geoffrey's epilogue, a later scribal addition of one sentence refers to the author as "Geoffrey Arthur of Monmouth."[4] Most significantly, where Geoffrey claims that he merely translated a "very old book" given to him by Archdeacon Walter, the author of the Variant says that he followed "the histories of the ancients," which set forth the deeds of all the British kings, from Brutus through Cadwallader. All manuscripts of the Variant include the Prophecies of Merlin, which were unquestionably written by Geoffrey himself. They had circulated as a separate *Libellus Merlini* as early as 1135, before Geoffrey's version of the *Historia* was completed. Unlike the rest of the Variant, however, the text of the Prophecies in chapters 112 to 117 is in all respects the same as that found in the Vulgate. The Prophecies were therefore probably not originally a part of the Variant but were added to the common ancestor of all surviving manuscripts from a copy of the Vulgate.[5]

On the basis of fundamental differences in vocabulary, syntax, and style, all scholars agree that Geoffrey himself did not write the Variant. Opinions as to the relationship between this text and Geoffrey's version have differed, with some regarding the Variant as an earlier version, and others as a later redaction of the Vulgate. The resolution of this question is central to understanding the nature of Geoffrey's unique contribution to medieval historiography and the development of Arthurian literature. If the Variant came first, then its author deserves much of the credit for the content and organization of Geoffrey's work, while Geoffrey's principal accomplishment was to supply the further narrative elaboration and rhetorical polish that ensured its widespread impact and enduring popularity.

ORDER OF THE VERSIONS

The first editor of the Variant, Jacob Hammer, assumed that it was the work of a later redactor who abbreviated Geoffrey's original text, added material from earlier sources such as Bede and Landolfus Sagax, and displayed a greater fondness for biblical phraseology. Shortly after Hammer's edition appeared, however, Robert A. Caldwell demonstrated that the Anglo-Norman poet Wace had used the Variant as the principal source for his *Roman de Brut,* completed in 1155.[6] Noting that Wace had also used the Vulgate in later sections of the *Brut,* Caldwell suggested that the Vulgate and Variant versions might be the same two books that Geffrei Gaimar described in the epilogue to his *Estoire des Engleis.* The first was a copy of the Vulgate, which Gaimar says Robert of Gloucester had caused to be translated from "books of the Welsh" about the kings of Britain. The second was "the good book of Oxford that belonged to Walter the Archdeacon," which Gaimar says he used to supplement what he found in the first. Since Gaimar had written even earlier than Wace, sometime in the 1130s, Caldwell suggested that the order and relationship of the Variant and Vulgate versions could be a question of major importance to the history of Geoffrey's work.

Beginning in 1957, Caldwell sought to address that question in a series of unpublished conference papers. The first examined the use of original sources in the two versions, particularly the Variant's inclusion of extraneous or contradictory information from Landolfus Sagax and Bede that was omitted from the Vulgate.[7] The second explored differences in style and narrative development, which suggested to Caldwell that the Vulgate must have been a revision of the Variant.[8] In his contribution to *Arthurian Literature in the Middle Ages,* Caldwell argued that the Variant "looks like an early draft put together from original sources," and the

Vulgate "like a deliberate revision," and he suggested that the question of authorship deserved further study.[9] It was only in his last contribution to the subject, an informal faculty lecture entirely overlooked by subsequent scholars, that Caldwell plainly stated his belief that the Variant was the "very old book" that Archdeacon Walter gave to Geoffrey, and that Walter himself was its author.[10]

Caldwell's views initially found acceptance among scholars, including R. S. Loomis, Lewis Thorpe, and Brynley Roberts.[11] In 1966 the French scholar Pierre Gallais tried to suggest that the author of the Variant must have followed Wace,[12] but his argument was refuted in 1977 by Hans-Erich Keller.[13] It was not until 1981 that R. William Leckie rejected Caldwell's theory, in part because it had been advanced in a brief note without detailed argumentation or supporting evidence.[14] According to Leckie, the author of the Variant departed from Geoffrey by describing the passage of dominion from the Britons to the Anglo-Saxons immediately after the siege of Cirencester in 595 (rather than after the death of Cadwallader in 689), and by signaling the crucial nature of that moment with the renaming of the island (an event that is not mentioned in the Vulgate).[15] Leckie concluded that the Variant represented an attempt by a later author to reconcile Geoffrey's account with prior authorities, all of which had assigned the passage of dominion to the period shortly after the arrival of the Saxons in 449. Neil Wright adopted Leckie's argument in the introduction to his edition of the Variant in 1988. Wright also relied on his own comparison of passages in which the Vulgate and Variant share material derived from Gildas and Bede.[16] He suggested that these passages show the author of the Variant had recast not the sources themselves, but the Vulgate text, including any borrowings it contained. Since 1988 all scholars have simply accepted the conclusions reached by Leckie and Wright, and the priority of the Vulgate over the Variant has been regarded as an established fact.

I believe, however, that Leckie overstated the difference between the two versions on the passage of dominion, and that Wright's discussion of the use of original sources was incomplete. The loss of dominion described in chapter 186/187 of the Variant is only temporary, as it is in the Vulgate. In both versions the Britons eventually regain control of the island under Cadwallon, and lose it permanently only after the death of Cadwallader. Wright's focus on the Variant's paraphrase of Bede in one sentence of chapter 188 ignored the fact that the same chapter contains additional material from Bede that does not appear in the Vulgate.[17] Indeed, several other chapters of the Variant (5, 54, 59, and 86) do likewise, as both Hammer and Caldwell had pointed out.[18] It is important to recognize that both versions sometimes make independent use of Gildas, Nennius, and Bede. The Variant contains language from Gildas in chapter 91 and quotations from Bede in 5, 54, 59, and 86 that are not derived from the Vulgate. Both texts often use the same material from Nennius, but in chapter 100 the Variant appears to quote from the "Vatican" version, while the Vulgate follows the "Harleian" recension.[19] The Variant's description of Britain in chapter 5 is taken almost entirely from Bede, while the Vulgate's is an amalgam of phrases borrowed from Gildas, Bede, and Nennius (and even one sentence from Henry of Huntingdon). In several places the Variant incorporates quotations from Bede that are not fully integrated with what follows, as in chapter 54 (describing Caesar's invasion of Britain before he crosses to the island) or in 86 (stating that Maximian was killed at Aquileia by Valentinian, while 89 later says that he was killed at Rome by friends of Gratian). Both of these quotations from Bede, and the inconsistencies they create, are omitted in the Vulgate.

Only where they do not make independent use of the same source can one safely assume that the version closer to the wording of that source must be the earlier text. One such case is a single sentence from pseudo-Hegesippus that is quoted almost verbatim in chapter 55 of the Variant, but more freely paraphrased in the Vulgate.[20] More instructive are the synchronisms with world history that accompany the first thirteen kings of Britain, from Brutus through Cunedagius. Both versions specify the number of years they ruled and coordinate their reigns with the pre-Roman kings of the Latins.[21] All of the synchronisms in the Variant come from Jerome's translation of Eusebius. In chapters 28 through 30, the Variant skips one generation before Capis Silvius (seventh king of the Latins) and seems to confuse him with his father, Aegyptus Silvius. The Vulgate corrects this omission, by inserting two additional synchronisms and making separate, successive references to both kings. Unlike the rest, these additional synchronisms do not come from Jerome but from the *Chronica Maiora* of Bede. If the Variant were a later revision of the Vulgate, it is unlikely that it would have retained all seventeen of the synchronisms taken from Jerome and deleted just the two that came from Bede.

Stylistic considerations also weigh against the view that the Variant was an abbreviation or abridgment of the Vulgate. Although the Variant is shorter, many of its individual chapters (at least thirty-four) use more words without adding anything in substance. Some are roughly the same in length, but are completely reworded, with differences in vocabulary and word order, and changes in the mood or tense of verbs. Overall, the Variant is generally inferior in style, displaying what Wright aptly described as a certain artless repetitiousness.[22] For example, the Variant says in chapter 177 that "succeeding him to the kingdom of Albany, Ywain was made king of the Albans," while the Vulgate reports more simply that "Ywain succeeded Auguselus to the kingdom." In chapter 24, where the Variant says that Estrildis "was so beautiful that no one could be compared to her in beauty," the Vulgate eliminates the redundancy by stating that she "was so beautiful that no one could easily be found to compare with her." A number of hackneyed phrases recur with monotonous regularity in the Variant. It says at least a dozen times that a region or populace was destroyed "by sword and fire," while the Vulgate uses this cliché on only three occasions.[23] In moments of heightened action, the Variant often shifts abruptly between the past and present tenses (sometimes within a single sentence); the Vulgate uses the historical present more sparingly and with greater consistency.[24] On the larger scale of narrative, the Vulgate is consistently an improvement over the Variant. Battle scenes are more vivid, dramatic, and suspenseful. Direct speeches are more eloquent and contribute more effectively to the motivation of the characters. After placing the two versions side by side, and comparing them sentence by sentence, I agree with Caldwell that one can more frequently and more easily explain the differences between the two if the Variant is regarded as an early draft of the Vulgate.[25]

Authorship

Wright acknowledged that if the Variant came first and was written by someone other than Geoffrey, the most obvious candidate as its author would be Archdeacon Walter, from whom Geoffrey claimed to have received the book he translated from British into Latin.[26] Many scholars have noted that Geoffrey was unlikely to have made such a claim without some degree of "collusion" by Walter.[27] What little we know about their relationship supports this assumption. Geoffrey's name appears in only a handful of documents between 1139 and 1151.[28] On three occasions Geoffrey serves as a witness to Walter's own archidiaconal *acta,* and in two others he appears together with Walter as a less senior witness to charters issued by local nobility in Oxford. On the basis of this evidence, it has been suggested that Geoffrey was a canon in the College of St. George, where Walter served as the provost; but it is equally possible that Geoffrey was a clerk or *magister* (a senior clerk with a university education) in Archdeacon Walter's own household.[29] In either case, Walter was not just a friend or acquaintance but Geoffrey's immediate supervisor, senior in both age and position. It would have been impossible for Geoffrey to have said what he did about the source of his "very old book" without Walter's knowledge and consent.

More important, we have the contemporary testimony of Geffrei Gaimar that, even before his patroness requested a copy of the Vulgate from Walter Espec, he had "previously obtained" *(ainz purchacé)* the book that belonged to Archdeacon Walter *(le bone livere de Oxeford / ki fust Walter l'arcediaen; Estoire,* lines 6462–65). Gaimar's additional comment that he had acquired this book "whether by right or by wrong" (*u fust a dreit u fust a tort*) suggests that Walter did not intend to make his book public. Ian Short has argued convincingly that Gaimar completed his poem during the fourteen-month period from March 1136 to April 1137.[30] If so, this means that Gaimar already had a copy of Walter's book near the end of 1135—several years before Henry of Huntingdon first saw Geoffrey's version at the Abbey of Bec, and quite possibly while Geoffrey himself was still at work.

The idea that Gaimar's second book was an early draft of the *Historia* was suggested by H. L. D. Ward in 1883, and independently restated by Short in 1994.[31] Caldwell and Keller believed it likely that the Variant was that draft. Neil Wright dismissed this idea as "wild speculation," arguing that there was no real evidence to support the identification of the Variant with the book described by Gaimar. But even though the first part of Gaimar's poem is lost, compelling evidence is provided by Gaimar's description of the event that both Leckie and Wright seized on as a defining feature of the Variant version: the renaming of Britain after the siege of Cirencester. The Variant says that after the Britons fled to Wales, the Saxons were called the English; their land was known as England, and it "lost the name of Britain" (*amisit terra nomen Britanniae;* 186/187.1). Gaimar introduces his account of the siege of Cirencester with strikingly similar language, describing it as the time when "*Bretaine perdi sun nun*" (*Estoire,* lines 27–32). Wace uses exactly the same words in the *Roman de Brut*—both before and after the siege—and he was unquestionably translating the Variant at this point (*Brut,* lines 13379–84 and 13641–56).

There are a number of avenues by which Gaimar could have gained access to what must have been the private draft of a book that belonged to the Archdeacon of Oxford. The College of St. George was located inside Oxford Castle. In the 1130s, the castellan of Oxford and patron of St. George's was Robert d'Oilly, hereditary royal constable under Henry I. Robert's immediate staff included the royal marshals, one of whom was Robert de Venoix, the father of Gaimar's patroness Constance fitz Gilbert.[32] Walter owed his position in the college to Robert d'Oilly, and his substantial prebend, including land in Walton and income from the Church of St. Mary Magdalene, depended on Robert's patronage. Either the constable or the marshal could have prevailed on Walter for a copy of his book. Another network of potential contacts emerges from the fact that Constance's mother (or stepmother) was the daughter of Herbert the Chamberlain.[33] Constance's grandfather and one of her uncles, Geoffrey fitz Herbert, both sat with Archdeacon Walter on the famous Treasury court held at Winchester in 1108 or 1111.[34] Another uncle, William fitz Herbert, was Treasure of York Cathedral by 1114 and served as archdeacon in the West Riding of Yorkshire until his consecration as archbishop of York in 1143.[35]

One may reasonably ask why, if the Variant was Walter's own work, he would have allowed or directed Geoffrey to revise it and take credit for the final version. I think the explanation lies in Walter's prominent position as a member of the Anglo-Norman administration. Unlike Geoffrey, Walter appears in dozens of official documents over a period of more than forty years, with a career that brought him into regular contact with leading members of the aristocracy. Although some have assumed that he was a Welshman,[36] he may have been born in Oxfordshire. The only thing we know about his family is that a paternal aunt left him some hereditary land in Shillingford (south of Oxford along the Thames between Dorchester and Wallingford).[37] He also held land across the river in Clapcot from Brian fitz Count, son of Alan IV and half brother to Conan III of Brittany.[38] Walter may have inherited the estate he held in Cutteslowe (north of Oxford) from the Aluredus *clericus* ("Alfred the cleric") who held that land from Roger d'Ivry in 1086. This Aluredus could have been the same individual who was Walter's immediate predecessor as archdeacon of Oxford.[39]

Walter was an archdeacon by 1104,[40] and he held that position until his death, in 1151. He served the first two decades of his career under Robert Bloet, bishop of Lincoln from 1097 until 1123. Bloet was a royal justice, vice-regent, and close advisor to Henry I, who witnessed 155 charters for the king.[41] In addition to being a canon in the collegiate church of St. George in Oxford, Walter was a canon *ex officio* at Lincoln Cathedral and a nonresident canon of St. Mary's collegiate church in Warwick.[42] As provost of St. George's, Walter managed a lavish endowment that received two-thirds of the tithes from at least sixty-eight manors in eight different counties.[43] H. E. Salter noted that Walter was even more prominent as a lawyer than as an ecclesiastic.[44] In 1108 or 1111 he participated in the earliest recorded session of the pre-exchequer court of the Treasury, held at Winchester in the presence of Queen Matilda, the bishops of Salisbury, Lincoln, and London, and eleven other prominent royal officials.[45] In 1125 King Henry sent Walter along with Richard Basset as his royal agents to take possession of Peterborough Abbey during the three-year vacancy following the death of its abbot.[46]

Walter retained both his position and his prominence throughout the Anarchy. King Stephen directed him to enforce the resolution of a property dispute in 1135.[47] At the beginning of 1139 he participated in the dedication of the church at Godstow Abbey, placing his own gift on the altar in the presence of King Stephen, Queen Matilda, the Archbishop of Canterbury, and the bishops of Lincoln, Salisbury, Worcester, Exeter, Bath, and Coutances.[48] At the end of that year he witnessed a writ issued by King Stephen at Salisbury, together with Bishop Robert of Hereford, Phillip de Harcourt, Waleran de Meulan, and other members of Stephen's household.[49] After Stephen was captured in the Battle of Lincoln in 1141, Walter appeared as witness to a charter issued in Oxford by Empress Matilda, together with King David of Scotland, Bishops Nigel of Ely and Bernard of St. David's, Robert of Gloucester, Robert d'Oilly, and Alexander de Bohun.[50] In the 1140s, he served as one of several judges in a famous dispute between Reading Abbey and the Abbey of St. Denis in Paris, together with the abbot of Gloucester (Gilbert Foliot), the bishop of Hereford, and the dean of St. Paul's.[51]

Need for Discretion

His record shows that Walter was a respected member of the royal administration, who managed to retain his standing in the Anglo-Norman aristocracy throughout a time of political turbulence and change. There are a number of reasons why he might not have wanted to publish under his own name an alternative history in which the Britons ruled the island through the late seventh century and hoped one day to rule again. The work risked controversy not so much for the legend of Trojan origins (which the Normans had embraced as well), or the fabulous exploits of Arthur (for which there was an eager audience), but because it systematically contradicted the canonical version of English history set forth in Bede and the *Anglo-Saxon Chronicle* and accepted by establishment historians such as William of Malmesbury and Henry of Huntingdon.[52] Walter's own bishop, Alexander of Lincoln, told Henry of Huntingdon to follow Bede wherever possible while writing the *Historia Anglorum*. According to Bede, the *Gewissae* were the early West Saxons, and Caedwalla and Ine were prominent members of the royal House of Wessex. For Walter and Geoffrey, the *Gewissae* were a British people, led by Octavius in the fourth century and by Vortigern in the fifth. The last king of the Britons, Cadwallader, was descended from the "noble race of the Gewissae" through his mother. Walter and Geoffrey's alternative history has this Cadwallader buried at Rome in 689 rather than Caedwalla, the West Saxon king described by Bede. Moreover, Cadwallader's son Ivor continues to lead the British resistance against the Saxons for another forty-eight years (sixty-nine in the Vulgate) at a time when English history tells us that Caedwalla's successor Ine ruled the island.

Regardless of whether the work was intended as parody or as a serious expression of the British historical myth—and it was perhaps a bit of both—Walter surely knew that his alternative vision of the past had the potential to offend some members of the royal family, and others among the

Anglo-Norman aristocracy to whom he owed his position and his livelihood. Henry's queen Matilda traced her lineage to the English kings of Wessex through her mother, Saint Margaret of Scotland, as did her daughter, the empress Matilda, and her niece, Stephen's queen, Matilda of Boulogne. It was Queen Matilda's interest in her relationship to Aldhelm (a member of the royal family of Wessex)[53] that prompted the monks of Malmesbury Abbey to undertake what became William of Malmesbury's *Gesta Regum Anglorum*. After her death William dedicated the work to her daughter the empress, noting that it showed how no one had a "more royal or glorious claim to the hereditary crown of England" than she. King Henry cited his daughter's descent from the House of Wessex as justification for demanding his barons' support for her succession to the throne. It is thus hardly surprising that Walter regarded his book as a private draft, allowing his younger protégé Geoffrey to take credit for the final version and seek the patronage of Robert of Gloucester. As Henry's illegitimate son, Robert did not share the queen's West Saxon royal blood. Robert's closest ally and regular companion at court was the Breton noble Brian fitz Count, who had been raised by Henry I and given the substantial honor of Wallingford. Robert's half sister Matilda, another illegitimate child of Henry I, was Duchess of Brittany, married to Brian's half brother Conan III.

The Vulgate goes even farther than the Variant in flattering the Bretons, while treating the Welsh with less respect than their relatives across the Channel. In a lengthy speech added to chapter 121, Hengist tells his troops not to fear the enemy because they have only a few "Armorican Britons," while the "insular Britons" are worthless and easily defeated.

In chapter 190 Edwin and Cadwallon are sent as young men to King Salomon of Brittany to learn the codes of knighthood and courtly manners—an anecdote that does not appear in the Variant. In chapters 194–95 the Vulgate inserts a lengthy dialogue in which Salomon expresses surprise that Cadwallon's subjects cannot resist the English, whom the Bretons hold in contempt. Cadwallon admits that his people had not maintained the dignity of their forebears, since the worthier men of the island *(nobiliores)* went to Brittany and only the unworthy *(ignobiles)* remained behind. At the same time, the Vulgate heightens the level of anti-Saxon rhetoric, calling them in chapters 119 and 204 a *nefandus populus* (accursed race) and adding in 191 a speech in which Brian harshly condemns their *proditio* (treason, betrayal) and *nequitia* (wickedness, worthlessness). When Geoffrey completed the Vulgate (somewhere between 1135 and 1138), Walter had been archdeacon of Oxford for over thirty years, and he would continue to serve in that capacity for another decade to come. It is understandable that a man in Walter's position would encourage his younger colleague to claim sole authorship of the *Historia,* allowing Geoffrey to name him only as the source of the "very old book" it pretended to translate.

Influence

If one accepts the premise that the Variant was earlier, and that it was Geoffrey's immediate source, then consideration of the changes he made to it is key to understanding the true nature of Geoffrey's literary accomplishment. Hammer and Wright have described some of the obvious differences between the two versions: the Vulgate contains more

and longer speeches, authorial asides are introduced, biblical phraseology is reduced while rhetorical passages mod-
eled on Gildas are added, entire sections are reorganized
and events reordered.[54] But this is a superficial catalog; the
deeper implications of these changes and what they can tell
us about Geoffrey's aims and methods have yet to be explored. It has been said that Geoffrey's first and last thought
was for literary effect,[55] but he made substantive changes
and additions to the Variant that go beyond simple improvements in style and narrative development. Closer examina-
tion of the manner in which Geoffrey revised, reworked,
and expanded what he found in the Variant may help to illu-
minate the perennial debate about his motives for writing
the *Historia*.

Geoffrey's version was wildly popular. His account of
early British history provided the basis for nearly every subsequent chronicle written in Latin.[56] Because the Variant
was a private draft not meant for publication, its survival
was probably an accident and its circulation was limited.
Nevertheless, its influence can be traced directly in some
versions of the Welsh *Brut y Brenhinedd*,[57] as well as in the
Old Norse *Breta sögur*.[58] It was also followed at the beginning
of the *Brut y Tywysogion*,[59] and in the preface to the C-Text
of the *Annales Cambriae*.[60] More important, because Wace
adopted it as the principal source for his *Roman de Brut*, the
Variant had an indirect impact on vernacular historiography that was far out of proportion to the small number of
its surviving manuscripts.[61] Wace's *Brut* was translated into
Middle English by Layamon and by Robert Mannyng of
Brunne. It was abridged and adapted in French by Peter
Langtoft and in the earliest Anglo-Norman Prose *Brut*. Versions of the latter were translated into both Latin and Eng-

lish; one English version was printed by Caxton in 1480 and reprinted twelve times by 1528. This vernacular *Brut* tradition, ultimately based on Wace's translation of the Variant, played a central role in shaping the popular conception of English history throughout the late medieval and early Renaissance periods.[62]

NOTES

1 On Geoffrey's unique contribution to English historiography, see Davies, *Matter of Britain*, 15–22.

2 See Leckie, *Passage of Dominion*, 3–19.

3 For a survey of the extensive scholarly debate concering Geoffrey's motives, humorous or otherwise, see Gillingham, "Context and Purposes," 99–115; and Monika Otter, *Inventiones: Fiction and Referentiality in Twelfth-Century English Historical Writing* (Chapel Hill, 1996), 69–84.

4 Geoffrey calls himself Galfridus Monemutensis in the Vulgate text and Galfridus de Monemuta in the *Life of Merlin*. His name appears in charters as Galfridus Arturus or Galfridus Monemutensis, but never as the combination of both. See Tatlock, *Legendary History of Britain*, 438–39.

5 See Notes to the Translation at 112.1.

6 Caldwell, "Wace's *Roman de Brut*."

7 "The Use of Sources in the *Variant* and Vulgate Versions of the *Historia Regum Britanniae* and the Question of the Order of the Versions," presented at the 1957 congress of the International Arthurian Society in Bangor, Wales; abstract in *Bulletin Bibliographique de la Société Internationale Arthurienne* 9 (1957): 123–24. In 2008, Caldwell's daughter, Dr. Elizabeth Kaplan, donated the original typescripts of this and the next paper to the University of North Dakota, where they are preserved at the Chester Fritz Library in the Elwyn B. Robinson Department of Special Collections. A third paper, now lost, supplemented the first two: "The Order of the Variant and Vulgate Versions of the *Historia Regum Britanniae*"; abstract published in *Proceedings of the Linguistic Circle of Manitoba and North Dakota* 1, no. 2 (November 1959): 15–16.

8 "On the Order of the *Variant* and Vulgate Versions of the *Historia Regum*

Britanniae," presented at the 1957 Modern Language Association meeting in Madison, Wisconsin; noted (with a shorter title) in *Proceedings of the Modern Language Association* 73, no. 2 (1958): 4.

9 Parry and Caldwell, "Geoffrey of Monmouth," 86–87.

10 Caldwell, "Prince of Liars," 49–51.

11 See Loomis's review of Walter F. Schirmer's *Die frühen Darstellungen des Arthurstoffes* in *Speculum* 34 (1959): 677–82, at 677; Thorpe, *History of the Kings of Britain,* 16; and Brynley Roberts, *Brut y Brenhinedd, Llanstephan MS. 1 Version* (Dublin, 1971), xiii. Thorpe and Loomis had both heard Caldwall's full presentation at the 1957 conference in Bangor.

12 Gallais, "La *Variant Version."*

13 Keller, "Wace et Geoffrey de Monmouth." Keller believed that the Variant was Geoffrey's source and suggested that Walter might have been its author.

14 Leckie, *Passage of Dominion,* 26–28.

15 Leckie, *Passage of Dominion,* 104–5.

16 Wright, *First Variant Version,* lxii–lxx. For Gildas he relied on his previous article arguing that the Variant did not contain any quotations from Gildas that were not also found, less freely rephrased and abbreviated, in the Vulgate; "Geoffrey of Monmouth and Gildas," 24–33. For Bede he provided one example (consisting of one sentence) in chapter 188, where Bede is directly quoted in the Vulgate but paraphrased in the Variant.

17 Augustine's conversion of the English and the baptism of King Ethelbert, taken from Bede, *HE* 1.23 and 25–26, are omitted from the Vulgate, as noted by Leckie, *Passage of Dominion* 106–7.

18 Wright, *First Variant Version,* lxi, discusses those chapters to prove that the Variant was not derived from Wace, but they also show that the Variant did not get them from the Vulgate.

19 All citations to Nennius refer to Mommsen's edition. I use the names assigned to different recensions in Michael Lapidge and Richard Sharpe, *A Bibliography of Celtic Latin Literature, 400–1200* (Dublin, 1985), 42–45.

20 The quotation is discussed by Jacob Hammer in "Les sources de Geoffrey de Monmouth *Historia Regum Britanniae, IV, 2," Latomus* 5 (1946): 79–82. The recent article by Neil Wright, "Twelfth-Century Receptions of a Text: Anglo-Norman Historians and Hegesippus," *Anglo-Norman Studies* 31

(2009): 177–195, does not address the difference in wording between the two versions of the *Historia*.

21 See Notes to the Translation at 22.2.

22 Wright, *First Variant Version,* lxiv.

23 Variant 37, 43, 75, 61, 62, 89, 137, 139, 154, 155, 184/186, 200; Vulgate 61, 89, 155.

24 See Variant 18, 19, 20, 21, 56, 60, 62, 91, 123, 165, 177, 178, and 203. All of these passages are translated in the past tense here. The Vulgate uses the historical present only in 19, 21, 177, and 203.

25 Caldwell, "Prince of Liars," 51.

26 Wright, *First Variant Version,* lxvi.

27 For example, by E. K. Chambers, *Arthur of Britain* (London, 1927), 55; Griscom, *Historia Regum Britanniae,* 152; Brooke, "The Archbishops," 231; and Curley, *Geoffrey of Monmouth,* 12.

28 Modern accounts of Geoffrey's life often state, incorrectly, that he first appears in 1129, based on the list of charters in H. E. Salter, "Geoffrey of Monmouth and Oxford," *English Historical Review* 34 (1919): 382–85. But Salter later showed that the first of those charters (for Oseney Abbey) must be redated to the 1140s, and the second was a forgery. See H. E. Salter, *Facsimiles of Early Charters in Oxford Muniments Rooms* (Oxford, 1929), nos. 65 and 101; and David Postles, "The Foundation of Oseney Abbey," *Bulletin of the Institute of Historical Research* 53 (1980): 242–44. Geoffrey's first genuine appearance in the record is actually in 1139 as a witness for Robert d'Oilly's gift to Godstow Abbey; E. A. Amt, *The Latin Cartulary of Godstow Abbey* (Oxford, 2014), no. 587.

29 Other members of Walter's archidiaconal household appear alongside Geoffrey in the surviving *acta;* see Brian Kemp, ed., *Twelfth Century English Archidiaconal and Vice-Archidiaconal Acta* (Woodbridge, 2001), nos. 166–71. The composition of an archdeacon's typical household staff is discussed by Kemp, xlix–lii; and by M. Brett, *The English Church under Henry I* (Oxford, 1975), 199–211.

30 Short, "Gaimar's Epilogue," 323–43.

31 H. L. D. Ward, *Catalogue of Romances in the Department of Manuscripts in the British Museum* (London, 1883), vol. 1, p. 214.

32 Constance's connection with the family of Venoix was first noted by Alexander Bell, "Gaimar's Patron: Raul le Fiz Gilebert," *Notes & Queries,*

12th ser. 8 (1921): 104–5. The implications were explored by Valerie Wall in her unpublished paper on "Culture and Patronage in Twelfth-Century Hampshire and Lincolnshire," summarized in *The Anglo-Norman Anonymous* 16, no. 3 (October 1998): 8–10.

33 In the Pipe Roll of 1130, Robert de Venoix accounts for the small remaining balance of a payment for the daughter of Herbert the Chamberlain and her dower *(dos),* indicating that she was a widow. Robert acquired two properties through this marriage: the first, in Soberton, was part of his wife's dowry *(maritagium)* from Herbert the Chamberlain. The second, in Eastleigh, had belonged to Henry the Treasurer, who may have been her first husband. The *Winton Domesday* shows that Henry had died by 1110 and that his widow acquired his house in Winchester.

34 H. W. C. Davis et al., eds., *Regesta regum Anglo-Normannorum, 1066– 1154* (Oxford, 1913–69), vol. 2, no. 1000, where it is dated to 1111. Richard Sharpe, "The Last Years of Herbert the Chamberlain," *Historical Research* 83 (2010): 588–601, argues for a date in 1108 and suggests that Walter and the two fitz Herberts were members of a jury drawn from the royal household.

35 A third uncle, Herbert fitz Herbert, was married to Sibyl Corbet, former mistress of Henry I and mother of his illegitimate children Reginald of Cornwall and Queen Sibyl of Scotland. On the connection of Robert de Venoix to this family, see Christopher Norton, *St William of York* (Woodbridge, 2006), 209 and Genealogical Table 2.

36 See M. Domenica Legge, "Master Geoffrey Arthur," in *An Arthurian Tapestry: Essays in Memory of Lewis Thorpe,* ed. Kenneth Varty (Glasgow, 1981), 22–27, at 23.

37 Amt, *Cartulary of Godstow,* no. 632. Her identity as Walter's paternal aunt *(amita)* was first noted by Julia Barrow in a review of Kemp, *Archidiaconal Acta,* in *The Journal of Ecclesiastical History* 54 (2003): 138–39. In the Godstow Cartulary her name appears as "Brityva"; London, P. R. O. E164/20, fol. 145. She is probably the "Bristeva" who in 1086 held lands from the bishop of Lincoln in nearby Dorchester and Marsh Baldon. See Berenice Wilson, "Beorhtgifu," in *Anglo-Saxon Women: A Florilegium,* ed. Emily Butler, et al. (in preparation).

38 H. E. Salter, *The Boarstall Cartulary* (Oxford, 1930), 311; Hubert Hall, *The Red Book of the Exchequer* (London, 1896), vol. 1, p. 310.

39 Kemp, *Archidiaconal Acta,* no. 166; Salter, *Oxford Charters,* no. 58; Henry of Huntingdon, *De contemptu mundi* 4 (ed. Diana Greenway, 592–93).

40 According to records that were available to White Kennett (bishop of Peterborough from 1718–1728).

41 Dorothy M. Owen, "Bloet, Robert (d. 1123)," *Oxford Dictionary of National Biography* (Oxford, 2004). Walter himself attested at least one royal charter, at Woodstock in 1111. Davis et al., *Regesta,* vol. 2, no. 1089.

42 Diana Greenway, ed., *Fasti Ecclesiae Anglicanae 1066–1300: Volume 3, Lincoln* (London, 1977), 117; Kemp, *Archidiaconal Acta,* nos. 170 and 171.

43 Salter, *Oxford Charters,* no. 58; Davis et al., *Regesta,* vol. 2, no. 1468; William Page, ed., *A History of the County of Oxford* (London, 1907), vol. 2, p. 160.

44 See Page, *History of the County of Oxford,* vol. 2, p. 6. In 1110–1111 Walter heard a plea along with the sheriff of Oxford to enforce compliance with a writ issued by Henry I. See J. Hudson, ed., *Historia ecclesie Abbendonensis* (Oxford, 2002), vol. 2, p. 174.

45 See note 34, above.

46 They are referred to as the king's "justices" *(iusticiares suos)* in W. T. Mellows, ed., *The Chronicle of Hugh Candidus* (Oxford, 1949), 99. Walter's detailed survey of the abbey's properties is preserved in the *Black Book of Peterborough,* and it is printed as an appendix to T. Stapleton, ed., *Chronicon Petroburgense* (London, 1849).

47 Davis et al., *Regesta,* vol. 3, no. 354.

48 Kemp, *Archidiaconal Acta,* no. 166; Amt, *Cartulary of Godstow,* nos. 7 and 415.

49 Davis et al., *Regesta,* vol. 3, no. 189.

50 Davis et al., *Regesta,* vol. 3, no. 629; Salter, *Oxford Charters,* no. 96.

51 The case is discussed in F. M. Stenton, "Acta Episcoporum," *Cambridge Historical Journal* 3 (1929): 1–14; and in Z. N. Brooke et al., *The Letters and Charters of Gilbert Foliot* (Cambridge, 1967), 100–101.

52 The *Historia*'s numerous departures from the conventional history of England are discussed by Wright, "Geoffrey of Monmouth and Bede"; and Flint, "Parody and Its Purpose." Davies, *Matter of Britain,* 10, refers to it as "counter-history," an outright challenge to the authorized account of the Saxon conquest found in Bede.

53 Walter's close friend Faritius, abbot of Abingdon from 1100 to 1117,

claimed that Aldhelm was King Ine's nephew (*Vita Aldhelmi* 1); William of Malmesbury disputed this (*Gesta Pontificum Anglorum* 5.186).

54 See Hammer, *Variant Version,* 8–12; Wright, *First Variant Version,* xvii–liv.

55 J. E. Lloyd, *History of Wales* (London, 1939), vol. 2, p. 528.

56 Fletcher provides a comprehensive survey in *Arthurian Material,* which is supplemented by Keeler, *Geoffrey of Monmouth and the Late Latin Chroniclers.*

57 See Roberts, *Brut y Brenhinedd,* xxxiv–xxxv.

58 See Stefanie Würth, *Der "Antikenroman" in der isländischen Literatur des Mittelalters* (Basel, 1998), 66–67.

59 See Thomas Jones, *Brut y Tywysogion or the Chronicle of Princes, Peniarth MS 20 Version* (Cardiff, 1952), 1. The Red Book of Hergest version, printed and translated in *Monumenta Historica Britannica* (London, 1848), 841, is essentially the same. The opening of the *Brenhinedd y Saesson* was based on the Vulgate.

60 Caroline Brett, "The Prefaces of Two Late Thirteenth-Century Welsh Latin Chronicles," *Bulletin of the Board of Celtic Studies* 35 (1988): 64–73. Comparison of the two prefaces shows that the so-called "Galfridian" additions to the C-Text were taken from the Variant, while those in the B-Text came from the Vulgate.

61 Alan MacColl, "The Meaning of 'Britain' in Medieval and Early Modern England," *Journal of British Studies* 45 (2006): 248–69.

62 See John Gillingham, "Gaimar, the Prose Brut, and the Making of English History," in *The English in the Twelfth Century: Imperialism, National Identity, and Political Values* (Woodbridge, 2000), 113–22.

PROLOGUE

Prologus

[5] Britannia, insularum optima, quondam Albion nuncupata est, in occidentali oceano inter Galliam et Hiberniam sita, octingenta milia passuum in longum, ducenta vero in latum continens. Terra opima frugibus et arboribus et alendis apta pecoribus ac iumentis, vineas etiam in quibusdam locis germinans; sed et avium ferax terra, fluviis quoque

2 multum piscosis ac fontibus aqua praeclara copiosis. Habet et fontes salinarum, habet et fontes calidos, venis quoque metallorum, aeris, ferri, plumbi et argenti fecunda. Eratque

3 quondam civitatibus nobilissimis viginti octo insignita. Insula haec Britones et Pictos et Scottos incolas recepit. Britones autem, a quibus nomen accepit, in primis a mari usque ad mare totam insulam insederunt; qui de tractu Armori-

4 cano, ut fertur, Britanniam advecti sunt. Qualiter vero et unde vel ubi applicuerunt restat calamo perarare sequendo veterum historias, qui a Bruto usque ad Cadwaladrum, filium Cadwalonis, actus omnium continue et ex ordine texuerunt.

Prologue

[5] Britain, the best of islands, was formerly known as Albion. Situated in the western sea between Gaul and Ireland, it is eight hundred miles long and two hundred miles wide. The land is rich in crops and trees and suitable for raising cattle and beasts of burden, even producing vines in certain areas; moreover the land is full of birds, and the water is remarkable with rivers teeming with fish and plentiful springs. It has salt springs, it has hot springs, and it is rich with veins 2 of metal—copper, iron, lead and silver. Britain was formerly distinguished by twenty-eight most noble cities. This island 3 was settled by Britons and Picts and Scots. The Britons, however, from whom it received its name, at first occupied the entire island from sea to sea; they sailed to Britain, it is said, from the Armorican region. Now it remains to inscribe 4 with my pen how and from what place they came and where they landed, following the histories of the ancients, who wove together the deeds of all of them, continuously and in order, from Brutus up to Cadwallader the son of Cadwallon.

BOOK ONE

Liber I

[6] Aeneas post Troianum excidium, cum Ascanio filio fugiens, Italiam navigio devenit. Ibique, a Latino susceptus, cum Turno Dauni Tuscorum regis filio dimicans, eum interemit. Regnumque Italiae et Laviniam filiam Latini adeptus est, de cuius etiam noomine Lavinium oppidum quod struxerat appellavit, et regnavit Aeneas Latinis annis quatuor.

2 Quo vita discedente regnum suscepit Ascanius qui et Iulius eiusdem filius dictus erat; quem apud Troiam ex Creusa filia Priami regis genuerat et secum in Italiam veniens adduxerat. Qui Ascanius, derelicto novercae suae Laviniae regno, Albam Longam condidit, deosque et penates patris sui Aeneae

3 ex Lavinio in Albam transtulit. Simulacra Lavinium sponte redierunt. Rursus traducta in Albam, iterum repetiverunt antiqua delubra. Educavit autem Ascanius summa pietate Postumum Silvium, fratrem suum ex Lavinia procreatum, et cum triginta quatuor annis regnasset, Silvium reliquit here-

4 dem. Et Ascanius cum quindecim esset annorum, genuerat

5 filium quem vocavit Silvium a Silvio fratre suo Postumo. Hic furtivae indulgens veneri, nupserat cuidam nepti Laviniae eamque fecerat praegnantem. Cumque id Ascanio patri suo compertum esset, praecepit magis suis explorare quem sexum puella concepisset. Dixerunt magi ipsam gravidam

Book 1

[6] After the destruction of Troy, fleeing with his son Ascanius, Aeneas came to Italy by ship. There, after he was received by Latinus, Aeneas killed Turnus (the son of Daunus the king of the Tuscans) while fighting with him. Aeneas won both the kingdom of Italy and Lavinia, the daughter of Latinus. The city that he built he called Lavinium after her, and Aeneas ruled over the Latins for four years. Upon his 2 death, the kingdom passed to Ascanius, who was his son, also known as Iulius, whom he had fathered in Troy upon Creusa the daughter of Priam and had brought with him when coming to Italy. Ascanius, having left the kingdom to his stepmother Lavinia, founded Alba Longa and transferred the statues of the gods and ancestors of his father Aeneas from Lavinium to Alba. The statues returned to Lavinium 3 of their own will. When carried back to Alba, they returned again to their former shrines. Ascanius raised his brother Silvius Postumus, the son of Lavinia, with the greatest piety, and after he had reigned for thirty-four years he left the kingdom to Silvius. And Ascanius, when he was fifteen 4 years of age, fathered a son whom he called Silvius after his brother Silvius Postumus. This boy, indulging a secret 5 passion, had married a certain niece of Lavinia, and made her pregnant. When his father Ascanius learned this, he sent his magicians to discover the sex of the child the girl had conceived. The magicians said that she was pregnant

esse puero qui et patrem et matrem interficeret; pluribus quoque terris in exilium peragratis ad summum tandem cul-
6 men honoris perveniret. Nec fefellit eos vaticinium suum. Nam ut dies partus venit, edidit mulier puerum et mortua est pariendo. Traditur autem puer ad nutriendum et vocatur Brutus. Et cum esset quindecim annorum, comitabatur patri in venatu sagittamque in cervos dirigens, inopino ictu sagittae patrem interfecit.

[7] Indignantibus ergo parentibus, in exilium pulsus est Brutus. Exulatus itaque navigio tendit in Graeciam, ubi pro-geniem Heleni filii Priami invenit, quae sub potestate Pan-drasi regis Graecorum in servitute tenebatur. Pirrus etenim, Achillis filius, post eversionem Troiae ipsum Helenum cum pluribus aliis inde secum in vinculis abduxerat, ut necem
2 patris sui in ipsos vindicaret. Agnita igitur Brutus suorum concivium prosapia, moratus est apud eos. Ibique in tantum militia et probitate vigere coepit, ut inter omnes patriotas valde amaretur. Divulgata itaque per universam terram fama probitatis ipsius, coeperunt ad eum confluere omnes qui de genere Troianorum ibidem morabantur, orantes ut si fieri posset a servitute Graecorum liberarentur. Quod fieri posse asserebant, si ducem haberent, qui eorum multitudinem in
3 bello contra Graecos gnaviter regere nosset. In tantum enim infra patriam multiplicati erant ut septem milia cum armis, exceptis parvulis et mulieribus, computarentur. Praeterea erat quidam nobilissimus iuvenis in Graecia, nomine Assara-cus, qui partibus eorum favebat, ex Troiana matre natus. Hic tria castella, quae sibi pater suus moriens donaverat, contra

with a boy, who would kill his mother and father; having traveled in exile through many lands he would finally arrive at the highest pinnacle of honor. Their prophecy did not 6 fail. For when the day of his birth arrived, the woman brought forth a boy but died in childbirth. The boy was given over for nursing, and called Brutus. When he was fifteen years of age, while accompanying his father on a hunt, and aiming an arrow at the stags, he killed his father with an unexpected blow from the arrow.

[7] Brutus was sent into exile by his outraged family. Thus exiled, he headed for Greece by ship, where he found the descendants of Helenus, the son of Priam, who were being held in slavery by Pandrasus, king of the Greeks. For after the destruction of Troy, Pyrrhus the son of Achilles had led Helenus away with him in chains, along with many others, to take revenge upon them for the death of his father. Rec- 2 ognizing their common family lineage, Brutus settled in among them. There he began to flourish so in military spirit and prowess that he was greatly admired among all his compatriots. Once word of his virtue had spread throughout the land, all those of Trojan descent who lived there began to gather around him, asking to be freed from slavery to the Greeks if any way could be found to do this. They assured him that it could be done if they had a leader to command their numbers valorously in battle against the Greeks. Their people had multiplied so much in that land that they 3 could now be reckoned as seven thousand in arms, excluding women and children. In addition, there was a certain noble youth among the Greeks called Assaracus, born of a Trojan mother, who favored their cause. He was vigorously defending three castles (which his father had left to him

fratrem suum viriliter tenebat; quae ei conabatur auferre
4 frater, quia ex concubina natus fuerat. Erat autem ille patre
et matre Graecus et asciverat regem ceterosque Graecos
parti suae favere. Inspiciens ergo Brutus et virorum multitudinem et munitionum opportunitatem securius petitioni illorum acquievit.

[8] Erectus itaque Brutus in ducem, convocat Troianos
undique et oppida Assaraci munivit. Ipse vero et Assaracus,
cum maxima multitudine virorum ac mulierum quae eis ad-
haerebant, nemora et colles occupant. Deinde per litteras
2 regem in haec verba affatur: "Pandraso regi Grecorum Brutus dux reliquiarum Troiae salutem. Quia indignum fuerat
gentem praeclaro genere Dardani ortam iugo servitutis
premi et tractari aliter quam nobilitatis eius serenitas expeteret, sese infra abdita nemorum recepit malens ferino ritu,
carnibus videlicet et herbis, vitam cum libertate tueri quam
3 divitiis et deliciis affluens iugo servitutis teneri. Quod si cel-
situdinem tuam offendit, non est imputandum eis cum com-
munis sit intentio captivorum velle ad pristinam dignitatem
redire. Misericordia itaque motus, amissam libertatem lar-
giri digneris et loca quae occupavit inhabitare permittas. Sin
autem, concede ut ad aliarum terras nationum cum pace li-
beri abscedant."

[9] Lectis igitur litteris, Pandrasus eorum quos in servitutem tenuerat admiratus audaciam continuo procerum

when he died) against his brother, who was trying to take them from him because he had been born to a concubine. The brother's father and mother were both Greek, and he 4 had won over the king and the rest of the Greeks to his side. Considering both the number of their men and the availability of these fortifications, Brutus agreed to their request with greater confidence.

[8] After he had been made their leader, Brutus summoned the Trojans from all directions and garrisoned the towns of Assaracus. He and Assaracus seized the forests and the hills with the great multitude of men and women who followed them. Then he addressed the king by letter in these words: "Greetings from Brutus, leader of the Trojan 2 remnant, to Pandrasus, king of the Greeks. Because it was beneath the dignity of a people descended from the illustrious line of Dardanus to be oppressed with the yoke of slavery and be treated otherwise than the dignity of their noble birth demands, they have retreated into the hidden recesses of the forests, preferring to lead a life of liberty like wild beasts, sustained by meat and grass, rather than to be confined by the yoke of servitude, overflowing with riches and delights. If this offends your dignity, you should not hold it 3 against them, since it is the common purpose of all captives to want to return to their former status. Therefore take pity upon them by considering it right to grant back their lost liberty, and allow them to inhabit the region they have occupied. Otherwise, agree to let them withdraw free and in peace to lands of other nations."

[9] Having read the letter, astonished by the audacity of those people he had up until now held in servitude, with the advice of his nobles Pandrasus immediately ordered his

suorum consilio exercitum colligere decrevit ut armis eos arctaret qui terras eius insolenter occupaverant. Oppidum-que mox Sparatinum adiit, cui Brutus cum tribus milibus fortium Troianorum obvius ex inproviso invasit et irrupti-
2 onem in Grecos et stragem magnam fecit. Porro Graeci stu-pefacti, nil tale verentes, omnes in partes dilabuntur et flu-vium Akalon qui prope fluebat transire festinant, in quo multi periclitati interierunt. Quos diffugientes Brutus inse-quitur et partim in undis, partim super ripam ferro pro-
3 sternit. Antigonus autem, frater Pandrasi, videns stragem suorum, indoluit revocavitque vagantes socios in turmam et feroci impetu in saevientes Troas se interserit. Densaque acie incedens hortatur suos viriliter resistere, telaque leti-fera totis viribus contorquet. Troes vero audacter insistentes caedem miserandam peregerunt et Antigonum captum re-tinuerunt.

[10] Brutus igitur, victoria potitus, oppidum sescentis militibus munivit, nemorum abdita petens, ubi Troiana plebs cum mulieribus et pueris delitescebant. At Pandrasus, ob fugam suam fratrisque captionem graviter maerens, nocte illa populum dilapsum coadunare non cessavit. Et, cum postera lux illucesceret, oppidum obsidere progressus est in quo Brutum et fratrem suum Antigonum, aestimabat clausos, assultumque moenibus intulit distributo exercitu per turmas in circuitu.

[11] Obsessi uero a muris viriliter resistentes, telis om-nium generum ac sulphureis taedis eorum machinationes

army to be assembled to surround with arms the Trojans who had insolently seized the territory they held. He came at once to the city of Sparatinum, against which Brutus unexpectedly launched an attack with three thousand hardy Trojans, violently assaulting and inflicting great slaughter on the Greeks. The astonished Greeks, who were fearing no 2 such thing, scattered in all directions and rushed to cross the River Akalon, which flowed nearby; many perished in the attempt. Brutus pursued those who were fleeing, and with his sword he cut down some of them in the water and some on the banks of the river. Observing the slaughter of 3 his own troops Antigonus, the brother of Pandrasus, was greatly distressed. He called his scattered comrades back into formation and with a ferocious charge against the raging Trojans, he threw himself into the fray. Advancing in tight formation, he urged his men to resist the enemy vigorously, and flung his deadly spears with all his strength. However, bravely pressing on, the Trojans completed the wretched slaughter and took Antigonus captive.

[10] After Brutus won the victory, he garrisoned the town with six hundred troops, and made for the depths of the forest where the Trojan people were hiding with their women and children. But Pandrasus, deeply distressed by his own rout and the capture of his brother, lost no time that night in reassembling his scattered people. When the next day began to dawn, he proceeded to besiege the town in which he thought Brutus and his brother Antigonus were enclosed, and with his troops arranged in squadrons all around, he launched an assault against the walls.

[11] However, fighting manfully from the walls, those besieged repelled their siege engines with all manner of

repellebant. Tandem cibi penuria et cotidiano labore afflicti, legatum ad Brutum mittunt, postulantes ut eis in auxilium festinaret, ne debilitate coacti oppidum deserere cogerentur. Brutus ergo audiens, suos in unum collegit et ad succurrendum oppidanis viriliter hortatur. Sed quia tantum non habuit exercitum ut campestre proelium inire adversus hostes auderet, callido usus consilio, proponit castra eorum noctu adire ipsosque soporatos, deceptis eorundem vigilibus interficere. Advocato itaque secreto Anacleto, Antigoni socio, quem cum Antigono captum tenebat, evaginato gladio in hunc modum affatus est: "Egregie iuvenis, finis vitae tuae Antigonique adest, nisi quae tibi dixero fideliter exsecutus fueris. Volo ergo per te in sequenti nocte vigiles Graecorum caute decipere, ut tutiorem aditum aggrediendi ceteros habeam. Tu vero callide negotium huiusmodi agens, in secunda noctis hora vade ad obsidionem, manifestaturus fallacibus verbis te Antigonum a carceribus et vinculis meis abstraxisse et usque ad convallem nemorum eduxisse illumque nunc inter frutices delitere nec longius abire posse propter insequentes Troianos, qui aditus viarum circumdederunt ne ad fratrem liberatus redeat. Sicque deludens adduces eos usque ad convallem hanc, ubi te et eos operiemur."

[12] Anacletus ergo, viso gladio, qui inter haec verba morti suae imminebat, perterritus valde promisit iureiurando sese rem quam intimaverat exsecuturum si sibi et Antigono vita daretur. Confirmata itaque huiusmodi proditione, versus obsidionem se agere coepit Anacletus et, cum iam prope castra incederet, ab exploratoribus Graecorum

missiles and sulfurous torches. Eventually, weakened by the shortage of food and the daily effort, they sent an envoy to Brutus, begging him to hasten to their aid so they would not be compelled by their overwhelming fatigue to abandon the city. Hearing this, Brutus called his men together and urged them to manfully relieve the people in the city. But, because he did not have a large enough force to risk entering into pitched battle directly against the enemy, he cunningly proposed to enter their camp at night, slip past the guards, and kill them while they were sleeping. He secretly summoned Anacletus, the companion of Antigonus, whom he held captive along with Antigonus, and after drawing his sword he addressed him as follows: "Distinguished youth, the end of your life and that of Antigonus is here, unless you are prepared to do exactly as I say. I want to use you carefully to deceive the Greek sentries tomorrow night, so that I may have safer access to attack the others. You must accomplish this cunning plan as follows. At the second hour of the night, go to the siege and deceitfully announce that you have rescued Antigonus from bondage in my prison and taken him to a ravine in the woods, and that he is now hiding among the bushes and cannot move further because of the pursuing Trojans, who blocked his escape so that he could not return free to his brother. After deceiving them in this way, lead them to this valley, where we shall await both you and them."

[12] Anacletus, eyeing the sword that threatened his death while these words were spoken, was thoroughly terrified and promised under oath that he would do as instructed if he and Antigonus were granted their lives. His treachery thus assured, Anacletus headed toward the siege and, as he approached the camp, he was taken and recognized by the

tenetur et agnoscitur. At ille, ingentem laetitiam simulans,

2 "Subvenite," ait, "viri, et si quis est non falsus amicus me, et Antigonum vestrum de manibus Troianorum eripite. Quem usque ad convallem hanc proximam nocte hac de carcere Bruti extractum eduxi. Et ecce inter vepres et nemorum densa delitescit, timens ne a Troianis iterum comprehendatur."

3 Audientes autem Graeci Anacleti verba, nihil haesitantes accelerant, arma arripiunt, et illum usque ad convaliem festinantes sequuntur. Illis denique inter frutecta progredientibus emergit se Brutus cum armatis catervis et prosilit in medium repente, factoque impetu occupat perterritos nil tale verentes ac caede durissima affecit; ulteriusque progressus per tres turmas socios suos divisit obsidionem Graecorum disturbare parans, praecepitque ut singulae turmae singulas castrorum partes adirent sine tumultu: nec caedem cuiquam inferrent, donec ipse, cum sua cohorte, tentorio regis potitus, lituo signum daret.

[13] Edocti itaque omnes Bruti oratione infra castra se recipiunt. Nec mora, insonante lituo, enses evaginant et stricto ferro hostes semisopitos invadunt; trucidant quosdam arma capessentes, quosdam inermes et somno oppressos haud segniter interficiunt. Ad gemitus morientium evigilant ceteri et, cum aliis stupefacti, ab hostibus caeduntur.

2 Neque enim tempus arma capiendi vel spatium fugiendi dabatur, cum Troes armati eos undique circumvenientes tamquam oves in caulis iugulabant. Quibus autem fugae

Greek scouts. Pretending to be overjoyed, he said: "Come 2
help me, men, if any of you is a true friend to me, and rescue
your Antigonus from the hands of the Trojans. For I brought
him to this nearby ravine tonight after freeing him from
Brutus's prison, and lo! he is hiding among the thorn bushes
in the depths of the forest, fearing to be captured again by
the Trojans."

As soon as they heard what Anacletus said, the Greeks 3
rushed without hesitation, seized their arms, and followed
him quickly to the ravine. And then, as they were making
their way among the thickets, Brutus emerged with an
armed band and charged unexpectedly into their midst; as
he made his assault, he overcame the terrified and unsuspecting guards and inflicted terrible slaughter upon them.
Moving on, he divided his troops into three bands, preparing to disrupt the Greeks' siege, and ordered them to proceed quietly in individual groups to the separate parts of the
fortress; they were not to kill anyone until he, after seizing
the king's tent with his personal guard, gave a signal with his
trumpet.

[13] Instructed by Brutus's speech, everyone withdrew inside the camp. Without delay, as soon as the horn was
sounded, they unsheathed their swords and attacked the
half-asleep enemy with weapons drawn. They slaughtered
some as they reached for their weapons, others they killed
without the slightest hesitation as they lay unarmed and half
asleep. At the groans of the dying the rest awoke and, stupe-
fied like the others, were killed by the enemy. Neither time 2
to take up arms nor space to flee was given while the fully
armed Trojans, surrounding them on all sides, butchered
them like sheep in pens. Those who chanced to flee were

beneficium contigit, scopulis elisi sub noctis tenebris prae-
cipitabantur. Cadentibus crura vel bracchia frangebantur.
Cui neutrum horum contingebat, inscius quo fugam faceret,
in prope fluentibus fluviis submergebatur. Vixque infortunium quisquam evadere potuit. Namque oppidani quoque
commilitonum adventu applaudentes, insiliebant armati atque cladem duplicabant.

[14] Brutus autem tentorium regis, ut praedictum est, aggressus sociis interfectis ipsum vivum retinere curavit. Ut
ergo sub luce aurorae ruina tanta patuit, Brutus, magno fluctuans gaudio, spolia peremptorum sociis iuxta modum cuiusque distribuere praecepit. Deinde cum Pandraso oppidum ingreditur, mortuorum cadavera sepelienda tradens.
2 Postera autem die dux inclitus Brutus maiores natu convocans, quaesivit ab eis quid de rege Pandraso agendum adiu-
dicarent quidque ab eo petendum laudarent. Qui mox diversis affectibus capti, pars partem regni ad inhabitandum
petere hortabatur, pars vero licentiam abeundi et ea quae
itineri necessaria forent. Cumque diu in ambiguo res extitisset, surrexit unus Membricius nomine ceterisque auscultan-
3 tibus ait: "Utquid haesitatis, patres et fratres, in his quae sa-
luti nostrae sunt utilia? Ultima haec sententia nobis tenenda
est, licentia videlicet abeundi, si vobis posterisque vestris
vitam et pacem adipisci desideratis. Nam si eo pacto vitam
concesseritis Pandraso, ut per eum partem Graeciae adepti
inter Danaum, invisum genus, cohabitare deliberatis, numquam diuturna pace fruemini, dum fratres et filii et nepotes
eorum, quibus tantam intulistis stragem, vobis immixti vel

thrown headlong when they smashed into boulders in the dark of the night. Their legs or arms were broken when they fell. Those who suffered neither fate, not knowing which way to run, were drowned in the streams flowing nearby. Scarcely anyone was able to escape misfortune. Celebrating the arrival of their compatriots, the townsfolk also leaped forth equipped with arms and redoubled the slaughter.

[14] After Brutus had attacked the king's tent, as he said he would, and killed his companions, he took care to keep the king himself alive. When the light of dawn revealed the magnitude of the enemy's defeat, Brutus, swelling with great joy, ordered the spoils of the dead to be distributed to his men, each according to his measure. Then he entered the city with Pandrasus, handing over the bodies of the dead to be buried. Next day the noble duke Brutus, summoning the 2 elders, asked them how they advised him to deal with King Pandrasus, and what they thought should be demanded from him. Then, seized by different emotions, some urged him to ask for a part of the kingdom to live in, others for permission to depart and provisions to sustain them on their journey. And after the matter had remained in doubt for some time, a man named Membricius stood up and, with everyone listening, said: "Why are you undecided, fathers 3 and brothers, about these things which are vital to our well-being? We must choose the latter alternative, namely permission to depart, if you wish to secure long life and peace for yourselves and your posterity. For if you choose to grant Pandrasus his life in return for being granted a part of Greece to inhabit among the Danaans, a hated people, you will never enjoy a lasting peace while the brothers and sons and grandsons of those upon whom you inflicted such

4 vicini fuerint. Memores caedis parentum, aeterno vos exsufflabunt odio; nec vobis minores vires habentibus, facile erit resistere, dum generatio eorum multiplicata generationi succedet. Eorum enim numerus cotidie augebitur, vester vero minuetur. Laudo itaque et consulo in parte mea, si ceteris videbitur, ut petatis ab illo filiam suam primogenitam, quam Innogen vocant, ut duci nostro copuletur et aurum et argentum, naves et frumentum et quae itineri neccesaria fuerint. Et si impetrare poterimus, licentia sua alias nationes petamus."

[15] Ut ergo finem dicendi fecit, acquievit tota multitudo atque suasit ut Pandrasus in medium adduceretur. Nec mora adductus, optio ei datur eligendi aut filiam suam, sicut praedictum est, Bruto coniugem dare aut suum interitum et fra-

2 tris. Qui respondens ait: "Nihil mihi vita praestantius, nihil iocundius censeo et, licet invitus et coactus sub mortis periculo externo viro et hosti filiam meam carissimam daturus sum, solacium tamen habeo quia probo eam copulo et nobili, quem ex genere Priami et Anchisae creatum fama declarat. Do ergo ei filiam meam primogenitam Innogen, do etiam aurum et argentum, naves et frumentum, vinum et oleum, et quicquid itineri vestro dixeritis esse neccesarium.

3 Et si, a proposito vestro divertentes, cum Graecis commanere volueritis, tertiam regni mei partem ad inhabitandum vobis concedo. Sin autem, cetera prosequar in vestra deliberatione."

4 Conventione itaque facta, diriguntur legati per universa Graecie litora colligere naves; quae collectae trecentae

slaughter are your neighbors and mingled among you. Re- 4
membering the slaughter of their relatives, they will despise
you with eternal hatred; nor will you, having smaller forces,
be able to resist them easily, while for them generation will
follow generation in ever greater numbers. Their population
will continuously be increased, while yours will be diminished. For my part, then, I recommend and advise, if the rest
of you approve, that you should ask for his firstborn daughter, whom they call Innogen, to be joined with our leader,
and for gold and silver, ships and grain, and whatever will be
necessary for our journey. And if we are able to obtain it,
with his permission let us seek out other nations."

[15] When he made an end to his speech, the entire gathering agreed and directed that Pandrasus be brought among
them. He was brought without delay, and was offered the
choice either to give his daughter in marriage to Brutus, as
just said, or to die along with his brother. In response, he
said: "I count nothing more important to me than life, noth- 2
ing more pleasant, and if I must give over my most beloved
daughter to a foreign husband and an enemy, reluctantly and
compelled by the threat of death, I take comfort in the fact
that I join her with a worthy and noble man whom public
opinion declares to be sprung from the line of Priam and
Anchises. Therefore, I give him my firstborn daughter Innogen, and I also give gold and silver, ships and grain, wine
and oil, and whatever you say is needed for your journey. If 3
you wish to change your plan and live among the Greeks, I
grant to you a third of my kingdom to live in. If not, I shall
proceed in accordance with your decision."

An agreement having thus been reached, messengers 4
were sent to gather ships from all the shores of Greece.

viginti quatuor erant numero et omni mox genere farris onerantur. Filia regis Bruto maritatur; quisque, prout dignitas expetebat, auro et argento donatur et, peractis cunctis, erectis velis, secundis ventis abscedunt.

[16] Prospero itaque cursu, duobus diebus et una nocte sulcantes maria, applicuerunt in quandam insulam nomine Leogetiam quae ab incursione piratarum vastata ac omni habitatore deserta antiqua tamen retinebat delubra. In qua feras diversorum generum reperientes copiose naves suas venatione refecerunt. Venientes autem ad quandam desertam civitatem, templum Dianae in ea reperiunt ubi imago

2 eiusdem deae responsa quaerentibus dabat. Qui, mox litatis victimis, a numine futuri itineris praesagia requirunt: quae vel qualis patria eis sedes certae mansionis debeatur. Communicatoque omnium assensu, assumpto Brutus secum Gerione augure et duodecim maioribus natu, circumdatus tempora vittis, abdita templi penetrans, ante vetustissimum delubrum, ubi ara deae statuta fuerat, vas sacrificii vino plenum et sanguine candidae cervae dextra tenens, erecto vultu ad effigiem numinis, silentium in haec verba dissoluit:

3   "Diva potens nemorum, terror silvestribus apris,
      cui licet anfractus ire per aethereos
    infernasque domos, terrestria iura resolve;
      et dic quas terras nos habitare velis.
    Dic certam sedem, qua te venerabor in aevum,
      qua tibi virgineis templa dicabo choris."

When assembled, there were three hundred twenty-four in all, and they were soon loaded with every kind of grain. The king's daughter was married to Brutus; to each man was given gold and silver according to his rank; and after everything was ready they departed with hoisted sails and following winds.

[16] Plowing through the waves on a favorable course for two days and one night, they landed at a certain island by the name of Leogetia which, although devastated by an attack of pirates and devoid of all inhabitants, nevertheless still featured an ancient temple. There, finding wild beasts of many kinds, they replenished their ships after a fruitful hunt. Coming to a certain deserted city, they found in it a temple to Diana where a statue of that goddess gave answers to those who questioned her. Once sacrifices had been offered, they asked the goddess for predictions about their future journey, and about which and what kind of country was destined to be their permanent home. By the common consent of all, Brutus entered the innermost precinct of the temple along with Gerion the augur and twelve most senior elders, with ribbons circling his brows. Standing before the most ancient shrine where the altar of the goddess had been set up, holding a consecrated vessel filled with wine and the blood of a white hind in his right hand, with his head upright, Brutus broke the silence with these words:

> "Mighty goddess of the forests, terror of the woodland boars, who can travel among the heavenly orbits and the infernal realms, unleash your earthly authority and tell us which lands you wish us to inhabit. Tell us of a settled home where we can worship you forever, and where I shall dedicate temples to you with choirs of virgins."

4 Haec ubi novies dixit, circuivit aram quater fuditque vinum quod tenebat in foco iuxta morem litantium ibi accenso. Postea recubuit super pellem cervae, quam ante aram extenderat, invitatoque somno obdormivit. Eratque tunc quasi tertia noctis hora. Tunc visum est illi deam astare ante ipsum et sese sic affari:

5 "Brute, sub occasu solis, trans Gallica regna
insula in Oceano est, undique clausa mari:
insula in Oceano est habitata gigantibus olim,
nunc deserta quidem, gentibus apta tuis.
Hanc pete: namque tibi sedes erit illa perennis;
hic fiet natis altera Troia tuis.
Hic de prole tua reges nascentur, et ipsis
totius terrae subditus orbis erit."

6 Tali visione dux expergefactus, vocatis sociis, rem per ordinem narravit ut sibi dormienti contigerat.

[17] Dehinc ad naves repedavit et, flante secunda aura, prospero cursu triginta dierum spatio venerunt ad Affricam, deinde ad Lacum Salinarum et ad Aras Philistinorum. Hinc navigauerunt inter Ruscicadam et Montes Azarae. Ibi ab incursione piratarum maximum passi sunt periculum; victo-

2 riam tamen adepti, spoliis eorum ditati sunt. Porro flumen Malvae transcurrentes applicuerunt in Mauritaniam. Quam penuria cibi et potus e navibus egressi vastaverunt a mari usque ad mare. Inde, refertis navibus, petierunt Columnas Herculis ubi Sirenes, monstra maris, apparuerunt eis; quae

He said this nine times, circled the altar four times, and   4
poured the wine he held upon the hearth, lit according to
the custom of those making a sacrifice. After that he lay
down upon the skin of the hind which he had spread before
the altar, and fell into a deep sleep. It was then about the
third hour of the night. Then the goddess seemed to stand
before him and to address him in this manner:

> "Brutus, beneath the setting sun, beyond the king-   5
> doms of Gaul, there is an island in the Ocean, sur-
> rounded on all sides by the sea: the island in the Ocean
> was formerly inhabited by giants, but now it is de-
> serted, and suitable for your people. Seek it out: for it
> shall be your home forever. Here shall rise up a new
> Troy for your offspring. Here kings shall be born from
> your descendants, and to them will be subjected the
> whole circle of the earth."

Awakened by this vision, the duke summoned his comrades   6
and told them exactly what had happened to him while he
slept.

[17] After that he returned to the ships and, with a following wind blowing, by a favorable course of thirty days time
they came to Africa, then to the Lake of the Salt Pans and to
the Altars of the Philistines. From here they sailed between
the Ruscicada and the Mountains of Azara. There they suffered great danger from an attack by pirates; but having won
victory, they were enriched with the pirates' booty. Further   2
on, passing over the River Malva, they landed in Mauritania.
Leaving their ships, they plundered it from sea to sea owing
to their shortage of food and drink. From there, after filling
up their ships, they made for the Pillars of Hercules, where
the Sirens, monsters of the sea, appeared to them; after the

ambiendo naves fere obruebant. Elapsi tamen inde Hispaniae oras praetermeant ubi iuxta litora invenerunt quatuor generationes de exulibus Troianis quae Antenoris fugam comitate fuerant. Quorum dux Corineus dictus erat, vir magnae virtutis et audaciae. Agnita itaque invicem veteris originis prosapia associatus est eis cum maxima populi parte cui praesidebat. Deinde Aquitaniam a dextra pretereuntes ostium Ligeris ingressi anchoras fixerunt. Moratique sunt septem diebus, situm regni explorantes.

[18] Regnabat tunc in Aquitannia Gofarius rex Pictus. Hic cum audisset, fama indicante, externam gentem in fines regni sui applicuisse, misit nuntios ad explorandum utrum pacem ferrent an arma. Nuntii autem classem petentes obviauerunt Corineo egresso iam cum ducentis viris ad venandum. Mox allocuti eum cur sine licentia saltus regis ad venandum invasissent (statutum enim ab antiquo fuerat neminem sine principis iussu ibidem debere feras capere), Corineus respondit se prohibitionem nescire sui regis neque etiam huiuscemodi rei alias prohibitionem audisse, sed nequaquam fieri debere. Quo dicto unus ex illis, Imbertus nomine, curvato arcu sagittam in ipsum direxit. Vitavit eam Corineus impetumque faciens in Imbertum ipso arcu quem tenebat capud ei in frusta conscidit. Diffugientes autem socii Gofario necem Imberti nuntiaverunt et hostes fortissimos adventasse. Rex ergo contristatus statim collegit exercitum grandem, ut in ipsos animadverteret mortemque

Sirens surrounded the ships they nearly sank them. Nevertheless, having escaped, the Trojans passed along the coast
of Spain, where near the shore they discovered four generations of Trojan exiles who had been Antenor's companions
in flight. Their leader was called Corineus, a man of great   3
virtue and boldness. Having mutually acknowledged their
descent from an ancient lineage, they joined forces with
him and the greater part of the people he ruled over. Then,
sailing past Aquitaine on their right, after they entered the
mouth of the Loire, they dropped anchor. There they stayed
for seven days exploring the situation of the kingdom.

[18] King Gofar the Pict then reigned in Aquitaine. When
he heard a rumor that foreign people had landed within the
borders of his kingdom, he sent messengers to find out
whether they were bringing war or peace. Approaching the
fleet, the messengers encountered Corineus, who had disembarked with two hundred men to go hunting. When they   2
demanded of him why his men had entered the king's forest
to go hunting without permission (it had been decreed from
antiquity that no one should take the game there without
their ruler's permission), Corineus replied that he knew
nothing about their king's prohibition, nor in addition had
he ever heard of the prohibition of this kind of thing elsewhere, and it should in no way be instituted. This said, one
of them, Imbert by name, bent his bow and shot an arrow at
him. Corineus dodged it and, making an attack on Imbert,   3
smashed his head to pieces with the very bow that Imbert
was holding. Running away, however, his comrades reported
Imbert's death to Gofar and told him that the most powerful enemies had arrived. Saddened, the king immediately
gathered a large army, in order to punish the newcomers and

4 nuntii vindicaret. At Brutus, divulgato eius adventu, naves munit, mulieres et parvulos infra transtra iubet commanere. Ipse autem cum multitudine virorum bellatorum obvius regi Gofario progreditur. Initoque certamine dira pugna utrobique committitur. Et cum diei multum in agendo consumpsissent, puduit Corineum Aquitanos tam audacter in eos re-

5 sistere, Troianos non triumphare. Unde, sumpta audacia, sevocavit in dextram partem proelii suos et, facto agmine, celerem impetum in hostes facit, ipsosque dextra laevaque caedit et penetrata cohorte cunctos in fugam coegit. Fortuna ei, amisso gladio, bipennem administravit qua cunctos, quos attingebat, a summo usque deorsum findebat. Miratur Brutus, mirantur socii, mirantur etiam hostes audaciam viri et virtutem. Qui, bipennem post fugientes librans, timorem

6 illorum his verbis coercebat: "Quo fugitis, timidi, quo segnes abitis? Revertimini, o revertimini et congressum cum Corineo facite. Pro pudor! Tot milia hominum solum fugitis? Sed habete solacium quod dextra haec solebat Tyrrhenos gigantes et fugare et prosternere ac ternos atque quaternos ad Tartara trudere."

7 Ad haec verba Corinei quidam consul nomine Suhardus, cum trecentis militibus, impetum faciens Corineum undique circumdedit. At Corineus non oblitus bipennis in ipsum consulem erectam vibrat, percussumque a summo usque ad

8 imum in duas partes dissecuit. Sed et confestim irruens in ceteros bipennem rotat stragem maximam faciens et nunc

avenge the death of his messenger. But Brutus, having been   4
warned of Gofar's approach, fortified his ships and ordered
the women and children to stay below the rowing benches.
He himself, with a multitude of his warriors, proceeded
against King Gofar. The battle was joined, and both sides
engaged in fierce fighting. When most of the day had been
consumed in the action, Corineus felt ashamed that the
Aquitainians were resisting so boldly and the Trojans were
not winning. Therefore, summoning his courage, he pulled   5
his men to the right side of the battle and, forming a line,
made a rapid assault against the enemy and cut them down
to the left and the right. Having penetrated their line, he
forced them all to flight. After he lost his sword, Fortune
provided him with a battle-ax with which he split from top
to bottom everyone he came near. Brutus was amazed, his
companions were amazed, even the enemy were amazed by
the boldness and valor of the man. Brandishing the battle-ax
after those in flight, he rebuked their cowardice with these
words: "Where are you fleeing to, where are you going, you   6
lazy cowards? Come back, come back and do battle with
Corineus. For shame! Do so many thousands of men run
from one alone? But take comfort that this right arm was accustomed to drive away and strike down the Tyrrhenian giants and to send them to Tartarus by threes and fours."

At these words of Corineus, a certain consul named Su-   7
hardus assaulted Corineus with three hundred soldiers and
surrounded him on all sides. But Corineus, not forgetting
the battle-ax, swung it on high against the consul, and when
he struck he split him in two from top to bottom. Then, im-   8
mediately rushing at the rest of them, he swung the ax, making great slaughter. Running here and there, he cut off the

hac nunc illac discurrens, huic bracchium cum manu amputat, illi scapulas a corpore separat, alii caput truncat. Omnes in ipsum solum et ipse solus in omnes ruit. Quod Brutus cernens a longe, motus probitate viri, cucurrit cum turma et
9 auxilium ei subrogat. Mox oritur ingens clamor et crebri ictus multiplicantur et fit caedes durissima. Nec mora, victoriam adepti sunt Troes et regem Gofarium cum suis in fugam vertunt.

[19] Fugiens itaque Gofarius partes Galliarum adivit, ut ab amicis et cognatis auxilium peteret. Erant tunc temporis duodecim reges in Gallia, quorum regimine tota patria pari dignitate regebatur. Qui benigne suscipientes eum promittunt sese unanimiter expulsuros a finibus Aquitanniae exter-
2 nam gentem. Brutus autem, victoria laetus, peremptorum spoliis socios ditat et in turmas et centurias resociatos per patriam ducit et dilatat, volens eam penitus delere. Agros igitur depopulatur, civitates incendit et gazas absconditas inde extrahit, stragem miserandam civibus ac plebanis in-
3 fert. Dumque tali clade Aquitaniae partes infestaret, venit ad locum ubi nunc est civitas Turonorum quam, ut Homerus testatur, ipse prior construxit atque ibidem castra metatus est ut, si necessitas urgeret, se suosque infra ipsa castra reciperet. Peractis itaque castris, post biduum, ecce Gofarius cum immenso exercitu collecto ex omni Galliarum parte adventavit.

[20] Torva igitur lumina in castra Troianorum retorquens, tristis in haec verba erupit: "Pro fatum triste! Castra etiam in regno meo statuerunt ignobiles exules. Armate vos, viri, armate celeriter et per ordinatas turmas ad pugnam

arm along with its hand of this one, severed the shoulder blades from the body of that one, and chopped off the head of another. They all ran at him alone, and he alone at them. Brutus, seeing this from afar and inspired by the valor of the man, hastened with a company of men and came to his aid. There soon arose a tremendous clamor and the frequent blows were multiplied. Soon the Trojans had won the victory and they drove King Gofar into flight with his men.

[19] Fleeing thus, Gofar entered the regions of Gaul, in order to seek aid from his friends and relatives. At that time there were twelve kings in Gaul, under whose control the entire country was ruled with equal standing. They received him kindly, and promised as one to drive the foreign people beyond the borders of Aquitaine. Brutus however, cheered by victory, gave the spoils of those who were slain to his men and, reorganizing them into squadrons and companies, he led them through the country and spread them out intending to destroy it completely. He plundered the fields, burned the cities and removed their hidden treasures, and inflicted miserable slaughter on the townspeople and the peasants. While terrorizing Aquitaine with such devastation, he came to the place where the city of the Turones is now, which, as Homer testifies, he himself first constructed. There he laid out his camp so that, if needed, he and his men could take refuge inside. The camp was completed after two days, and then Gofar suddenly arrived with a huge army assembled from all parts of Gaul.

[20] Casting a fierce look at the Trojans' camp, in sorrow he burst out with these words: "O sorrowful fate! These ignoble exiles established a camp in my own kingdom. Arm yourselves, men, quickly, and march to battle in close order.

incedite. Nulla mora erit quin semimares istos velut oves intra caulas capiemus atque captos captivos per regna nostra mancipabimus."

2 Armaverunt se socii omnes ad praeceptum regis Gofarii et, per duodena agmina statuti, hostes invadunt. Hostes econtra, dispositis turmis, eos audacter suscipiunt. In congressu ergo praevaluerunt Troes et caedem magnam ex ho-

3 stibus fecerunt, fere ad duo milia hominum. Galli autem, quia eorum maior numerus erat et magis ac magis augmentabatur, undique convenientes impetum in Troas acriter fecerunt et eos in castra regredi coegerunt. Obsessi itaque a Gallis sub noctis silentio consilium inierunt, ut Corineus cum suis per quaedam divortia, intempesta nocte egrederetur et in nemore quod prope erat usque ad diem deliteret ut, cum Brutus diluculo egressus cum eis dimicaret, ipse cum cohorte gentis suae inprovisus a dorso superveniret et sic

4 utrimque attonitos Gallos invaderent. Quod ita factum est. Et dum mane die illucescente Brutus, cum gente sua de castris exiens, cum Gallis decertaret, mutuis vulneribus prosternuntur et, antequam Corineus cum suis se exercitui manifestaret, cecidit nepos Bruti, Turnus nomine, vir magnae audaciae, quo fortior sive audacior nullus excepto Corineo inter Troas aderat. Hic solus solo gladio sescentos viros straverat; sed ab irruenti multitudine dum eos per-

5 sequitur, a suis avulsus, multis vulneribus confossus est. De nomine itaque ipsius civitas Turonis vocabulum sumpsit,

There shall be no delay in our catching those eunuchs like sheep in their pens and, having captured them, we shall sell them throughout our kingdom as slaves."

All his allies armed themselves as ordered by King Gofar 2 and, arrayed in twelve columns, attacked the enemy. Their enemies, on the other hand, having arranged their troops, received them fearlessly. The Trojans therefore prevailed in the engagement and made great slaughter among their enemies, killing nearly two thousand men. However, because 3 their numbers were greater and were increasing more and more, coming together from every direction, the Gauls made a sharp assault upon the Trojans and forced them to retreat into the camp. Thus besieged by the Gauls, in the quiet of the night the Trojans formed a plan, by which Corineus and his men would sneak out by a certain side road in the dead of night and hide until daylight in a nearby wood, so that, when Brutus emerged to fight with the Gauls at dawn, he and the cohort of his people could fall upon them unexpectedly from behind, and thus they could attack the astonished Gauls from both directions. And so it happened. 4 Early in the morning, as dawn was breaking, when Brutus left the camp with his people in order to fight with the Gauls, they were struck down with injuries on both sides and, before Corineus was revealed with his army, a nephew of Brutus named Turnus was killed, a man of great boldness, than whom there was no one stronger or bolder among the Trojans except Corineus. He alone with only his sword struck down six hundred men; but he was fatally stabbed with multiple wounds by the onrushing multitude when he was pursued by them and separated from his men. From his 5 name the city of Tours took its title, because Turnus was

quia ibidem sepultus est Turnus. Interea, superveniente Corineo a tergo, hostes invadit. Troes audaciores et multo acriores propter mortem Turni vindicandam insurgentes sternunt Gallos et trucidant undique sine intermissione. Tandem fugam arripiunt Galli et campum deserere festi-

6 nant; quos Troes animosi usque ferientes insecuntur. Patrata igitur victoria, Brutus receptui lituum sonans reverti et co-adunari ad castra facit suos, decernitque cum eis naves re-petere ne, iterum hostes conglobati et pluriores prioribus effecti, sustinere eos nequirent sed magis periclitarentur. Contione itaque peracta, classem repetunt et de praeda di-vitiarum diversarum eam replent. Prosperis denique ventis, diis faventibus terram divinitus promissam petunt et in portu Dertae fluminis, qui Totonesium dicitur, applicant.

[21] Insulae huic tunc nomen Albion erat, quae a nemine exceptis paucis gigantibus inhabitabatur. Diffusi itaque Troes per patriam gigantes reperiunt, quos statim ad caver-nas montium fugant. Quadam autem die, dum in eodem portu navium diis libamina ex more solvuunt et victimis cae-sis festivum diem celebrant, supervenit Goemagog gigas cum aliis viginti gigantibus, illos a sacrificio incepto distur-bans et quosdam de Bruti sociis lapidibus et contis obrue-

2 runt. At Troes, undique confluentes, omnes interfecerunt praeter solum Goemagog. Hunc ergo Brutus vivum con-servari praecepit, volens videre luctam inter ipsum et

buried there. Meanwhile Corineus, arriving in the rear, attacked the enemy. The Trojans, rising up more boldly and much more sharply to avenge the death of Turnus, scattered the Gauls and butchered them everywhere without pause. Finally, the Gauls took flight and hastened to abandon the camp; the Trojans followed, striking them furiously all the way. Having achieved victory, Brutus sounded retreat with 6 his horn, turned back and assembled his men at the camp; he decided to get back to the ships with them just in case, if their enemies assembled a second time and in greater numbers than those before, the Trojans should be unable to withstand them and be placed in even greater danger. Once the assembly was completed, they returned to the fleet and filled it up with a booty of various riches. Then, with prosperous winds, and the favor of the gods, they sailed for the divinely promised land and landed in the harbor at the mouth of the River Dart, which is known as Totnes.

[21] At that time the name of this island was Albion, which was inhabited by no one except a few giants. After they spread through the country, the Trojans encountered some giants whom they quickly chased away to caverns in the mountains. One day, however, while they scattered offerings to the gods in their accustomed manner in the same port where their ships were located, and they celebrated the feast day with slaughtered sacrifices, Goemagog the Giant arrived with twenty other giants; disturbing the Trojans as they began the sacrifice, they overwhelmed one of Brutus's companions with stones and wooden staves. But the Tro- 2 jans, gathering from all directions, killed every one of them except Goemagog alone. Brutus therefore ordered him to be kept alive, wanting to see a wrestling match between him

35

Corineum. Corineus vero audiens de montibus accurrit et videns gigantem ad luctandum provocat. Inito deinde certamine, hinc stat Corineus tunica succinctus, hinc stat gigas ad luctam paratus; et exsertis bracchiis alter in alterum tendens dorsa vinculis bracchiorum adnectunt crebris flatibus auras vexantes. Nec mora, Goemagog Corineum totis viribus astringens, pectore pectus illius allisit fortiter tribus Corineo fractis costis. Mox ille, in iram accensus, revocat vires et toto conamine amplexatus de litore proximo super rupes excussit. At ille, per abrupta silicum ruens, in frusta dilaceratus, exspiravit fluctusque sanguine maculavit. Locus ergo ille nomen ex casu illius sortitus est usque in presentem diem.

4   Hinc Troes agros incipiunt colere, domos aedificare ut in brevi tempore terram diu inhabitatam censeres. Postea Brutus de nomine suo insulam Britanniam appellat, sociosque suos Britones. Unde postmodum loquela gentis, quae prius Troiana nuncupabatur, dicta Britannica est. Corineus quoque, ad occidentem portionem regni sortitus, ab appellatione nominis sui Corineiam vocat; quae nunc vel a cornu Britanniae quia ceu cornu ea pars terrae in mari producta est, vel per corruptionem praedicti nominis Cornubia appellatur.

    [22] Potitus tandem regno Brutus affectavit civitatem aedificare. Ad quam aedificandam congruum quaerens locum pervenit ad Thamensem fluvium locumque nactus est proposito suo perspicuum. Condidit itaque ibidem civitatem

and Corineus. When he heard about this, Corineus ran from the mountains and, seeing the giant, challenged him to wrestle. At the outset of the contest, Corineus stood on one side with his tunic bound up, the giant stood on the other ready to wrestle; each one approaching the other with arms outstretched, they joined together with their arms around each other's back, disturbing the air with their constant grunts. Without delay, squeezing all the strength out of Corineus, Goemagog strongly crushed the other's chest with his own, and three of Corineus's ribs were broken. Instantly, inflamed with rage, he recovered his strength and seizing Goemagog with all his power he dashed him upon the rocks of the nearby shore. Torn to pieces by smashing down upon the rocks, he died and stained the waves with his blood. That spot is named after his fall even to the present day. 3

From that point on, the Trojans began to till the fields and to build houses, so that in a short while you would have thought the land had been inhabited for a long time. Afterward, Brutus called the island Britain from his own name, and his comrades Britons. Whence after that the language of the people, which had previously been know as Trojan, was called British. Corineus also, having been assigned the western portion of the realm, from the pronunciation of his own name called it Corinea; now it is called Cornubia (Cornwall), either from the horn of Britain (because that area extended into the sea just like a horn) or from a corruption of the former name. 4

[22] Having won the kingdom, Brutus desired to construct a city. Searching for a suitable place to build, he came to the River Thames and found that place to be suitable for his purpose. He built a city there and called it New Troy,

eamque Novam Troiam vocat, quae postmodum per corrup-
2   tionem vocabuli Trinovantum dicta est. Condita ergo civitate munivit eam civibus iure victuris deditque legem qua
pacifice tractarentur. Regnabant tunc in Troia filii Hectoris,
expulsis Antenoris reliquiis. Praeerat in Iudaea Heli sacerdos
et Arca Testamenti capta erat a Philisteis. Regnabat in Italia
Silvius Aeneas, Aeneae filius, avunculus Bruti, Latinorum
tertius.

which was later called Trinovantum through corruption of
the name. After building the city, he furnished it with citi-   2
zens to live there by right and he gave them law so they
could conduct their affairs peacefully. At that time the sons
of Hector were reigning in Troy, the survivors of Antenor
having been expelled. Eli the priest was in charge of Judea
and the Ark of the Testament was captured by the Philistines. Silvius Aeneas, son of Aeneas, uncle of Brutus and
third of the Latins, was reigning in Italy.

BOOK TWO

Liber II

[23] Cognoverat autem Brutus Innogen uxorem suam et ex ea genuit tres filios quorum nomina erant Locrinus, Albanactus, Kamber. Mortuo autem Bruto, vicesimo quarto anno adventus sui in Britanniam, sepelierunt eum filii sui infra urbem quam condiderat et diviserunt regnum Britanniae inter se et habuit quisque partem suam. Locrinus, qui et primogenitus, sortitus est eam partem quae postea de nomine suo appellata est Loegria; Kamber autem partem illam quae est ultra Sabrinum flumen, quae nunc Gualia dicitur, sed de nomine suo prius Kambria nomen retinuit. Unde adhuc gens illa lingua Britannica sese Kambro appellat. Albanactus iunior possedit partem quae de nomine suo Albania dicta est, sed nunc Scotia appellatur.

[24] Illis deinde concordi pace inter se regnantibus, applicuit Humber rex Hunorum in Albaniam et, commisso proelio cum Albanacto, interfecit eum et magnam gentis suae partem. Ceteri vero ad Locrinum diffugerunt. Locrinus igitur, audito rumore, indoluit accitoque fratre Kambro cum magno exercitu perrexit vindicare fratrem suum. Rex autem Hunnorum eis obvius fuit circa Humbrum fluvium et, congressu facto, compulsus est rex Hunnorum cum suis fugam arripere quousque in flumen praecipitatus est et nomen suum flumini reliquit. Locrinus itaque et Kamber, potiti

Book 2

[23] Meanwhile, Brutus had slept with his wife Innogen and by her he fathered three sons, whose names were Locrinus, Albanactus, and Kamber. When Brutus died in the twenty-fourth year after his arrival in Britain, his sons buried him beneath the city that he had founded, and divided the kingdom of Britain among themselves, each having his own part. To Locrinus, the firstborn, was assigned the region that was later called Loegria after him. To Kamber was given the region that is across the Severn River, which is now called Wales, but previously took the name Cambria after him—hence the people there call themselves Cambrians in the British tongue. The youngest, Albanactus, took possession of the region which was called Albany after him, but is now known as Scotland.

[24] After that, as they were reigning in peace and harmony among themselves, Humber, king of the Huns, arrived in Albany and made war upon Albanactus and killed him and a great part of his people. The rest fled away to Locrinus. When Locrinus heard this news, he was deeply saddened, and summoning his brother Kamber, he proceeded with a large army to avenge his brother Albanactus. The king of the Huns confronted them near the River Humber, and after the battle was joined, the king of the Huns was forced to flee with his men until he was hurled into the river, and he gave his name to the river. Locrinus and Kamber,

victoria, naves hostium petunt, spolia diripiunt, et sociis lar-
giuntur. Tres puellas ibidem mirae pulchritudinis invenerunt, quarum una fuit filia regis Germaniae quam praedictus
3 Humber cum ceteris rapuerat dum patriam vastaret. Erat
nomen illius Estrildis et tantae pulchritudinis fuit quod
nulla ei in pulchritudine comparari posset. Amore itaque illius captus Locrinus praecepit eam sibi servari ut in uxorem
duceret. Quod cum Corineo compertum esset, indignatus
est quoniam Locrinus pactus ei antea fuerat sese filiam ipsius ducturum. Adiit ergo regem et bipennem in dextra
4 manu librans taliter illum allocutus est iratus: "Haeccine re-
pendis mihi, Locrine, ob tot vulnera quae in obsequio patris
tui perpessus sum, dum proelia cum ignotis committeret
gentibus ut, filia mea postposita, barbaram sibi praepo-
neres? Non inpune feres dum vigor huic inerit dextrae quae
tot gigantibus causa mortis exstitit."
5   Hoc autem iterum iterumque replicans, librabat bipennem quasi percussurus, cum utrorumque sese interposu-
erunt amici. Sedato vero Corineo, Locrinum regem quod
pepigerat exsequi laudaverunt ac si coegissent. Duxit itaque
Corinei filiam Locrinus nomine Guendoloenam; nec tamen
Estrildis amoris oblitus est sed, facto intra Urbem Trinouan-
tum subterraneo, inclusit eam ac servandam familiaribus
suis tradidit ibique furtivam venerem agens septem annis
6 eam frequentavit. Quotienscumque igitur adibat illam, fin-
gebat se velle occulta libamina diis suis reddere. Interea

having won the victory, made for the enemies' ships, took the spoils, and bestowed them lavishly upon their comrades. There they found three young women of amazing beauty, one of whom was the daughter of the king of Germany, whom the aforesaid Humber had abducted with others when he laid waste to that country. Her name was Estrildis, and she was of such beauty that no one could be compared to her in beauty. Seized with love for her, Locrinus ordered that she be kept for himself, so that he could take her as his wife. When this was revealed to Corineus, he was indignant, because Locrinus had previously made a pact with him to take his own daughter in marriage. He therefore approached the king and, swinging a battle-ax in his right hand, spoke to him thus in anger: "Is this is how you repay me, Locrinus, for all the wounds I suffered under your father's command when he was fighting battles against foreign nations, that you cast my daughter aside and set a barbarian girl above her? You will not do this without punishment, while I retain the strength in this right arm that has caused the death of so many giants." 4

Repeating this again and again, he swung the battle-ax as if to strike him, until friends of both of them intervened. After they calmed Corineus, they recommended and indeed compelled Locrinus to do as he had promised. So Locrinus married Corineus's daughter, who was called Guendolena; but he did not forget his love for Estrildis. Having constructed a chamber beneath the city of London, he shut her up there and entrusted her to his closest servants, and there he visited her, conducting a secret affair for seven years. Whenever he went to her, he pretended that he wanted to make a private offering to his gods. Eventually, Estrildis 6

45

gravida facta est Estrildis ediditque filiam mirae pulchritudinis quam vocavit Habren. Gravida etiam facta est Guendoloena genuitque filium cui impositum est nomen Maddan. Hic Corineo avo suo traditus est nutriendus, cuius doctrinam et mores exsecutus est.

[25] Subsequente deinde tempore, defuncto Corineo, deseruit Locrinus Guendoloenam et Estrildem in reginam sublimavit. Indignata ergo Guendoloena secessit in partes Cornubiae collectaque totius patriae iuventute coepit Locrinum inquietare. Consertoque tandem utrorumque exercitu, commiserunt proelium iuxta flumen Sturam ibique

2 Locrinus ictu sagittae occubuit. Mortuo itaque Locrino, Guendoloena suscepit regni gubernacula, paterna furens insania. Iubet deinde Estrildem et filiam eius praecipitari in fluvium Sabrinae fecitque edictum ut flumen nomine puellae vocaretur in posterum, tantum honoris tribuens pro eo quod eam genuerat Locrinus, vir suus. Unde usque in hodiernum diem appellatum est flumen Sabrina a nomine

3 Habren puellae per corruptionem. Regnavit deinde Guendoloena quindecim annis, cum Locrinus antea secum decem regnasset annis. Et, cum vidisset Maddan filium suum aetate adultum, sceptro regni insignivit eum, contenta regione Cornubiae dum viveret. Tunc Samuel propheta regnabat in Iudaea et Silvius Aeneas adhuc vivebat et Homerus clarus habebatur.

[26] Insignitus igitur Maddan duxit uxorem et ex ea genuit duos filios, Mempritium et Malim, regnumque cum pace quadraginta annis tenuit. Quo defuncto, discordia orta est inter praedictos fratres propter regnum quia uterque

became pregnant and gave birth to a girl of astonishing beauty, whom she called Habren. Guendolena also became pregnant, and gave birth to a son who was given the name Maddan. He was given over to be raised by his grandfather Corineus, whose teaching and customs he followed.

[25] With the passing of time, after Corineus had died, Locrinus abandoned Guendolena and raised up Estrildis as his queen. Indignant, Guendolena therefore withdrew to the region of Cornwall and, having gathered the youth of that whole region, began to harass Locrinus; when both of their armies came together, they engaged in battle next to the River Stour, where Locrinus was struck down by the blow of an arrow. After Locrinus died, Guendolena took control of the kingdom, raging with all of her father's madness. She ordered Estrildis and her daughter to be thrown into the River Severn and issued an edict that the river should henceforth be called by the girl's name, granting her that much honor because her own husband Locrinus had fathered her. Thus to the present day the river is called the Severn, as a corruption of the name of the girl Habren. Then Guendolena reigned for fifteen years, after Locrinus had previously reigned with her for ten years, and when her son Maddan appeared to her to be of adult age she honored him with the scepter of the realm, being content to keep the region of Cornwall for the remainder of her life. At that time the Prophet Samuel was reigning in Judea, and Silvius Aeneas was still alive, and Homer was at the height of his fame.

[26] After he was crowned, Maddan took a wife and fathered two sons by her, Mempritius and Malim, and he held the kingdom in peace for forty years. After his death, a dispute over the kingdom arose between the two brothers,

totum possidere volebat. Mempritius ergo Malim fratrem suum, in dolo simulata pace colloquio postulans, inter pro-loquendum ipsum interfecit solusque regni monarchiam adeptus in tantam tyrannidem exarsit ut quemque fere

2 nobilissimum interficeret. Sed et totam progeniem suam exosus, quemcumque suspectum in regni successione habe-bat, aut vi aut dolo perimebat. Relicta etiam propria con-iuge, ex qua inclitum iuvenem Ebraucum genuerat, sese so-domitico operi—pro nefas!—subdidit. Tandem vicesimo regni sui anno, dum venatum iret, a sociis avulsus in quan-dam convallem, a multitudine rabiosorum luporum dilace-ratus interiit. Tunc Saul regnabat in Iudaea et Euristeus in Lacedaemonia.

[27] Defuncto itaque Mempritio, Ebraucus filius suus, vir magnae staturae et mirae fortitudinis, regimen Britanniae suscepit et sexaginta annis rexit. Hic primus post Brutum classem in partes Galliae direxit provinciasque mari prox-imas caede virorum et praedationibus affecit, ditatusque auri argentique copia spoliisque diversis in Britanniam re-

2 versus est. Deinde trans Humbrum condidit civitatem quam de nomine suo vocavit Kaerebrauc, id est civitatem Ebrauci. Aedificavit et aliam civitatem Alclud nomine versus Alba-niam et oppidum Montis Agned, quod nunc Castellum

3 Puellarum dicitur, et Montem Dolorosum. Et tunc David rex regnabat in Iudaea et Silvius Latinus in Italia et Gad, Nathan, et Asaph in Israel prophetabant. Genuit quoque vi-ginti filios ex viginti coniugibus necnon et triginta filias. Erant autem nomina filiorum eius: Brutus Viride Scutum, Margadud, Sisillius, Regin, Morvid, Bladud, Iagon, Bodloan,

ecause each one wanted to hold it all. Therefore, deceitfully asking his brother Malim for a meeting under the pretense of peace, Mempritius killed him while in the act of speaking. After he assumed the monarchy alone he burned with such tyranny that he killed almost all of the highest nobility. Moreover, hating his whole family as well, he killed by force or by treachery whomever he suspected of having designs on the succession of the kingdom. He abandoned his lawful wife, by whom he had fathered the outstanding youth Ebraucus, and surrendered himself—what shame!—to acts of sodomy. Finally, in the twentieth year of his reign, lured by his companions into a certain valley while out hunting, he was torn to pieces by a band of rabid wolves and died. At that time Saul was reigning in Judea and Eurystheus in Sparta.

[27] After Mempritius died, his son Ebraucus, a man of great stature and remarkable strength, assumed control of Britain and ruled for sixty years. He was the first after Brutus to send a fleet to the regions of Gaul, and he harassed the provinces near the sea with pillaging and slaughter. He returned to Britain enriched with an abundance of gold and silver and various spoils. After that he founded a city beyond the Humber, which he named Kaerebrauc after himself, that is to say the City of Ebraucus. He built another city called Aldclud, toward Albany, and the town of Mount Agned (which is now called the Castle of the Maidens) and the Dolorous Mount. And at that time King David was reigning in Judea and Silvius Latinus in Italy, and Gad, Nathan, and Asaph were prophesying in Israel. He also fathered twenty sons by twenty wives, as well as thirty daughters. The names of his sons were Brutus Greenshield, Margadud, Sisillius, Regin, Morvid, Bladud, Iagon, Bodloan,

Kincar, Spaden, Gaul, Dardan, Eldad, Ivor, Cangu, Hector,
4 Kerin, Rud, Assarach, Buel. Nomina autem filiarum: Gloigin, Innogin, Otidas, Guenlian, Guardid, Angarad, Guenlodee, Tangustel, Gorgon, Medlan, Methael, Ourar, Mailure,
Kambreda, Ragan, Gad, Ecub, Nest, Chein, Stadud, Gladus,
Ebrein, Blangan, Aballac, Angues, Galaes (omnium pulcher-
5 rima), Edra, Anor, Stadiald, Egron. Has omnes direxit pater
in Italiam ad Silvium Albam qui post Silvium Latinum regnabat. Fueruntque ibi maritatae nobilibus Troianis, quorum
cubilia et Latinae et Sabinae diffugiebant. At filii, duce Assa-
raco fratre, duxerunt classem in Germaniam et auxilio Silvii
Albae usi subiugato populo adepti sunt regnum.

[28] Brutus autem cognomento Viride Scutum cum patre
remansit regnique gubernacula post illum adeptus duodecim annis regnavit. Huic successit Leil filius suus, pacis
amator et aequitatis, qui urbem constituit de nomine suo
Kaerleil in aquilonali parte Britanniae. Vixit Leil post sump-
tum regnum viginti quinque annis, sed regnum in fine tepide
rexit. Quocirca civilis discordia in regno orta est.

[29] Post hunc regnavit filius suus Rudhudibras triginta
novem annis. Iste populum a civili discidio in concordiam
revocavit condiditque Kaerkein, id est Cantuariam civitatem, et Kaergueint, id est Wintoniam, atque oppidum Mon-
2 tis Paladur, quod nunc Septonia dicitur. Ibi tunc, ut dicitur,
aquila locuta est dum murus aedificaretur. Tunc Salomon
coepit aedificare templum Domini in Ierusalem et Aggeus,
Amos, Ieu, et Ioel et Azarias prophetabant. Et tunc Silvius
Egypti patri Albae in Italia successit.

Kincar, Spaden, Gaul, Dardan, Eldad, Ivor, Cangu, Hector, Kerin, Rud, Assarach, Buel. The names of his daughters 4 were Gloigin, Innogin, Otidas, Guenlian, Guardid, Angarad, Guenlodee, Tangustel, Gorgon, Medlan, Methael, Ourar, Mailure, Kambreda, Ragan, Gad, Ecub, Nest, Chein, Stadud, Gladus, Ebrein, Blangan, Aballac, Angues, Galaes (the most beautiful of all), Edra, Anor, Stadiald, Egron. Their father sent them all into Italy to Silvius Alba, who was 5 ruling after Silvius Latinus. There they were wedded to Trojan nobles, whose marriage beds both the Latin and Sabine women were avoiding. But the sons, led by their brother Assarach, took a fleet to Germany and with the help of Silvius Alba they conquered the people and secured the kingdom.

[28] Brutus, however, surnamed Greenshield, stayed behind with his father, succeeded him in the government of the realm, and reigned for twelve years. His son Leil followed him, a lover of peace and justice, who founded a city in the northern part of Britain that was named Kaerleil after him. He lived for twenty-five years after assuming royal power, but he ruled the kingdom weakly in his last years. Because of this civil unrest arose in the kingdom.

[29] After this Leil's son Rudhudibras reigned for thirty-nine years. He brought the people back from civil unrest into harmony, and he founded Kaerkein, or the city of Canterbury, and Kaerguint, or Winchester, as well as the fortress of Mount Paladur, which is now called Sephtonia. In that 2 place, it is said, the Eagle spoke while the wall was being constructed. At that time Solomon began to build the temple of the Lord in Jerusalem, and Ahias, Amos, Jehu, Joel, and Azarias were prophesying. Also at that time Silvius the son of Aegyptus succeeded his father at Alba in Italy.

[30] Successit deinde Bladud, filius Rudhudibrae, rexitque regnum pacifice viginti annis. Hic aedificavit urbem
Kaerbadum, quae nunc Bada nuncupatur, fecitque ibidem
calida balnea ad usus mortalium, quibus praefecit numen
Minervae. In cuius aede inextinguibiles posuit ignes, qui
numquam deficiunt in favillas, sed ex quo tabescere inci-
2 piunt in saxeos globos ferventes vertuntur. Quod per nigro-
mantiam artem addidicit facere: adeo ingeniosus fuit. Multa
et alia prestigia fecit et ad ultimum ceu Daedalus, alis sibi
factis, per aera volare praesumpsit. Unde summo infortunio
lapsus cecidit super templum Apollinis infra Urbem Trinovantum, membrisque confractis miserabiliter exspiravit.

[31] Quo defuncto, Leir filius eiusdem in regem erigitur
qui sexaginta annis viriliter regnum rexit. Aedificavit autem
super flumen Soram civitatem de nomine eius dictam Kaerleir; Saxonice vero Leircestra nuncupatur. Huic natae sunt
tres filiae denegata masculini sexus prole: nomina earum
2 Goronilla, Regau, Cordeilla. Pater eas paterno amore sed
magis iuniorem Cordeillam diligebat. Cumque in senectutem vergere coepisset, cogitavit regnum suum ipsis dividere
et cum parte regni maritis copulare. Sed, ut sciret, quae illa-
rum parte regni potiore dignior esset, interrogationibus suis
3 singulas temptavit, scilicet quae magis illum diligeret. Inter-
roganti igitur Goronilla maior natu numina caeli testata
est ipsum se magis diligere quam vitam suam. Cui pater:
"Quoniam senectutem meam vitae tuae praeposuisti, te

[30] Then followed Bladud the son of Rudhudibras, and he ruled the kingdom peacefully for twenty years. He built the city of Kaerbadum, which is now known as Bath; and there he made hot baths for the use of mortal men, which he put under the protection of the goddess Minerva. In her temple he placed inextinguishable fires that are never reduced to ashes, but when they begin to diminish are turned into glowing balls of stone. Because he was so clever, he 2 learned to achieve this through the art of necromancy. He created many other wonders and in the end, having made wings just like Daedalus, he presumptuously attempted to fly through the air. Whereupon, by a stroke of the greatest misfortune, he fell and crashed upon the temple of Apollo in the city of London and died miserably with his limbs completely shattered.

[31] After he died his son Leir was made king, who ruled the kingdom vigorously for sixty years. He built a city on the River Soar called Kaerleir after him; in the Saxon speech, however, it was called Leicester. Male children were denied to him, but he had three daughters; their names were Goronilla, Regau, and Cordeilla. Their father loved them with pa- 2 ternal affection, but especially the youngest, Cordeilla. And when he began to approach old age, he thought about dividing his kingdom among them, and joining each of them to husbands along with their part of the kingdom. But in order to know which of them deserved the more important part of the kingdom, he questioned each of them in turn in order to learn which of them loved him the most. Upon question- 3 ing, Goronilla, the eldest, swore to the gods above that she loved him more than her own life. To which her father replied: "Because you have placed my old age before your own

carissimam filiam maritabo iuveni quemcumque elegeris in regno meo cum tertia parte regni."

4   Deinde Regau secunda exemplo sororis suae benivolentiam patris captans, iureiurando respondit se super omnes creaturas eum diligere. Credulus ergo pater, eadem dignitate qua primogenitam cum tertia parte regni maritare spopondit. At Cordeilla iunior, cum intellexisset sororum adulatio-

5 nibus acquievisse, temptare cupiens patrem respondit: "Est uspiam, pater mi, filia quae patrem suum plusquam patrem praesumat diligere? Nempe ego semper dilexi te ut patrem et adhuc a proposito non desisto; et si ex me amplius extorquere vis, audi amoris certitudinem quem tecum habeo et interrogationibus tuis finem impone. Etenim quantum habes tantum vales tantumque te diligo."

6   Porro pater iratus eam ex iracundia aut derisione taliter responsum dedisse indignans stomachando ait: "Quoniam sic patris senectutem sprevisti ut vel eo amore quo me sorores tuae diligunt dedignata es respondere, ego dedignabor te in tantum ut in regno meo cum sororibus tuis partem non habebis. Quippe cum te plusquam ceteras hucusque dilexerim, tu me minus quam ceterae diligere fateris."

7   Nec mora, consilio procerum suorum praedictas puellas dedit unam duci Cornubiae et alteram regi Albaniae. Quibus post decessum suum totam regni monarchiam concessit. Contigit interea quod Aganippus rex Francorum uxore

life, I will give you in marriage, my dearest daughter, to whatever young man in my kingdom you will choose, along with a third part of my kingdom."

Then Regau, his second daughter, trying to win her father's kindness by following her sister's example, replied upon oath that she loved him above all living things. Her credulous father accordingly promised to give her in marriage along with a third part of his kingdom and the same status as his firstborn daughter. But Cordeilla, the youngest, wanting to test her father after she realized how he had succumbed to the flattery of her sisters, replied: "My father, is there anywhere a daughter who presumes to love her father more than as a father? Of course I have always loved you as a father and I do not abandon that principle now; if you wish to wring more out of me, listen to the truth about the love I have for you and put an end to your questioning. For truly, as much as you have, so much are you worth, that is how much I love you."

Then her father became irate, seething with indignation that she had responded in this way out of anger or contempt, and said: "Because you have despised your father's old age so much that you refused to answer even with the same love shown to me by your sisters, I will refuse you so much, that you will have no part in my kingdom with your sisters. For in fact, while I have loved you more than the others until now, you admit that you love me less than the others do."

Immediately, following the advice of his nobles, he gave the first two girls away in marriage, one to the Duke of Cornwall and the other to the king of Albany. He arranged to leave the whole rule over his kingdom to them after his death. It happened meanwhile that Aganippus, king of the

carens, audita fama pulchritudinis Cordeillae, nuntios diri-
8 git ad regem Britonum ut illam sibi coniugio copularet. Pater autem, nondum filiae responsionibus oblitus, ait se eam
sibi daturum, sed sine dote: duabus etenim prioribus regnum suum diviserat. Quod cum Aganippo intimatum esset,
amore virginis inflammatus, remisit iterum ad regem dicens
se satis auri et argenti et terrae possidere, neque dote alia
indigere nisi tantummodo puelle nobilis coniugio, de qua
sibi postmodum heredes procrearet. Confirmato igitur nuptiali foedere, mittitur Cordeilla ad regem Aganippum et ei
in uxorem coniungitur.

9   Post multum vero temporis, ut Leir rex senio affectus
torpere coepit, insurrexerunt in eum duces quibus filias
praedictas locaverat et abstulerunt ei regnum et regiam potestatem. Concordia tamen inter eos habita rex Albaniae
Maglaunus alter generorum illum secum retinuit cum quadraginta militibus ne inglorius esset propter filiam eius con-
10 iugem suam. Moram itaque apud eum illo faciente, indignata
aliquanto filia sua Goronilla, ob multitudinem militum secum commorantium, quia ministris eiusdem conviciaban-
tur. Maritum suum affata, iussit patrem suum contentum
esse debere obsequio triginta militum. Indignatus ille re-
licto Maglauno secessit ad Henninum ducem Cornubiae,
11 sponsum alterius filiae. Apud quem moratus, infra annum
orta est discordia inter utrorumque famulos; unde iussus est
a filia pater senex familiam totam deserere praeter quinque

Franks, lacking a wife and having heard the report of Corde-illa's beauty, sent messengers to the king of the Britons so that he could be joined with her in marriage. Her father, 8 however, still mindful of his daughter's response, said that he would give her to Aganippus, but without a dowry: for he had already divided his kingdom between the two older daughters. After this was reported to King Aganippus, in-flamed with love for the maiden he sent back again to the king, saying that he had enough gold and silver and land, and did not need any other dowry except only marriage with a noble young woman, by whom he might afterward produce heirs. Once the wedding compact was confirmed, Cordeilla was sent to King Aganippus and became his wife.

After a long time, when King Leir, affected by old age, be- 9 gan to grow weak, the dukes that he had found for these daughters rose up against him and took his kingdom and royal power away from him. Once peace was established be-tween them, Maglaunus the king of Albany, one of his two sons-in-law, kept Leir with himself along with forty soldiers. He did this on account of his wife, Leir's daughter, so that Leir would not be humiliated. As Leir stayed on with them, 10 his daughter Goronilla became somewhat resentful about the multitude of soldiers residing with them, because they were insulting her servants. She spoke with her husband, and then told her father he would have to be content with a retinue of thirty soldiers. Being resentful, Leir left Maglau-nus and withdrew to Henninus, Duke of Cornwall, the spouse of his second daughter. While he stayed there, within 11 a year a disagreement arose between the two households; because of that his daughter ordered that her aged father should abandon his entire household except for five men

qui ei obsequio satis essent. Porro pater, ultra quam dici potest, tunc anxius et tristis reversus est iterum ad primogenitam sperans mutato animo se cum tota familia honorifice
12 velle retinere. At illa per numina caeli iuravit quod nullatenus secum commaneret nisi, relictis omnibus, solo milite
contentus esset. Paruit ille tristis et cum solo milite illi adhaesit. Recordatus subinde honoris pristini et dignitatis
amissae, detestando miseriam ad quam redactus erat, cogi-
tare coepit quod iuniorem filiam expeteret. Aestimans eam
pietate posse moveri paterna, transfretavit ad Gallias et in
transfretando haec apud se cogitando memorabat:

13   "O irrevocabilia seria fatorum, quo solito cursu fixum iter
tenditis? Cur, inquam, me ad instabilem felicitatem promo-
vere voluistis, cum maior poena sit ipsam amissam recolere,
14 quam sequentis infelicitatis praesentia urgeri? O irata fortuna! O Cordeilla filia, quam vera sunt dicta illa quae ques-
tionibus meis sapienter respondisti: ut quantum haberem
tantum valerem tantumque me diligeres! Dum igitur habui
quod dare possem, visus fui valere his qui non mihi sed donis
meis applaudebant. Interim dilexerunt me, sed abeuntibus
muneribus et ipsi abierunt. Sed qua fronte tamen, filia mea
carissima, tuam audebo faciem videre vel me ipsum tibi
praesentare qui, quasi vilem et abiectam, te deterius et sine
dote quam sorores tuas inter extraneos locare curavi?"

who would be enough for his retinue. At once her father, more anxious and sad than he could say, went back again to his eldest daughter hoping that, with a change of heart, she would be willing to keep him honorably with his whole reti- nue. But she swore by the gods above that he could not pos- 12 sibly stay with them unless, dismissing them all, he would be content with a single knight. Sorrowful, he complied and stayed with her with a single knight. But as he often recalled his former honors and lost dignities, loathing the wretched- ness to which he was reduced, he began to think that he might try to find his youngest daughter. Reckoning that she might be moved by a sense of duty toward her father, he passed over the sea to Gaul, and while he was passing over, he turned his mind to thoughts such as these:

"O irreversible course of the fates, where are you direct- 13 ing your unchangeable route with your usual speed? Why, I say, did you wish to move me forward to insecure happiness, when it is a greater punishment to recall that happiness which is lost than to be burdened with the presence of mis- fortune which follows it? O angry fortune! O Cordeilla my 14 daughter, how true those words are with which you wisely responded to my questions: that as much as I had was how much I was worth and how much you would love me! There- fore, while I had things I could give, I seemed worthy to those who were applauding not me but my gifts. In the meantime they loved me, but once my presents were gone, they too were gone. But with what countenance, my dearest daughter, shall I dare to look upon your face or to present myself to you, when I took pains to send you away among foreigners, as if you were a worthless and humble person, without a dowry and inferior in status to your sisters?"

15   Dum ergo haec et his similia in mente volveret, applicuerunt in Gallias et venit Karitiam ubi filia sua erat. Cum autem veniret ad urbem ubi ipsa tunc manebat, erubuit ingredi
ad eam solus in paupere veste, retinensque pedem per nun-
tium qui solus armiger sibi adhaerebat, indicavit eius adven-
16   tum, historiam miseriae suae pandens. Manifestato itaque
patris infortunio, contrita est corde et flevit amare celerique
consilio usa, tradidit clam nuntio qui haec sibi indicaverat
auri argentique copiam, praecipiens ut ad aliam civitatem
patrem deduceret, ibique se infirmum fingeret ac balneis et
optimis cibis indulgeret et foveret vestibusque melioribus
ornaret. Iussit quoque ut quadraginta milites pariter secum
retineret et tunc demum regi Aganippo viro suo adventum
suum et causam adventus per internuntios manifestaret.
17   Quo facto atque completo secundum reginae praeceptum
post paucos dies notificato regi eius adventu veniunt ad eum
rex et regina magna stipati militum caterva atque honorifice
illum susceperunt. Dederuntque ei potestatem in toto regno
suo, donęc in pristinam dignitatem illum restituissent.
18   Interea collecto grandi per totam Galliam exercitu, Cordeilla cum patre in Britanniam transivit, commissoque
proelio cum generis, triumpho potitus est atque dominium
totius regni adeptus. Tribus annis post imperavit genti Bri-
19   tonum restituens quemque potestati suae. Defuncto autem
eo in senectute bona, suscepit Cordeilla regni gubernacula

While he turned over these and similar thoughts in his 15
mind, they landed in Gaul and he came to Karitia, where his
daughter was. But when he came to the town where she was
staying at that time, he was ashamed to enter it alone in the
clothes of a pauper and, pausing in his steps, sent word of his
arrival via a messenger, the only squire still attached to him,
who explained the story of his suffering. When her father's 16
misfortune was thus revealed to her, Cordeilla was contrite
in her heart and wept bitterly and, quickly taking counsel,
she secretly handed over an ample supply of gold and silver
to the messenger who had brought word of this to her, in-
structing him to bring her father to another city, and there
to pretend he was sick and indulge and maintain him with
baths and the finest foods and dress him in better clothing.
She also ordered that he should keep forty soldiers with
him, and finally sent word via messengers to her husband
Aganippus about Leir's arrival and the reason for his arrival.
Once this was finished and done according to the queen's in- 17
structions, and the king alerted after a few days about his
arrival, the king and queen came to him, surrounded by a
large troop of soldiers, and gave him an honorable reception. They also gave him power throughout their whole
kingdom until such time as they should have restored him
to his former dignity.

Meanwhile, having gathered a large army from the whole 18
of Gaul, Cordeilla crossed over with her father into Britain
and, after engaging in battle with his son-in-law, he achieved
victory and attained dominion over the whole kingdom. He
ruled the race of the Britons for three years after that, bringing everyone back under his own authority. When he died in 19
his ripe old age, Cordeilla took the helm of the kingdom and

sepelivitque patrem in quodam subterraneo supra fluvium Soram infra Leircestriam. Erat autem subterraneum illud in honore bifrontis Iani dedicatum, ubi gens idolatriae data totius anni opera in sollemnitate eiusdem dei auspicabantur.

[32] Mortuo quoque Aganippo rege, Cordeilla regnum Britanniae per quinquennium in pace bona rexit donec a filiis sororum suarum inquietata, Margano videlicet et Cunedagio (his enim nominibus insigniti erant), post multis proeliis commissis ad ultimum devicta ab eis et capta miserias carceris sortita est; ubi ob amissionem regni dolore obducta

2 sese interemit. Exinde partiti sunt iuvenes regnum et pars illa quae est trans Humbrum cessit Margano; alia vero pars regni quae vergit ad occasum submittitur Cunedagio. Emenso deinde biennio, accesserunt quibus regni turbatio placebat ad Marganum animumque illius pulsabant, dicentes dedecus et iniustum fore, cum primogenitus esset, totius

3 regni dominium non habere. Cumque sic a perversis hominibus incitatus esset, duxit exercitum per provincias Cunedagii, ferroque et incendio vastare coepit. Orta igitur inter fratres discordia, obvius venit Morgano Cunedagius cum maxima exercitus multitudine, factoque congressu caedes inmensa utrimque facta est et Marganus in fugam vertitur.

4 Quem secutus Cunedagius fugientem a provincia in provinciam, tandem intercepit eum in pago Kambriae et eo interfecto de nomine suo illi pago usque in hodiernum diem nomen dedit. Potitus itaque victoria, Cunedagius monarchiam totius regni adeptus triginta tribus annis gloriose rexit. Tunc

buried her father in a certain underground tomb on the River Soar below Leicester. The tomb was dedicated to the honor of two-faced Janus, and it was where the people, who were given to idolatry, made a ceremonial start to the whole year's work in ritual observance to that same deity.

[32] After King Aganippus died, Cordeilla ruled the kingdom of Britain in peace for five years until it was disrupted by her sisters' sons, namely Marganus and Cunedagius (for those were the names they had been given), and after many battles were fought she was finally defeated and captured by them and consigned to the miseries of prison. There she killed herself, overwhelmed with grief for the loss of the kingdom. After that the young princes divided the kingdom 2 and that part which is beyond the Humber fell to Marganus; the other part which lies toward the west was given to Cunedagius. Two years having passed, some men who took pleasure in stirring up trouble in the kingdom approached Marganus and roused his spirit, saying that it would be disgraceful and unjust, since he was the eldest, not to have dominion over the entire kingdom. After he was incited in this 3 way by these evil men, he led an army through the provinces of Cunedagius and began to lay waste with sword and fire. A war broke out between the brothers, and Cunedagius came against Marganus with a great host; after battle was joined there was immense slaughter on both sides and Marganus was driven away in flight. Cunedagius pursued him as he fled 4 from province to province, until he eventually caught up with him in a district of Wales and killed him. Marganus gave that district the name which it bears to the present day. After he achieved victory, Cunedagius obtained the monarchy of the entire realm and ruled gloriously for thirty-three

Isaias et Osee prophetabant et Roma condita est a geminis fratribus Remo et Romulo undecimo kalendis Maii.

[33] Postremo, defuncto Cunedagio, successit ei Rivallo filius eius, iuvenis fortissimus et prudens, qui regnum cum diligentia gubernavit. In tempore eius cecidit pluvia sanguinea per tres dies et muscarum affluencia homines moriebantur. Rivallo successit Gurgustius filius eius: cui Sisillius; cui Iago Gurgustii nepos; cui Kinmarcus Sisillii filius; cui Gor-

2 bodiago. Huic nati sunt duo filii, Ferreus et Porrex, inter quos orta est contentio regni, vivente adhuc patre sed vergente in senium. At Porrex, regni cupiditate accensus, fratrem suum dolo interficere parat. Quod cum illi compertum fuisset, vitatis insidiis transfretavit in Gallias ususque auxilio Suhardi regis Francorum reversus est et cum fratre dimi-

3 cavit. Pugnantibus autem illis, interfectus est Ferreus et omnes sui. Porro mater eorum, nomine Indon, de morte filii commota quia artius eum diligebat, in odium et iram adversus victorem fratrem incitata est. Nacta ergo tempus vindicandi, filium aggreditur somno oppressum cum ancillis suis et in plurimas sectiones dilaceravit. Exinde civilis discordia multo tempore populum afflixit et regnum quinque regibus submissum est qui sese mutuis cladibus infestabant.

[34] Succedente tempore, surrexit quidam iuvenis Dunwallo Molmutius nomine, filius Clotenis ducis Cornubiae, specie et audacia omnes reges Britanniae excellens. Qui ut patris hereditatem suscepisset, surrexit in Pinnerem regem

years. At that time Isaiah and Hosea were prophesying, and Rome was founded by the twin brothers Remus and Romulus on the twenty-first day of April.

[33] Eventually, Cunedagius died and his son Rivallo succeeded him, a most powerful and sensible young man, who governed the kingdom with diligence. In his time a bloody rain fell for three days and men died from a swarm of flies. Rivallo was succeeded by his son Gurgustius; he by Sisillius; he by Iago the nephew of Gurgustius; he by Kinmarcus the son of Sisillius; he by Gorbodiago. Gorbodiago had two sons, Ferreus and Porrex. While their father was still living but approaching old age, a dispute over the kingdom arose between them. Inflamed with a desire for the kingdom, Porrex planned to kill his brother by treachery. When Ferreus learned of this, he avoided the ambush and sailed over to Gaul, obtained help from Suhardus, the king of the Franks, returned, and battled with his brother. During the battle, however, Ferreus was killed with all his men. Afterward their mother, Indon by name, was upset by the death of her son because she loved him dearly, and she was stirred to hatred and anger against his victorious brother. So when she found a suitable time to take revenge, she attacked her son with her maidservants while he was sound asleep and tore him into many pieces. After that civil war afflicted the people for a long time and the kingdom was subject to five kings who attacked each other with mutual devastation.

[34] With the passage of time a certain young man by the name of Dunwallo Molmutius arose, the son of Clotenus the Duke of Cornwall, exceeding all the kings of Britain in his appearance and boldness. When he had received the inheritance from his father, he rose up against Pinnerus, the

Loegrie et facto congressu interfecit eum. Deinde convenerunt Rudaucus rex Kambriae atque Staterius rex Albaniae
confirmatoque inter se foedere duxerunt exercitus suos in
2 terram Dunwallonis omnia depopulantes. Quibus venit obvius Dunwallo cum triginta milibus virorum et proelium
commisit. Ut autem multum diei pugnatum est et adhuc victoria staret utrisque in ambiguo, sevocavit Dunwallo ad se
sescentos audacissimos iuvenes et armis interemptorum armavit eos. Ipse quoque proiectis illis quibus armatus erat similiter fecit. Deinde duxit eos in catervas hostium quasi ex
3 ipsis essent. Nactus ergo locum quo Rudaucus et Staterius
erant, commilitonibus dixit ut in ipsos irruerent et fortiter
ferirent. Facto itaque impetu, perimuntur praedicti duo reges et plures alii cum illis. At Dunwallo timens ne a suis op-
primeretur, proiectis hostium armis et suis resumptis, ad
suos revertitur et ruens acriter in hostium catervas victoria
potitus est, fugatis partim caesisque partim hostibus ter-
4 raque omnis siluit in conspectu eius. Cumque totam Britanniam dominio suo subiugasset, fecit sibi diadema ex auro et
regnum in pristinum statum reduxit. Hic leges quae Mol-
muntinae dicuntur inter Britones statuit, quae usque ad hoc
tempus inter Anglos celebrantur. Statuit quoque inter cetera, ut templa deorum et civitates tali dignitate pollerent,
ut quicumque fugitivus sive reus ad ea confugeret, liber ab
omni impedimento et securus abiret et ad propria rediret.
5 Decretum est etiam ut in itinere templi et civitatis et fori

king of Loegria, and killed him in battle. Then Rudaucus, the king of Wales, and Staterius, the king of Albany, came together and having reached an alliance between themselves they led their armies into the land of Dunwallo, laying waste to it all. Dunwallo came against them with thirty thousand ₂ troops and engaged in battle. However, when they had been fighting for much of the day and the victory of either side still appeared uncertain, Dunwallo called to himself six hundred of his most courageous young men and armed them with the arms of the fallen. He himself, casting aside what he had been armed with, did the same. Then he led them among the enemies' troops as if they belonged there. He ₃ found where Rudaucus and Staterius were located and told his comrades to attack them and strike boldly. The assault was launched, and those two kings were slain and many others with them. Dunwallo, fearing that he might be attacked by his own men, cast aside the enemies' armor and resumed his own. He returned to his own men and by sharply attacking the enemy host he achieved victory. Some of the enemies were put to flight, some were killed, and the whole land grew quiet before him. And when he had subjected all of ₄ Britain to his dominion, he made himself a crown of gold, and restored the kingdom to its former state. He established among the Britons what are called the Molmutine laws, which are celebrated up to the present time among the English. He established among other things that the temples of the gods and the cities should enjoy such respect that whatever fugitive or criminal took sanctuary in them could leave them safe and free from any impediment and return to their own territory. It was also decreed that the same law would ₅ apply to the roads leading to temples, cities and courts, and

necnon et culturae aratri eadem lex haberetur. Cessabant ergo in diebus eius latronum mucrones et raptorum rapinae nec erat usquam qui violentiam alicui inferret. Hac pace et quiete cum quadraginta annis regnum administrasset, diem clausit ultimum in Urbe Trinovantum et prope templum Concordiae sepultus est, quod ipse ad confirmationem legum construxerat.

also to the tilling of the fields. In his days the swords of bandits and the robbery of robbers ceased, and there was no one anywhere who would do violence to anyone. After he had administered the kingdom with peace and quiet for forty years, he ended his days in the city of London and was buried near the Temple of Concord, which he had built himself as a monument to the law.

BOOK THREE

Liber III

[35] Dunwalloni successerunt filii eius Belinus et Brennius. Qui cum de regno inter se contenderent, censuerunt proceres terrae regnum hac ratione dividendum ut Belinus in parte sua Loegriam et Kambriam necnon et Cornubiam possideret. Erat enim primogenitus poscebatque Troiana

2 consuetudo ut hereditatis dignior pars ei proveniret. Brennius vero iunior Nordhamhumbriam ab Humbro usque Cathenesiam obtineret et fratri subderetur. Confirmato igitur super his foedere, rexerunt terram cum pace et iustitia per quinquennium. Interea surrexerunt adulatores quidam, mendacii fabricatores, Brennium adeuntes et sic affantes:

3 "Utquid te occupat ignavia qua fratri Belino subiciaris, cum idem pater et mater eademque generis nobilitas te ei parificet? Adde quod in militia praevales, totiens expertus vires tuas in duce Morianorum Cheulfo, terra marique Albanorum provinciam vastante; cui resistere et de regno fugare potuisti. Rumpe ergo foedus quod tibi dedecori est et contra generositatem tuam fecisti et fac, consilio procerum tuorum, ut ducas filiam Elfingii regis Norguegensium et ipsius auxilio dignitatem amissam recuperes."

Book 3

[35] Dumwallo was succeeded by his two sons, Belinus and Brennius. When they were fighting over the kingdom between themselves, the leading men of the country recommended that the kingdom be divided in such a way that Belinus for his part would possess Loegria and Wales and also Cornwall. For he was the firstborn, and Trojan custom demanded that the more worthy part of the inheritance should come to him. Brennius, the younger brother, would receive 2 Northumbria from the Humber to Caithness, and be made subordinate to his brother. Once an agreement was confirmed on these terms, they ruled the land with peace and justice for half a decade. Meanwhile certain flatterers arose, makers of lies, approaching Brennius and addressing him as follows: "Why does this idleness overtake you, by which you 3 are subjected to your brother Belinus, when the same father and mother and also the same nobility of birth make you equal to him? Moreover, you excel over him in warfare, having so often tested your powers against Cheulfus, Duke of the Morini, whom you were able to withstand and drive from the kingdom when he was laying waste to the province of the Albans by land and sea. Therefore break this pact which is dishonorable to you and which you made contrary to your nobility, and see to it that, with the consent of your nobles, you marry the daughter of Elfingius, king of the Norwegians, and with his help regain your lost dignity."

4   Ut igitur his et aliis animum iuvenis corruperunt, acquievit consilio eorum et transiens in Norguegiam duxit regis filiam.

[36] Quod cum fratri nuntiatum esset, indignatus quod sine sui licentia se inconsulto id egisset adiit cum exercitu Nordamhumbriam occupavitque comprovincialium civitates et munitiones et custodibus suis tradidit custodiendas. Porro Brennius peracto negotio cum uxore et magnis copiis

2 Norguegensium parato navigio redit Britanniam. Rumor enim innotuerat de fratre, quia urbes et munitiones suas armato milite invaserat; cumque iam in altum aequora sulcaret, Gudlacus rex Dacorum ex insidiis prosiliens, invasit classem et dimicans cum Brennio cepit forte navem in qua puella fuerat illatisque uncis illam intra consocias naves attraxit. Ardebat enim eius amore et duxisset eam uxorem nisi

3 Brennius praepedisset. Interea ruunt ex adverso venti factoque turbine navigium dissipant et in diversa litora compellunt. Rex autem Dacorum, vi tempestatis actus, quinque dierum cursu rabie ventorum pulsus, applicuit cum puella in

4 Britanniam, nesciens quam esset nactus patriam. Captus itaque a pagensibus ductus est ad Belinum regem, qui et ipse super maritima fratris adventum praestolabatur. Erant autem cum nave Gudlaci tres aliae naves, quarum una fuerat ex Brennii navigio lapsa; quorum hominum relatu rei causa et

After they had corrupted the young man's mind with 4
these and other arguments, he accepted their advice,
crossed over to Norway, and took the king's daughter in
marriage.

[36] When this was reported to his brother, incensed that
Brennius had acted without his permission and indeed without even consulting him, he went with an army to Northumbria and occupied the cities and fortresses of the locals and
handed them over to his own guards to be guarded. At this
point Brennius concluded his business, prepared his fleet,
and returned to Britain with his wife and a great force of
Norwegians. For news had spread that his brother had in- 2
vaded his cities and strongholds with armed soldiery. But as
Brennius was already plowing across the high seas Gudlacus,
king of the Danes, rushing forth from ambush, attacked the
fleet and while fighting with Brennius happened to lay hold
of the ship the young woman was in and dragged it with a
grappling hook into the midst of his own ships. For he too
was burning with love for her and would have taken her as
his wife, had Brennius not interfered. Meanwhile the winds 3
rushed in from an adverse quarter and caused a whirlwind,
scattering the fleet and driving it to different shores. But
the king of the Danes, driven by the force of the storm and
battered for five days by the course of the raging winds,
landed with the young woman in Britain, not knowing what
country he had reached. After he was captured by the peas- 4
ants he was taken to King Belinus, who was at the coast
himself, expecting the arrival of his brother. Along with
Gudlacus's ship there were three other ships, one of which
had been lost from Brennius's fleet; from the report of
its men the reason for the affair and their misfortunes was

infortunium patuit Belino. Captus igitur rex Gudlacus cum puella et ceteris qui in navibus erant, custodiae mancipatur.

[37] Emensis deinde aliquot diebus, ecce Brennius resociatis navibus in Albaniam applicuit. Qui cum audisset et uxoris retentionem et regni sui occupationem, misit nuntios fratri ut uxor et regnum restituerentur sibi. Sin autem testatus est caeli numina se totam Britanniam a mari usque ad mare ferro et igne vastaturum. Audiens ergo Belinus negavit plane quod petebat collectoque omni exercitu venit obviam fratri pugnaturus. Brennius quoque, fidens in Norguegensibus suis et exercitu undecumque collecto, occurrit illi obviam in nemore quod vocatur Calaterium, ubi congredientes magnam caedem utrimque fecerunt. Postremo, praevalentibus Britonibus, diffugiunt Norguegenses vulnerati ad naves, Belino insequente et stragem magnam patrante. Ceciderunt in illo conflictu quindecim milia hominum, nec ex residuis mille superfuerunt qui illaesi abscederent. At Brennius, vix unam navim nactus, ut fortuna dedit, Gallicana litora petivit; ceteri quoque, quo casus ducebat, fuga delituerunt.

[38] Cum igitur Belino victoria cessisset, convocavit regni proceres infra Eboracum, consilio illorum tractaturus, quid de rege Dacorum faceret. Mandaverat namque illi ex carcere quod sese regnumque Daciae sibi submitteret tributumque singulis annis daret, si liber cum amica sua sineretur abire, pactumque hoc fidei iuramento et obsidibus datis

revealed to Belinus. So Gudlacus was taken prisoner along with the young woman and the others who had been in the ship, and placed in custody.

[37] After some days had passed, Brennius regrouped his ships and landed in Albany. When he had heard about his wife's captivity and the occupation of his kingdom, he sent messengers to his brother demanding that his wife and his kingdom be restored to him; otherwise he swore by the heavens that he would destroy all of Britain with sword and fire from sea to sea. Hearing this, Belinus flatly refused what 2 he asked and, mustering his entire army, he went out to meet his brother and do battle with him. Brennius, confident in his Norwegian allies, with an army assembled from every quarter, also rushed out to meet him in the forest called Calaterium, where they joined in battle and inflicted great slaughter on both sides. Finally, the Britons prevailed and 3 the Norwegians ran wounded to their ships, with Belinus following them and inflicting great slaughter. Fifteen thousand men fell in that battle, and there did not remain a thousand among the survivors who could withdraw uninjured. But Brennius, having found only a single ship, as luck would have it, sailed to the coast of Gaul; the rest, as chance directed them, took refuge in flight.

[38] Consequently, when the victory had been granted to Belinus, he called the elders of the kingdom together in York to elicit their counsel about what to do with the king of the Danes. For the latter had sent word from prison that he would submit himself and the kingdom of Denmark to Belinus and would pay tribute each year if he was allowed to depart as a free man with his beloved, and that he would seal this agreement by an oath of loyalty and by giving hostages.

firmaret. Audita igitur huiuscemodi pactione, consilio et assensu baronum, rex Dacorum e carcere solutus liber cum suis abire permittitur atque in Daciam sospes rediit.

[39] Rex itaque Belinus, totius Britanniae dominio potitus, leges quas pater adinvenerat confirmavit, addens quoque ut strata viarum quae ducebant ad civitates ex caemento et lapidibus fabricarentur—quae scilicet a Cornubiensi mari usque ad Catinensium litus in introitu Albaniae, id est
2 ab australi plaga in septentrionem, protenderentur. Iussit etiam aliam fieri in latitudinem regni a Menevia urbe, quae super Demeticum mare sita est, usque ad Portum Hamonis, id est ab oriente in occidentem, ut ducatum praeberet ad urbes infra positas. Alias quoque duas ex obliquo terrae vias construere praecepit ut utroque latere accessus ad urbes et municipia paterent. Erat enim terra lutosa et aquosa, utpote insula intra mare sita; nec ante Dunwallonem patrem Belini extiterat quisquam qui viarum aut pontium curam haberet
3 in toto regno. Deinde sancivit eas Belinus omni honore omnique dignitate iurisque sui esse praecepit ita ut de illata super eas violentia supplicium sumeretur. Si quis autem scire desiderat omnia quae de ipsis praeceperit, legat Molmuntinas leges, quas Gildas historiographus de Britannico in Latinum, rex vero Aluredus de Latino in Anglicum transtulit, et reperiet luculenter scripta quae optat.

After the agreement had been accepted on these terms, with the advice and consent of the barons the king of the Danes was released from prison and permitted to depart as a free man with his companions, and he returned safe and sound to Denmark.

[39] And so King Belinus, having obtained dominion over all of Britain, confirmed the laws which his father had established, adding also that the pavement of the roads that led to the cities should be made from cement and stones and that those should be extended from the Cornish sea to the shore of Caithness at the entrance to Albany, that is from the southern region to the north. He also ordered that another should be built, across the breadth of the kingdom, from the city of St. David's, which is situated on the Demetian sea, to Southampton, that is from east to west, in order to provide a route to the cities located along the way. He commanded another two roads to be built diagonally across the land in order to allow access to the cities and towns on either side. For the land was muddy and wet, inasmuch as the island was situated in the midst of the ocean; and before Belinus's father Dunwallo no one had been put in charge of the roads or bridges for the whole kingdom. Then Belinus dedicated them with every honor and every dignity and declared it to be his law that punishment would be administered for any violence inflicted upon them. But if anyone wants to know all that he decreed about them, he should read the Molmutine laws, which Gildas the historian translated from British into Latin, and King Alfred from Latin into English, and he will find what he wishes clearly set forth.

[40] Belino autem regnum cum pace et tranquillitate re-
gente, frater eius Brennius in Gallias ut praedictum est appulsus, principes regni duodecim tantum militibus commitatus adiit, casum suum singulis ostendens atque auxilium
2   ab eis petens quo honorem amissum recuperare queat. Venit
tandem ad Seginum Allobrogum ducem, a quo gratanter
susceptus, tum quia nobili prosapia ortus, tum quia curiali-
ter erat edoctus, per temporis spacium retentus est. Erat
enim pulcher aspectu, venatu et aucupatu omnibus prae-
cellens. Cum igitur in amicitiam et familiaritatem ducis in-
cidisset, statuit dux consilio suorum fidelium unicam filiam
quam habebat sibi copulare, cum ducatu Allobrogum si
3   masculino careret herede. Nec mora desponsatur ei puella
principesque terrae ei subduntur. Et vix annus emensus erat;
suprema die adveniente mortuus est dux. Brennius itaque
principatu potitus, quos prius amicitia et obsequiis illexerat,
largitionibus donorum accumulat.

[41] Procedente ergo tempore, per totam Galliam collecto exercitu, in Britanniam profectus est; congregato in
Neustriam ab omni litore navigio, inde secundis velis in Britanniam applicuit. Divulgato autem eius adventu, Belinus
armatorum stipatus caterva proelium cum illo commissurus
2   obvius venit. Sed cum hinc inde cohortes se ad bellum pararent, mater amborum ducum, Tonwenna nomine, adhuc
vivens se mediam aciebus interserit, per dispositas incedens

[40] While Belinus was ruling the realm in peace and tranquility, his brother Brennius, having been driven to Gaul as said before, went to the princes of that realm, with an escort of only twelve knights, explaining his misfortune to each one of them and asking for help from them, so that he might be able to recover his lost throne. Eventually he came 2 to Seginus, Duke of the Allobroges, by whom he was received with joy, either because he was born of a noble family or because he had been raised at court, and was kept for a period of time. For he was handsome in appearance, surpassing all others in hunting and fowling. When, therefore, he had entered into friendship and familiarity with the duke, the duke decided, on the advice of his faithful advisers, to join Brennius with his only daughter, along with the leadership of the Allobroges if he should die without a masculine heir. Without delay, the girl was betrothed to Bren- 3 nius, and the princes of the land were placed under him. And when barely a year had passed, the duke's last day arrived and he died. Once Brennius obtained the leadership, through lavish distribution of gifts he increased the number of followers he had previously attracted by friendship and services.

[41] As time went by, he gathered an army throughout Gaul and made for Britain; a fleet was assembled in Neustria from every shore, and from there, with a following wind, he sailed to Britain. When his arrival was announced, Belinus came to meet him to engage in battle, surrounded by a host of armed men. But as the forces on either side were prepar- 2 ing for combat, the mother of the two commanders, Tonwenna by name, who was still alive, planted herself between the front lines of the advancing forces. For she was burning

turmas. Aestuabat enim filium videre quem multo tempore non viderat. Ut igitur tremulis gressibus ad locum quo ipse erat pervenit, brachia materna collo filii innectit, optata carpens oscula, nudatisque uberibus illum in hunc modum affata est, sermonem impediente singultu:

3   "Memento, fili, memento uberum istorum quae suxisti, maternique uteri, unde te rerum opifex in hominem cum non esses creavit. Anxietatum igitur quas pro te pertuli, reminiscens petitioni meae acquiesce atque inceptam iram compesce. Nam quod dicis te a natione tua per fratrem tuum expulsum, si rei veritatem consideres, tu ipse te expulisti non ille, sicut nosti, quando regem Norguegensium eo inconsulto ut fratrem gravares adisti. Denique fugiens ad

4   summum honoris culmen provectus es. Plus profecisti in fuga quam si stares in patria. Subditus namque illi partem regni quae tibi contigerat possidebas et adhuc, si voluisses, habere potuisses. Quam ut dimisisti, par sibi aut maior factus es regnum Allobrogum adeptus. Quid igitur fecit nisi quod ex paupere te in sublimem erexit ducem? Adde quod gentem barbaram super eum adduxisti, qui te et illum forsitan regno privassent, si partes vestras debiliores aspexissent."

5   Brennius igitur, super matris lamentationibus motus, sedato animo acquievit et deposita galea secum ad fratrem perrexit. Belinus quoque, pacifico vultu, abiectis armis obviam ei venit et in amplexus, cum osculo pacis, se invicem

to see the son on whom she had not laid her eyes for a long time. Accordingly, when she came with trembling steps to where he stood, she fastened her motherly arms around her son's neck and, stealing wished-for kisses, with her breasts laid bare, she addressed him in this manner, her speech interrupted by sobs:

"Remember, my son, remember these breasts which you 3 sucked, and the maternal womb wherein the maker of all things brought you into being as a man when you did not exist. Remembering the pains that I suffered for you, grant my plea and curb your growing anger. For while you say you were driven from your country by your brother, if you consider the truth of the matter, it was you who drove yourself out, not your brother, as you realized when you approached the king of Norway without his permission in order to make trouble for him. And then while fleeing you were carried to the highest summit of honor. You accomplished more in 4 flight than if you had stayed in this country. For when you were subject to him, you possessed only the part of the realm that belonged to you, and if you had wanted it you would have it still. When you lost it, you became equal or greater than him, because you gained the kingdom of the Allobroges. What has he therefore done if not to raise you up from a pauper to an exalted leader? Moreover, you brought a barbaric people against him, which perhaps would have deprived you and him of the kingdom had they found your side to be weaker."

Inspired by his mother's lamentations, Brennius obeyed 5 her with a calm spirit, removed his helmet, and went with her to his brother. Belinus, too, with a peaceful countenance laid his arms aside and came to meet him; with a kiss of

brachiis fraternis innexuerunt. Nec mora, amici facti sunt et Urbem Trinovantum pariter ingressi sunt. Ibique consilio capto communem exercitum parant et cum magno navigio ad Gallias simul transfretaverunt.

[42] Quod cum per nationes divulgatum fuisset, convenerunt omnes reguli Francorum in unum exercitum contra eos ut bellando eos vi de terra sua eicerent. At Belino et Brennio victoria favente, fractis catervis atque diffusis, Franci fugam

2 arripiunt. Fugientes ergo Francos Britones et Allobroges insecuntur, caedunt, interimunt et quosdam capiunt; captos compedibus et manicis ferreis tradunt, ipsos quoque regulos deditioni coegerunt, urbibusque eversis et munitionibus captis, totum Galliae regnum infra annum submiserunt.

[43] Postremo, petentes Romam, Italiam ferro et igne depopulantur. Erant tunc temporis Romae duos consules creati, Gabius et Porsenna; qui cum nullam fiduciam resistendi super gentem suam haberent, assensu et consilio senatorum concordiam et amicitiam petentes, auri et argenti copia plurimisque diversis donariis largiendo, quod petebant impetraverunt, singulis annis tributum de Italia et

2 censu Romanorum paciscentes. Acceptis itaque obsidibus et foedere firmato, in Germaniam duxerunt exercitum ad bellandos eiusdem terrae populos. Exeuntibus autem illis de Romanorum finibus, terrore sublato, piguit Romanos praefati foederis et resumpta audacia a tergo eos oppugnare coe-

3 perunt. Germanis itaque a fronte resistentibus et Italis a

peace they hugged each other in a brotherly embrace. They immediately became allies and entered into London together. There they took counsel, raised a joint army, and together they passed over to Gaul with a great fleet.

[42] When news of this had spread among the peoples of Gaul, all of the minor kings of the Franks came together in one army against them in order to do battle and drive them out of their land by force. Belinus and Brennius were favored by victory and the Franks took flight, their troops broken and scattered. As the Franks were fleeing, the Britons and the Allobroges pursued them, struck them down, killed them, and captured a few; they put iron shackles and manacles on the captives and forced the kings to surrender, destroyed the cities, and captured the fortifications, and within the year they subjugated the entire kingdom of Gaul.

[43] After that, making for Rome, they laid waste to Italy with sword and fire. At that time there were two consuls in Rome, Gabius and Porsenna. Because they had no confidence in their own people to resist, seeking peace and friendship with the advice and consent of the senate, by lavishly giving an abundance of gold and silver and a great many other offerings, they obtained what they desired by agreeing to send a tribute once a year from Italy and the wealth of the Romans. After hostages were accepted and a treaty established, Belinus and Brennius led the army into Germany to make war upon the people of that land. But as they were leaving the territory of the Romans, because the fear of them had been lifted, the Romans repented of the treaty just mentioned and, recovering their courage, began to attack Belinus and Brennius from the rear. As the Germans were resisting in front of them and the Italians were harass-

tergo infestantibus, terror invasit Britones et Allobroges. In tanta tamen anxietate positi, festino utuntur consilio fratres ut Belinus, scilicet cum Britonibus suis, oppugnare Germanos insisteret, Brennius vero cum suis Romam rediret et
4 rupti foederis iniuriam in Romanos vindicaret. Reverso ergo Brennio in Italiam Romani, qui ad Germanos auxiliandos exercitum Allobrogum et Britonum per notas vias praeterierant, Romam redire coeperunt et Brennium praecedere festinabant. Belinus autem, praecognito per exploratores eorum transitu, Alpium itinera occupat vallemque nactus qua hostes futura nocte transituri erant, infra illam cum suis
5 delituit, omnem strepitum suorum compescens. Venientes itaque Itali ad eundem locum, nil tale verentes, insidias Belini compererunt. Et cum vallem armis hostium fulgere ad lunae radios cernerent, stupefacti in fugam versi sunt. Quos gradu propero insequens Belinus, stragem non modicam illucescente aurora incepit Italis inferre. Nec cessavit gladius eius a mane usque ad vesperam Romanos caedere, donec nox superveniens eorum impetum compescuit atque diremit. Prostratis itaque Romanis atque dispersis, flectit iter post Brennium atque Romam petit.
6 Ut igitur communem exercitum simul fecerunt, Romam undique obsidione cinxerunt; invadentes muros machinis ad terram prosternunt et Romanis immensum terrorem inferunt. Romani ergo econtra viriliter resistentes a muris propulsabant fundibulis et ballistis eorum ferocem audaciam et lapidibus immensis muros infestantes obruebant.

ing them to the rear, the Britons and the Allobroges were overcome with fear. In a position of such anxiety, the brothers quickly made the decision that Belinus would stay with his Britons to fight the Germans, while Brennius would return with his troops to Rome and take revenge upon the Romans for breaking the treaty. After Brennius returned to Italy the Romans, who had overtaken the army of the Britons and Allobroges by routes known to them in order to lend help to the Germans, started back to Rome and hurried to get ahead of Brennius. Belinus, however, having been forewarned by his scouts about their passage, occupied the route across the Alps and, having found a valley which the enemy would be passing through the next night, he concealed himself in it with his men, suppressing all their noise. The Italians came to that place without suspecting a thing 5 and came across Belinus's ambush. And when they saw the valley glittering in the moonlight with the arms of their enemies they were stunned and turned back in flight. Following them at a speedy pace, as the dawn began to break Belinus commenced a great slaughter of the Italians. His sword did not cease to kill Romans from morning until night, and when darkness came he blocked and cut off their attack. With the Romans overthrown and scattered, he turned his path to follow after Brennius and made for Rome.

As soon as they joined their forces, they surrounded 6 Rome with a blockade on all sides; attacking the walls with siege engines, they knocked them to the ground and caused immense terror among the Romans. So the Romans, resisting them vigorously, repulsed their ferocious courage from the walls using their catapults and ballistae, and crushed them with immense stones as they were attacking the walls.

Quod cum duces ambo Brennius et Belinus aspexissent, in-
doluerunt de strage suorum et accensi ira obsides, quos a
Romanis susceperant, scilicet viginti quatuor ex nobiliori-
7 bus, patibulis ante portas affixerunt. At Romani, proter-
viores propter contumeliam filiorum et nepotum effecti,
freti legatione consulum, Gabii scilicet et Porsennae, qui ut
congregarent exercitum de Apulia et Italia praecesserant,
eadem die qua illos adesse noverunt eis in auxilium, statutis
agminibus, urbem egrediuntur et cominus cum ducibus
congrediuntur. Hinc Gabius et Porsenna, hinc Romani, ho-
8 stes inparatos occupare temptant. Porro fratres ambo, cum
cladem commilitonum tam subito illatam inspexissent, convocato exercitu in turmas et centurias suos resociaverunt et
irruptionem in hostes audacter facientes retrocedere coegerunt. Postremo, innumerabilibus utrimque caesis victoria
cessit fratribus. Interempto namque in certamine Gabio et
Porsenna capto, urbem victores subintrant, diversi generis
opibus ditati.

[44] Capta itaque, sicut dictum est, Roma Belinus in Britanniam reversus est. Brennius vero in Italia remansit, populum inaudita tyrannide premens. Cuius vitam et actus tex-
tus Romanae Historiae declarat. Belino autem in Britanniam
reverso, renovare coepit urbes veteres ubicumque collapsae
fuerant et quasdam novas aedificare ubi prius non fuerant.
2 Inter quas condidit unam super Oscam flumen prope

When both commanders, Brennius and Belinus, had seen this, they were distressed by the slaughter of their men and, inflamed with anger, they fastened the hostages they had accepted from the Romans, twenty-four individuals of the highest nobility, to gibbets in front of the gates. But the Romans were made all the more aggressive because of the indignity done to their sons and grandsons, and relied upon an embassy from the consuls, namely Gabius and Porsenna, who had proceeded to gather an army from Apulia and Italy. Assembling an army on the same day they learned the consuls were coming to help them, they marched out from the city and joined in close combat against the two commanders. On this side Gabius and Porsenna, on that side the Romans, each tried to catch the enemy unprepared. When both brothers witnessed from afar the disaster so suddenly inflicted upon their fellow soldiers, having summoned their army, they immediately reassembled their men in squadrons and companies and charging boldly against the enemies forced them to retreat. Finally, after an immense number had been cut down on either side, victory fell to the brothers. Gabius was killed in the battle and Porsenna taken captive; the victors entered the city, enriched by many kinds of treasure.

[44] After Rome was captured, in the way we said, Belinus returned to Britain. Brennius however stayed in Italy, oppressing the people with unheard-of tyranny. The text of the Roman History describes his life and deeds. Belinus, however, having returned to Britain, began to restore the old cities wherever they had fallen into ruins, and to build some new ones where they had not been before. Among those he founded one on the River Usk near the Severn Sea

Sabrinum mare, quae Kaerusc appellata, metropolis Demetiae facta est; quae postea a Romanis urbs Legionum dicta est pro eo quod in eadem legiones Romanorum hiemare solebant. Fecit etiam in Urbe Trinovantum portam mire fabricae super ripam Thamensis fluvii quam postea Saxones

3 Angli Belnesgata appellaverunt. Desuper vero portam aedificavit turrim mire magnitudinis, portumque subtus navibus idoneum. Leges quoque paternas in regno renovavit et firmas teneri praecepit, constanti iustitiae indulgens. In diebus eius tanta copia terram refecit quantam nec retro ulla aetas habuisse meminit, nec subsequens subsecuta fuit.

4 Cum ergo summa tranquillitate rexisset populum, ultimum clausit diem in Urbe Trinovantum. Cuius corpus combustum in aureo cado repositum in summitate turris quam fecerat decenter collocatum est.

[45] Successit ei filius eius Gurguint Barthruc nomine, vir modestus et prudens, qui per omnia patris actus imitans pacem et iustitiam amavit. Interea contigit Dacos non reddere tributum quod diebus patris et pacti sunt reddere et sibi persolvebant. Quod graviter ferens transivit cum magna classe in Daciam. Afflictoque durissimis proeliis populo, regem Dacorum interfecit et regnum pristino iugo subdidit.

[46] Ea tempestate, cum dispositis omnibus pro voluntate sua, domum per insulas Orcadum rediret, invenit ibi triginta naves viris et mulieribus plenas. Causam ergo adventus eorum quaerens, accessit ad illum dux classis eiusdem, Partholoum nomine, et adorato eo veniam rogavit et

2 pacem. Qua impetrata, dixit se ex partibus Hispaniarum

which was called Kaerusk and became the capital of Demetia; later it was called the City of Legions by the Romans because the Roman legions were accustomed to pass the winter there. He also made a gate of marvelous workmanship in London on the bank of the River Thames, which the Anglo-Saxons later called Billingsgate. Above the gate he built a ₃ tower of marvelous size and under it a harbor suitable for ships. Granting consistent justice, he also renewed his father's laws throughout the kingdom and ordered them to be held firm. In his days such plenty revived the land as no age recalled having before, nor any later age experienced. After ₄ he had ruled the people with the greatest tranquility, he ended his life in the city of London. After his body was burned and placed in a golden urn, it was fittingly laid to rest at the top of the tower he had made.

[45] His son Gurguint Barthruc succeeded him, a modest and prudent man, who loved peace and justice, imitating his father in all of his deeds. Meanwhile it happened that the Danes did not render the tribute which they had both promised to render in his father's days and used to pay in full. Taking this very seriously, he passed over to Denmark with a great fleet. The people were crushed by very harsh battles, he killed the king of the Danes, and he reduced the kingdom to its former submission.

[46] At that time, with everything arranged according to his wishes, while returning home through the Orkney Islands he found thirty ships there full of men and women. When he asked about the reason for their arrival, the leader of the fleet, named Partholoum, approached and did homage to him and asked for his pardon and for peace. When ₂ that was granted, he said that he had been banished from

expulsum et maria circuire, ut locum mansionis inveniret. Petiit ergo ut portiunculam Britanniae ad inhabitandum praestaret, ne odiosum iter maris diutius pererraret; quod

3 iam per annum unum et dimidium fecerat. Quo audito rex haud petitioni eius defuit et ad inhabitandam non Britanniam sed Hiberniam eis indulsit insulam, quae intacta adhuc hominum accessu fuerat, ductoresque eis de suis tradidit qui

4 eos illuc usque dirigerent. Ubi cum venissent, invenerunt terram opimam et apricam, nemoribus ac fluminibus et omni Dei munere opulentam; coeperuntque continuo ibi tabernacula sua aedificare et terram colere, creveruntque et multiplicati sunt ibidem usque in hodiernum diem. Gurguint vero rex, peracto vitae suae cursu, mortuus est et sepultus in Urbe Legionum.

[47] Post hunc Guizelinus diadema regni suscepit; quod satis modeste omni tempore vitae suae rexit. Erat ei nobilis uxor, Marcia nomine, omnibus artibus erudita; quae inter plurima proprio ingenio reperta legem quam Britones Marcianam appellant adinvenit. Hanc rex Aluredus inter cetera

2 transtulit et Saxonica lingua Merchenelaga vocavit. Mortuo autem Guizelino gubernaculum regni praedicte reginae remansit. Erat enim ei filius septem annorum, Sisillius nomine, cuius aetas nondum apta erat regimini. Sed postquam adolevit in virum diademate regni potitus est. Mortuo Sisillio, Kinewarus filius suus regnum obtinuit. Cui successit Danius eiusdem frater.

[48] Huic successit Morpidus ex concubina genitus. Is probitate famosissimus esset nisi plus nimio crudelitati

the regions of Spain and was roaming the seas in order to find a place to live. He then asked if he could lend them a small part of Britain to inhabit, so that he would no longer have to wander through his tiresome journey by sea, which he had now been doing for a year and a half. Hearing this, the king did not refuse his petition, and he granted to them not Britain but the island of Ireland to inhabit, which had until then been untouched by the arrival of men, and he gave them pilots from his own men who could guide them all the way there. When they came there, they found a fertile and sunny land, rich in forests and streams and every gift of God; there they immediately began to build their own dwellings and to cultivate the land, and in that place they multiplied and increased in number up to the present day. King Gurguint, however, having completed the course of his life, died and was buried in the City of Legions.

[47] After him Guizelinus received the crown of the kingdom; he ruled with innate moderation for his entire life. He had a noble wife named Marcia, learned in all the arts; among many other discoveries of her own making she invented the law which the Britons call Marcian. King Alfred translated this among other things and called it the *Merchenelaga* in the Saxon language. When Guizelinus died the government of the kingdom remained with this queen. For she had a seven-year-old son named Sisillius, who because of his age was not yet prepared to rule. But after he reached manhood he took possession of the crown of the kingdom. When Sisillius died his son Kinewarus obtained the kingdom. His brother Danius succeeded him.

[48] Morpidus, born to Danius's mistress, succeeded him. He would have been very famous for his uprightness had he

indulsisset. Iratus namque modum non habebat, nec cuiquam parcebat, sed proprio telo interficiebat. Pulcher tamen erat aspectu et in dandis muneribus profusus, nec erat
2 alter tantae fortitudinis in regno. Temporibus eius applicuit
quidam dux Morianorum cum magna classe armatorum in
Nordamhumbriam et devastare coepit patriam. Cui Morpidus occurrens cum valida manu Britonum, congressus est et
victoria potitus; ipse solus plus in proelio illo profecit quam
maxima pars sui exercitus. Et post victoriam vix superfuit
unus quem propriis manibus non interficeret, ut vel sic tru-
3 culentiam suam satiaret. At postquam perimendo fatigatus
est, vivos excoriari praecipiebat et excoriatos comburi. Inter
haec saevitiae suae acta, contigit a parte Hibernici maris
beluam inauditae magnitudinis et feritatis advenisse, quae
incolas secus maritima repertos miserabiliter lacerabat et
4 devorabat. Cuius fama cum aures eius pulsasset, accessit ad
illam solus viribus fidens et congressus est cum illa. At cum
omnia tela in ea consumpsisset, arreptum faucibus apertis
ipsum velut pisciculum devoravit.

[49] Genuerat ipse quinque filios, quorum primogenitus,
Gorbonianus nomine, solium regni suscepit. Nullus ea tempestate iustior erat aut amantior aequi, nec qui populum
maiori diligentia tractaret. Inter haec et plurima innatae
probitatis ipsius bona, debita naturae solvens, ab hac luce
migravit et in Urbe Trinovantum sepultus est.

[50] Successit illi Archgallo, frater eius, qui in actibus suis

not indulged in even more excessive cruelty. For when he was angry he had no restraint, nor did he spare anyone but killed them with his own weapon. Nevertheless, he was handsome in appearance and generous in giving gifts, and there was no one else of such strength in the kingdom. In 2 his time a certain duke of the Morini arrived in Northumbria with a great fleet of armed men and began to lay waste to the country. Marching out to meet him with a strong force of Britons, Morpidus joined him in battle and won the victory; he accomplished more by himself in that fight than most of his army. And after the victory hardly a single person was left that he did not kill with his own hands, in order to satisfy his ferocity to the utmost. And after he was 3 tired of killing, he ordered that the living be flayed and the flayed to be burned. In the midst of these acts of cruelty there happened to arrive from the region of the Irish Sea a whale of unheard-of size and ferocity which mercilessly tore apart and devoured the inhabitants it found along the coast. When news of this reached his ears, Morpidus approached 4 it alone, trusting in his strength, and joined in battle with it. But after he had used all his spears against it, the whale seized him with open jaws and devoured him like a little fish.

[49] Morpidus had five sons of whom the oldest, Gorbonianus by name, took the throne of the kingdom. There was no one in his time who was more just or more devoted to equity, and no one who treated the people with greater diligence. Amid these and many other good deeds arising from his innate virtue, repaying the debt to nature, he departed from this life and was buried in London.

[50] His brother Archgallo succeeded him, who proved

germano dissimilis exstitit. Nobiles namque deponere, ignobiles exaltare affectavit et quibusque sua auferre, thesauros accumulare non destitit donec regni fortiores diutius ferre non valentes, eum a solio deposuerunt et Elidurum, fratrem suum, in regem erexerunt. Qui postea, propter mi-

2 sericordiam quam in fratrem fecit, Pius vocatus est. Nam ubi Archgallo per quinquennium notos et ignotos provinciales circuisset, ut amissum honorem per eorum auxilium recuperaret, nec a quoquam exauditus fuisset, paupertate cogente reversus est ad fratrem Elidurum regem. Cui mox rex occurrens in nemore Calaterio, amplexatus est eum, os-

3 cula dans innumera. Et ut aliquamdiu fraternis amplexibus et fletibus invicem consolati sunt, duxit illum secum Elidurus in civitatem Aldclud et in thalamo suo occuluit et aegrotare finxit se, nuntios mittens per totius regni barones ut ad se visitandum venirent. Qui cum venissent, praecepit ut unusquisque singulatim et sine strepitu thalamum ingrederetur. Dicebat enim sermonis tumultum plurimum capiti

4 nociturum. Singulis ergo quiete ingredientibus praecipiebat Elidurus satellitibus ad hoc praeparatis, ut capita truncarentur extractis gladiis nisi se iterum fratri suo Archgalloni sicut prius fuerant submitterent. Sic igitur separatim de cunctis agens omnes Archgalloni mediante timore pacifica-

5 vit. Confirmato itaque omnium foedere duxit fratrem ad Eboracum, cepitque diadema de capite suo et fratris capiti imposuit. Unde postea, quia pius in fratrem extitit, nomen Pius suscepit. Regnavit deinde Archgallo decem annis et ab

to be different from his brother in his actions. For he aimed
to pull down the nobles, raise up the lowborn, and take away
everyone's possessions; he did not cease to accumulate treasures until the most powerful men of the kingdom, unable
to bear it any longer, deposed him from the throne and
raised up his brother Elidurus as king. He was later called
the Dutiful because of the mercy he showed his brother. For 2
after Archgallo had wandered among the inhabitants of familiar and unfamiliar provinces for half a decade in order to
recover his lost throne through their help, but had not been
heeded by anyone, he was compelled by poverty to return to
his brother, King Elidurus. The king, going out immediately
to meet him in the Calaterian forest, embraced him, giving
him innumerable kisses. And after they had consoled each 3
other for a while with brotherly hugs and tears, Elidurus
took him with him to the city of Dumbarton and hid him in
his bedchamber and pretended to be ill, sending messengers
to the barons throughout the kingdom that they should
come to visit him. When they had come, he ordered each of
them to enter the bedchamber alone and without a sound.
For he said that much noise from talk would hurt his head.
As each of them quietly entered, Elidurus ordered his re- 4
tainers, prepared for this, to cut off their heads with drawn
swords, unless they would once again submit to his brother
Archgallo as they had before. Doing this with all of them
separately, by means of fear he reconciled every one to Archgallo. After securing the promise of all, he led his brother 5
Archgallo to York and took the crown from his head and
placed it on his brother's head. Afterward, because he had
proved to be loyal to his brother, he received the name of
the Dutiful. Archgallo then ruled for ten years and, having

antecepta nequitia correptus iustior et mitior omnibus apparuit. Superveniente denique languore obiit et in urbe Kaerleir sepultus est.

[51] Erigitur Elidurus iterum in regem et pristinae dignitati restituitur. Sed dum Gorbonianum, fratrem suum primogenitum, in omni bonitate sequeretur, duo residui fratres eius Ingenius et Peredurus illum lacessere et infestare bello temptant. Congressi itaque potiti sunt victoria et ipsum captum turri Urbis Trinovantum custodiae mancipaverunt.

2 Deinde partiti regnum in duo diviserunt; Ingenio ab Humbro flumine usque in occidentem tota terra cessit, Pereduro Albania usque Humbrum. Emensis autem septem annis, obiit Ingenius et totum regnum cessit Pereduro; ipsumque post temporis spatium mors repentina surripuit. Elidurus igitur, carcere ereptus, tertio in regni solium sublimatur. Et cum totum tempus vitae suae bonis moribus et pietate iustitiaque explesset, ab hac luce migrans exemplum pietatis successoribus reliquid.

[52] Eliduro successit nepos eius, Gorboniani filius, avunculum moribus et prudentia imitatus. Post hunc regnavit Marganus Archgallonis filius. Qui etiam exemplo parentum serenatus, gentem suam cum tranquillitate rexit. Cui successit Ennianus, frater suus. Hic tractando iniuste populum et cum tyrannide exercens, sexto regni sui anno a regia

2 sede depositus est. In loco cuius positus est cognatus eius Idwallo, Ingenii filius; cui successit Runo, Pereduri filius; huic Gerontius, Eliduri filius; post hunc Catellus, filius suus;

been punished for his former wickedness, he appeared more just and mild to all. Overcome by infirmity at last, he died and was buried in the city of Kaerleir.

[51] Elidurus was raised again as king and restored to his former dignity. But while he imitated his eldest brother Gorbonianus in all good deeds, his two remaining brothers Ingenius and Peredurus tried to harass and vex him with war. Having joined in battle they won the victory and after they captured Elidurus they delivered him to the Tower of London for safekeeping. Then they divided the kingdom in two; all the land from the River Humber to the west went to Ingenius, that from Albany to the Humber to Peredurus. After seven years Ingenius died, and the entire kingdom fell to Peredurus; and after a space of time sudden death took him away. Consequently, Elidurus was freed from prison and raised to the throne of the kingdom for the third time. And since he completed all the time of his life with good behavior and loyalty and justice, departing from this world he left behind a model of loyalty for his successors.

[52] Elidurus was succeeded by his nephew, the son of Gorbonianus, who resembled his uncle in character and prudence. After him ruled Marganus, the son of Archgallo. Enlightened by the example of his ancestors, he ruled his people in peace. His brother Ennianus succeeded him. Because he treated the people unjustly and ruled with tyranny, in the sixth year of his reign he was removed from the throne. His relative Idwallo, the son of Ingenius, was put in his place; he was succeeded by Runo, the son of Peredurus; he by Gerontius the son of Elidurus; after him by his son Catellus; after Catellus by Coillus; after Coillus by Porrex;

post Catellum Coillus; post Coillum Porrex; Porreci successit Cherin. Huic nati fuerunt tres filii, Fulgenius videlicet et Eldaldus necnon et Andragius, qui omnes alter post alterum 3 regnaverunt. Post hos successit Urianus Andragii filius; cui Eliud; cui Cledaucus; cui Clotenus; cui Gurgutius; cui Merianus; cui Bledudo; cui Capenronius; cui Sisillius; cui Bledgabred. Hic omnes cantores quos retro aetas habuerat et in modulis et in musicis instrumentis excessit, ita ut deus iocu4 latorum diceretur. Post hunc regnavit Archmail frater suus; post hunc Eldol; huic successit Redion; cui Rederchius; cui Samuil Penissel; cui Pir; cui Capoir; cui Eligueillus, Capoiri filius, vir in omnibus actibus modestus et prudens.

[53] Post hunc Heli filius eius, regnumque quadraginta annis rexit. Hic tres generavit filios, Lud scilicet, Cassibellaunum, Nennium. Quorum primogenitus, id est Lud, regnum post obitum patris suscepit. Hic gloriosus urbium aedificator existens, renovavit et sublimavit prae ceteris muros Urbis Trinovantum et plurimis turribus eam circumcinxit. Praecepitque civibus ut palatia in eadem construerent, ita ut non esset in longe positis regnis civitas quae huic posset pa2 rificari. Iste Lud bellicosus et satis probus extitit et in dandis epulis profusus; et cum plures civitates possideret, hanc prae ceteris ornavit. Unde postmodum de nomine suo Kaerlud dicta est, ac deinde per corruptionem nominis Kaerlondem. Succedente tempore, per commutationem linguarum dicta est Lundene et postea Lundres, applicantibus alienige3 nis qui patriam linguam in suam commutaverunt. Defuncto tandem Lud, corpus eius reconditum est in praedicta civitate iuxta portam illam quae adhuc de nomine suo Portlud

and Porrex was succeeded by Cherin. To him were born three sons, namely Fulgenius and Eldadus and also Andragius, who all ruled one after the other. They were succeeded ₃ by Urianus, the son of Andragius; he by Eliud; he by Cledaucus; he by Clotenus; he by Gurgutius; he by Merianus; he by Bledudo; he by Capenronius; he by Sisillius; he by Bledgabred. This man surpassed all singers from previous ages both in melody and in playing musical instruments, so that he was said to be the god of minstrels. His brother ₄ Archmail ruled after him; then Eldol; he was succeeded by Redion; he by Rederchius; he by Samuil Penissel; he by Pir; he by Capoir; he by Eligueillus, the son of Capoir, a man who was modest and prudent in all of his actions.

[53] After him came his son Heli, and he ruled the kingdom for forty years. He had three children, namely Lud, Cassibellaunus, and Nennius. The eldest, that is Lud, inherited the kingdom after the death of his father. Becoming a famous builder of cities, he restored and raised the walls of London above all the rest, and he surrounded it with many towers. He also directed the citizens to build palaces there, so that there would not be a city in any far-off kingdom that could equal this one. This Lud was warlike and very honor- ₂ able and he was generous in giving feasts; and although he possessed many cities, he adorned this one above the others. It was later called Kaerlud after him, but then became Kaerlondem through corruption of the name. As time passed, through alteration of the language it was called Lundene, and after that Lundres by the arrival of strangers who altered the native language to their own. When Lud finally ₃ died, his body was concealed in that city next to the gate which is still known from his name as Portlud in British and

Britannice, Saxonice vero Ludesgata nuncupatur. Nati fuerant ei filii duo, Androgeus et Tenuantius. Qui cum aetate adhuc iuniores regni administrationi minime sufficerent, Cassibellaunus eorum avunculus loco illorum in regnum sublimatur. Mox, diademate insignitus, tanta coepit largitate ac probitate pollere ut fama eius undique divulgaretur, etiam in extrema regna. Nepotibus deinde adultis et ad virilem aetatem excretis pietati indulgens noluit illos omnino expertes regni esse sed in partes tamquam ascivit, Urbem Trinovantum cum ducatu Cantiae tribuens Androgeo, ducatum Cornubiae Tenuantio. Ipse diademate praelatus, ipsis et totius regni principibus imperabat.

Ludesgata in Saxon. Two sons were born to him, Androgeus and Tenuantius. Because of their age the younger men were still not ready for the administration of the kingdom, so their uncle Cassibellaunus was raised to the throne in their place. Soon, honored with the crown, he began to distinguish himself by such liberality and uprightness that his fame spread everywhere, even to far-off kingdoms. When his nephews were adult and grown to a mature age, yielding to his sense of loyalty, he did not want them to be entirely lacking a share in royal power, but in some regions he made them his associates, so to speak, giving the city of London along with the leadership of Kent to Androgeus, and the leadership of Cornwall to Tenuantius. He himself, preeminent because of the crown, retained sovereignty over them and the leaders of the whole realm.

4

BOOK FOUR

Liber IV

[54] Interea contigit, ut in Romanis reperitur historiis, Iulium Caesarem subiugata Gallia in Britanniam transisse. Sic enim scriptum est: anno ab urbe condita sescentesimo nonagesimo tertio, ante vero incarnationem Domini anno sexagesimo, Iulius Caesar primus Romanorum Britannias bello pulsavit, in navibus onerariis et actuariis circiter octo-

2 ginta advectus. Cum enim ad litus Rutenorum venisset et illinc Britanniam aspexisset, quaesivit a circumstantibus quae patria, quae gens inhabitasset. Cumque nomen regni didicisset et populi, ait: "Hercle! Ex eadem prosapia nos Romani descendimus quia ex Troiana gente processimus. Nobis Aeneas post destructionem Troiae primus pater fuit, illis autem Brutus, Silvii Aeneae filius. Sed, nisi fallor, valde a nobis degenerati sunt, nec quid sit militia noverunt, cum infra

3 Oceanum extra orbem commaneant. Leviter cogendi erunt tributum nobis dare et obsequium Romanae dignitati praestare. Prius tamen per nuntios requirendi sunt ut Romanis subiciantur et vectigal reddant ut ceterae gentes."

Quod cum litteris regi Cassibellauno intimasset, indignatus rex epistulam suam ei remisit haec verba continentem:

Book 4

[54] Meanwhile it came to pass, as one finds in the Roman histories, that Julius Caesar, having conquered Gaul, crossed over to Britain. Thus it is written: in the six hundred ninety-third year after the founding of Rome, the sixtieth year before the incarnation of the Lord, Julius Caesar, the first of the Romans who made war upon the Britons, was carried to the island in about eighty transport and passenger ships. When he had come to the coast of the Ruteni and gazed ₂ from there upon Britain, he asked those around him what land it was and what race lived there. When he had learned the name of the kingdom and its people, he said: "By Hercules! We Romans descend from the same lineage, since we come from the Trojan race. Aeneas was our first father after the destruction of Troy, theirs was Brutus, the son of Silvius Aeneas. But, unless I am mistaken, they are much degenerated in comparison to us, nor do they know anything about real warfare, since they dwell outside the world in the middle of the ocean. They will easily be forced to give us tribute ₃ and to show obedience to Roman authority. First they must be required by our envoys to become subject to the Romans and pay tax like other races."

When he had related this in writing to King Cassibellaunus, the king was indignant and sent back his own letter, containing these words:

[55] "Cassibellaunus, rex Britonum, Gaio Caesari. Miranda est, Caesar, Romanorum cupiditas quae quicquid est usquam auri vel argenti in toto orbe terrarum sitiens, nos extra orbem positos praeterire intactos non patitur. Censum exigis, tributarios nos facere quaeris qui perpetua libertate hactenus floruimus, qui a Troiana nobilitate sicut Ro-

2 mani descendimus. Opprobrium generi tuo, Caesar, si intelligis, postulasti qui isdem ortos natalibus iugo servitutis premere non erubuisti. Libertatem autem nos in tantum consuevimus et tam nobis ab antecessoribus familiaris est, ut quid sit in genere nostro servitus penitus ignoremus.

3 Quam libertatem si dii ipsi quoque conarentur auferre, nos omni nisu elaboraremus ne, quod nobis tamquam insitum a natura par cum diis tanto tempore tenuimus, per hominem mortalem amitteremus. Liqueat igitur tibi, Caesar, pro regno nos et libertate, dum vita comes fuerit, indefessos communiter stare, etiam mortem subire paratos si nostrae dissolutionis tempus forte institerit."

[56] His itaque lectis, Caesar navigium parat. Ventis et mari se committens vela erigit ac aura flante prospera in ostio Thamensis fluvii cum toto navigio applicuit. Vix terram attigerant, et ecce Cassibellaunus rex cum omni Britonum exercitu Dorobernum advenit, paratus pugnantium copiis

2 non impiger occurrere Caesari. Aderat secum Belinus, princeps militiae suae, cuius consilio et providentia totius regni

[55] "Cassibellaunus, king of the Britons, to Gaius Caesar. It is astonishing, Caesar, the greed of the Romans, which thirsting for whatever there is of gold or silver anywhere in the entire world, cannot allow us placed beyond the world to escape untouched. You claim our property, you seek to make us your tributaries who have flourished thus far in perpetual liberty, and who are descended from Trojan nobility just like the Romans. If only you could understand, Caesar, 2 what you have demanded is a disgrace to your entire people, that you were not ashamed to oppress those born of the very same ancestry with the yoke of servitude. Moreover, we have been so accustomed to liberty, and it is so familiar to us from our predecessors, that in our race we are completely ignorant of what servitude is. If even the gods them- 3 selves had tried to take away our liberty we would have resisted with all our power, so we would not lose through a mortal man that which we have so long preserved, as if ingrained in us by nature and equal with the gods. It should therefore be clear to you, Caesar, that while life is with us we will stand together, indefatigable, for our kingdom and our liberty, and ready to endure death if by chance the time of our destruction draws near."

[56] Having read these things, Caesar prepared his fleet. Entrusting himself to the winds and the sea, he raised his sails and, a with favorable breeze blowing, he arrived with his entire fleet in the mouth of the River Thames. They had scarcely touched land when King Cassibellaunus with the entire army of the Britons came to Dorobernum, prepared for fighting with his troops not at all reluctant to go against Caesar. Belinus was present with him, leader of his army, 2 with whose counsel and foresight the governance of the en-

monarchia tractabatur. Duo quoque nepotes sui, viri stre-
nuissimi, Androgeus scilicet, dux Trinovantum et Tenuantius, dux Cornubiae, latus eius stipabant necnon tres sibi
subditi reges, Cridious Albaniae et Guertaet Venodotiae
3 Britaelque Demetiae. Qui omnes ad libertatem tuendam
animati dederunt consilium ut in hostes, antequam se castris munissent, haud segnis insiliret et a regno suo eos viva-
citer perturbaret. Dispositis itaque agminibus ad bellum
intrepidi procedunt, hostibus se cominus offerunt; pila pilis
obviant ac tela omnium generum utrimque vibrantur. Hinc
inde mox corruunt vulnerati, telis infra vitalia receptis.
4 Manat tellus cruore morientium ac super ipsa cadavera fero-
citer pugnatur. Concurrentibus itaque catervis, optulit casus Nennium et Androgeum duces cum Cantuariis quibus
praeerant, aciei in qua Caesar erat inserere. Et cum ictus
mixtim ex utraque parte multiplicarent, sors dedit Nennio
5 congressum in ipsum Caesarem faciendi. Irruens ergo in illum toto conamine laetatur se posse vel solum ictum tanto
viro inferre. Quem Caesar ut videt impetum in se velle facere, praetenso clipeo excepit et nudato gladio quantum vires
dederunt ipsum super cassidem et scutum quo erat ille pro-
tectus tanto conamine percussit ut gladius inde extrahi a
6 Caesare nequaquam posset. Irruentibus ergo turmis coactus
est Caesar gladium Nennio relinquere. Nennius itaque, gladio imperatoris insignitus, in eo pugnavit toto certamine et
quemcumque eo percutiebat letaliter vulnerabat. Illi ergo in

tire kingdom was managed. Two of his nephews also stood by his side, namely Androgeus, Duke of London, and Tenuantius, Duke of Cornwall, most vigorous men, along with three kings subordinate to him, Cridious of Albany, Guertaet of Venedotia and Britael of Demetia. They had given advice to all that to safeguard their liberty they should spring upon the enemy troops without delay, before they could fortify their camps, and should drive them vigorously from the kingdom. With their troops arranged, the Britons advanced fearlessly to battle and met their enemies in hand to hand combat; javelins beat against javelins and spears of every kind flew from both sides. Soon the wounded fell on both sides, their vital parts pierced with weapons. The earth was drenched with the blood of the dying while the battle was fought fiercely above their bodies. While the troops were thus engaged in battle, the dukes Nennius and Androgeus with the Kentishmen they commanded happened to come amid the battle line that Caesar was in. And as the blows mixed and multiplied on either side, fate granted that Nennius should encounter Caesar himself. Rushing against him with all his strength, Nennius was overjoyed to be able to deal even a single blow to such a man. Caesar, who saw that Nennius wished to make an assault upon him, warded him off with his shield held high and, with his naked sword, using all his strength, struck him on the helmet and the shield he was protected by with such force that the sword could not be dislodged by Caesar in any way. With the troops attacking headlong, Caesar was thus forced to relinquish his sword to Nennius. And so, equipped with the emperor's sword, Nennius fought with it through the entire battle, and he gave a lethal wound to every man he struck with it. While

hunc modum hostes prosternenti obviavit Labienus, Roma-
7 norum tribunus, et a Nennio peremptus est. Sicque dimi-
cantibus Romanis et Britonibus magna caedes ex utraque
parte facta est plurima parte diei. Nocte superveniente
castra petunt Romani, telorum ictibus graviter vulnerati
et labore diurno mirabiliter fatigati, sumuntque mox consilium nocte eadem naves ingredi et ad Gallias redire.

[57] Abeuntibus itaque Romanis Britones quidem gratu-
lantur de victoria, sed contigit statim dolere et tristari, Nennio viro egregio ac bellicoso de vulnere Caesaris infra quindecim dies moriente. Quem in Urbe Trinovantum delatum
sepelierunt iuxta aquilonalem portam, exsequias ei regias
facientes pro eo quod frater regis erat, gladium quoque Caesaris, quem in congressu scuto suo retinuerat, in sepulchro
iuxta illum ob memoriam probitatis collocantes. Nomen
gladii scriptum erat in eo Crocea Mors, quoniam vix eo quis
percussus mortis periculum poterat evadere.

[58] Caesare itaque in Gallias appulso, rebellionem moliuntur Galli, dominium Romanorum formidantes. Fugae
enim eorum fama divulgata, minus terrori illis erant quorum
dominium inviti et coacti susceperant. Crebrescebat quoque fama cotidie, totum mare Britonum navibus plenum ad
fugam Romanorum insequendam. Audaciores igitur effecti
2 cogitabant qualiter Caesarem a finibus suis arcerent. Quod
Iulius callens, timuit anceps bellum cum feroci populo
committere, apertisque thesauris maiores atque nobiliores
terrae muneribus donavit promissisque maioribus sibi eos

he was striking the enemy down in this way, the Roman tribune Labienus met him, and he was killed by Nennius. With   7
the Romans and Britons fighting like this for most of the
day, great slaughter was made on either side. When night
came, the Romans made for their camps, gravely wounded
by weapon blows and totally exhausted from the daylong
struggle, and they soon decided to board their ships that
night and return to Gaul.

[57] After the Romans left, the Britons certainly rejoiced
at their victory, but they quickly turned to grieving and lamenting when Nennius, an outstanding and warlike man,
died fifteen days later from the wounds inflicted by Caesar.
Carrying him to the city of London, they buried him next to
the northern gate, giving him a royal funeral because he was
the brother of the king, and also placing in the tomb next to
him, in memory of his probity, the sword of Caesar, which
he had caught in his shield during the battle. The name of
the sword, Yellow Death, was written upon it, because anyone it struck could hardly avoid the peril of death.

[58] After Caesar was driven back to Gaul, the Gauls
mounted a rebellion, fearing the dominion of the Romans.
News of the Romans' flight having spread, they were less of
a terror to those who unwilling and compelled had accepted
their dominion. News also spread daily that the whole sea
was filled with the Britons' ships in order to pursue the Romans in their flight. Growing bolder, the Gauls considered
how to keep Caesar away from their territories. Aware of   2
this, Caesar was afraid to engage in war on two fronts with
the defiant people and, with his treasury thrown open, he
gave gifts to the magnates and nobles of the land, and won
them over with extravagant promises, pledging that, if with

allexit, pollicens si fortuna iuvante a Britannia subiugata victor rediret populo libertatem, exheredatis restitutionem,

3 principibus munificentiae largitatem velle facere. Sicque delinitos et pacificatos in tantum amorem sibi omnes devinxit, ut non solum rebellare sed etiam Britonum iniuriam et ferocem audaciam se cohercere et vindicare secum promitterent.

[59] Paratis itaque omnibus quae ad tantum negotium pertinebant, biennio emenso, navibusque sescentis utriusque commodi comparatis, iterum Britanniam adiit et per Thamensem fluvium prosperis velis evectus Urbem Trinovantum primo aggredi temptat. Verum Britones praemuniti ita alveum fluminis palis ferreis per totum amnem fixis constipaverunt, ut nulla navis illaesa et sine periculo transmeare flumen posset.

[60] Venientes ergo Romani ad illam palorum Charybdim infiguntur palis, perforantur naves, aquis absorbentur; et in hunc modum plures periclitantur. Caesar, videns stragem suorum, indoluit et dimisso itinere alvei quod coeperat ad terram divertere classem imperat. Qui vix elapsi de periculo paucis submersis terram subeunt, navibus egrediuntur,

2 castra figunt. Et ecce Cassibellaunus haud segnis comparatis copiis descendit in proelium datoque signo irruit in Romanos et eos caedere audacter coepit. Romani autem, quamquam periculum passi, viriliter Britonum primam invasionem sustinuerunt et eos a castris procul pepulerunt; audaciam pro muro habentes non minimam ex hostibus stragem fecerunt. At Britones suorum agminibus constipati,

good luck he should return as the victor after conquering Britain, he would be willing to give liberty to the people, restitution to the disinherited, and abundance of largesse to the magnates. Thus he bound them all to himself, mollified 3 and pacified, in such affection that they promised not simply to revolt, but to restrain and punish along with him the offense and defiant insolence of the Britons.

[59] Two years later, having prepared everything that was needed for such an undertaking, and with six hundred ships of both types assembled, Caesar approached Britain again and, carried by favorable winds up the River Thames, he tried first to attack the city of London. However, the Britons had taken precautions, and had so crowded the channel of the river with iron stakes fixed throughout the stream that no ship could navigate the stream unharmed and without risk.

[60] Coming to that Charybdis of stakes, the Romans were fixed upon the stakes, their ships were pierced and engulfed with water, and in this manner many were put in peril. Caesar was distressed upon seeing the slaughter of his men and, abandoning the route of the channel that had trapped them, he ordered the fleet to turn to land. Having barely escaped the danger, with only a few being sunk, they came to shore, disembarked from their ships, and established their camps. And behold, Cassibellaunus, with no hesitation and 2 his troops prepared, marched down to battle and after giving the signal attacked the Romans and boldly began to kill them. But the Romans, although faced with peril, vigorously held back the first assault and drove the Britons away from their camps; having great boldness as their rampart they slaughtered the enemy. But then the Britons amassed their

multo maiorem numerum armatorum quam prius conflave-
rant, ita ut aestimarentur tricies maiorem numerum habere;
augmentabantur praeterea omni hora supervenientibus tur-
3 mis undique. Caesar autem videns eorum multitudinem
atque vesanam rabiem non posse sustinere receptui canens
certamen diremit; suos ad castra redire coegit ne maius periculum sustinerent. Navesque protinus ingreditur et ad Gal-
4 lias aura flante prospera quantocius devenit. Ibi prope litus
turrim ingressus, quam antea sibi praeparaverat propter du-
bios belli eventus, tuto se collocavit loco. Turri illi Odnea
nomen erat, ubi exercitum misere dilaceratum longa admo-
dum quiete refecit et proceres terrae ad se collocutum venire fecit.

[61] Cassibellaunus autem, secundo de Romanis trium-
phans magno exultans gaudio, statuit vota diis omnipoten-
tibus solvere atque pro tanto eventu sacrificiorum ritus
adimplere. Monuit itaque omnes qui erant in exercitu ut
constituto termino convenirent ad Urbem Trinovantum
cum uxoribus et filiis et caris suis, quatinus ibidem pro
2 adepta victoria dies exultationis secum agerent. Cumque
omnes absque mora advenissent, diversa libamina facientes
prout cuique suppetebat litaverunt. Numerus holocausti
illius comprehensus est in quadraginta milia vaccarum et
centum milia ovium et triginta milia silvestrium ferarum
cuiusque generis collectarum, praeterea diversorum gene-
3 rum volatilia quae numero comprehendi difficile fuit. Liba-
minibus itaque diis pro more peractis, refecerunt se residuis

troops, brought together a much greater number of soldiers than before, so that they might be reckoned to have thirty times the larger number; moreover they were increased every hour with troops arriving from all around. Caesar, on the 3 other hand, seeing that it was not possible to hold back their multitude and their frenzied madness, sounded the retreat and departed from the conflict; he compelled his men to return to the camps in order to avoid greater danger. They boarded their ships immediately and came to Gaul all the sooner because a favorable wind was blowing. There, having 4 entered a tower near the shore, which he had prepared for himself because of the doubtful outcome of the war, he established himself safely in that location. The name of that tower was Odnea, in which the wretchedly mangled army after a long rest fully recovered and summoned the leading men of the land to confer with them.

[61] Cassibellaunus on the other hand, having triumphed over the Romans a second time, exulting with great joy, decided to fulfill his vows to the all-powerful gods, and to perform rites of sacrifice for so great an outcome. Therefore he directed all who were in the army to come together at the appointed place in the city of London with their wives and daughters and dear ones so that they could conduct the days of celebration with them in that place for the victory they had won. And when everyone had come without delay, of- 2 fering up various libations they made such sacrifices as each one could afford. That number of burned offerings included forty thousand cows and one hundred thousand sheep and thirty thousand wild animals of every kind gathered from the woods, in addition to birds of diverse species that it would be difficult to number. After the offerings to the gods 3

epulis, ut fieri assolet in huiusmodi sacrificiis atque per-
functi diversorum generum ferculis, quod reliquum fuit diei
ludis exultantes indulserunt. Interea contigit inclitos iuvenes palaestra exercitari; inter quos erat nepos regis, Hireglas nomine, alter vero Androgei ducis nepos, Evelinus dic-

4 tus. Qui caestibus contendentes invicem se ad iracundiam
indignando provocaverunt. Quorum alter Evelinus Androgei nepos Hireglas regis nepotem gladio arrepto interfecit.
Perturbata igitur curia, rumor ad Cassibellaunum regem
pervenit et de laetitia qua prius fluctuabat in maerorem con-
versus est. Advocatoque Androgeo praecepit ut nepos suus
Evelinus sibi ad iustitiam protinus praesentaretur et senten-

5 tiam quam proceres dictarent subiret. Cumque animum
regis ira commotum dubitasset Androgeus, respondit sese
suam curiam habere et in illa definiri debere calumniam
suorum. Si igitur morem antiquitus statutum intemeratum
custodire vellet, die statuto praesto erat ut in curia sua iuvenem legibus coerceret et de praesenti calumnia satisfaceret.
Rex indignans recessit iratus, Androgeo gladium et mortem

6 comminatus. Nec distulit quin mox terras et possessiones
eius ferro et flammis vastaret. Androgeus ergo, iram regis
sustinere non valens, per internuntios coepit regem compel-
lare et eius iracundiam mitigare. Sed cum furorem eius nullatenus posset refrenare, diversis cogitationibus angebatur,

were completed in the accustomed manner, they refreshed themselves with the leftovers from the feast as was usually done with sacrifices of this kind, and after finishing off the various kinds of dishes they joyfully indulged in games for the rest of the day. During this time, it happened that wrestling was being practiced by the prominent youths, among whom were the king's nephew, named Hireglas, and the nephew of Duke Androgeus, called Evelinus. Fighting with gloves, they provoked each other to anger with insults. The second of the two, Evelinus the nephew of Androgeus, seized a sword and killed Hireglas the nephew of the king. With the court thrown into confusion, the news reached King Cassibellaunus, and from the joy that overflowed before he was plunged into sorrow. Having called for Androgeus, he directed that his nephew Evelinus should be brought before him immediately for justice, and submit to the sentence that the nobles declared. Because Androgeus worried about the king's intentions being motivated by anger, he responded that he had his own court, and that the charges against the boy should be settled there. If, therefore, the king wished to observe the strict custom anciently established, a day would be set immediately when he could punish the boy in his court according to law and resolve the charges against him. Indignant, the king withdrew in anger, threatening Androgeus with the sword and death. He did not delay, but immediately ravaged Androgeus's lands and possessions with sword and flames. Androgeus, therefore, not strong enough to sustain the wrath of the king, through intermediaries tried to appeal to the king and soothe his passion. But when he was completely unable to restrain the king's fury, he struggled with various ideas about how he

qualiter regi valeret resistere. Itaque omni alia spe decidens auxilium Caesaris expetere decrevit litterasque illi in hanc direxit sententiam:

7   "Gaio Caesari Androgeus dux Trinovantum post optatam mortem optandam salutem. Paenitet me adversum te egisse dum regem meum ad Romanos expellendos de terra nostra viribus meis adiutus sum. Si enim me bello subtraxissem, Cassibellaunus Romanorum victor non extitisset. Cui post triumphum tanta irrepsit superbia ut me, per quem trium-

8 phavit, a finibus meis exterminare praesumat. Numina caelorum testor, me non promeruisse iram illius, nisi dicar promereri, quia diffugio nepotem meum curiae suae tradere iudicandum morte; quem iniuste iratus exoptat damnare. Quod ut manifestius discretioni tuae liqueat, causam rei adverte. Contigerat nos ob laetitiam triumphi libamina diis patriis offerre. In quibus, dum celebraremus quae agenda sunt sollemnia, iuventus nostra ludos mutuos componens, inter ceteros inierunt duo nepotes nostri palaestram exem-

9 plo aliorum ducti. Cumque meus triumphasset, succensus est alter iniusta ira festinavitque eum percutere. At ille vitato ictu cepit socium per manum qua extractum ensem tenebat, volens eripere ne sibi noceret. Interea cecidit nepos regis super mucronem, confossusque morti subiacuit. Quod cum regi notum esset, praecepit ut puerum meum traderem curiae suae ad ulciscendum nepotem suum, ut pro homici-

10 dio supplicio plecteretur. Cui dum contradixissem, venit

could win against the king. Finally, with all other hope cut
off, he decided to ask Caesar for help and sent him a letter
to this effect:

"To Gaius Caesar, Androgeus, Duke of London, after 7
wishing for your death now wishes for your health. It pains
me to have acted against you when, along with my men I
helped my king to drive the Romans out of our land. If I had
removed myself from the battle, Cassibellaunus would not
have proved to be the victor over the Romans. Pride has so
crept into him since his triumph, that he presumes to expel
me, through whom he triumphed, from my own territories.
I swear to the gods of the heavens, I do not deserve his an- 8
ger unless I could be said to deserve it because I avoid handing my nephew over to his court to be sentenced to death;
unjustly angered, he longs to condemn him. To make this
clearer to you, consider the facts of the case. We happened
to present offerings to our native gods out of joy for our victory, during which, after we had celebrated the solemnities
that must be performed, while our young men were organiz-
ing games among themselves, among the rest our two nephews arrived in the wrestling ring, drawn by the example of
the others. And when mine had triumphed, the other was 9
incensed with unjust anger and rushed to strike him. But he,
avoiding the blow, grabbed his fellow by the hand in which
he held a drawn sword, wanting to grab it away so he would
not be injured. Meanwhile the king's nephew fell on the
point of the sword and after being stabbed he succumbed to
death. When this became known to the king, in order to
avenge his nephew he directed that I should hand my boy
over to his court, so that he could suffer the penalty for murder. When I objected, he came with an army and ravaged my 10

cum exercitu terras meas et possessiones ferro et igni vastare. Unde a serenitate maiestatis tuae auxilium peto, quatinus per te dignitati meae restitutus, tu per me Britannia potiaris. De hoc autem nihil haesitaveris, quia omnis abest proditio. Ea enim condicione moventur mortales, ut post inimicitias amici fiant, et post fugam ad triumphum accedant."

[62] His Caesar inspectis, consilium mox capit a familiaribus suis, ne verbis solummodo Androgei invitatus Britanniam adiret, nisi tales dirigerentur obsides quibus securius incederet. Nec mora misit ei Androgeus Scevam, filium suum, et triginta nobiles iuvenes ex propinquis suis. Transiens itaque Caesar applicuit in Rutupi Portu et terram ingre-

2 diens venit inprovisus usque Dorobernum. Interea obsidere Cassibellaunus Urbem Trinovantum parat. Sed ut Caesaris adventum cognovit, exercitum congregat; ei ire obviam festinat. Ut igitur vallem prope Doroberniam intravit, aspexit in eadem Romanorum castra et tentoria fixa: ductu etenim Androgei illuc convenerant. Nec mora advenientes Britones

3 statuerunt se per catervas, cum Romanis pugnaturi. Androgeus autem cum quinque milibus armatorum in prope sito nemore delituit, ut auxilium Caesari ferret. Ut ergo hinc inde convenerunt, tela iaciunt et invicem vulnerantur; et dimissis telis iam cominus certamen ensibus agere meditantur, cum Androgeus nemore egrediens cum suis Cassibellauni aciem a tergo invadit. Unde Britones attoniti stationem

4 suam dimittere et aciem dirimere coacti sunt. Fugam itaque

lands and possessions with sword and fire. For this reason I ask for help from your serene highness, so that, with my dignity restored by you, through me you will win control over Britain. Have no hesitation about this, because there is no treachery involved. For it is in the nature of mortal men, that after enmity they become friends, and after flight they achieve triumph."

[62] After he read these words, Caesar then took advice from his counselors that he should not go to Britain invited merely by the words of Androgeus, unless suitable hostages were sent so that he might advance more safely. Without delay Androgeus sent his own son Sceva and thirty noble youths from among his relatives. Crossing over, therefore, Caesar arrived at Richborough and moving inland he came unexpected all the way to Canterbury. Meanwhile Cassibellaunus prepared to besiege London. But when he learned about Caesar's arrival, he assembled his army and hastened to attack him. When he entered a valley near Canterbury, he saw established therein the camps and tents of the Romans; they had assembled there because they were led by Androgeus. As soon as they got there the Britons arranged themselves in companies in order to fight with the Romans. Androgeus, however, hid in a wood located nearby with five thousand armed soldiers he brought to help Caesar. As both sides came together, they cast their spears, and each was wounded by the other; then, with their spears abandoned, they were expecting to engage in close combat with swords, when Androgeus, emerging with his men from the wood, attacked the battle line of Cassibellaunus from behind. From there, surprised by the Britons, they were forced to abandon their stations and break up their line. Immediately taking to

validam simul arripientes, montem petunt in loco prope situm, rupibus et coriletis obsitum, cuius summitatem nacti
ab hostibus se tuentur et iaculis ac lapidibus tamquam de
munitione celsa in terram proiectis a se longius propellunt.
Caesar itaque montem obsedit et Britones undique circum-
vallavit, obstruens vias et aditus ne quis eorum evadat, me-
5 mor dedecoris fugarum praeteritarum. O admirabile genus
Britonum, qui ipsum cui totus mundus nequivit resistere bis
fugere coegerunt; devicti quoque et fugati resistunt, parati
mortem pro patria et libertate subire. Emenso igitur die
primo ac secundo, cum non haberent quid comederent obsessi, cum fame captionem Caesaris formidantes et iram
eius abhorrentes, misit nuntios Cassibellaunus Androgeo,
orans ut sese cum Iulio pacificaret ne dignitas gentis suae,
6 quarum stirpe ortus erat, ipso deleto deleretur. Mandavit
etiam supplicans se nondum promeruisse ut mortem suam
optaret, licet inquietudinem sibi intulisset. At Androgeus
nuntiis respondens ait:

"Dii caeli et terrae, orat me nunc herus meus cui prius
despectui eram et quem iniuriis lacessierat! Pacificarine
Caesari se per me desiderat rex Cassibellaunus, qui exustis
ferro et flammis possessionibus meis, ceu pro nihilo ducens
7 exheredare cogitarat? Non est valde timendus terrae princeps vel diligendus qui in pace ferus est ut leo et in bello timidus ut lepus. Vereri tamen debuerat ne illum iniuriose
tractaret per quem tantus vir, videlicet Romanus imperator

headlong flight, they made for a mountain located nearby, covered with rocks and thickets of hazel trees, from the summit of which they protected themselves against the enemy and, by virtue of the lofty fortification as much as the javelins and rocks thrown at the ground below, they drove the enemy far away. Caesar therefore besieged the mountain and surrounded the Britons on every side, blocking the approaches and entries so none of them could escape, mindful of his previous humiliating retreat. O admirable race of 5 Britons, who twice forced him to flee, whom the whole world was unable to resist; they resist even when defeated and put to flight, prepared to suffer death for their country and their freedom. When the first day and the second had passed, besieged without having anything to eat, since their hunger made them fear a loss to Caesar and shrink from his anger, Cassibellaunus sent messengers to Androgeus asking whether he could make peace with Julius, so that the dignity of their race, from which lineage he was born, would not be destroyed with his own destruction. He also begged Andro- 6 geus not to wish for his death, which he did not deserve even though he had caused trouble for him. Responding to the messengers, Androgeus said:

"O gods of heaven and earth, my master now pleads with me who was despised before and whom he provoked with injuries! Does King Cassibellaunus desire to make peace with Caesar through me, having destroyed my possessions with sword and flames just as if, taking me for nothing, he thought to disinherit me? An earthly prince is not greatly to 7 be feared who in peace is fierce as a lion and in war is timid as a hare. Nevertheless he should have taken care not to wrongfully mistreat one by whom so great a man, namely

ac totius orbis victor, bis devictus est et fugatus. Insipientia obducitur qui commilitones quibus triumphat iniuriis et contumeliis infestat. Non enim unius ducis est victoria, immo omnium commilitonum qui pro duce suo se et sanguinem suum fundunt. Quiescat ergo rex noster amodo praesumere se victorem absque aliis extitisse, per quos tota victoria patrata est. Et ego, licet indigne me exacerbasset, pacificabo eum Caesari, non reddens malum pro malo. Satis vindicata est iniuria quam mihi intulit, cum misericordiam meam et auxilium supplex imploret."

[63] Haec dicens, festinus venit ad Caesarem amplexisque eius genibus, sic allocutus est eum: "Ecce, satis vindicasti te, Caesar, in Cassibellaunum, cum ad deditionem et tributum reddendum compulisti. Quid amplius ab eo exigere censes quam subiectionem sui et vectigal Romanae dignitati? Nulla virtus clementia dignior est imperatori. Esto igitur ei propitius et clemens et non reddas ei secundum opera sua."

Cumque ad haec verba Androgei Caesar nihil respondisset, sed quasi surda aure illum praeterisset, indignatus Androgeus Caesari iterum ait: "Hoc solum me pepigisse tibi, Caesar, memini ut submisso Cassibellauno Britanniam Romano imperio subdere laborarem; ecce, quod pepigi habere potes. Quid ultra tibi debeo? Nolit caeli terraeque rector ut dominum meum et avunculum, se tali iustitie offerentem, patiar aut captum vinculis teneri aut dira morte interimi.

the emperor of Rome and conqueror of the entire globe, was twice defeated and put to flight. He is overtaken by foolishness who heaps injuries and abuses on the comrades by whom he triumphs. The victory is not the leader's alone, 8 but on the contrary it is that of all his fellow soldiers who sacrifice themselves and their blood for their leader. Our king must then be nodding off to expect that in the future he will be victorious without the others, through whom all victory was accomplished. And I, although it will aggravate me undeservedly, will make peace for him with Caesar, not returning evil for evil. It shall be sufficient vindication for the injury he has done to me that he begs for my mercy and help."

[63] That said, he went with haste to Caesar, and after embracing his knees, he spoke to him in this manner: "Behold, Caesar, you have sufficiently vindicated yourself on Cassibellaunus, when you compelled him to surrender and pay tribute. What more do you think to extract from him than subjection to you and tribute for the dignity of Rome? No virtue is more fitting to an emperor than clemency. Therefore be favorably inclined and merciful to him and do not pay him back according to his own misdeeds."

When Caesar had not responded to these words of Androgeus, but had ignored him as if with a deaf ear, Androgeus was indignant and said again to Caesar: "This alone I had agreed to with you, Caesar, I remember, that by the submission of Cassibellaunus I would labor to subject Britain to the Roman Empire; behold, what I agreed to, you can have. What further do I owe to you? The ruler of heaven and earth would not want me to let my lord and uncle, when offering such justice, be held captive in chains or destroyed by

Non est facile Cassibellaunum interfici me vivente, cui auxilium in tanta necessitate denegare non possum, nisi petitionem meam pro eo benigne susceperis."

3   Hac ergo oratione mitigatus, Caesar concessit Androgeo quod petebat. Datis itaque obsidibus et tributo de Britannis quoque anno tria milia librarum argenti aerario Romano assignato, concordes facti Caesar et Cassibellaunus dextras sibi invicem dederunt et oscula pacifica; sicque contione separata quisque in sua cum gaudio remearunt. Caesar autem tota hieme in Britannia remansit; vere redeunte in Gallias transfretavit. Inde Romam cum omni exercitu suo se contulit sicut in historia legitur Romanorum. Postea, cum Cassibellaunus septem annis supervixisset, mortuus est et in Eboraco sepultus.

[64] Cui successit Tenuantius dux Cornubiae: nam Androgeus, frater eius, Romam cum Caesare profectus fuerat. Qui diademate insignitus regnum cum diligentia quoad vixit tractavit. Post illum Kimbelinus filius suus, miles strenuus, suscepit imperium; quem Caesar Augustus Romae nutrierat, armis decoraverat. Hic in tantam amicitiam Romanorum venerat ut, cum posset tributum eorum detinere, gratis dabat. His diebus natus est salvator noster Iesus Christus in Bethlehem, sicut evangelica narrat historia.

[65] Huic Kimbelino nati sunt duo filii, Guiderius et Arviragus; et cum rexisset feliciter decem annis regnum Britanniae, moriens dimisit sceptrum regni Guiderio primogenito. Hic cum tributum Romanis denegaret, missus est Claudius imperator a senatu cum exercitu ad Britanniam

an awful death. It will not be easy to kill Cassibellaunus while I live, for I cannot deny help to him in such need, unless you graciously accept my petition for him."

Softened by this speech, Caesar granted to Androgeus 3 what he sought. Therefore, after hostages were given and also an annual tribute from the Britons of three thousand pounds of silver allotted to the Roman treasury, Caesar and Cassibellaunus were reconciled and gave each other their right hands and kisses of peace; after the assembly dispersed they returned to their own men with joy. Caesar, however, stayed in Britain the whole winter; with the return of spring he passed over to Gaul. Thence he conveyed himself with his entire army to Rome, as it is told in the history of the Romans. Afterward, when Cassibellaunus had lived on for seven years, he died and was buried in York.

[64] Tenuantius the Duke of Cornwall succeeded him: for his brother Androgeus had gone to Rome with Caesar. Once he was crowned, he managed the kingdom with diligence as long as he lived. After that his son Kimbelinus, a mighty soldier, assumed supreme authority; Augustus Caesar had raised him in Rome, and honored him with arms. He revered the Romans with such friendship that, when he could have withheld their tribute, he gave it freely. In his time our savior Jesus Christ was born in Bethlehem as gospel history relates.

[65] To this Kimbelinus were born two sons, Guiderius and Arviragus; and when he had ruled the kingdom of Britain happily for ten years, upon his death he left the scepter of the realm to his firstborn son, Guiderius. When he refused to pay tribute to the Romans, the Emperor Claudius was sent to Britain with an army by the Senate to subjugate

ut iterum subiugaret eam et tributum redderet. Princeps militiae Claudii Lelius Hamo vocabatur cuius consilio et ope Claudius nitebatur. Venientes ergo in Britanniam applicuerunt Porcestriam civitatem supra mare sitam.

Quam cum obsedisset Claudius et portas eius muro praeclusisset ut vel sic fames afflictos cives eius deditioni cogeret, [66] supervenit Guiderius cum exercitu Britonum commissoque proelio cum Romanis, maiorem partem exercitus et ipsum Claudium ad naves fugere coegit. Sed inter bellandum Hamo praefatus princeps militiae, versuto usus consilio proiectis armis propriis capit Britannica arma defunctorum in bello et quasi ex ipsis contra suos pugnabat, exhortans Britones ad insequendum Romanos, citum pro-

2 mittens de illis triumphum. Noverat enim linguam Britannicam, quam didicerat Romae inter obsides Britonum. Deinde accessit paulatim iuxta regem adituque invento quod cogitarat explevit et regem, nihil tale timentem, mucrone percussum suffocavit. Elapsus deinde ab hostium catervis

3 sese inter suos recepit. Frater autem regis, ut illum peremptum invenit, deponens arma sua regiis se induit armis, hinc inde Britones ad perstandum exhortans, tamquam esset Guiderius. Qui nescientes casum regis, stragem non minimam de hostibus, usque ad naves persequendo egerunt.

4 Caedentibus itaque Britonibus divisi sunt Romani in duas partes: Claudius cum quadam parte suorum naves ingreditur; Hamo autem, quia naves ingredi non licuit, nemorum

it again and hand over the tribute. The leader of Claudius's army was called Lelius Hamo, whose counsel and help Claudius depended upon. Coming therefore to Britain, they landed at the city of Portchester, located by the sea.

When Claudius had besieged the town and blocked its gates with a wall, so that he could force the citizens thus thoroughly afflicted with hunger to surrender, [66] Guiderius arrived with an army of Britons, and doing battle with the Romans, he forced the greater part of their army and Claudius himself to retreat to their ships. But during the fighting Hamo, the leader of the army mentioned before, used a cunning strategy and casting off his own arms, grabbed up the British arms of those who had died in battle, and fought as if one of them against his own men, exhorting the Britons to pursue the Romans and promising a quick triumph over them. He knew the British language which he 2 had studied among the British hostages in Rome. Then, little by little, he drew near the king, and when the moment came that he intended to exploit, with the king fearing nothing, he killed him with a blow from his sword. Then, slipping away from the enemy's front line, he took himself back among his own men. But when the king's brother 3 learned the king had been killed, he put off his own arms and dressed himself in the king's arms, exhorting the Britons here and there to stand firm as if he were Guiderius. Unaware of the king's demise, they accomplished no little slaughter of their enemies, pursuing them all the way to their ships. And so, yielding to the Britons, the Romans 4 were divided into two groups: Claudius with one group of his men boarded the ships; Hamo, however, who was unable to board the ships, sought protection in the woods.

tutamina petit. Arviragus igitur, existimans in comitatu Hamonis Claudium esse, persequitur fugientes de loco ad 5 locum nec cessavit eos insequi usque ad litus maris. Ibi, dum in portu navium Hamo se de equo misisset, ut in una nave mercatorum ascenderet et de instante mortis periculo se eriperet, mox supervenit Arviragus et stricto ense eum interfecit nomenque dedit loco, qui usque hodie Portus Hamonis appellatur.

[67] Interea Claudius resociatis sociis oppugnat praedictam civitatem — quae tunc Kaerperis, nunc autem Porcestria dicitur. Nec mora, moenia diruit civibusque subactis insecutus est Arviragum iam Wintoniam ingressum. Obsedit civi- 2 tatem diversisque machinis oppugnat. Arviragus vero, se obsessum indignans, copias suorum per catervas disponit apertisque portis ad proeliandum educit; sed intervenientibus ex utraque parte maioribus natu concordiam facere statuerunt ne strages populi amplior fieret. Requisitus Claudius pacemne an bellum mallet, respondit se salvo Romano honore malle pacificari; neque enim adeo humanum cru- 3 orem sitiebat, ut extra rationem eos debellare vellet. Ductis igitur usque ad id loci sermonibus pactus est Claudius sese filiam suam Arvirago daturum, tantum ut se cum regno Britanniae potestati Romanae subiectum cognosceret. Postpositis ergo debellationibus utrimque suaserunt maiores natu Arvirago huiuscemodi pactionibus acquiescere. Paruit itaque et subiectionem Caesari fecit.

Arviragus therefore, thinking Claudius to be in Hamo's company, pursued them as they ran from place to place and did not cease to follow them all the way to the coast of the sea. There, Hamo had just released his horse in the seaport 5 so that he could embark on one of the merchant ships and snatch himself away from the imminent threat of death, when Arviragus soon arrived and, drawing his sword, killed him and gave his name to that place, which up to this day is called Hamo's Port.

[67] Meanwhile Claudius, his men reassembled, besieged the city mentioned before—which was then Kaerperis, but is now called Portchester. Without delay, he demolished the walls, and having conquered the citizens he followed after Arviragus, who had now entered Winchester. He besieged the city and attacked it with various machines. Arviragus, 2 however, indignant that he was besieged, arranged his troops into companies and after the gates were opened led them forth to battle; but being intercepted by superior numbers on every side, they decided to make a settlement to avoid an even greater slaughter of the people. When asked whether he preferred peace or war, Claudius responded that, subject to the demands of Roman honor, he preferred to make peace; nor indeed did he thirst for human blood to such a degree that he would wish beyond reason to fight it out with them. Their conversation having led to this 3 point, Claudius promised he would give his own daughter to Arviragus if he would acknowledge that he and the kingdom of Britain were subject to the power of Rome. With the fighting thus suspended on either side, his elders persuaded Arviragus to agree to this bargain. He therefore complied and submitted to Caesar.

[68] Confestim Claudius Romam mittens natam suam ut Arvirago sponsaretur adduci praecepit. Interea auxilio Arviragi usus, Orcades et proximas Britanniae insulas potestati Romanae adquisivit. Porro, emensa hieme, redierunt legati cum filia, Genuissa nomine, et Arvirago nuptiali copulata toro celebrarunt nuptias iuxta Sabrinum fluvium in confinio
2 Demetiae et Loegriae. Unde rex, locum eundem celebrem post se esse cupiens, suggessit Claudio ut ibidem civitas aedificaretur et de nomine eius Kaerglou—id est Claudiocestria—appellaretur. Quidam tamen ipsam traxisse nomen a Gloio duce aiunt quem Claudius in illa generauerat; cui post Arviragum gubernaculum Demetici ducatus cessit. His itaque patratis, reversus est Claudius Romam, ubi tunc temporis Petrus apostolus, de Anthiochia veniens, praedicationem evangelii Romanis intimabat.

[69] Post discessum Claudii a Britannia, Arviragus in superbiam elatus despexit Romanae potestati subiacere. Missus est igitur Vespasianus a senatu in Britanniam, ut Arviragum et gentem rebellem compesceret et tributum restitueret. Cum autem navigaret et in Rutupi Portu applicare vellet, Arviragus de adventu illius premunitus a portu eum prohibuit; retraxit igitur se Vespasianus a portu illo, retortisque velis in Totonesio litore se contulit et, exiens in terram, civitatem Kaerpenhuelgoit, quae nunc Exonia vocatur,
2 adiit. Cumque eam septem diebus obsedisset, supervenit Arviragus cum exercitu forti; congressusque cum Romanis, totum diem consumpserunt ambo exercitus lacessentes

[68] Sending immediately to Rome, Claudius ordered his daughter to be brought so that she could be married to Arviragus. Meanwhile, with Arviragus's help, he added the Orkneys and nearby islands of Britain to the dominion of Rome. After that, when winter had passed, the envoys returned with his daughter, named Genuissa, and, after she was married to Arviragus, they celebrated their nuptials next to the Severn River at the border of Demetia and Loegria. For that reason the king, desiring the spot to be celebrated after him, suggested to Claudius that a city should be built there and be called Kaerglou—that is, the City of Claudius—after his name. Others, however, say that its name is derived from Duke Gloius, whom Claudius fathered in that city; after Arviragus the government of the dukedom of Demetia passed to him. After these things were done, Claudius returned to Rome, where at that time the apostle Peter, having come from Antioch, was preaching the message of the evangelists to the Romans.

[69] After the departure of Claudius from Britain, Arviragus, filled with pride, declined to submit to the power of Rome. Therefore, Vespasian was sent to Britain by the Senate in order to restrain Arviragus and the rebellious race and to reinstate their tribute. However, as he was sailing and wanted to land at Richborough, Arviragus had been forewarned about his arrival and denied him entry into the port; Vespasian therefore withdrew himself from that port and adjusting his sails he took himself to the coast of Totnes and, coming ashore, approached the city of Kaerpenhuelgoit, which is now called Exeter. And after he laid siege to it for seven days, Arviragus arrived with a strong army; they joined in battle with the Romans, and both armies spent the entire

invicem vulneribusque utrimque lacerati. Superveniente noctis crepusculo, quieverunt. Mane autem facto, mediante Genuissa regina concordes effecti sunt Vespasianus et Arvi-
3 ragus. Hieme vero emensa navigavit Vespasianus in Galliam et inde Romam rediit. Rexit deinde Arviragus regnum Britanniae cum pace et tranquillitate usque in senectutem vergens dilexitque senatum et gentem Romanam propter uxorem suam quam diligebat; quae de Romanis, sicut prae-dictum est, originem duxerat. Ut igitur dies vitae suae exple-vit, mortuus est et sepultus Claudiocestriae, in templo quod in honorem Claudii dicaverat.

[70] Successit Arvirago filius suus Marius, vir mirae pru-dentiae et sapientiae. Regnante itaque illo, quidam rex Pic-torum, nomine Rodric, de Scithia adveniens cum magna classe applicuit in Albaniam coepitque provinciam vastare. Collecto igitur Marius exercitu, obviam ei venit et congres-sus cum illo interfecit eum et victoria potitus erexit lapidem in signum triumphi in loco qui postea de nomine suo dicta est Westmaria; in quo titulus scriptus memoriam eius usque
2 in hodiernum diem testatur. Perempto vero Rodric, dedit devicto populo qui cum eo venerat partem Albaniae ad inha-bitandum; quae pars Cathenesia nuncupatur. Erat autem terra deserta, nullo habitatore antea culta. Cumque uxores non haberent, a Britonibus natas et cognatas uxores sibi pe-
3 tentes, repulsam passi sunt. Transeuntes igitur in Hiber-niam, duxerunt de populo illo uxores ex quibus orta soboles in magnam multitudinem creverunt; et exinde Picti Britan-niam incoluerunt. At Marius, cum totum regnum summa

day attacking each other in turn, and each side was covered in wounds. When evening came, they rested. In the morning, however, through the mediation of Queen Genuissa, Vespasian and Arviragus were reconciled. After winter had 3 passed, Vespasian sailed to Gaul and from there he returned to Rome. Then Arviragus ruled over the kingdom of Britain with peace and tranquility until he neared old age, and he loved the Roman Senate and people because of his wife, whom he loved. She traced her origin to the Romans as said before. When, therefore, the days of his life ran out, he died and was buried in Claudiocestria in the temple that he had dedicated to the honor of Claudius.

[70] His son Marius succeeded Arviragus, a man of wonderful prudence and wisdom. While he was reigning, a certain king of the Picts named Rodric coming from Scythia with a great fleet landed in Albany and began to lay waste to the province. Marius therefore, having assembled an army, attacked him and after meeting him in battle he killed him, and with victory achieved he raised a stone as a sign of his triumph in that place, which afterward was called Westmorland after his name; on the stone an inscription bears witness to his memory even to the present day. After Rodric 2 was killed, Marius gave the conquered people who came with him a part of Albany to live in; that part is called Caithness. It was an empty land, having been settled by no inhabitants before. And since they did not have wives, they sought from the Britons their daughters and kinswomen as wives, but were refused. Passing over therefore to Ireland, they 3 took wives from that people and with their offspring they multiplied in great numbers; and after that the Picts lived in Britain. But after he had united the entire kingdom in the

pace composuisset, coepit cum Romanis dilectionem habere, tributa solvens et, exemplo patris incitatus, iustitiam
et leges paternas atque omnia honesta sectabatur.

[71] Cumque cursum vitae suae explesset, moriens filio
suo Coillo regni gubernaculum dimisit. Hic ab infantia Romae nutritus, mores Romanorum edoctus, in amicitiam eorum incidit et tributa libenter eis reddens, adversari eis in
nullo volebat.

[72] Interim natus est ei unicus filius, cui nomen Lucius
impositum est. Hic post mortem patris regni diademate insignitus, omnem viam prudentiae atque actus patris bo-
nosque mores insecutus, ab omnibus ad quos fama bonitatis
illius pervenerat, amabatur et colebatur. Audiens quoque
Christianitatem Romae et in aliis regnis exaltari, primus
omnium regum Britonum Christi nomen affectans epistulas
dirigit Eleutherio papae, petens ut ad se mitteret personas
2 tales a quibus Christianitatem suscipere deberet. Serenave-
rant enim mentem eius miracula quae Christi discipuli et
praedicatores per diversas nationum gentes ediderant. Et
quidem in omnem terram exivit sonus eorum et in fines
orbis terrae verba eorum. Et quia ad amorem vere fidei an-
3 helabat, piae petitionis effectum consecutus est. Siquidem
praedictus pontifex, gloriam in excelsis Deo canens, duos
religiosos doctores, Faganum et Duvianum, de latere suo
misit Britanniam, qui verbum Dei caro factum et pro hominibus passum, regi populoque praedicarent et sacro baptis-
4 mate insignirent. Nec mora, concurrentes undique populi

greatest peace, Marius began to show favor to the Romans, rendering tribute and, inspired by the example of his father, he adhered to justice and the paternal laws and everything that was honorable.

[71] And when the course of his life had finished, upon his death he left the government of the kingdom to his son Coillus. Raised in Rome from infancy and schooled in Roman ways, he had become friendly with them, and rendering tribute to them freely, he wished to be their adversary in nothing.

[72] Meanwhile a single son was born to him, to whom the name Lucius was given. Endowed with the crown after the death of his father, he emulated all the ways of wisdom and good customs of his father, and he was loved and cherished by all to whom his reputation for integrity had reached. Hearing that Christianity was being praised in Rome and other kingdoms, he was the first of all the kings of the Britons to yearn for the name of Christ, and he sent letters to Pope Eleutherius, asking that he send to him the sort of persons from which he should receive Christianity. The miracles that the preachers and disciples of Christ had 2 related to peoples of many nations had enlightened his mind. And indeed their sound had gone forth into all the earth: and their words unto the ends of the world. And because he aspired to the love of the true faith, it came about that his devout petition was granted. Accordingly, the pope 3 mentioned before, chanting glory to God on high, sent two doctors of religion, Fagan and Duvian, from his side to Britain to preach about the word of God made flesh and his suffering for mankind to the king and the people, and to honor them with holy baptism. Without delay, the people of many 4

diversae nationis, exemplum regis sequentes, lavacro sacro intinguntur atque omnipotenti Deo subduntur, idola despicientes et minutatim confringentes. Beati igitur doctores, cum paganismum de gente Britonum in maiori parte delevissent, templa quae in honore plurimorum deorum fundata fuerant, mundatis ruderibus, uni Deo consecraverunt et viris religiosis custodienda tradiderunt. Fuerant tunc in Britannia per regiones constituti viginti octo flamines et tres archiflamines qui tura diis ex ritu gentilium cremabant atque libamina de pecudibus litabant. Haec itaque ex apostolica doctrina idolatriae eripientes, episcopos ubi erant flamines, archiepiscopos ubi archiflamines consecraverunt.

6 Sedes principales archiflaminum sicut in nobilioribus civitatibus fuerant, Londoniis scilicet et Eboraci et in Urbe Legionum, quae super Oscam fluvium in Glamorgantia sita est, ita in his tribus evacuata superstitione tribus archiepiscopis dicaverunt; in reliquis episcopos ordinaverunt divisisque parochiis unicuique ius suum assignaverunt. Metropolitano Eboracensi Deira et Albania, sicut magnum flumen Humbri eas a Loegria secernit, in parrochiam cessit. Londoniensi vero submissa est Loegria et Cornubia, quas provincias seiungit Sabrina a Kambria, id est Gualia, quae Urbi Legionum subiacuit. His ita Dei nutu constitutis, redierunt Romam antistites praefati et cuncta quae fecerant a beato papa confirmari impetraverunt. Palliis itaque ac ceteris

nations hastened together from everywhere and, following the example of the king, they were dipped in the holy font and placed under God almighty, despising the idols and breaking them to pieces one by one. So then the blessed teachers, since they had for the most part erased the paganism of the British race, took the temples that had been founded in honor of multiple gods and, after they were cleaned of rubbish, placed them in the custody of religious men. There were then in Britain, organized by regions, 5 twenty-eight priests and three archpriests, who burned incense to the gods according to the heathen custom and obtained omens from offerings of sheep. Therefore, converting the temples from idol worship according to apostolic teaching, they consecrated bishops where there were priests, archbishops where there were archpriests. As the 6 principal seats of the archpriests were in the most noble cities, namely London and York and the City of Legions (which is located next to the River Usk in Glamorgan) so in these three cities, after they were purged of superstition, they committed the seats to three archbishops; in the rest they appointed bishops and assigned to each his own jurisdiction after the parishes were divided. As the great stream of the 7 Humber separated them from Loegria, Deira, and Albany fell within the province of the metropolitan see of York. Loegria and Cornwall were made subject to that of London, since the Severn keeps those regions separate from Cambria—that is, Wales—which was placed under the City of Legions. After these things had been arranged with God's 8 help, the prelates just mentioned returned to Rome and asked that everything they had accomplished be confirmed by the blessed pope. Accordingly, fittingly adorned with the

honoribus decenter ab ecclesia Romana insigniti, reversi sunt in Britanniam cum pluribus viris religiosis comitati, quorum doctrina et praedicatione gens Britonum in fide Christi roborata et aucta est; quorum actus in libro quem Gildas historiographus composuit lucide scripti reperiuntur.

BOOK 4

pallia and other honors by the Roman church, they returned
to Britain accompanied by many religious men through
whose instruction and preaching the British race was reinforced and strengthened in the Christian faith; their acts
will be found clearly set forth in the book that Gildas the
historian composed.

BOOK FIVE

Liber V

[73] Interea gloriosus ille rex Lucius cum cultum verae fidei crescere et exaltari in regno suo vidisset, magno fluctuans gaudio possessiones et territoria, quae prius templa idolorum possederant, in meliorem usum vertens, ecclesiis fidelium habenda concessit augmentavitque illas amplioribus

2 agris et mansis omnique libertate donavit. Peracto igitur feliciter vitae suae cursu, ab hac luce migravit in urbe Claudiocestrie et in ecclesia primae sedis honorifice sepultus est anno ab incarnatione Domini centesimo quinquagesimo sexto. Defuncto eo contentio inter Britones orta est quis heres eius esse deberet. Carebat enim sobole quae ei hereditario iure succederet.

[74] Sed ut Romae nuntiatum est, misit senatus Severum senatorem duasque legiones cum illo, ut patria Romanae potestati restitueretur. Mox, ut terram ingressus est, rebellabant Britones adversus eum. Quorum pars sibi continuo submissa est; pars autem quae subici Romanae potestati renuit trans Humbrum usque in Scotiam ab ipso imperatore

2 fugata est. At illa duce Fulgenio omni nisu Severo resistens irruptiones molestas consociatis sibi Pictis in regnum Deirae, dum procul abesset, faciebat. Quam irruptionem

Book 5

[73] Meanwhile, that glorious king Lucius, filled with great joy after he had seen the worship of the true faith thrive and become exalted in his kingdom, turned the possessions and territories that the temples of idolatry had possessed to better use by giving them over to be held by the churches of the faithful, and he endowed those churches with more ample fields and dwellings and granted them every freedom. The 2 course of his life happily completed, he departed from this world in the city of Gloucester and was honorably laid to rest in the cathedral church in the one hundred and fifty-sixth year after the incarnation of the Lord. Upon his death a dispute arose among the Britons as to who should be his heir. For he was without offspring that could succeed him by hereditary right.

[74] When this news arrived in Rome, the Senate sent senator Severus and two legions with him so that the country could be restored to Roman control. As soon as he entered the land, the Britons rebelled against him. A part of them remained in submission to him, but another part, which refused to be subject to Roman control, fled from that emperor across the Humber all the way to Scotland. But 2 led by Fulgenius, resisting Severus with all their strength, they made troublesome assaults, having allied themselves with the Picts in the kingdom of Deira, though it was far away. Taking this incursion seriously, the emperor ordered a

graviter ferens imperator, iussit vallum construi inter Deiram et Albaniam ut vel sic eorum impetus arceretur ne longius nocere posset. Facto igitur vallo a mari usque ad mare Fulgenius, quia terram sibi obstrui videt, marinum petit auxilium, navigavitque in Scithiam ut Pictorum auxilio

3 dignitati restitueretur. Reversus itaque cum magno navigio Eboracum obsedit, ubi magna pars Britonum Severum deserens Fulgenio adhaesit. Sed Severus, convocatis ceteris Britonibus atque Romanis, viriliter adiit obsidionem; congressique pariter, inter pugnandum occubuit Severus cum pluribus suorum et Fulgenius letaliter vulneratus est. Sepultusque est Severus Eboraci, sicut legiones suorum Romanorum postulaverunt, cum regali honore et reverentia.

[75] Reliquit ipse duos filios post se, Basianum et Getam; quorum Geta matre Romana generatus erat, Basianus Britannica. Romani ergo arripientes Getam sublimaverunt in regem, Britanni vero Basianum elegerunt. Orta itaque inter eos altercatione, pugnare invicem coeperunt fratres. Con-

2 festim Geta perempto Basianus regno potitur. Ea tempestate erat in Britannia iuvenis quidam, nomine Carausius, ex infima gente natus. Qui cum virtutem suam et probitatem in multis negotiis examinasset, profectus est Romam; petivitque a senatu et optinuit ut maritima Britanniae ab incursione barbarica navigio tueri liceret, promisitque rei publice

3 augmentum in tributis. Reversus itaque cum signatis chartis in Britanniam, mox collectis undicumque navibus cum magna iuvenum turba novitates affectantium tamquam pirata crudelis mare ingressus est. Proxima igitur aggressus

rampart to be built between Deira and Albany, so that their
assault could be resisted and could no longer cause harm.
After the rampart was built from sea to sea, Fulgenius, who
saw the land barricaded against him, sent for help by sea.
And he sailed to Scythia so that his power could be restored
with the help of the Picts. Having returned with a large 3
fleet, he laid siege to York, where a great part of the Britons,
deserting Severus, went over to Fulgenius. But Severus, summoning other Britons as well as Romans, vigorously attacked the blockade; and having joined together in battle,
during the fight Severus was struck down with many of his
men, and Fulgenius was mortally wounded. And, as his Roman legions demanded, Severus was buried at York with
royal honor and respect.

[75] He left two sons after him, Bassianus and Geta; of
the two Geta was born of a Roman mother, Bassianus of a
British one. The Romans therefore seized upon Geta and
raised him up as king, but the Britons chose Bassianus. Thus
a dispute arose between them and the brothers began to
fight with each other. After killing Geta, Bassianus immediately seized the throne. At that time there was a certain 2
young man in Britain named Carausius, born from a lowly
tribe. When he had tested his virtue and probity in many ac-
tivities, he departed for Rome; he asked the Senate and obtained permission that he be allowed to protect the coast of
Britain against barbarian incursion with a fleet. And he
promised an increase in tribute to the state. Returning then 3
to Britain with signed charters, he soon collected ships from
everywhere, along with a great crowd of young men looking
for adventure, and he put to sea like a savage pirate. Then,
attacking the nearby coast, he did not cease to waste the

litora, urbes et villas finitimorum depopulari ferro et igne non cessabat. Insulis quoque comprovincialibus appulsus, 4 omnia sua incolis atrociter eripiebat. Sic itaque illo agente, confluxit ad eum non minima multitudo perditorum hominum aliena rapere hanelantium, ita ut in brevi tantum congregaret exercitum quantus uni regno sufficeret ad possidendum. Elatus ergo in superbiam petivit a Britonibus ut sese regem facerent et ipse Romanos omnes de regno exterminaret. Quod cum impetrasset, confestim dimicans cum 5 Basiano interfecit eum. Quippe proditus est a Pictis quos dux Fulgenius, matris suae frater, in Britanniam locaverat. Nam dum his confidens dimicaret, promissis et donis Carausii corrupti, a Basiano mox in ipso congressu se subtraxerunt et inter Carausii copias se inserentes de commilitonibus hostes facti sunt. Unde Carausio victoria ocius cessit. Ut autem regni gubernacula Carausius adeptus est, dedit Pictis locum mansionis in Albania, ubi Britonibus admixti in aevum subsequens permanserunt.

[76] Cum ergo Carausii invasio Romae nuntiata foret, legavit senatus Allectum, fortem virum et prudentem, cum tribus legionibus in Britanniam ut tyrannum illum de regno deleret et tributum Romanae potestati restitueret. Nec mora, veniens Allectus in Britanniam proelium commisit cum Carausio illoque interfecto regni solium suscepit. Deinde persecutus est Britones, qui relicta re publica Carausio 2 adhaeserant. Britones igitur id graviter ferentes erexerunt in regem sibi Asclepiodotum, ducem Cornubiae, communique

cities and farms of the neighboring districts with sword and fire. Also, having landed on the neighboring islands, he violently snatched away all of their inhabitants. As he was doing this, no small multitude of degenerate men flocked to him, eager to snatch away the property of others, so that in a short time he assembled an army so large it would suffice to seize an entire kingdom. Swollen with pride, he proposed to the Britons that if they would make him king he would banish all the Romans from the kingdom. When this was granted, immediately fighting with Bassianus, he killed him. Of course Bassianus was betrayed by the Picts, whom Duke Fulgenius, his mother's brother, had stationed in Britain. For when he trusted they would fight, seduced by the promises and gifts of Carausius, they soon abandoned Bassianus in that battle and, joining among the troops of Carausius, they became enemies instead of allies. From that point the victory quickly fell to Carausius. Once Carausius took control of the kingdom, he gave the Picts a place to settle in Albany where they subsequently remained, mixed among the Britons.

[76] When Carausius's invasion became known in Rome, the Senate sent Allectus to Britain, a strong and prudent man, with three legions, to erase his tyranny from the kingdom and reinstate the payment of tribute to the dominion of Rome. Coming to Britain without delay, Allectus made war on Carausius and, having killed him, assumed the throne of the kingdom. Then he hunted down the Britons who, abandoning the state, had followed Carausius. Taking this badly, the Britons therefore raised up as their king Asclepiodotus the Duke of Cornwall, and pursuing Allectus by

assensu persecuti sunt Allectum inveneruntque eum Londoniae festum patriis diis celebrantem. Qui cum Asclepiodoti
adventum comperisset, intermisso sacrificio egressus est
contra eum in campum; et proelium committentes, dissipa-
tus est Allectus cum gente sua fugiensque interfectus est.

3 Livius ergo Gallus, Allecti collega, reliquos convocans Romanos in urbe, clausis portis resistere Asclepiodoto parat,
turribus ac muris armato milite munitis. Asclepiodotus ob-
sidens civitatem misit ocius nuntios ducibus regni ut sibi
festinarent in auxilium, quatinus gens Romanorum de regno
exterminaretur ne amplius dominium eorum super se pate-
rentur. Ad edictum ergo illius venerunt Demeti, Venedoti,
Deiri et Albani, et quicumque ex genere Britonum erant.

4 Cumque omnes simul convenissent, machinis muro admotis
cum balistis et sagittariis civitatem undique invadentes,
dirutis muris ac portis, urbem ingrediuntur, stragem de Romanis non modicam facientes. Interfectis itaque Romanis
praeter unam legionem, suaserunt Gallo ut deditioni se et

5 eos traderet quatinus vivi abscedere sinerentur. Assensum
ergo praebens Gallus tradidit se cum ceteris, fide interpo-
sita, ut vivi de regno Britanniae exirent. Cumque Asclepiodotus misericorditer illis assentiret, supervenerunt Venedoti et facto impetu omnes decollaverunt super rivum qui
per mediam fluit civitatem, qui postea de nomine ducis Britannice Nentgallin, Saxonice vero Galabroc nuncupatus est.

common consent, they found him in London celebrating a feast to the gods of his ancestors. When he learned of the arrival of Asclepiodotus, Allectus interrupted the sacrifice and came out against him in the field; but, engaging in battle, he was routed along with his people and killed as he fled. Then Livius Gallus, a colleague of Allectus, assembling the 3 remaining Romans together in the city of London, with the gates closed, prepared to resist Asclepiodotus, with the towers and walls garrisoned with soldiers. Besieging the city, Asclepiodotus quickly sent messengers to the dukes of the kingdom that they should hasten to his assistance, so that the Roman people would be banished from the kingdom, and the Britons would no longer have to endure their dominion. In response to this edict therefore came the Demetians, the Venedotians, the Deirans, and the Albans, and all the others who belonged to the British race. And after all 4 had come together at once, they brought siege engines up to the walls and attacked the city from every direction with ballistae and archers. The walls and the gates were demolished and they entered the city, making no little slaughter of the Romans. After all the Romans except for one legion had been killed, the Britons persuaded Gallus to surrender along with his men, so that they would be allowed to depart with their lives. Agreeing to this, Gallus therefore surrendered 5 himself with the others, giving his word that, if they lived, they would leave the kingdom of Britain. Although Asclepiodotus would have agreed with them out of mercy, the Venedotians intervened and, making an attack, beheaded all the Romans next to the river which flowed through the middle of the city, which afterward was known by the name of their leader, as Nentgallin in British, or Galabroc in Saxon.

[77] Triumpho itaque peracto, cepit Asclepiodotus regni diadema et capiti suo populo concedente imposuit. Rexitque terram cum iustitia et pace decem annis latronum saevi
2 tiam atque raptorum compescens. His diebus orta est persecutio Diocletiani in Christianos et, edicto eius grassante per universum orbem, missus est Maximianus Herculius trans
3 Alpes in Gallias edicta principis facturus. Perveniens ergo dira haec examinatio usque in Britanniam, trucidatis episcopis ac sacerdotibus necnon et de populo innumeris inter ceteros passus est sanctus Albanus Verolamius, Iulius quoque et Aaron Urbis Legionum cives.

[78] Surrexit interea Cohel, dux Kaercolim, in regem Asclepiodotum et conserto proelio interfecit eum regnique diademate se insignivit. Quod ubi Romae nuntiatum est, gavisus est senatus de morte illius quia per omnia Romanam
2 potestatem turbaverat atque deleverat. Recolentes quoque damnum quod pro amisso tributo sustinebant, legaverunt in Britanniam Constantium senatorem, qui antea Hispaniam Romanis subdiderat, virum sapientem, audacem, et bellicis rebus studentem, rei publicae fidelem. Porro Cohel cum adventum illius in Britanniam nosset, timuit ei bello occurrere quia fama ipsum virum fortem atque bellicosum ubique
3 praedicabat. Direxit ergo Cohel nuntios Constantio pacem petens et subiectionem cum tributo promittens. Acquievit Constantius pacemque receptis obsidibus confirmaverunt. Emenso deinde mense uno, gravi aegritudine correptus Cohel infra octo dies mortuus est. Constantius ergo regni

[77] Having thus achieved victory, Asclepiodotus took the crown of the kingdom and placed it on his own head with the people's consent. He ruled the land with justice and peace for ten years, while curbing the ferocity of bandits and robbers. In those days began the persecution of Diocletian against the Christians, and as his edict spread throughout the entire world, Maximianus Herculius was sent across the Alps into Gaul to implement the imperial edicts. Coming therefore all the way to Britain with his awful inquisition, after the bishops and the priests were slaughtered, along with countless numbers of people, among others there suffered Saint Alban of Verulamium, and also Julius and Aaron, citizens of the City of Legions.

[78] Meanwhile Coel, Duke of Kaercolim (Colchester), arose against King Asclepiodotus and, after engaging him in battle, killed him and adorned himself with the crown of the kingdom. As soon as this news reached Rome, the Senate rejoiced over the death of one who had disrupted and erased Roman authority everywhere. Also recalling the damage they sustained through lost tribute, they sent senator Constantius as an envoy to Britain, a wise man who had previously subjugated Spain to the Romans, bold and schooled in matters of war, faithful to the state. When he learned about his arrival, Coel feared to meet him in battle because his reputation everywhere declared him to be a strong and warlike man. Coel therefore sent messengers to Constantius seeking peace and promising submission along with tribute. Constantius agreed and, after hostages were accepted, they confirmed the peace. After one month had passed, Coel was seized with a grave disease, and within eight days he was dead. Constantius having therefore gained the crown of the

diademate insignitus, duxit filiam Cohel, Helenam nomine, pulchram valde ac formosam artibusque liberalibus edoc-

4 tam. Nec erat regi Cohel filius qui regni solio potiretur. Unde ita patri cara extiterat, ut artibus omnibus inbui eam faceret, quo facilius et sapientius post illum regnum regere nosset. Cum igitur illam in societatem tori recepisset, Constantius generavit ex ea filium vocavitque eum Constanti-

5 num. Subsequente deinde tempore, cum undecim anni praeterissent, Constantius Eboraci obiit, regnum filio suo Constantino relinquens. Qui ut solio sublimatus est, probitatem patris excedens infra paucos annos magnanimus et prudens omnibus apparuit. Latronum ac tyrannorum rapacitatem coercuit et iustitiam pacemque populo donavit.

[79] Tempore itaque illo Maxentius Romani imperii curam agens, tyrannidem gravissimam exercuit; rem publicam opprimere ac nobiles quosque senatores exterminare non destitit, donec saevitia illius exterminati ad Constantinum in Britanniam diffugerunt. Qui ab eo honorifice accepti

2 querimonias graves de Maxentio ei attulerunt. Audiens ergo Constantinus, lamentationibus eorum incitatus, Romam adiit cum infinito exercitu, ducens secum tres Helenae avunculos, Loelinum videlicet et Trahern Mariumque, ipsosque in senatorium ordinem promovit.

[80] Interea surrexit Octavius, dux Gewisseorum, in proconsules Romanae dignitatis quibus permissa fuerat a Constantino potestas Britanniae et illis peremptis solio regni potitus est. Cumque id Constantino nuntiatum esset, direxit Trahern, avunculum Helenae, in Britanniam cum

kingdom, he married Coel's daughter, named Helena, who was very pretty, indeed beautiful, and schooled in the liberal arts. There was no son of King Coel's who could obtain the throne of the kingdom. Therefore, her father had taken care to see that she was steeped in all the arts so that she would know how to rule the realm after him more easily and more wisely. After he had taken her to bed, Constantius produced with her a son and called him Constantine. Then, as time went by, when eleven years had passed, Constantius died in York, leaving the kingdom to his son Constantine. When he was raised to the throne, he exceeded the probity of his father, and in a few years showed himself to be noble in spirit and prudent. He punished the greediness of brigands and tyrants and gave justice and peace to the people.

[79] In his time Maxentius, conducting the administration of the Roman Empire, exercised the most oppressive tyranny, never ceasing to oppress the state and to banish the nobles and also the senators until, banished by his cruelty, they fled to Constantine in Britain. After they were honorably received by him, they conveyed to him serious complaints about Maxentius. Hearing these, Constantine, inspired by their lamentations, went to Rome with an immeasurable army, taking with him three uncles of Helena, namely Loelinus, Trahern, and Marius, and promoted them to senatorial rank.

[80] Meanwhile Octavius, Duke of the Gewissae, rebelled against the proconsuls of Roman authority, to whom the rule of Britain had been entrusted by Constantine, and after they were killed he obtained the throne of the kingdom. When this was reported to Constantine, he sent Trahern, Helena's uncle, to Britain with three legions, to punish

2 tribus legionibus ut ausum Octavii vindicaret. Appulsus itaque in litore iuxta urbem Kaerperis, infra duos dies recepit civitatem illam a civibus sibi redditam. Deinde tendens Wintoniam obviavit illi Octavius cum grandi exercitu non longe a Wintonia in campo qui Britannice Maisuram appel-

3 latur, coepitque proeliari et victoria potitus est. Trahern autem fugiens cum suis naves petit ingressusque altum mare Albaniam aequoreo itinere adiit et provinciam totam depraedatus spoliis Albanorum ditatus est. Quod cum Octavio

4 nuntiatum esset, resociatis suis tendit Albaniam. Sed Trahern citra Albaniam in provincia quae Westmarialanda dicitur evagatus audacter bello Octavium suscipiens devicit atque fugavit. Insecutusque eum toto regno privavit. At ille fugiens navigio Norwegiam petit, regem Gumperium adiens

5 ut auxilio eius regno Britanniae restitueretur. Interea Trahern a quodam familiari Octavii interfectus periit. Edixerat enim Octavius recedens quibusdam familiaribus suis ut insi-

6 dias ei pararent et se de illo vindicarent. Comes igitur oppidi municipii qui eum prae ceteris diligebat, complens Octavii votum, dum Trahern ex Urbe Londoniarum quadam die recederet, delituit cum centum militibus in quadam nemorosa valle, qua ille transiturus erat, atque praetereuntem inopinate inter commilitones suos interfecit, mittensque post

7 Octavium nuntiavit ei rei eventum. Octavius igitur gaudens reversus est in Britanniam et dissipatis Romanis solium regni recuperavit. Exin regnum cum pace obtinuit; copiam

the outrageous conduct of Octavius. Putting ashore on the 2
coast near the town of Portchester, within two days he re-
captured that city, returning it to its citizens. Then, as he
was heading for Winchester, Octavius came against him
with a great army not far from Winchester, in a field which is
called Maisuram in British, began to fight and achieved the
victory. Trahern, however, fleeing with his men, made for 3
the ships, and after he embarked on the high seas he went
via the ocean to Albany. He plundered the entire province,
and was enriched with the spoils of the Albans. When this
was reported to Octavius, he regrouped his men and made
for Albany. But Trahern quickly left Albany for the province 4
called Westmorland, and boldly taking up the battle with
Octavius, he defeated him and drove him away. Pursuing
him, Trahern deprived him of the entire kingdom. But Octavius fled to Norway with his fleet, seeking out King Gum-
perius in order to be restored to the kingdom of Britain with
his help. Meanwhile Trahern was struck down by a certain 5
follower of Octavius and perished. For Octavius had told
certain of his followers as he retreated that they should prepare an ambush for Trahern and should take revenge for Octavius by that means. Therefore the count of a fortified 6
town, who cared for him more than the others, complied
with Octavius's wish and, when Trahern withdrew from the
city of the Londoners one day, hid himself with a hundred
soldiers in a certain wooded ravine that Trahern would be
passing through and killed him as he passed unsuspecting
among his fellow soldiers. Sending after Octavius the count
reported this turn of events to him. Octavius, therefore, re- 7
joicing, returned to Britain and, with the Romans scattered,
he recovered the throne of the kingdom. After that he held

auri et argenti ac divitias innumeras congregans, in thesauro reposuit. Regnum itaque Britonum ab illo tempore usque in diebus Gratiani et Valentiniani feliciter rexit.

[81] Denique, senio confectus, Octavius cogitavit de regno disponere qualiter post mortem suam pace hereditaria frueretur. Neque enim erat ei filius, sed unam tantum filiam habens optabat eam post se in regni solio sublimari. Consilium igitur a familiaribus fidelibus sumens, fuerunt qui filiam alicui nobilium Romanorum locare laudarent, ut fir-

2 miori pace regnum tueretur. Fuerunt quoque qui censerent Conanum Meriadocum, nepotem suum, heredem facere; filiam vero alicui principi extra regnum, cum magna auri et argenti copia copulandam. Dum ergo haec inter se cum ambiguitate gererent, surrexit Caradocus, dux Cornubiae, sententiamque dedit potiorem, quatinus puella donaretur Maximiano senatori Romano, nobili ac prudenti viro, ut

3 heres esset regni post fata Octavii. Erat autem patre Britannus, filius Loelini avunculi Constantini, matre vero et natione Romanus, et ex utraque parte regalem protrahebat dignitatem. Unde spes omnibus dabatur, tum propter affinitatem, tum propter puellae regalem et hereditariam dignitatem, tranquilla pace diebus eorum post se regnum Britanniae florere.

4 His auditis, Conanus qui priorem de se sententiam audisse gaudebat omnique nisu ad regnum hanelabat, totam

the kingdom in peace; collecting a wealth of gold and silver and innumerable riches, he restored them to the treasury. He ruled the kingdom of the Britons happily from that time up until the days of Gratian and Valentinian.

[81] Finally, having grown old, Octavius thought about how to arrange control of the kingdom so that after his death his heirs could enjoy it in peace. For he had no son, but only a daughter, and he wished for her to be raised the throne of the kingdom after him. When he took counsel about this from his faithful retainers, there were those who recommended that he should find someone from the Roman nobility for his daughter, so that he could protect the kingdom with a more solid peace. There were also those 2 who thought he should make his nephew, Conan Meriadoc, his heir, and marry his daughter to some other prince outside the kingdom, along with a great wealth of gold and silver. While they were considering these things among themselves with uncertainty, Caradoc the Duke of Cornwall rose to his feet and offered his opinion that it would be better if the girl were given to Maximian the Roman senator, a noble and prudent man, so he could be heir to the kingdom after the death of Octavius. Moreover he was a Briton because of 3 his father, being the son of Loelinus the uncle of Constantine, and he was a Roman because of his mother and his birth, and on both sides he descended from royal blood. From this hope was given to everyone, in part because of his lineage and in part because of the royal and hereditary standing of the girl, that the kingdom of Britain would flourish after him with tranquil peace in their days.

After hearing these things, Conan, who before hearing 4 Caradoc's opinion about the matter had been delighted and

fere curiam perturbavit, indignans quod contra se dux Cornubiae sententiam dedisset. At Caradocus, vilipendens temerarii iuvenis exactionem, ex consilio et voluntate regis misit Mauricium, filium suum, Romam ut ex senatus con-

5 sultu Maximianum adduceret. Veniens itaque Mauricius Romam, invenit Romam turbatam et magnam inquietudinem inter ipsum Maximianum et duos imperatores, Gratianum videlicet et fratrem suum Valentinianum, qui ambo vi imperii potestatem usurpaverant, repulso Maximiano ab imperii societate quam petebat. Mauricius ergo evocans seorsum Maximianum intimavit ei super legatione et negotio pro quo venerat.

[82] Quibus auditis Maximianus laetus suscepit hanc legationem et iter arripiens cum Mauricio in Britanniam venit.

[83] Rex igitur Octavius, cum honore summo suscipiens Maximianum, dedit ei filiam suam et heredem regni constitvit. Quod videns Conanus, nepos ipsius, indignatus secessit in Albaniam et exercitum collegit quantum potuit. Venitque cum multitudine Pictorum ac Britonum trans Humbrum

2 flumen quasque provincias depopulans. At Maximianus, collecto fortiori exercitu, contra illum venit et cum illo dimicans in fugam coegit et cum victoria domum rediit. Conanus iterum resociatis turmis inquietabat regnum Britanniae.

3 Sed Maximianus commissis proeliis quandoque cum triumpho, quandoque superatus abibat, ut assolet in dubio eventu

was hoping with all his might to obtain the kingdom, threw nearly the whole court into confusion, resentful that the duke should have offered this opinion in opposition to him. But Caradoc, ignoring the demand of the reckless young man, and in line with the purpose and desire of the king, sent his son Mauricius to Rome so that he could bring Maximian back by decree of the Senate. Coming therefore to Rome, Mauricius found a state of confusion in Rome and a great disturbance between that Maximian and the two emperors, namely Gratian and his brother Valentinian, who had both usurped the imperial power by force, while Maximian had been driven away from the imperial partnership which he sought. Mauricius therefore, calling Maximian apart from the others, told him about the legation and the business for which he had come.

[82] After he heard about it, Maximian received this legation happily and, taking to the road, he went to Britain with Mauricius.

[83] Therefore King Octavius, receiving Maximian with the highest honor, gave him his daughter and appointed him as the heir to the kingdom. Seeing this, his nephew Conan became indignant, withdrew to Albany and assembled as large an army as he could. And he came with a multitude of Picts and Britons across the River Humber, laying waste to those provinces. But Maximian, having assembled a more powerful army, came against him and engaging in battle with him he put him to flight and returned home with the victory. Once his troops were united again, Conan harassed the kingdom of Britain. When battles were fought, Maximian went away sometimes with victory, sometimes defeated, as is customary in the uncertain course of war. Finally, through

belli. Tandem annitentibus viris sapientibus et amicis eorum concordes facti sunt et amici adinvicem.

[84] Post quinquennium, congregatis copiis auri et argenti ac innumerabilium divitiarum, Maximianus navigium parat atque in Galliam transiens Armoricum regnum, quod nunc Britannia dicitur, primitus adiit et populum qui terram incolebat debellare coepit. At Franci audientes duce Humbalto venerunt cum exercitu; et congredientes pugnam ini-
2 erunt Franci et Britones. Sed Franci maiori parte debilitati fugam arripiunt, Britones vero insequentes quindecim milia eorum fere trucidaverunt. Maximianus itaque victoria potitus ad castra cum suis rediit gratulans quia terram sibi subdendam leviter aestimabat. Vocatoque ad se Conano se-
3 paratim extra turbam subridens ait: "Ecce, subiugavimus partem Galliae, Francos devicimus. Ecce, spem ad cetera subicienda nobis habemus. Festinemus ergo urbes et oppida nostro dominio subiugare, antequam rumor in ultiorem Galliam evolans adversum nos universos populos excitet. Nam si regnum istud retinere poterimus, non dubito quin totam Galliam per hunc aditum potestati nostrae subdamus. Ne igitur pigeat te regnum Britanniae mihi cessisse, quia quicquid in illa amisisti tibi in hac patria restaurabo.
4 Regem enim te faciam esse regni huius et erit haec altera Britannia eamque ex nostro genere pulsis indigenis replebimus. Terra enim haec fertilis est omni fructu repleta, flumina piscosa et piscibus copiosa, nemora et saltus venatibus apta; nec est uspiam meo iudicio gratior tellus."

the efforts of wise men and their friends, they were reconciled and became friends with each other.

[84] After five years, having gathered an abundance of
gold and silver and innumerable riches, Maximian prepared
a fleet and, passing over to Gaul, he went first to the Armorican kingdom, which is now called Brittany, and began
to subdue the people who lived in that land. But when the
Franks heard about this, they came with an army led by
Duke Humbaltus, and meeting together the Franks and
Britons entered into battle. But after the greater part of 2
them were incapacitated the Franks took flight, and the
Britons, following after, slew almost fifteen thousand of
them. Having thus achieved the victory, Maximian returned
to camp with his men, rejoicing because he expected the
land would be subjected to him easily. After he called Conan
to him apart from the army, he said, smiling: "Behold, we 3
have conquered part of Gaul, we have defeated the Franks.
Behold, we have hope the rest will be made subject to us.
Let us therefore hasten to subject the cities and towns to
our rule before news spreads to remoter Gaul and provokes
the entire people against us. For if we can retain this kingdom, I have no doubt that in addition to this we can reduce
all of Gaul to our power. Therefore it should not distress you
to have ceded the kingdom of Britain to me, because whatever you lost in that I will restore to you in this country. For 4
I will make you king of this kingdom and this will be another
Britain, and after the natives are driven out we will fill it
again with our people. For this land is fertile, filled with all
crops, with rivers for fishing and full of fish, with forests and
woods suitable for hunting, nor is there anywhere, in my
judgment, a more pleasing land."

Ad haec submisso capite grates egit Conanus promisitque se fidelem sibi omni tempore vitae suae fore.

[85] Post haec, convocatis militum turmis, Redonum civitatem petunt quam mox eadem die cives eis reddiderunt. Quidam enim eorum audita Britonum audacia et peremptorum casu diffugerant ad nemora, relictis mulierculis et infantibus. Quippe ubicumque vi vel sponte intrabant, quod erat masculini sexus interficiebant, solis mulieribus parcentes. Cumque universam terram ab incolis delevissent, munierunt civitates et oppida suis armatis et castra in diversis promontoriis statuerunt.

[86] Sed deerant habitatores qui totam occuparent terram. Misit ergo in Britanniam et edicto praecepit ut centum milia plebanorum colligerentur sparsim per regiones regni et triginta milia militum quibus totam terram incolendam
2 contraderet. Qui cum ad eius iussionem convenissent, distribuit eos per partes regni et habitatores fecit et Conanum eis in regem promovit. Ipse deinde cum suis ulteriorem Galliam penetrans, gravissimis proeliis illatis, subiugavit eam necnon et totam Germaniam, civitate Treveri solium imperii sui constituens. Postea in Gratianum et Valentinianum imperatores vim sui furoris exacuens, uno perempto alte-
3 rum a Roma fugavit. Ipse vero Romae imperator factus quadragesimus ab Augusto imperium rexit anno ab incarnatione Domini trecentesimo septuagesimo septimo. Valentinianus

To this, with his head bowed, Conan gave thanks, and he pledged to be faithful to him for all the time of his life.

[85] After this, having assembled troops of soldiers, they attacked the city of Rennes, which its citizens surrendered soon on the same day. Certain of them, having heard of the boldness of the Britons and the fate of the fallen, fled to the woods, their women and children abandoned. For indeed, wherever the Britons entered, either freely or by force, they killed those who were of the masculine sex, sparing only the women. And when they had left the whole land empty of its inhabitants, they garrisoned the cities and towns with their soldiers, and they established camps on various promontories.

[86] But residents were lacking to occupy the whole land. Therefore, Maximian sent an edict to Britain and ordered that one hundred thousand commoners should be assembled from here and there throughout all regions of the kingdom, along with thirty thousand soldiers, with whom he caused the whole land to be inhabited. When they had come 2 together in response to his command, he divided them throughout all parts of the kingdom and made them its residents, and appointed Conan as their king. Then he himself entered the remoter parts of Gaul with his men and, after the most serious battles were fought, he conquered them and also the whole of Germany, setting up the throne of his empire in Trier. After that, he pointed the force of his anger against Gratian and Valentinian, and after one was killed he chased the other away from Rome. He himself was made 3 emperor of Rome, the fortieth after Augustus, and he ruled the empire in the three hundred and seventy-seventh year after the incarnation of the Lord. Valentinian, however, the

autem, frater Gratiani, ad Theodosium in Orientem fugiens, imperio per Theodosium restitutus est et Maximianum subinde apud Aquileiam fratrem vindicans interfecit.

[87] Interea infestabant Conanum in Armorica Galli et Aquitani crebrisque irruptionibus inquietabant. Quibus ipse viriliter resistens, commissam sibi patriam ab eorum

2 incursionibus protexit. Cumque sibi de omnibus cessisset victoria, volens commilitonibus suis uxores dare ut ex eis nascerentur heredes qui terram hereditate possiderent, decrevit ut ex Britannia sortirentur uxores quibus maritarentur. Direxit ergo legatos ad Dionotum ducem Cornubiae, qui Caradoco fratri successerat, et curam huius negotii ami

3 cabiliter inpendit. Erat iste Dionotus totius regni custos dum Maximianus aberat et principatum Britanniae sub eo regebat dum Maximianus maioribus negotiis intenderet. Habebat et filiam mirae pulcritudinis cui nomen erat Ursula, quam Conanus sibi in uxorem delegerat.

[88] Dionotus igitur, auditis Conani legationibus, paruit libens collectisque per diversas provincias filiabus nobilium numero undecim milia, de plebanis vero sexaginta milia, omnes convenire in urbe Londonia praecepit. Inde per Thamensem fluvium navibus collocatis in altum se dederunt et maria sulcantes versus terram Armoricanorum navigabant.

2 Nec mora, insurgunt venti contram in classem illam et in brevi per totum pelagus dissipaverunt. Periclitatae sunt

brother of Gratian, fleeing to Theodosius in the East, was restored to the empire by Theodosius, and immediately after that, avenging his brother, he killed Maximian near Aquileia.

[87] Meanwhile, the Gauls and the Aquitanians were harassing Conan in Armorica, and troubling him with constant attacks. Resisting them boldly, he protected the country entrusted to him against their incursions. And when victory 2 had been conceded to him by them all, wanting to give wives to his fellow soldiers so that heirs would be born to them who could take possession of the land by inheritance, he decreed that wives whom they could marry should be selected from Britain. He therefore sent messengers to Dionotus, the Duke of Cornwall, who had succeeded his brother Caradoc, and in a friendly fashion entrusted the supervision of this business to him. This Dionotus was the guardian of the 3 whole kingdom while Maximian was absent, and he ruled the dominion of Britain under him while Maximian was attending to more important business. He also had a daughter of marvelous beauty, whose name was Ursula, whom Conan had selected as a bride for himself.

[88] Having listened to Conan's messengers, Dionotus willingly complied, and after eleven thousand daughters of the nobility and sixty thousand of the commoners had been assembled from diverse provinces, he ordered them all to convene in the city of London. From there, once the ships were assembled, by way of the River Thames they committed themselves to the high seas, and, plowing through the waves, they navigated toward the land of the Armoricans. Without delay, the winds arose against their fleet and in a 2 short space of time they were scattered across the whole

ergo quaedam, in maiori parte submersae. Sed quae periculum evaserunt appulsae sunt in barbaras insulas et ab ignota
3 et nefanda gente sive trucidatae sive mancipatae sunt. Inciderant siquidem in dirum exercitum Gwanii et Melgae, quorum Gwanius rex Hunorum, Melga Pictorum rex fuerat; qui mittente Gratiano maritima Germaniae dira clade vexabant. Hi itaque, obviantes navigio predictarum puellarum, rapuerunt eas ad se volentes lascivire cum eis. Sed cum abhorrerent puellae eorum immundam dementiam, quaedam absque ulla pietate ab eis trucidatae sunt, quaedam ad exteras nationes venundatae. Deinde cum didicissent praedicti
4 pirate Britanniae insulam armato milite fere evacuatam, direxerunt iter ad illam et applicuerunt in Albaniam. Agmine igitur facto, invaserunt regnum quod rege et defensore carebat, vulgus inerme caedentes. Nam, ut praedictum est, Maximianus omnem iuventutem validam secum abduxerat et colonos simul, qui si forte affuissent hostibus istis resistere potuissent. Praefati itaque tyranni Gwanius et Melga,
5 postquam grassati sunt pro voluntate sua super vulgus inerme, urbes et munitiones sibi subdentes, totam Britanniam suo dominio subiugaverunt. Cum igitur haec calamitas
6 niam suo dominio subiugaverunt. Cum igitur haec calamitas Maximiano Romae nuntiata fuisset, misit Gratianum municipem cum duabus legionibus in Britanniam ut auxilium ferret oppressis. Qui venientes, disturbatis hostibus qui se per totam terram tamquam municipes locaverant, acerrima caede affectos, in Hiberniam, quotquot evasere periculum, fugaverunt.

sea. Some were thus placed in danger, and the majority were sunk. But those who escaped danger were driven ashore on barbarous islands and they were either slaughtered or enslaved by strange and wicked people. For indeed they encountered the wicked army of Gwanius and Melga, in which Gwanius was king of the Huns, and Melga king of the Picts; sent by Gratian, they were troubling the coast of Germany with awful devastation. Attacking the ship of the women just mentioned, these men seized them, wishing to indulge their lust upon them. But when the young women shrunk back from their foul madness, some were slaughtered by them without any mercy, while others were sold to foreign nations. Then, when these pirates learned that the island of Britain was nearly emptied of armed soldiers, they turned their path toward it and landed in Albany. After a column had been formed, they invaded the kingdom, which was without a king or protector, cutting down the defenseless rabble. For, as said before, Maximian had taken all the strong young men with him, and likewise the farmers who, if by chance they had been present, would have been able to resist these enemies. And so the tyrants just mentioned, Gwanius and Melga, after they had marched at will against the defenseless rabble, making the towns and fortresses subordinate to themselves, subjugated all of Britain to their rule. Accordingly, when this calamity was announced to Maximian in Rome, he sent the citizen Gratian with two legions into Britain, to bring help to the oppressed. When they arrived, they dislodged the enemies who had positioned themselves throughout the land like citizens, reduced them by the most terrible slaughter, and drove whatever number escaped from danger to Ireland.

7   Interea interfecto Maximiano Romae ab amicis Gratiani
et Britonibus qui cum eo venerant dissipatis et in parte ne-
catis, [89] Gratianus regnum Britanniae adeptus est et tyrannidem non modicam in populum exercuit donec catervatim se stipantes plebani et irruentes in eum interfecerunt.
Quod audientes praedicti hostes ex Hibernia navigium educentes, secum Scotos, Norguegenses, Dacos cum magna
manu conducentes, Britanniam a mari usque ad mare ferro
2   ac flammis vastaverunt. Mittuntur ergo legati cum epistolis
Romam ad senatum lacrimosis suspiriis postulantes auxilium, voventes se in perpetuum servituros si ab hac dira oppressione hostium liberarentur. Quibus mox committitur
legio, praeteriti mali non immemor; quae ut advenit in Britanniam, cum hostibus congressa magnam multitudinem
stravit atque reliquos usque in Alban iam fugere coegit.
3   Sicque Dei nutu a tam atroci oppressione exempti, vallum
cum muro inmensum inter Albaniam et Deiram a mari usque ad mare construxerunt arcendis hostibus oportunum,
indigenis vero magnum tutamen et defensionem facturum.
Erat autem tunc Albania penitus barbarorum incursione
vastata ita ut indigenis expulsis receptaculum esset omnium
perditorum.

[90] Romani ergo depulsis hostibus Romam reverti decreverunt, denuntiantes Britonibus nequaquam se tam laboriosis expeditionibus posse ulterius fatigari et ob erraticos
latrunculos Romanam iuventutem ac potestatem terra marique tam frequentibus expeditionibus vexari; malle potius
toto tributo fraudari quam tot laboriosis occursionibus subiacere. Convocatis itaque in urbe Londonia optimatibus terrae repedare se Romam profitentur.

Meanwhile, after Maximian was killed at Rome by friends 7
of Gratian, and the Britons who came with him were scattered and part of them killed, [89] Gratian was raised to the
throne of Britain and exercised an unrestrained tyranny
over the people until, surrounding him en masse and rushing upon him, the commoners killed him. Hearing this, the
enemy mentioned before brought their ships over from Ireland along with a great force of Scots, Norwegians, and
Danes and laid waste to Britain with sword and fire from sea
to sea. Ambassadors were therefore sent with letters to the 2
Senate in Rome, begging for help with tearful sighs, offering
to serve forever if they were delivered from the awful oppression of the enemy. They were soon provided with a legion not at all mindful of past offenses which, when it arrived in Britain and engaged the enemy, killed a great many
and forced the rest to flee all the way to Albany. And in or- 3
der, God willing, to be freed from the savage oppression,
they constructed a massive rampart with a wall from sea to
sea between Albany and Deira suitable to guard against the
enemy, effectively creating protection and defense for the
natives. But Albany had been completely devastated by the
invasion of the barbarians so that, with the natives driven
away, it had become a refuge for all marauders.

[90] Then the Romans, having driven off the enemy, determined to return to Rome, warning the Britons that in no
way could they be bothered again by such laborious expeditions nor could Roman youth and power be troubled by
such frequent expeditions over land and sea on account of
wandering brigands. They would rather be deprived of all
tribute than be subjected to such laborious visits. After the
leading nobles of the land were assembled in the city of London, the Romans announced they were going back to Rome.

[91] Atque ut se ab incursione erraticorum hostium tueantur, turres in litore, quo navigium piratarum applicare formidabant, struendas decernunt ut, sicut murus praefatus in terra ad munitionem erat, ita et turres a mari sibi pro munimento fierent. Armorum quoque instruendorum exemplaria a Romanis habuerunt, peltis et pilis suadentes seipsos, coniuges, liberos, opes, et, quod maius his erat, libertatem vi propria atque armorum defensione viriliter dimicando tue-

2 rentur. Sicque vale dicto Romani tamquam ultra non reversuri profecti sunt. Quo audito Gwanius et Melga navibus quibus fuerant in Hiberniam vecti emergentes cum Scotis et Norguengensibus, Dacis et Pictis, omnem Albaniam murotenus capessunt. Contra hos constituuntur in edito murorum rudes ad pugnam, qui leviter prostrati atque telorum grandine territi, muris deiciuntur et fugam arripiunt. Hostes

3 itaque deiecto ad solum muro fugientes persecuntur, persequendo interimunt, quosdam mancipatos carceribus tradunt et fit tanta strages quanta nullis temporibus antea fuerat facta. Igitur rursum nihilominus miserae Britonum reliquiae mittunt Romam epistolas ad Agitium, summum Romanae potestatis virum, in hunc modum: "Agitio ter con-

4 suli gemitus Britonum." Et post pauca querentes adiciunt: "Nos mare ad barbaros, barbari ad mare repellunt. Interea oriuntur duo funerum genera: aut enim submergimur aut iugulamur." Verum Romani nulla commoti pietate auxilium ferre recusant, pretendentes eorum saepissime laboriosam

[91] However, in order to protect the Britons against the attack of roving enemies, they decreed that towers should be built on the shore which the ships of the pirates would fear to approach and thus, just as the wall mentioned before was a fortification on land, the towers would give them fortification against the sea. They also received from the Romans patterns for the fabrication of arms, encouraging them to use spears and shields to protect themselves, their wives, their children, their wealth, and, what was greater than these, their liberty by fighting vigorously with their own strength and defense of arms. And thus, having bid 2 farewell as if never to come again, the Romans departed. As soon as they heard this, Gwanius and Melga, appearing with Scots and Norwegians, Danes, and Picts in the ships by which they had been conveyed to Ireland, seized all of Albany as far as the wall. Against these were set up on the heights of the walls men unprepared to fight, who, easily struck down and terrified by a hail of javelins, were knocked from the walls and took to flight. Those who were thrown to 3 the ground the enemies pursued as they were fleeing; while pursuing they killed them; they handed some of them over to prison in chains; and such a slaughter was made as had never been made before. Nevertheless, the wretched remnant of the Britons therefore sent letters to Aegidius in Rome, a man of the highest Roman power, in this way: "To 4 Aegidius, thrice consul, the groans of the Britons." And after a few complaints they add, "The sea drives us to the barbarians, the barbarians to the sea. Meanwhile there arise two kinds of death: either we are drowned or we are butchered." But the Romans, not at all moved by pity, refused to bring help, alleging as an excuse their frequent laborious

in Britanniam expeditionem et praeterea de tributis frauda-
tionem. Legati tristes redeunt atque huiuscemodi repulsam
denuntiant.

[92] Inito ergo consilio, transfretavit Guizelinus, Lon-
doniensis metropolitanus, in minorem Britanniam, quae
tunc Armorica sive Letavia dicebatur, ut auxilium a confra-
tribus postularet. Regnabat tunc in illa Aldroenus, quartus a
2 Conano primo duce. Qui viso tantae reverentiae viro excepit illum cum honore cognitaque sui adventus causa, tristis
ac maestus de persecutione agnatorum et patriae, subsidium
se ferre quale posset promisit. Tradiditque sibi Constantinum fratrem suum bellicosum et duo milia militum ex electis Britonibus.

[93] Qui mare ingressi in portu Totonesio applicuerunt.
Nec mora, collecta multitudine senum ac iuvenum atque
utriusque aetatis virorum regni, cum hostibus congressi victoriam adepti sunt. Exin confluxerunt undique prius dispersi Britones et in abditis locorum latitantes factaque intra
Silcestriam contione erexerunt Constantinum in regem
2 regnique diadema capiti suo imposuerunt. Tunc erumpens
Guizelinus pontifex, qui illum adduxerat, in vocem laetitiae
cantando gratulanter ait: "Christus vincit, Christus regnat,
Christus imperat! Ecce quod desideravimus, ecce rex Britanniae desertae, ecce defensio nostra—assit modo Christus!"

3 Dimissa itaque contione illa cum exultatione, dederunt
regi suo coniugem ex nobili genere Romanorum ortam,
quam ipse Guizelinus archiepiscopus secum educaverat. De
qua progenuit tres filios, quorum nomina sunt Constans,

expeditions to Britain and, in addition, the withholding of tribute. The ambassadors returned downcast, and reported on the nature of their rejection.

[92] Therefore, after taking counsel, Guizelinus, the archbishop of London, passed over to lesser Britain, which was then called Armorica or Letavia, to ask for help from their brethren. Aldroenus then ruled that land, the fourth after Conan, its first leader. Upon seeing a man of such reverence, Aldroenus received him with honor, and learning the reason for his visit he was saddened and mournful about the persecution of his relatives and their country, and he promised to bring such relief as he could. He gave to him his warlike brother Constantine and two thousand soldiers from those chosen by the Britons.

[93] Having put to sea, they landed in the port of Totnes. Without delay, after collecting a multitude of the old and the young and men of both ages from the kingdom, they engaged their enemies, and won the victory. After that the Britons, previously scattered and hiding in secret locations, drew together from every direction and, assembled in Silchester, they raised Constantine as king and placed the crown of the kingdom on his head. Then Guizelinus the bishop, who had brought him there, burst out and chanted gratefully in a joyful voice: "Christ conquers, Christ rules, Christ commands! Behold what we longed for, behold the king of forsaken Britain, behold our protection—if only Christ is with us!"

Once the assembly was dissolved, with exultation they gave that king a wife born of the Roman nobility, whom Archbishop Guizelinus himself had raised. By her he fathered three sons, whose names were Constans, Aurelius

Aurelius Ambrosius, Utherpendragon. Constantem primogenitum tradidit ecclesiae Amphibali nutriendum infra

4 Wintoniam, ubi etiam monasticum suscepit ordinem. Ceteros, videlicet Aurelium et Utherpendragon, Guizelino praesuli nutriendos commisit. Cumque decem annis regnasset Constantinus, quidam Pictus qui in obsequio suo fuerat accessit ad eum quasi colloquium secretum habiturus in virgulto quodam semotis omnibus arbitris et cum cultro dolose interfecit eum.

[94] Defuncto itaque Constantino, dissensio facta est inter proceres regni de duobus fratribus, quis eorum in regem sublimaretur. Erant siquidem ambo adhuc pueri infra aetatem tanti culminis regendi. Cumque diu contendissent et alii hunc, alii illum acclamarent, accessit vir gnarus quidem sed dolosus, Vortigernus, dux Gewisseorum, qui et ipse ad regnum toto nisu anhelabat, et persuasit optimatibus regni, quatinus Constantem primogenitum, qui in monasterio

2 Wintoniensi degebat, in regem eligerent. Quod cum quidam propter monasticum ordinem abhorrerent, ipse se ultro ad hoc opus praesto esse atque iuvenem de monasterio exempturum spopondit. Relictis ergo illis Wintoniam tendit, monasterium ingreditur atque colloquium regalis iuvenis deposcit. Cumque extra claustrum eductus esset, verba

3 huiuscemodi auribus illius secreto instillavit: "Ecce pater tuus defunctus est et fratres tui propter aetatem sublimari in regem nequeunt, nec alium habemus praeter te de genere tuo quem nobis regem eligamus. Acquiesce ergo consilio

Ambrosius, and Utherpendragon. Constantine gave his firstborn son Constans to the church of Amphibalus in Winchester to be raised, where Constans also joined the monastic order. The others, namely Aurelius and Utherpendragon, 4 he committed to Guizelinus the bishop to be raised. And after Constantine had ruled for ten years, a certain Pict who was in his retinue approached him as if to have a secret conversation in a certain thicket secluded from all onlookers and treacherously killed him with a knife.

[94] After Constantine was dead, a disagreement arose among the leading men of the kingdom about which of the two brothers should be raised up as king. Both were still boys below the age they had to reach in order to rule. And after they had debated this for some time, and some had approved this one, others that one, Vortigern approached, a knowing but deceitful man, leader of the Gewissae, who himself aspired to the kingdom with all his strength, and he persuaded the nobles of the kingdom to choose as their king Constans, the firstborn, who was passing his time in the monastery at Winchester. Although some were averse to 2 this because of his monastic vows, Vortigern himself was ready and willing to do this and promised to remove the young man from the monastery. Leaving those others behind, he made for Winchester, entered the monastery, and demanded an audience with the royal youth. When Constans was led outside the cloister, Vortigern secretly poured words of this nature into his ears: "Behold, your father is 3 dead and your brothers are not old enough to be raised as king, nor do we have anyone else from your family other than you whom we can choose as our king. Therefore, listen

meo et, si possessionem meam augmentare volveris, sua-
debo populum et in affectum convertam sublimandi te in
regem et ex hoc habitu mutatis vestibus te abstraham."

4 Quod cum audisset Constans, magno exultans gaudio
quod petebat se libenter exsequi confessus est et quicquid
callebat ipsum velle iureiurando confirmavit. Assumpsit
itaque eum Vortigernus, vellent nollent monachi, atque mutato habitu regiis ornamentis mox indutum Londonias se-
5 cum duxit. Sed tunc temporis, defuncto Guizelino pontifice,
ecclesia illa carebat nec affuit alter qui eum inungere et coronam imponere presumeret. Arripiens igitur ipse Vortigernus propter instantem necessitatem coronam, capiti illius
manibus suis imposuit.

[95] Sublimatus itaque Constans totam regni curam Vortigerno commisit, necnon et semetipsum consilio et mode-
rationi eiusdem tradidit. Elapso autem tempore, cum totas
regni habenas ipse Vortigernus pro voto moderaretur, coepit apud se deliberare et intenta mente excogitare qualiter
quod desiderabat de regno compleret. Videbat namque con-
gruum tempus adesse quo id ad effectum duceret, cum ei
totius regni dominium cessisset et regis Constantis fatuitas
2 pateret universis. Quippe in claustro enutritus nullam dis-
pensationis curam vel providentiam regni gerebat, omnia
Vortigerno tantum committens. Duo autem fratres illius
tamquam in cunis adhuc nutriebantur. Praeterea regni proceres maiores natu mortibus diversis omnes fere obierant et

to my advice and, if you are willing to enlarge my possessions, I will persuade the people and change their minds so
as to raise you up as king, and I will extricate you from this
monastic habit with a change in robes."

When Constans had heard this, exulting with great joy,   4
he freely agreed to do what Vortigern asked, and whatever
he understood him to want he confirmed under oath. And
so Vortigern took him up, whether the monks were willing
or not, and having altered his habit and quickly adorned him
with royal trappings, he took him with himself to London.
However, with Bishop Guizelinus being dead by then, that   5
church had no one, nor did another come forward, who
would presume to anoint him and put the crown on his
head. Therefore, snatching it up because of the pressing
need, Vortigern himself placed the crown on Constans's
head with his own hands.

[95] After he was raised on high, Constans entrusted the
government of the entire kingdom to Vortigern, and he also
surrendered himself to his counsel and direction. However,
once time had passed, when Vortigern himself handled the
reins of the kingdom as he wished, he began to deliberate
and give careful thought to how he could fulfill what he desired from the kingdom. For it seemed the appropriate time
had come when he could make it happen, since the control
of the entire kingdom had passed to him and the foolishness
of King Constans was obvious to everyone. Obviously, hav-   2
ing been raised in the cloister, Constans bore no responsibil-
ity for the management or oversight of the kingdom, simply
leaving everything to Vortigern. His two brothers were, in
effect, still being raised in their cradles. Moreover, the more
senior nobles of the kingdom had nearly all died by various

erat terra omni consilio destituta nisi quantum in se erat. Haec itaque in animo volvens, excogitavit fraudem pravi consilii et accessit quadam die ad Constantem, dolenti simi-

3 lis dicens: "Moveor propter te, carissime domine, quia regnum tuum inquietare affectant collaterales insulani, et maxime Norguegenses et Daci. Rumor enim et fama late vagans innotuit terram hanc carere viris et senioribus morte deletis, et te ipsum nihilominus iuvenem cum fratribus tuis puerili inniti consilio. Quamobrem provida te oportet uti deliberatione, quatinus ab imminentibus hostibus, antequam quod moliuntur incipiant praemunitus eripiaris et regnum in pace et tranquillitate perseveret."

4 Cui Constans, "Nonne," ait, "omnia dispositioni tuae commisi? Fac ergo quaecumque ad salutem meam et regni pacem noveris utilia fore."

5 Ad haec Vortigernus: "Si in manum meam commiseris munitiones terrae, urbes et castra et cetera quibus regnum ab incursione hostium tuear, thesauros quoque quibus milites et viri bellicosi per universas terrae regiones disponantur, non vereor eo te roborari consilio ut facile caveas hostium circumvenientium temeritatem."

6 Respondit rex: "Sicut tibi omnem regni curam commisi, ita fac ad libitum tuum universa quae dixisti."

"Oportet ergo," ait ille, "te aliquos ex Pictis tecum in familia habere et curiam tuam talibus munire custodibus qui

causes and the land was devoid of all capacity for judgment except his. Turning this over in his mind, he conceived a plan of corrupt design, and on a certain day he approached Constans, appearing troubled, and said: "I am worried about 3 you, dearest lord, because neighboring islanders are trying to disturb your kingdom, most of all the Norwegians and the Danes. Indeed, as rumor and report spread abroad, this land is known to be lacking in men, and the elders to have been taken by death, with yourself nevertheless still young with only your brothers' childish counsel to lean on. Because of this it is necessary for you to use deliberation so that being forewarned you are rescued from the threatening enemy before they start to make trouble, and the kingdom can continue in peace and tranquility."

Constans replied to him: "Did I not commit everything 4 to your discretion? Do therefore whatever you think will be useful for my safety and the peace of the kingdom."

To this Vortigern replied: "If you will entrust to my hand 5 the defenses of the land, the cities and camps and everything else, with which I will protect the kingdom against enemy attacks, and also the treasury, by means of which soldiers and warriors shall be stationed through all regions of the land, I have no doubt that you will be strengthened by that advice so that you easily avoid the impetuosity of the encircling enemy."

The king responded: "As I committed the care of the en- 6 tire kingdom to you, therefore do everything you just said, however you want."

"It is appropriate, then," said Vortigern, "for you to have some Picts in your household and to strengthen your court with as many guards as can step forth to be mediators

mediatores inter te et hostes existant et eorum machinationes explorent quo tutius in domo et in curia esse possis."

7   Haec dicens misit ocius nuntios in Scotiam, invitans Pictos ad regis praesidium. Quibus adductis honorabat eos
Vortigernus supra omnes regis familiae tirones et donariis
ditabat; cibis et potibus, quibus gens illas nimis indulgebat,
cottidie usque ad crapulam et ebrietatem replebat. Unde
Vortigernum magis pro rege habebant quam ipsum Constantem. Inebriati ergo per plateas et vicos, tamquam fana-
8   tici acclamabant: "Dignus est Vortigernus imperio, dignus
est Britanniae sceptro!"

Sub his autem favoribus diu latere non potuit versuti ac
dolosi viri animus, utpote qui ad argumenta suae nequitiae
haec omnia preparabat. Quadam ergo die dum inebriati ex
more fuissent Picti, accessit Vortigernus subtristis, simulans
se velle de regno Britanniae recedere ut ampliores adquireret possessiones et sibi suisque possent stipendia sufficere.

9   Neque enim id tantillum quod possidebat quinquaginta militibus ut unusquisque modicum quid acciperet satis esse
ducebat. Sic loquens, Pictos ebriosos ad scelus animavit et
se ad hospitium suum contulit, illos in aula regia potantes
dimittens. Illi vero adinvicem murmurantes quod talem
tamque honoratum virum tamque munificum amitterent,
arbitrantes verum esse quod ille falso ac simulato ore pro-
10 tulerat, dixerunt furore repleti: "Utquid monachum istum
vivere permittimus? Utquid non interficimus eum ut Vortigernus regno potiatur? Dignus namque est imperio regni
et honore, dignus etiam omni dignitate qui nos ditare non
cessat."

between you and the enemies and investigate their tricks so that you can be safer in your household and court."

Saying this, he quickly sent messengers to Scotland, summoning Picts to the king's garrison. Once they were brought there, Vortigern honored them above all the recruits of the royal household and enriched them with gifts; with food and drink, which that people indulged in too much, he filled them daily to the point of drunkenness and intoxication. Because of this they would rather have had Vortigern as king than Constans himself. Being drunk, therefore, they shouted through the streets and avenues: "Vortigern deserves to rule, he deserves the scepter of Britain!"

In the face of this acclaim, the mind of the cunning and deceitful man could no longer lie hidden, inasmuch as he was preparing all this for the conclusion of his wickedness. On a certain day, when the Picts were drunk as usual, Vortigern came to them frowning, pretending he wanted to leave the kingdom of Britain in order to acquire more extensive possessions, and income that could support him and his men. For he did not consider the pittance he possessed to be enough for fifty knights even if he paid each one the smallest amount he would take. Talking like this, he inspired the drunken Picts to wickedness and brought them to his lodging, leaving them in the inner court of the king, drinking heavily. Whispering to each other that they would miss a man who was so great and so much honored and such a benefactor, judging it to be true what he mentioned with his lying and deceitful mouth, they said full of anger: "Why should we allow this monk to live? Why should we not kill him so that Vortigern can obtain the kingdom? For he deserves the kingdom and the honor, and he also deserves every dignity, who never ceases to enrich us."

7

8

9

10

[96] Irruentes ergo in thalamum, impetum fecerunt in Constantem et amputato eius capite coram Vortigerno detulerunt. Quod cum vidisset, in fletum quasi contristatus erupit convocatisque civibus Londoniae civitatis—nam id in ea contigerat—iussit omnes proditores alligari atque teneri et ad ultimum decollari, qui tantum scelus perpetrave-

2 rant. Vindicta itaque de Pictis peracta fuerunt in populo qui aestimarent, etsi proloqui non auderent, proditionem illam et regis interfectionem per Vortigernum machinatam fuisse, Pictos siquidem nullatenus nisi assensu illius tale facinus ausos fuisse. Fueruntque qui eum a tali crimine verbis contra-

3 dicentibus purgarent. Re tandem in ambiguo relicta, nutritores duorum fratrum assumentes eos fugerunt in minorem Britanniam, timentes ne idem contingeret eis quod primogenito factum fuerat. Ibique eos rex Budicius cum honore quo decebat excepit et summa diligentia educavit.

[97] At Vortigernus, diadema regni capiti suo inponens, duabus cotidie angustiis vehementer angebatur, videlicet reatus sui conscientia atque Pictorum mortem suorum vindicare volentium infesta contumacia. Detrimentum suae gentis non modicum et totius regni inquietationem sustinens, accedebat quoque ad cumulum doloris sui interminatio duorum fratrum Constantis; quorum fama adventare eos in proximo super se, faventibus illis terrae optimatibus, divulgabatur.

[96] Running therefore to his bedchamber, they attacked Constans and, after his head was cut off, they carried it away to Vortigern in person. When he saw it, he burst forth in tears as if saddened, and, after summoning the citizens of the city of London—for it was there the deed was done—he ordered all the traitors who had perpetrated such a crime to be bound and held and ultimately beheaded. After vengeance had been taken against the Picts, there were those among the people who believed, although they dared not speak out, that this treachery and the assassination of the king had been engineered by Vortigern, since the Picts would never have dared to do such a thing without his consent. There were also those who would have absolved him of such a crime with contrary arguments. With the matter left in so much doubt, those who were caring for the two brothers, gathering them up, fled to lesser Britain, fearing that the same thing would be done to them that had happened to their eldest brother. And there King Budicius received them with fitting honor, and raised them with the utmost diligence.

[97] But Vortigern, placing the crown upon his own head, was exceedingly distressed every day by two troubles, namely the knowledge of his guilt and the hostile behavior of the Picts wanting to avenge the death of their men. While he was sustaining great harm to his people, and disturbance of his whole kingdom, the threat presented by the two brothers of Constans also added to the height of his suffering; news had spread that they were about to come against him, and would be supported by the well-known nobles of the land.

BOOK SIX

Liber VI

[98] Interea applicuerunt tres ciulae, quas longas naves dicimus, in partibus Cantiae plenae de armatis militibus; quorum duces Horsus et Hengistus dicebantur. Erat tunc temporis Vortigernus Doroberniae, quae nunc Cantuaria dicitur. Cui cum nuntiatum esset viros ignotae linguae magnaeque staturae in longis navibus advenisse, missis nuntiis cum pace ad se venire fecit. Mox ut adducti sunt, vertit oculos in duos praefatos germanos. Nam et ipsi prae ceteris
2 statura et decore eminebant. Intuitusque eos ait: "Quae patria, o iuvenes, vobis materna est aut quae causa huc in regnum nostrum appulit? Edicite!"

Cui Hengistus, ut erat prae ceteris amplioris et maturioris aetatis persona, pro omnibus respondit: "Rex tuorum nobilissime, Saxonica tellus, quae una est ex regionibus Germaniae, nos editos huc appulit. Causam itineris nostri et profectionis de terra nostra, si placet audire, in pacis securitate disseremus."

3 Concessa igitur a rege loquendi cum pace facultate sic orsus est: "Mos et consuetudo patriae nostrae est, bone rex, ut, cum abundantia virorum in ea excreverit, conveniant principes terrae et totius regni iuventutem, in annos quindecim aut eo amplius excretam, coram se venire compellunt positaque sorte, potiores atque fortiores in exteras regiones

Book 6

[98] Meanwhile three keels, which we call longships, landed in the region of Kent, filled with armed soldiers, whose leaders were called Horsa and Hengist. At that time Vortigern was in Dorobernum, which is now called Canterbury. When it was announced to him that men of unknown language and great stature had arrived in longships, messengers were sent in peace to summon them to him. As soon as they came, he turned his eyes to the two brothers just mentioned, because they stood out from the others in their stature and appearance. After he looked at them he said: "Young men, what country is your homeland, and what reason drove you here to our kingdom? Explain!"

Since he was an older and more important person than the others, Hengist answered for them all: "Most noble king of your people, the Saxon land, which is one of the regions of Germany, drove us here as exiles. If you wish to hear the reason for our journey and departure from our land, we will discuss it with your assurance of peace."

Accordingly, after the opportunity to speak in peace was granted by the king, Hengist began as follows: "Good king, the custom and practice of our country is that when the number of men in it has grown excessive, the leaders of the land assemble and force all the young men of the kingdom, fifteen years of age or older, to appear before them and, after they cast lots they order the better and stronger ones to be

tamquam in exilio relegatos dirigunt ut patria ipsa a multitu-
4 dine superflua vacuetur. Est enim terra nostra fecundior hominum procreandorum ubertate quam ceterorum anima-
lium, licet ipsa quoque ferarum abundantia atque divitiarum
copia in suo genere nequaquam fraudetur. Sic itaque a patria
sorte praefata deiecti istis in oris, Mercurio duce, advecti
sumus."

Audito igitur nomine Mercurii, interrogavit rex qua reli-
5 gione deum colerent. Cui Hengistus: "Deos patrios, Satur-
num, Iovem, Mercurium atque ceteros quos coluerunt
patres nostri veneramur atque colimus, maxime Mercurium
quem Woden lingua nostra appellamus. Huic maiores nostri
quartam feriam dicaverunt, quae usque in hodiernum diem
lingua nostra nomen Wodnesdai de nomine ipsius sortita
est. Post hunc colimus deam inter ceteras potentissimam,
nomine Fream, cui etiam dicaverunt sextam feriam quam de
nomine ipsius Friedai vocamus."

6 "De religione vestra, quae potius irreligio dici potest," ait
Vortigernus, "vehementer doleo. De adventu autem vestro
non modicum laetor, si moram nobiscum placuerit vobis per
spatium temporis agere. Sive enim Deus sive fortuna vos
huc appulerit, congruo tempore neccessitati nostrae auxilium ferre potestis. Infestant enim nos quidam latrunculi,
inimici nostri, undique, quos vestra ope longius abigere a
terra nostra et in speluncas terrae suae nequissime latitare
optarem aut omnino, si fieri posset, exterminare. Unde vos
quotquot venistis in regnum meum honorifice retinebo et
diversis muneribus et agris ditabo."

banished to foreign lands as if in exile, in order for our country to be emptied of the surplus population. Indeed our land 4 is more fruitful in its plenty of men for begetting children than of other animals, although in its own way it is by no means diminished in its population of wild beasts and its abundance of resources. And thus, after our lot was determined and we were expelled from our land, we were carried to these shores by the guidance of Mercury."

When he heard the name of Mercury, the king asked in what religion they worshiped this god. Hengist replied to 5 him: "We venerate and worship our ancestral gods, Saturn, Jove, Mercury, and others which our fathers worshiped, most of all Mercury, whom we call Woden in our language. To him our ancestors dedicated the fourth day of the week, which up to the present day in our language is assigned the name Wednesday after his name. After him we worship the most powerful goddess among the others, by the name of Frea. To her they dedicated the sixth day of the week, which after her name we call Friday."

"I am exceedingly sorry about your religion," said Vor- 6 tigern, "which can rather be called irreligion. However, I am delighted about your arrival if you are willing to behave according to our customs for a period of time. Indeed, whether God or Fortune drove you here, you can bring help exactly in our time of need. For certain brigands, our enemies, harass us everywhere, and with your help I want to drive them far away from our land and make them hide wretchedly in the caves of their land, or to exterminate them entirely, if it should be possible to do so. In return, however many of you came into my kingdom I will retain with honor and enrich with various rewards and estates."

7 Paruerunt barbari et foedere firmato curiam repleverunt proceribus et validis viris et ad bellum strenue edoctis, stipendia accepturi pro consuetudine legis suae. Nec mora, emergentes ex Albania Picti exercitum grandem valde in fines Britannorum et ultra eduxerunt magnamque partem

8 terrae vastaverunt. Contra quos Vortigernus Saxones barbaros cum exercitu suorum dirigens, trans Humbrum obvius venit illis et congressus magnam stragem ex eis faciens in fugam eos coegit. Sed quia consueverant antea prioribus bellis esse superiores, duriter resistendo multos Britonum, plures suorum vulneratos ac telis confossos amiserunt.

[99] Rex ergo, per Saxones victoria potitus, donaria sua ampliavit eis atque Hengisto dedit agros et mansiones plurimas in Lindiseia regione quibus se suosque sustentaret. Cumque se necessarium Hengistus regi sentiret et eius amicitiam atque benivolentiam pro virtute ac probitate sua erga se pronam aspiceret fidenter quadam die accessit ad eum in

2 iocunditate regia, dicens: "Domine mi rex, patere, si placet, me ad te pauca proloqui de statu regni atque tuorum fidelitate: comperi enim ex quo tibi adhaesi quia pauci sunt ex tuis qui te perfecte diligant et honorem tuum defendant. Omnes fere tibi malum interminant, dicentes nescio quos fratres, heredes regni iustiores te, in proximo ascituros ex Armorico tractu ut te deponant et illos promoveant.

The barbarians complied and, once a treaty was con- 7
firmed, they filled the court with nobles and powerful men
and those vigorously trained in warfare, with wages to be received in accordance with the customary practice of their
law. Without delay, emerging from Albany, the Picts vigorously led a great army to the very borders of Britain and beyond, and laid waste to a great part of the land. Vortigern, 8
directing the barbarous Saxons with their army across the
Humber, came against them in battle, making a great slaughter of them, and drove them to flight. But because the Picts
had been accustomed to being superior in previous battles
before this, by fiercely opposing many of the Britons they
lost more of their own men, wounded and pierced with
spears.

[99] Then the king, having achieved victory through the
Saxons, increased his gifts to them and gave to Hengist
many estates and dwellings in the region of Lindsey, with
which he could support himself and his men. And when
Hengist sensed that he was necessary to the king, and saw
that he was inclined to friendship and benevolence toward
him, because of his virtue and probity, he came to him confi-
dently one day in royal merriment, saying: "My lord king, if 2
you please, let me say a few words to you about the state of
the kingdom and the faithfulness of your men: for you will
find among your adherents that there are few among your
men who love you completely and defend your honor.
Nearly all of them threaten you with mischief, declaring
that they will soon receive from the Armorican region certain brothers unknown to me, more worthy heirs to the
kingdom than you, in order to depose you and promote

3   Nunc igitur, si tibi videbitur consilium ut de gente nostra invitemus aliquos ad tuendam patriam ab hostium incursione et tuorum proditione, palam manifestare ne dubites, ut numerus nostrorum augeatur in tuam fidelitatem et terreantur externi et privati hostes, cum te ac regnum tuum cinxerit ac protexerit fortissimorum virorum robur."

4   Ad haec Vortigernus: "Mitte ut dixisti ad terram tuam et invita quos volueris, tantum ut fideles vos in mea dilectione semper inveniam, et pete a me quod volueris; nullam patieris repulsam."

Qui audiens regem erga se benivolum inclinato capite gratias multimodas de benivolentia egit et adiecit: "Ditasti," inquid, "me largis mansionibus et agris sed, cum desit civitas aut munimentum in quo me meosque in necessitate reci-

5   piam, securus non sum de vita aut possessione. Concedat ergo dominus rex servo suo fideli Hengisto, quantum corrigia una possit ambire terrae in aliqua mansionum mearum ut ibi aedificem domum cum propugnaculis ad defensionem nostram si contigerit ab hostibus circumveniri. Et ego interim mittam pro uxore ac liberis et parentibus et amicis ut securior de nobis, quicquid commiserim, existas."

6   Motus itaque rex, petitioni eius acquievit. Nec mora, missa in Germaniam Hengistus legatione coepit corium tauri in unam redigere corrigiam. Nactus saxosum locum ad munimentum quod magna elegerat cautela, circuivit cum corrigia et infra spatium metatum castrum aedificavit. Quod aedificatum traxit nomen ex corrigia: Saxonice

them. Now then, if it seems wise to you that you should in- 3
vite some of our people in order to defend the country
against invasion by the enemy and betrayal by your own
men, make it openly known that you have no doubt the
number of us in fealty to you should be increased, and both
your external and internal enemies will be terrified when the
strength of the most powerful men surrounds and protects
you and your kingdom."

To this Vortigern replied: "Send as you have said to your 4
land and invite those you wish, for I always find your retainers pleasing to me, and ask of me what you wish; you will
suffer no refusal."

Hearing that the king felt kindly toward him, with bowed
head Hengist gave many thanks for this kindness, and
added: "You have given me lavish manors and estates but,
since there is no city or fortress in which I can protect myself and my men in need, I do not feel safe about my life or
property. Therefore, lord king, grant to your faithful servant 5
Hengist as much land as a single thong can surround in any
of my manors so that I can build there a dwelling with ramparts for our defense if it should happen to be surrounded
by enemies. And meanwhile I will send for my wife and children and parents and friends so that you may rest more secure because of us, whatever I shall be able to arrange."

Persuaded by this, the king granted his request. Without 6
delay, having sent an embassy to Germany, Hengist began to
cut a bull hide into a single thong. Having found a rocky
place to fortify which he had chosen with great care, he encircled it with the thong and in the area measured out he
built a fortress. When it was built, it took its name from the

Thancastre vel Twangcastre, Britannice vero Kaercarrei, quod Latino verbo Castrum Corrigie sonat.

[100] Interea reversi e Germania nuntii adduxerunt octodecim naves electis militibus plenas, inter quos adducta fuerat filia Hengisti, vocabulo Ronwen, pulchra facie ac venusto corpore. Patrato igitur Hengistus aedificio suo invitavit ad prandium regem ut et domum novam et novos milites videret. Qui non distulit venire privatim et absque multitudine

2 ut delectaretur cum fideli suo Hengisto. Ut autem descendit, rex laudavit opus gnaviter aedificatum ac milites e Germania invitatos secum retinuit. Postquam regiis epulis refecti sunt, egressa est puella de thalamo, filia Hengisti, aureum vas vino plenum manu ferens, accedensque propius

3 regi flexis genibus lingua sua ait: *"Washeil, lauerd king."* At ille, mox visa puella, miratus faciem decoram cum venusto corpore incaluit, interrogavitque interpretem suum quid puella sermone suo dixerat et quid eodem sermone respondere deberet. Cui interpres, "Vocavit te," ait, "dominum regem et vocabulo salutationis honoravit. Quod autem ei respondere debes ita est, *Drincheil.*"

4 Respondens Vortigernus ait, *"Drincheil,"* et iussit puellam potare recepitque scyphum de manu eius et ex more Saxonico osculatus est eam et potavit. Ab illo ergo die usque in hodiernum diem remansit consuetudo illa in Britannia inter convivantes et potantes ut per *"Washeil"* et *"Drincheil"* se

5 invicem salutarent. Rex autem multo diversi generis potu

thong: in Saxon "Thancaster" or "Twangcaster," but in British "Kaercarrei," which in the Latin speech means "Castle of the Thong."

[100] Meanwhile, having returned from Germany, the messengers brought eighteen ships full of chosen soldiers, among whom was brought a daughter of Hengist called Ronwen, with a beautiful face and attractive body. His building completed, Hengist then invited the king to lunch so that he could see his new home and his new soldiers. The king did not hesitate to come alone and without a crowd to be entertained by his faithful man Hengist. When he dismounted, however, the king praised the cunningly constructed fortification, and took the knights invited from Germany as his own retainers. After they were refreshed by the royal entertainments, a girl emerged from the bedroom, the daughter of Hengist, carrying a golden goblet full of wine in her hand, and coming near the king, on bended knee, in her own language she said: "*Washeil, lauerd king.*" As soon as he saw the girl, amazed by her comely face with her attractive body, he was inflamed and asked his interpreter what the girl had said in her language, and how he should respond in the same language. The interpreter replied to him: "She called you 'lord king' and honored you with a term of salutation. To which you should respond: *Drincheil.*"

Responding, Vortigern said, "*Drincheil,*" and ordered the girl to drink and took the goblet from her hand and kissed her in the Saxon fashion and drank. Consequently, from that day up to the present day, it remains the custom in Britain among those dining and drinking together to salute each other with "*Washeil*" and "*Drincheil.*" The king, however, intoxicated with many different kinds of drink, with

inebriatus instigante Satana, puellam adamavit et ut sibi daretur a patre postulavit, licet gentilis et non Christiana esset. Hengistus ergo cognita regis levitate consuluit Horsum, fratrem suum, ceterosque maiores natu de gente sua, qui omnes pariter in unum consenserunt, videlicet ut fieret regis petitio et peteret ille Cantiae provinciam in dotem dari

6 puellae. Nec mora, data est puella Vortigerno et Cantia Hengisto, nesciente Gorangono comite qui in eadem regnabat. Nupsit itaque rex eadem nocte paganae puellae, nil verescens de sua Christianitate. Quae cum placuisset ei, coepit eam tamquam reginam habere ac diligere; unde iram et inimicitiam procerum suorum et filiorum brevi temporis spatio incurrit. Genuerat namque antea filios tres de uxore priore, quorum nomina erant Vortimer, Katigern, Paschent.

[101] Hengistus autem accedens ad regem ait: "Ego sum quasi pater tibi et consiliarius tuus esse debeo. Noli praeterire consilium meum et omnes inimicos tuos virtute gentis meae superabis. Invitemus igitur adhuc, si placet, Octam filium meum e Germania cum fratruele suo Ebissa; bellatores enim viri sunt et expugnabunt nobiscum omnes inimicos

2 tuos maris et terrae. Da eis regiones a Pictis vastatas quae sunt iuxta murum inter Deiram et Scotiam. Ibi enim locati impetum Pictorum et adventantium barbarorum viriliter sustinebunt et sic in pace citra Humbrum remanebis."

3 Paruit Vortigernus iussitque invitare quoscumque sciret ad munimentum militiae et augmentum sibi valere. Missis

prompting by Satan, lusted after the girl and demanded that she be given to him by her father, although she was a heathen and not a Christian. Then Hengist, recognizing the fickleness of the king, consulted with his brother Horsa and other elders of his people, who all agreed together as one, namely to do as the king asked and to ask him to give the province of Kent as the girl's bride-price. Without delay, the 6 girl was given to Vortigern and Kent to Hengist, without the knowledge of Count Gorangonus who was ruling there. And so the king was married that night to the pagan girl, not caring about her Christianity. When she had pleasured him he took her as his queen to have and to cherish; because of this, in a short space of time, he incurred the anger and enmity of his nobles. For he had, before this, fathered three sons by his previous wife, whose names were Vortimer, Katigern, and Pascent.

[101] Approaching the king, however, Hengist said: "I am like a father to you and I ought to be your counselor. Do not neglect my counsel and you will overcome all your enemies with the strength of my people. Then, if it pleases you, we should still invite my son Octa from Germany with his younger brother Ebissa; for they are warlike men and with us they will conquer all your enemies at sea and on land. Give them the regions wasted by the Picts which are next to 2 the wall between Deira and Scotland. For, being stationed there, they will vigorously hold back the advances of the barbarians and thus you will remain in peace on this side of the Humber."

Vortigern complied and allowed him to invite whomever 3 he knew would be strong enough for the protection of his army and the increase of his men. Ambassadors were sent

ilico legatis, venerunt Octa et Ebissa et Cherdich cum trecentis navibus armatorum virorum, quos omnes suscepit rex
benigne magnisque ditavit muneribus. Post hos etiam alii
atque alii per invitationem Hengisti venerunt et paulatim
4 totam terram repleverunt. Quod cum vidissent Britones,
timentes proditionem dixerunt regi nimium se indulgere atque credere Saxonibus paganis, in tantum ut fere iam totam
terram cooperirent mixti cum Christianis; nec erat iam facile dinoscere qui forent pagani, qui Christiani. Insuper
tanta multitudo emerserat ut omnibus essent terrori. Dis-
suadebant ergo et adiudicabant neminem illorum amplius
5 suscipere sed de his qui supervenerant aliquos emittere. At
Vortigernus, quia diligebat coniugem suam filiam Hengisti
et per eam gentem suam, consiliis eorum acquiescere renuit.
Videntes igitur Britones se apud regem esse despectui et
consilia eorum fore derisui, omnes unanimiter adversus illum insurrexerunt et statim convenientes Londoniae Vorti-
6 mer, filium suum, in regem erexerunt. Qui mox congregato
exercitu non modico in Saxones barbaros atque paganos
aciem tendit et quatuor cum eis, patre adherente, bella ges-
sit atque devicit: primum proelium super flumen Derwend;
secundum super vadum Episford, ubi simul congressi Horsus et Katigernus, alter filius Vortigerni, alterutrum se letaliter vulneraverunt; tertium bellum super litus maris Cantiae
7 iuxta naves ipsorum Saxonum. Diffugientes enim ab Albania per longum Britanniae usque illuc contriti proeliis et afflicti impetum Britonum sustinere non valentes naves ingressi sunt et insulam Thaneth pro refugio adierunt. At
Britones nihilominus insequentes navali proelio cotidie illos

immediately, and Octa and Ebissa and Cherdich came with three hundred ships of armed men. The king received them all warmly and gave them gifts. After them more and more came as well at the invitation of Hengist and gradually filled the whole land. When the Britons had seen this, fearing 4 treachery they said to the king that he indulged and trusted the pagan Saxons excessively, to the point that they had already overwhelmed nearly the whole land, mixed with the Christians; it was not easy now to discern who were the pagans and who the Christians. On top of that, such a crowd had arrived that they were a terror to everyone. Therefore they advised and resolved that no more should be received, and that some who had already arrived should be expelled. But Vortigern, because he loved his wife, the daughter of 5 Hengist, and Hengist's people on account of her, refused to accept their advice. Then the Britons, seeing themselves looked down upon by the king and their counsel scorned, all unanimously rebelled against him and, gathering immediately in London, they raised his son Vortimer as king. Quickly raising a large army, he aimed his vanguard against 6 the barbarous and pagan Saxons and, with his father taking their side, he fought four battles and defeated them: the first battle by the River Derwent; the second by the ford called Episford, where Horsa and Katigern, the second son of Vortigern, having both come together, lethally wounded each other; the third battle on the shore of the sea in Kent, next to the Saxon's own ships. Fleeing from Albany across 7 the length of Britain all the way there, crushed and overthrown by battles, unable to sustain the onslaught of the Britons, they boarded their ships and sought refuge on the Isle of Thanet. But the Britons followed nonetheless and

infestabant et undique telis ac sagittis circumveniebant.

8 Cumque diutius talem assultum sustinere nequirent, coartati undique et fame iam afflicti miserunt Vortigernum regem suum, qui cum illis in omnibus affuerat socius, ad filium suum Vortimerium, petentes licentiam abeundi absque detrimento sui. Et dum colloquium inde Britones cum Vortigerno haberent, Saxones elapsi maria sulcare remis et vento coeperunt relictisque mulierculis suis et liberis Germaniam redierunt.

[102] Victoria itaque potiti Britones cum rege suo Vortimerio possessiones concivibus suis ereptas reddere primo non distulerunt. Deinde iubente et annitente sancto Germano, Autisiodorensi episcopo, ecclesias dirutas renovare et fidem Christi in quibusdam locis corruptam restaurare non destiterunt, donec ad perfectum reconciliati fuerunt.

2 Ad confirmandam enim fidem, quae per haeresim primum Arianam vel Pelagianam deinde per istos gentiles Saxones in Britannia corrupta erat, venerat sanctus Germanus cum Lupo Trecacensi episcopo missi a papa Romano, ut verbo praedicationis et luce evangelii gens quae errorum tenebris et ignorantiae a statu fidei susceptae deciderat, iterum eorum admonitionibus Deo per omnia cooperante corroboraretur et ecclesiae catholicae redderetur. Multa per eos mira-

3 cula fecit Deus in regno Britanniae quae Gildas in tractatu suo luculenter exposuit. Postquam ergo restituta est fides Christi per totum regnum Britanniae ad integrum hostesque

harassed them daily with naval battles and surrounded them on all sides with spears and arrows. And when they could no longer sustain such assaults, huddled together everywhere and by now afflicted with hunger, they sent their king Vortigern, who had been their close ally in everything, to his son Vortimer, asking permission to depart without harm to him. And then, while the Britons were having this discussion with Vortigern, the Saxons, escaping by sea, began to plow through the deep using their oars and the wind and, with their wives and children left behind, they returned to Germany.

[102] And so, after victory was achieved, the Britons with their king Vortimer wasted no time in restoring first of all the properties snatched away from their fellow citizens. Then, with the holy bishop Germanus of Auxerre directing and supporting them, they continued to renew the demolished churches, and to reestablish the Christian faith that was corrupted in certain areas, until they were completely restored. For to confirm the faith, which had been corrupted in Britain at first by the Arian or Pelagian heresy, and then by those heathen Saxons, Saint Germanus had come with Bishop Lupus of Troyes, sent by the Roman Pope so that, by the word of preaching and the light of the evangelists, the people who had fallen from the state of faith through the darkness of error and ignorance could be strengthened and returned to the catholic church once again through their admonition, with God assisting in all. God worked many miracles in the kingdom of Britain through them, which Gildas clearly related in his treatise. After that, once the faith of Christ was restored to integrity throughout the whole kingdom of Britain, and the enemies

deleti qui et fidem et populum inpugnabant, invidia diaboli qui Ronwen novercam Vortimerii ad hoc nefas instigavit ve-

4 neno periit Vortimerius. Convocans itaque Vortimerius milites et bellatores per quos vicerat, indicata morte, distribuit eis aurum et argentum et quicquid ab atavis in thesauris suis antea congestum fuerat, exhortans ut pro patria pugnantes

5 eam ab hostili irruptione tuerentur. Praecepit quoque pyramidem in litore maris a parte Germaniae strui in qua, collocato eius corpore, terrori esset Saxonibus et universis barbaris. At ubi defunctus est, postposita pyramide in Urbe Trinovantum illum sepelierunt.

[103] Vortigernus postea in regem restitutus, precibus coniugis suae misit in Germaniam pro Hengisto ut iterum in Britanniam rediret, sed privatim et cum paucis, ne iterum discordia inter se et Britones oriretur. Hengistus ergo audito obitu Vortimerii laetus efficitur et navigio parato cum trecentis milibus armatorum sulcavit aequora usque in Britan-

2 niam. Sed cum tantae multitudinis exercitus Vortigerno et principibus regni nuntiatus esset, expavit rex et ceteri indignati sunt; initoque consilio, memores admonitionis Vortimerii, constituerunt proeliari tamquam cum hostibus atque a litoribus expellere antequam terram occuparent.

3 Quod cum Hengisto per internuntios indicatum foret, excogitavit malignum apud se consilium illudque per complices suos, sceleris sui conscios, tractare coepit, videlicet ut

were destroyed who had attacked both the faith and the people, through the hatred of the devil who incited Ronwen, the stepmother of Vortimer, to this wicked deed, Vortimer died by poison. Calling together the soldiers and warriors with whom he had conquered, after his approaching death was revealed, Vortimer distributed to them the gold and silver and everything in his treasury that had been previously collected from their ancestors, urging them to protect themselves against hostile attacks by fighting for their country. He also instructed them to construct a pyramid on the shore of the sea facing Germany, with his body placed inside, which would be a terror to the Saxons and all barbarians. But after he died, they set the pyramid aside, and they buried him in the city of London.

[103] After that Vortigern was restored as king and, at the request of his wife, he sent to Germany for Hengist to return again to Britain, but in a private capacity and with few men, so that the discord between him and the Britons would not arise again. Hengist, having heard about the death of Vortimer, happily complied and, once his fleet was ready, he plowed through the sea with three hundred thousand soldiers all the way to Britain. But when an army of so great a number was reported to Vortigern and the leaders of his kingdom, the king grew frightened and the rest were indignant; and after they took counsel with Vortimer's advice in mind, they resolved to do battle as if they were enemies and to drive them from the shores before they could occupy the land. When this was revealed to Hengist by his messengers, he devised an evil plan in his mind, and began to implement it through his accomplices, who were aware of his wickedness, namely to approach the king and his people under the

regem et gentem suam sub specie pacis adoriretur et dispositioni regis et optimatum regni committeret, quatinus de
tanto numero Saxonum suorum quot vellent secum rema-
nere, quot in Germaniam redire sub obtentu pacis decer-
4 nerent. Pacem enim quaerebant et cum pace et tranquillitate in regno Britanniae, in quo plurimum iam laboraverant
cum ipsis, degere toto aevo suo affectabant. Quod cum per
internuntios regi suisque manifestasset, placuit eis optio
huiuscemodi, nihil verentes de proditione Saxonum. Die
igitur statuta mandavit cum legatis rex Hengisto ut cum
paucis adveniret.

[104] Interea Hengistus, nova proditione usus, praecepit
suis commilitonibus quos ad id facinus ex omni multitudine
elegerat ut unusquisque cultrum ex utraque parte inciden-
tem infra caligas in vaginis reconderet et, cum ventum foret
ad colloquium, dato a se hoc signo proditionis, "*Nimat ore
saxas,*" statim extractis cultris universos occuparent inermes
2 et interficerent. Nec mora, die praestituta, quae fuit kalendis Maii, iuxta coenobium Ambrii convenerunt Britones et
Saxones, sicut condictum fuerat, sine armis pacem consti-
tuere. Ut autem horam proditioni suae idoneam nactus fuisset Hengistus, vociferatus est lingua sua: "*Nimat ore saxas.*"
3 Ipse autem regem per chlamydem arripiens tenuit, donec in
alios scelus perficeretur. Extractis ilico cultris, sicut prae-
moniti fuerant, universos fere principes nil tale metuentes
iugulaverunt circiter quadringentos sexaginta, omnes barones aut consules.

[105] Dum autem fieret quasi de ovibus haec caedes,

guise of peace, and to comply with the decision of the king and the nobles of the kingdom to the extent that such number of his Saxons as the Britons wanted would remain with him, but as many as the Britons determined would return to Germany under the pretext of peace. For they were seeking 4 peace and they desired to spend all their days with peace and tranquility in the kingdom of Britain, in which many had already worked together with them. When this had been made clear through intermediaries to the king and his men, the suggestion pleased them, suspecting nothing about the treachery of the Saxons. He therefore directed through ambassadors to Hengist that he should appear on a specified date with only a small group of people.

[104] Meanwhile Hengist, engaging in unprecedented treachery, ordered each of his comrades, whom he had selected from the whole crowd for that deed, to conceal whatever knives they could find in sheaths inside their boots and, after they came to the meeting, when he gave this signal— "*Nimat ore seaxas!*"—with their knives drawn quickly, to seize everyone unarmed and kill them. Without delay, on the ap- 2 pointed day, which was the first of May, the Britons and Saxons came together near the monastery of Ambrius, as had been arranged, without arms to establish peace. But when Hengist found a suitable moment for his treason, he shouted in his language: "*Nimat ore seaxas!*" Seizing the king himself 3 by his cloak, he held him while the crime was committed against the others. With their knives drawn immediately, as ordered, the Saxons slit the throats of nearly all the nobles, who were fearing no such thing—roughly four hundred and sixty of them, all barons or earls.

[105] But while they were being slaughtered like sheep,

Britones qui evadere periculum potuerunt aut fugiendo aut lapides in hostes mittendo et palis et fustibus defendendo plures interemerunt. Eldol vero, consul Claudiocestriae, sustulit palum quem forte offenderat et defensioni vacavit et multos per palum confractis cervicibus ad Tartara legavit; nec prius destitit donec septuaginta ex illis palo suo interfectis divertit se ab eis equumque velocem ascendens civita-

2 tem suam quam citius potuit adiit. Peracto itaque scelere voluerunt regem ipsum interficere mortemque comminantes vinxerunt eum fortiter loris postulaveruntque sibi civitates et castra munitionesque regni omnes contradi si

3 mortis periculum evadere vellet. Cumque id iureiurando confirmasset, solventes eum a vinculis Urbem Trinovantum primitus adeuntes susceperunt, deinde Eboracum et Lindocolinum necnon et Wentanam civitatem. Ut ergo ab eis evadere potuit Vortigernus, secessit in partibus Kambriae, ignorans quid sibi agendum foret contra nefandam gentem.

[106] Vocatis denique magis suis, consuluit quid faceret. Dixeruntque omnes pariter ut aedificaret sibi turrim fortissimam quae foret sibi munimentum contra hostes nefarios

2 qui dolo sibi regnum surripuerant. Peragratis igitur quibuscumque locis ut in congruo loco turrim statueret, venit tandem ad montem Erir, ubi coadunatis caementariis et artificibus diversis coepit fundamenta turris iacere. Et cum ponerentur in fundamento lapides cum caemento, quicquid in die ponebatur in nocte absorbebatur, ita ut nescirent

the Britons who were able to escape danger, either by fleeing or by taking up stones against their enemies and defending themselves with stakes and clubs, killed even more. Eldol, the Earl of Gloucester, took up a staff that he happened
to find and had time to defend himself, and using the staff
he sent many to the infernal regions with their heads
smashed; nor did he stop until, after seventy of those had
been killed by his staff, he turned himself away from them
and mounting a fast horse he came to his own city as quickly
as possible. Having accomplished their crime, the Saxons 2
wanted to kill the king himself and, threatening him with
death, they bound him firmly with leather straps and demanded that he hand over all the cities and camps and fortresses of the kingdom if he wanted to avoid the risk of
death. And when he had confirmed this under oath, releas- 3
ing him from his bonds and going first to the city of London, they captured it; then York, and Lincoln, and also the
city of Winchester. When Vortigern was able to escape from
them, he retreated into the region of Wales, not knowing
what he could do against the wicked people.

[106] In the end, he summoned his magicians and asked
them what should be done. And they all said together that
he should build a very strong tower for himself that would
be a fortress for him against the evil enemies who had stolen
his kingdom through treachery. After he traveled through 2
many locations, in order to build it in an appropriate spot,
he came finally to Mount Erir where, having assembled ma-
sons and various craftsmen, he began to lay down the foundation of the tower. But when the stones had been laid in
the foundation layer with cement, whatever had been laid
down that day was swallowed up in the night, so that they

3   quorsum opus evanesceret. Cumque id Vortigernus comperisset, consuluit iterum magos ut rei causam indicarent. Qui
dixerunt ut iuvenem sine patre quaereret quaesitumque interficeret et sanguine ipsius caementum et lapides asperge-
rentur. Id profecto asserebant certissimum experimentum
ut fundamentum staret. Nec mora mittuntur legati per pro-
4   vincias Demetiae quaerere talem hominem. Qui cum in urbem quae Kaermerdin dicitur venissent, invenerunt pueros
et iuvenes utriusque sexus ante portam civitatis ludentes.
Accesseruntque ad ludum ut aspicerent cum ceteris, explorantes quod quaerebant. Interea lis exoritur inter duos
iuvenes, quorum unus Merlinus dicebatur, alter Dinabutius.
5   Certantibus ergo illis dixit Dinabutius ad Merlinum: "Quid
mecum, fatue, contendis? Non est aequa nobis nativitatis
prosapia: ego enim ex regibus duxi originem, tu autem ignoras quis tibi pater sit."

Audientes itaque legati, exploratores Vortigerni, iuvenes
in hunc modum decertantes, intuentes in Merlinum quae-
sierunt a circumstantibus quis esset vel unde oriundus. Responderunt dicentes quia nesciretur quis ei pater esset, sed
mater quae eum genuerat, filia regis Demetiae, in ecclesia
sancti Petri monialis adhuc in eadem urbe viveret.

[107] Festinantes igitur venerunt ad urbis praefectum
praeceperuntque ex parte regis ut Merlinus cum matre sua
ad regem mitteretur. Praefectus ilico complevit iussum regis
mittens Merlinum matremque eius ad eum. Cumque in
praesentia eius adducti fuissent, excepit rex diligenter illos

did not know where the work had vanished to. And when 3
Vortigern had learned of this, he asked his magicians again
to explain the reason for this. They said that a youth without a father should be sought, and once found he should be
killed and his blood should be sprinkled on the cement and
the stones. They assured him on the basis of reliable experience that, after that was done, the foundation would stand.
Without delay, envoys were sent through the provinces of
Demetia to seek for such an individual. When they came to 4
the city which is called Kaermerdin, they found boys and
young people of both sexes playing in front of the city gate.
And they approached the game to watch with the others,
looking for what they were seeking. Meanwhile, a quarrel
broke out between two youths, one of whom was called
Merlin, the other Dinabutius. While they were fighting,
Dinabutius said to Merlin: "Why do you argue with me, you 5
fool? Our lineage is not equal: for I am descended from
kings, while you do not know who your father is."

Hearing the youths fighting in this manner, the envoys,
scouts of Vortigern, stared at Merlin and asked the bystanders who he was and where he was born. They responded by
saying that it was unknown who his father was, but the
mother who gave birth to him, the daughter of the king of
Demetia, still lived in the same city as a nun in the church of
Saint Peter.

[107] Hurrying therefore, they came to the prefect of the
town and ordered on the king's behalf that Merlin and his
mother should be sent to the king. The prefect immediately
complied with the king's command, sending Merlin and
his mother to him. And when they were brought into his
presence, the king received them attentively and began to

et coepit a matre perquirere de quo viro iuvenem con-
2 cepisset. Cui illa ait: "Vivit anima tua, rex, et vivit anima mea
quia neminem agnovi qui illum in me generaverit. Unum autem scio quia, cum essem in thalamo parentum puella, apparuit mihi quidam in specie formosa iuvenis, ut videbatur, et
amplectens me strictis brachiis saepissime deosculabatur et
statim evanescebat, ita ut indicium hominis non appareret;
loquebatur aliquando non comparens. Cumque in hunc modum me diu frequentasset, tandem in specie humana mis-
cuit se mihi et gravidam dereliquit. Sciat ergo prudentia tua
me aliter virum non cognovisse."

3   Admirans autem Vortigernus hos mulieris sermones ad se
vocari fecit Maugantium magum ut sibi ediceret si id quod
dixerat mulier fieri potuisset. Adductus ergo magus coram
rege auditisque his quae mater Merlini edixerat inquit: "In
libris philosophorum et plurimis historiis reperimus multos
4 huiuscemodi habuisse generationes. Nam, ut Apuleius de
deo Socratis perhibet, inter lunam et terram habitant spiritus immundi quos incubos demones vocant. Hii partim habent naturam hominum, partim vero angelorum et, cum vo-
lunt, assumunt sibi humanas figuras et cum mulieribus
coeunt. Forsitan aliquis eorum huic mulieri stuprum intulit
et in ea iuvenem hunc generavit."

[108] Cumque omnia haec auscultasset, Merlinus accessit
ad regem et ait: "Utquid in praesentia tua huc adducti sumus?"

Cui rex, "Magi," inquit, "mei dederunt consilium ut
hominem sine patre perquirerem quatinus opus inceptum
sanguine ipsius irroratum firmius staret. Volens enim turrim

inquire of the mother by what man she had conceived the youth. She said to him: "I swear on your soul and mine, king, that I acknowledge no one who engendered him in me. But I do know someone who, when I was a girl in my parents' bedchamber, appeared to me in the guise of a handsome youth, so it seemed, and, embracing me tightly with his arms, kissed me very often and immediately vanished, so that no sign of the man was visible; sometimes he spoke to me without appearing. And when he had visited me in this way for a long time, finally he joined with me in human form and left me pregnant. In your wisdom, therefore, you understand that I have not been with a man in any other way."

Marveling at the woman's words, Vortigern had Maugantius the magician called to him so that he inform him if what the woman had said was possible. After the magician was brought before the king, and heard these things that Merlin's mother had declared, he said: "In the books of the philosophers and in many histories we find many to have this manner of birth. For, as Apuleius holds in *On the God of Socrates,* between the moon and the earth live unclean spirits which they call incubus demons. These have partly the nature of men, partly that of angels and, when they wish, they assume human forms and lie with women. Perhaps one of them brought dishonor to this woman and engendered this youth in her."

[108] And when he had listened to all this, Merlin approached the king and said: "Why are we brought here into your presence?"

The king answered him and said: "My magicians counseled me that I should search everywhere for someone without a father so that, sprinkled with his blood, the building under construction would stand more firmly. Although I

215

aedificare, non possunt fundamenta eius in loco isto consistere quin quod in die construitur in nocte a terra devoretur."

2   Tunc ait regi Merlinus: "Iube magos tuos adesse et convincam illos per omnia mentitos."

Acciti ergo magi sederunt coram rege. Quibus ait Merlinus: "Nescientes quid fundamenta inceptae turris inpediat, laudavistis regi ut sanguis meus funderetur in caementum, quasi opus ideo constare deberet. Sed dicite mihi, si magi estis, quid sub fundamento lateat. Nam aliquid sub illo esse oportet quod structuram stare non permittit."

3   Attoniti ergo magi conticuerunt omnes. Tunc intendens Merlinus in regem dixit: "Domine mi rex, voca operarios et iube fodere terram loci huius usque quo perveniatur ad stagnum quod subter latet, pro quo stare opus non valet."

Quod cum factum esset, repertum est stagnum sicut dixerat Merlinus et credidit rex illi in his et aliis quae locutus est postea Merlinus. Vertens se deinde Merlinus ad magos, "Dicite," inquid, "mendaces et fatui, si nostis quid sit

4   sub stagno."

Nec unum verbum proferentes obmutuerunt. "Praecipe," ait ad regem Merlinus, "hauriri stagnum per rivulos et videbis in fundo duos concavos lapides et in illis duos dracones dormientes."

5   Credidit ergo rex quia verum prius dixerat de stagno et fecit hauriri stagnum; sed super omnia Merlinum ammirabatur. Ammirabantur etiam cuncti qui aderant tantam in eo sapientiam, existimantes numen esse in illo.

want to build the tower, its foundations cannot not stand firm in this place without that which is built during the day being swallowed up by the earth at night."

Then Merlin said to the king: "Order your magicians to come and I will prove they are complete liars." 2

After the magicians were summoned, they sat in the presence of the king. Merlin said to them: "Not knowing what impairs the foundation of the tower under construction, you recommended to the king that my blood should be poured in the cement, as if the building ought to stand for that reason. But tell me, if you are magicians, what lies beneath the foundation. For there must be something that does not allow the structure to stand."

Astonished, the magicians all fell silent. Then turning to the king, Merlin said: "My lord king, call your workmen and order them to dig up the earth in this spot until they have come to the pond that lies beneath it, because of which the building is not able to stand." 3

When this was done, a pond was found just as Merlin said and the king believed him in these and other things that Merlin afterward said. Then turning himself to the magicians Merlin said: "Tell me," he said, "you liars and fools, if you know what is under the pond." 4

But, not speaking a word, they were silent. Merlin said to the king, "Direct the pond to be drained through channels and you will see at the bottom two hollow stones and in them two dragons sleeping."

Because he had told the truth before about the pond the king trusted him and had the pond drained; but above all he marveled at Merlin. All the rest who were present likewise marveled at so much wisdom, supposing it to be divine inspiration. 5

BOOK SEVEN

Liber VII

[111] Sedente itaque Vortigerno super ripam exhausti stagni, egressi sunt duo dracones de praedictis rupibus concavis, quorum unus erat albus, alter rubeus. Cumque invicem appropinquassent, commiserunt diram pugnam cernentibus
2   cunctis ita ut ignis de ore et naribus eorum exhalaret. Praevaluit autem albus draco rubeumque usque ad extremitatem lacus fugavit. At ille, cum se expulsum doluisset, fecit impetum in album et retro ire coegit. Illis ergo in hunc modum certantibus, praecepit rex Ambrosio Merlino—sic enim cognomen erat ei—dicere quid proelium draconum portenderet. Mox ille in fletum erumpens spiritum hausit prophetiae et ait:

[112] "Vae rubeo draconi nam exterminatio eius festinat. Cavernas ipsius occupabit albus draco, qui Saxones quos invitasti significat. Rubeus vero gentem designat Britanniae, quae ab albo opprimetur. Montes itaque eius ut valles aequabuntur et flumina vallium sanguine manabunt. Cultus reli-
2   gionis delebitur et ruina ecclesiarum patebit. Praevalebit tandem oppressa et saevitiae exterorum resistet. Aper etenim Cornubiae succursum praestabit et colla eorum sub pedibus suis conculcabit. Insulae Oceani potestati illius subdentur et Gallicanos saltus possidebit. Tremebit Romulea domus saevitiam ipsius et exitus eius dubius erit. In

Book 7

[111] And so, while Vortigern was sitting on the bank of the emptied pond, two dragons emerged from the hollow stones mentioned before, of which one was white, the other red. And when they drew near to each other, they engaged in a fierce battle, with it appearing to everyone as if fire breathed out of their mouths and nostrils. The white dragon prevailed and drove the red one to flee to the far side of the lake. But when it grieved at being driven off, it charged at the white one and forced it to retreat. While they were fighting in this way, the king ordered Ambrosius Merlinus — for that was his full name — to say what was portended by the battle of the dragons. Soon, bursting into tears, he was filled with the spirit of prophecy and said:

[112] "Woe to the red dragon, for its end is near. Its dens will be occupied by the white dragon, which signifies the Saxons you invited here. The red dragon indicates the people of Britain, who will be oppressed by the white one. Its mountains will become level with its valleys, and the streams of the valleys will flow with blood. The practice of religion will be destroyed and the ruin of the churches will be plain to see. At length the oppressed will overcome and fight back against the fury of the invaders. For the boar of Cornwall will lend his aid and will trample their necks beneath his feet. The islands of the ocean will be subject to his power and he will possess the forests of Gaul. The house of Romulus will tremble before his fury and his end will be unknown.

ore populorum celebrabitur et actus eius cibus erit narranti-
3 bus. Sex posteri eius sequentur sceptrum, sed post ipsos
exsurget Germanicus vermis. Sublimabit illum aequoreus
lupus quem Affricana nemora comitabuntur. Delebitur iterum religio et transmutatio primarum sedium erit. Dignitas
Londoniae adornabit Doroberniam et pastor Eboracensis
septimus in Armorico regno frequentabitur. Menevia pallio
Urbis Legionum induetur et praedicator Hiberniae propter
infantem in utero crescentem obmutescet. Pluet sanguineus
4 imber et dira fames mortales afficiet. His supervenientibus
dolebit rubeus, sed emenso labore vigebit. Tunc infortunium albi festinabit et aedificia hortulorum eius diruentur.
Sceptrigeri septem perimentur et unus eorum sanctificabi-
tur. Ventres matrum secabuntur et infantes abortivi erunt.
Erit ingens supplicium hominum, ut indigenae restituantur.
Qui faciet haec, aeneum virum induet et per multa tempora
5 super aeneum equum portas Londoniae servabit. Exin in
proprios mores revertetur rubeus draco et in se ipsum sae-
vire laborabit. Superveniet itaque ultio Tonantis, quia omnis
ager colonos decipiet. Arripiet mortalitas populum cunc-
tasque nationes evacuabit. Residui natale solum deserent et
exteras culturas seminabunt. Rex benedictus parabit navi-
6 gium et in aula duodecim inter beatos annumerabitur. Erit
miseranda regni desolatio et areae messium in fruticosos
saltus redibunt. Replebuntur iterum hortuli nostri alieno

He will be celebrated in the mouth of the people and his deeds will be food for those who relate them. Six of his successors will attain the throne, but after them the German worm will rise up. The wolf of the sea will raise him up, accompanied by the forests of Africa. Religion will be destroyed again and the location of the metropolitan sees will be altered. The dignity of London will adorn Canterbury and the seventh pastor of York will be followed in the kingdom of Armorica. St. David's will be clothed with the pallium of Caerleon and the preacher of Ireland will fall silent before an infant growing in the womb. A rain of blood will fall and a bitter famine will afflict mankind. Following these things the red dragon will be grieved, but once the trial is past he will grow strong. Then misfortune will quickly befall the white one, and buildings of its gardens will be destroyed. Seven who bear the scepter will be killed, and one of them will become a saint. The bellies of the mothers will be cut open and infants will be aborted. There will be an enormous suffering of men, in order to restore the native population. He that accomplishes these things will put on a man of bronze, and for a long time he will guard the ports of London atop a bronze horse. After that the red dragon will return to its old habits and will turn all its fury against itself. And thus the revenge of the Thunderer will come upon it, because the field of every farmer will fail. Mortality will snatch away the people and will exterminate all the nations. The remnant will abandon their native soil and will sow in foreign fields. The blessed king will prepare a fleet and will be placed as the twelfth in the court among the saints. There will be a miserable desolation of the kingdom and the threshing floors will return to fruitful glades. Our gardens

semine et in extremitate stagni languebit rubeus. Exin coronabitur Germanicus vermis et aeneus princeps humiliabitur. Terminus illi positus est quem transvolare nequibit.

[113] "Centum namque quinquaginta annis in inquietudine et subiectione manebit, ter centum vero insidebit. Tunc exsurget in illum aquilo et flores quos Zephyrus procreavit eripiet. Erit deauratio in templis, nec acumen gladiorum cessabit. Vix obtinebit cavernas suas Germanicus 2 draco, quia ultio proditionis eius superveniet. Vigebit tandem paulisper, sed decimatio Neustriae nocebit. Populus namque in ligno et ferreis tunicis superveniet, qui vindictam de nequitia eius sumet. Restaurabit pristinis incolis mansiones et ruina alienigenarum patebit. Germen albi draconis ex hortulis nostris abradetur et reliquiae generationis eius decimabuntur. Iugum perpetuae servitutis ferent matrem- 3 que suam ligonibus et aratris vulnerabunt. Succedent duo dracones, quorum alter invidiae spiculo suffocabitur, alter vero sub umbra nominis redibit. Succedet leo iustitiae, ad cuius rugitum Gallicanae turres et insulani dracones tremebunt. In diebus eius aurum ex lilio et urtica extorquebitur et 4 argentum ex ungulis mugientium manabit. Calamistrati varia vellera vestibunt et exterior habitus interiora signabit. Pedes latrantium truncabuntur, pacem habebunt ferae, humanitas supplicium dolebit. Findetur forma commercii,

will be filled again with foreign seed and the red dragon will languish at the edge of the pool. After that the German worm will be crowned and the bronze man will be humbled. A limit is set for the red dragon, beyond which he will not be able to fly.

[113] "For one hundred and fifty years he will endure trouble and submission, but he will remain in place for three hundred. At that time the north wind will rise against it and will snatch away the flowers that the west wind produced. There will be gilding in the temples, and the point of the sword will not rest. The German dragon will barely reach its lairs, because retribution for its treason will intervene. At 2 length he will flourish for a little while, but the decimation of Neustria will harm him. For a people will arrive in wood and tunics made of iron, who will take revenge for his wickedness. They will restore the original inhabitants to their dwellings and the ruin of the foreigners will be plain to see. The seed of the white dragon will be swept from our little gardens and the remnants of its generation will be decimated. They will bear the yoke of perpetual servitude and they will wound their mother with mattocks and plows. Two 3 dragons will follow, one of which will be killed by the sting of envy, while the other will return under the shadow of a name. The lion of justice will follow, at whose roar the towers of Gaul and the dragons of the island will tremble. In its days gold will be wrung from the lily and the nettle, and silver will pour from the hooves of those that bellow. Those 4 who curl their hair will put on various fleeces and their outward demeanor will signify their inward character. The feet of those that bark will be cut off, the wild things will have peace, humanity will suffer punishment. The shape of com-

dimidium rotundum erit. Peribit miluorum rapacitas et
5 dentes luporum hebetabuntur. Catuli leonis in aequoreos
pisces transformabuntur et aquila eius super montem Ara-
vium nidificabit. Venedotia rubebit materno sanguine et
domus Corinei sex fratres interficiet. Nocturnis lacrimis
madebit insula, unde omnes ad omnia provocabuntur.

[114] "Nitentur posteri transvolare superna, sed favor no-
vorum sublimabitur. Nocebit possidenti ex impiis pietas,
donec sese genitore induerit. Apri igitur dentibus accinctus,
2 cacumina montium et umbram galeati transcendet. Indignabitur Albania et convocatis collateralibus sanguinem
effundere vacabit. Dabitur maxillis eius frenum, quod in
Armorico sinu fabricabitur. Deaurabit illud aquila rupti
3 foederis et tertia nidificatione gaudebit. Evigilabunt rugi-
entes catuli et postpositis nemoribus infra civitatum moenia venabuntur. Stragem non minimam ex obstantibus facient et linguas taurorum abscident. Colla rugientium
onerabunt catenis et avita tempora renovabunt. Exin de
primo in quartum, de quarto in tertium, de tertio in secun-
4 dum rotabitur pollex in oleo. Sextus Hiberniae moenia subvertet et nemora in planitiem mutabit. Diversas portiones
in unum reducet et capite leonis coronabitur. Principium
eius vago affectui subiacebit, sed finis ipsius ad superos
convolabit. Renovabit namque beatorum sedes per patrias

merce will be divided, the half will be rounded. The rapacity of kites will pass away and the teeth of wolves will be blunted. The cubs of the lion will be transformed into fishes 5 of the sea and its eagle will nest atop Mount Snowdon. Venedotia will grow red with maternal blood and the house of Corineus will kill six brothers. The island will be wet with tears in the night, so that all will be provoked to all things.

[114] "Posterity will strive to fly above the highest places, but the acclamation of newcomers will be exalted. Goodness will harm those who possess from the wicked, until it dresses itself as its creator. Then, girded with the teeth of the boar, it will rise above the peak of the mountain and the shadow of the helmeted man. Albany will be angry and, after 2 its neighbors are summoned, it will spend its time in the shedding of blood. A bit will be placed in its jaws, that will be made in the bay of Armorica. The eagle of the broken treaty will cover it with gold and will rejoice in its third nesting. The roaring cubs will keep watch and after they leave 3 the woods they will hunt within the walls of the city. They will cause great slaughter among those who stand against them and they will cut off the tongues of bulls. They will burden the necks of those that roar with chains and they will renew the times of their ancestors. After that the thumb will be rolled in oil from the first to the fourth, from the fourth to the third, from the third to the second. The sixth 4 will overturn the walls of Ireland and will turn the woods into a plain. He will reduce the various parts into one and he will be crowned with the head of a lion. His beginning will be subject to his wandering state of mind, but his end will fly up to the heavens. And he will restore the seats of the blessed throughout the lands and settle the pastors in fitting

et pastores in congruis locis locabit. Duas urbes duobus palliis induet et virginea munera virginibus donabit. Promerebitur inde favorem Tonantis et inter beatos collocabitur.

[115] "Egredietur ex eo lynx penetrans omnia, quae ruinae propriae gentis imminebit. Per illam enim utramque insulam amittet Neustria et pristina dignitate spoliabitur. Deinde revertentur cives in insulam, nam discidium alienigena-

2 rum orietur. Niveus quoque senex in niveo equo fluvium Perironis divertet et cum candida virga molendinum super ipsum metabitur. Cadwaladrus vocabit Conanum et Albaniam in societatem accipiet. Tunc erit strages alienigenarum, tunc flumina sanguine manabunt, tunc erumpent Armorici montes et diademate Bruti coronabuntur. Replebitur Kambria laetitia et robora Cornubiae virescent. Nomine Bruti vocabitur insula et nuncupatio extraneorum peribit.

3 Ex Conano procedet aper bellicosus, qui infra Gallicana nemora acumen dentium suorum exercebit. Truncabit namque quaeque maiora robora, minoribus vero tutelam praestabit. Tremebunt illum Arabes et Affricani, nam impetum

4 cursus sui in ulteriorem Hispaniam protendet. Succedet hircus Venerii castri, aurea habens cornua et argenteam barbam, qui ex naribus suis tantam efflabit nebulam, quanta tota superficies insulae obumbrabitur. Pax erit in tempore suo et ubertate glebae multiplicabuntur segetes. Mulieres incessu serpentes fient et omnis gressus earum superbia

5 replebitur. Renovabuntur castra Veneris nec cessabunt

locations. He will clothe two cities with two pallia and he will give virginal gifts to the virgins. For this he will earn the favor of the Thunderer and he will be placed among the blessed.

[115] "A lynx will emerge from him and passing through all things, which will threaten the ruin of its own people. Indeed, through it Neustria will lose both islands and be deprived of its former dignity. Then the citizens will return to the island, for dissention will arise among the foreigners. A ₂ white-haired old man on a snow-white horse will also divert the flow of the Peridon, and with a white rod he will measure out a mill beside it. Cadwallader will summon Conan and enter into an alliance with Albany. Then there will be a slaughter of the foreigners, the rivers will flow with blood, the mountains of Armorica will burst forth, and they will be crowned with the diadem of Brutus. Wales will be filled with joy and the oaks of Cornwall will flourish. The island will be called by the name of Brutus and the name it was given by strangers will pass away. From Conan a warlike boar will pro- ₃ ceed, which will exercise the sharpness of its tusks among the forests of Gaul. For it will cut the branches from all the larger oaks, but it will offer protection to the smaller ones. The Arabs and the Africans will tremble before him, for the impact of his assault will extend to farthest Spain. The ram ₄ of the castle of Venus will follow, having golden horns and a silver beard, and it will blow such a cloud from its nostrils that it will cast a shadow over all the surface of the island. There will be peace in its time and the crops will be multiplied by the fruitfulness of the soil. Women will become serpents by their gait and every step they take will be full of pride. The camp of Venus will be restored and the arrows of ₅

sagittae Cupidinis vulnerare. Fons Annae vertetur in sanguinem et duo reges duellum propter leaenam de Vado Baculi
committent. Omnis humus luxuriabit et humanitas forni-
6 cari non desinet. Omnia haec tria saecula videbunt, donec
sepulti reges in urbe Londoniarum propalabuntur. Redibit
iterum fames, redibit mortalitas et desolatione urbium do-
lebunt cives. Superveniet aper commercii, qui dispersos greges ad amissa pascua revocabit. Pectus eius cibus erit egenti-
bus et lingua eius sedabit sitientes. Ex ore ipsius procedent
7 flumina, quae arentes hominum fauces rigabunt. Exin super
turrim Londoniarum procreabitur arbor, quae tribus solummodo ramis contenta superficiem totius insulae latitudine
foliorum obumbrabit. Huic adversarius Boreas superveniet
atque iniquo flatu suo tertium illi ramum eripiet. Duo vero
residui locum exstirpati occupabunt, donec alter alterum
8 foliorum multitudine annihilabit. Deinde vero locum duorum obtinebit ipse et volucres exterarum regionum susten-
tabit. Patriis volatilibus nocivus habebitur, nam timore um-
brae eius liberos volatus amittent. Succedet asinus nequitiae
in fabricatores auri velox, sed in luporum rapacitatem piger.

[116] "In diebus illis ardebunt quercus per nemora et in
ramis tiliarum nascentur glandes. Sabrinum mare per septem ostia discurret et fluvius Oscae per septem menses fer-
vebit. Pisces illius calore morientur et ex eis procreabuntur
serpentes. Frigebunt Badonis balnea et salubres aquae eorum mortem generabunt. Londonia necem viginti milium

Cupid will constantly inflict wounds. The source of the Anna will turn to blood and two kings will fight a battle over the lioness of Stafford. All of the ground will grow luxuriantly and humankind will not cease to fornicate. All these 6 things three ages will see, until the kings buried in the city of London are made visible. Famine will return again, death will return and the citizens will grieve for the desolation of their cities. The boar of commerce will arrive, who will call the scattered flocks back to their lost pasture. Its chest will be food for the needy and its tongue will bring relief to those that are thirsty. From his mouth rivers will flow, which will water the parched throats of men. After that a tree will be 7 grown above the tower of London, which, having only three branches, will overshadow the entire surface of the island with the breadth of its foliage. The north wind will come against it and will tear away its third branch with a hostile breeze. However, the two remaining branches will occupy the place of the one destroyed, until one annihilates the other with the multitude of its leaves. Then it will take the 8 place of the other two and it will give sustenance to birds of foreign lands. It will prove harmful to the native birds, for they will lose their freedom of flight through fear of its shadow. The ass of wickedness will follow swiftly against the makers of gold, but slowly against the rapacity of wolves.

[116] "In those days the oaks will burn throughout the forests and acorns will grow upon the branches of linden trees. The Severn will flow through seven mouths and the river Usk will boil for seven months. Fishes will be killed by its heat and serpents will be born from them. The baths of Badon will grow cold and their healing waters will bring death. London will mourn the death of twenty thousand

lugebit et Thamensis in sanguinem mutabitur. Cucullati ad nuptias provocabuntur et clamor eorum in montibus Alpium audietur.

2   "Tres fontes in urbe Wintonia erumpent, quorum rivuli insulam in tres portiones secabunt. Qui bibet de uno, diuturniori vita fruetur nec supervenienti languore gravabitur. Qui bibet de altero, indeficienti fame peribit et in facie ipsius pallor et horror sedebit. Qui bibet de tertio, morte subita periclitabitur nec corpus ipsius subire poterit sepulchrum. Tantam ingluviem vitare volentes, diversis tegumentis eam occultare nitentur. Quaecumque ergo moles superposita fuerit, formam alterius corporis recipiet. Terra namque in lapides, lapides in lignum, lignum in cineres, cinis
3   in aquam, si superiecta fuerint, vertentur. Ad haec ex urbe Canuti nemoris eliminabitur puella ut medelae curam adhibeat. Quae, ut omnes artes inierit, solo anhelitu suo fontes nocivos siccabit. Exin, ut sese salubri liquore refecerit, gestabit in dextera sua nemus Colidonis, in sinistra vero murorum Londoniae propugnacula. Quocumque incedet passus
4   sulphureos faciet, qui duplici flamma fumabunt. Fumus ille excitabit Rutenos et cibum submarinis conficiet. Lacrimis miserandis manabit ipsa et clamore horrido replebit insulam. Interficiet eam cervus decem ramorum, quorum quatuor aurea diademata gestabunt. Sex vero residui in cornua bubalorum vertentur, quae nefando sonitu tres insulas Britanniae commovebunt. Excitabitur Danerium nemus et in
5   humanam vocem erumpens clamabit: 'Ascende, Kambria, et

and the river Thames will be changed into blood. Those who wear cowls will be provoked to marriage and their cries will be heard in the mountains of the Alps.

"Three springs will burst forth in the city of Winchester, whose streams will cut the island into three parts. Whoever drinks from the first will enjoy long life and will never be overcome by illness. Whoever drinks from the second will die of starvation and paleness and dread will settle upon his face. Whoever drinks from the third will be struck down by sudden death and his body will not be able to be buried. Wishing to avoid such voraciousness, they will try to hide it with various coverings. Consequently, whatever mass is placed over it will take the form of another body. And thus earth will be turned to stones, stones to wood, wood to ashes, ashes to water if they are thrown upon it. At this a girl will be sent forth from the city of the forest of Canute to apply a cure. After she has applied all her skills, she will dry out the noxious springs with her breath alone. After that, as soon as she has refreshed herself with the beneficial liquid, she will carry the forest of Colidon in her left hand, but in her right the ramparts of the walls of London. Wherever she goes she will make sulfurous tracks, which will smoke with a double flame. That flame will incite the Flemings and will provide food for those that live beneath the sea. She will shed pitiable tears and will fill the island with a frightful outcry. A stag with ten branches will kill her, four of which will bear golden diadems. The remaining six will be turned into the horns of gazelles, which will provoke the three islands of Britain with a dreadful noise. The forest of Dean will be roused and bursting out in a human voice it will shout: 'Come, Wales, and join Cornwall to your side and say to

iunge lateri tuo Cornubiam et dic Wintoniae: absorbebit te tellus; transfer sedem pastoris ubi naves applicant et cetera membra caput sequantur. Festinat namque dies qua cives ob periurii scelera peribunt. Candor lanarum nocuit atque tincturae ipsarum diversitas. Vae periurae genti, quia urbs inclita propter eam ruet.'

6   "Gaudebunt naves augmentatione tanta et unum ex duobus fiet. Reaedificabit eam ericius oneratus pomis, ad quorum odorem diversorum nemorum convolabunt volucres. Adiciet palatium ingens et sescentis turribus vallabit illud. Invidebit ergo Londonia et muros suos tripliciter augebit. Circuibit eam undique Thamensis fluvius et rumor operis

7   transcendet Alpes. Occultabit infra eam ericius poma sua et subterraneas vias machinabitur. In tempore illo loquentur lapides et mare quo ad Galliam navigatur infra breve spatium contrahetur. In utraque ripa audietur homo ab homine et solidum insulae dilatabitur. Revelabuntur occulta sub-

8   marinorum et Gallia prae timore tremebit. Post haec ex Calaterio nemore procedet ardea, quae insulam per biennium circumvolabit. Nocturno clamore convocabit volatilia et omne genus volucrum associabit sibi. In culturas mortalium

9   irruent et omnia genera messium devorabunt. Sequetur fames populum atque dira mortalitas famem. At cum calamitas tanta cessaverit, adibit detestabilis ales vallem Galabes atque eam in excelsum montem levabit. In cacumine quoque ipsius plantabit quercum atque infra ramos nidifica-

10   bit. Tria ova procreabuntur in nido, ex quibus vulpes et lupus

Winchester: the earth will swallow you up; move the seat of the pastor to the place where ships land and the rest of the members will follow the head. For the day draws near when citizens will perish because of their crimes of perjury. The whiteness of your wools has harmed you as well as the diversity of their dyes. Woe to the perjured nation, because the famous city will be ruined due to them.'

"The ships will rejoice because of such an increase and 6 one will be made out of two. A hedgehog adorned with apples will rebuild the city, to the scent of which the birds of different forests will flock. It will add a huge palace and wall it around with six hundred towers. London will envy it and enlarge its own walls three times over. The river Thames will surround it on every side and news of the work will pass beyond the Alps. The hedgehog will hide its apples within it 7 and will devise passages beneath the earth. At that time the stones will speak and the sea that leads to Gaul will shrink into a narrow channel. A man on either bank will be heard by those on the other side and the solid ground of the island will be enlarged. The secrets of the deep will be revealed and Gaul will tremble with fear. After these things a heron will 8 emerge from the forest of Calaterium, which will fly around the island for two years in a row. With its cry in the night it will summon the winged creatures and make an alliance with every species of bird. They will overrun the fields of mankind and devour every kind of harvest. A famine will 9 follow the people, and a grievous mortality will follow the famine. But when this calamity ends, the accursed bird will go to the valley of Galabes and raise it up into a lofty mountain. At its summit the bird will plant an oak and nest among the branches. Three eggs will be laid in the nest, from which 10

et ursus egredientur. Devorabit vulpes matrem et asininum caput gestabit. Monstro igitur assumpto terrebit fratres suos ipsosque in Neustriam fugabit. At illi excitabunt aprum dentosum in illa et navigio revecti cum vulpe congredientur.

11 Quae, cum certamen inierit, finget se defunctam et aprum in pietatem movebit. Mox adibit ipse cadaver, dumque superstabit anhelabit in oculos eius et faciem. At ipsa non oblita praeteriti doli, mordebit sinistrum pedem illius totumque ex corpore evellet. Saltu quoque facto eripiet ei dextram aurem et caudam et infra cavernas montium delitebit.

12 Aper ergo illusus requiret lupum et ursum ut ei amissa membra restituant. Qui, ut causam inierint, promittent ei duos pedes et aures et caudam et ex eis porcina membra component. Acquiescet ipse promissamque restaurationem exspectabit. Interim descendet vulpes de montibus et sese in

13 lupum mutabit et quasi colloquium habitura cum apro, adibit illum callideque ipsum totum devorabit. Exin transvertet sese in aprum et quasi sine membris exspectabit germanos. Sed et ipsos, postquam advenerint, subito dente interficiet atque capite leonis coronabitur.

14 "In diebus eius nascetur serpens qui neci mortalium imminebit. Longitudine sua circuibit Londoniam et quosque praetereuntes devorabit. Bos montanus caput lupi assumet dentesque suos in fabrica Sabrinae dealbabit. Associabit sibi greges Albanorum et Kambriae, qui Thamensem potando

15 siccabunt. Vocabit asinus hircum prolixae barbae et formam ipsius mutuabitur. Indignabitur igitur montanus vocatoque

a fox and a wolf and a bear will hatch. The fox will devour its mother and wear the head of an ass. In this monstrous disguise it will terrify its own brothers and drive them away to Neustria. But they will arouse the tusked boar against it and returning in a ship they will attack the fox. When the battle begins, it will pretend to be dead and move the boar to compassion. Soon the boar will approach the fox's body and while standing over it will breathe upon its eyes and face. But the fox, mindful of its old cunning, will bite the boar's left foot and pull it from its body. Leaping up, it will also tear off its right ear and its tail and hide within the caverns of the mountains. The deluded boar will then require the wolf and the bear to restore its lost members. As soon as they begin work, they will promise it two feet and ears and a tail and from these they will fashion the members of a swine. The boar will agree with this and await the promised restoration. Meanwhile the fox will descend from the mountains and change itself into a wolf and, as if to have a conversation with the boar, it will approach him and will cunningly devour the whole of him. After that the fox will transform itself into a boar and await its brothers as if it had lost its members. But after they arrive, it will suddenly kill them with its tusk and it will be crowned with the head of a lion.

"In its days a serpent will be born that will threaten mankind with death. It will surround London with its length and will devour all those who pass by. The mountain ox will put on the head of a wolf and polish its teeth in the workshop of the Severn. It will make an alliance with the flocks of Albany and Wales, which will dry up the Thames as they drink. The ass will call the goat with the bushy beard and change into its shape. Then the mountain ox will be enraged, and after it

lupo cornutus taurus in ipsos fiet. Ut autem saevitiae indulserit, devorabit carnes eorum et ossa, sed in cacumine Uriani
16 cremabitur. Favillae rogi mutabuntur in cygnos, qui in sicco, quasi in flumine natabunt. Devorabunt pisces in piscibus et homines in hominibus deglutient. Superveniente vero senectute efficientur submarini luces atque submarinas insidias machinabuntur. Submergent navalia et argentum non
17 minimum congregabunt. Fluctuabit iterum Thamensis convocatisque fluminibus ultra metas alvei procedet. Urbes vicinas occultabit oppositosque montes subvertet. Adhibebit sibi fontem Galabes, dolo et nequitia repleti. Orientur ex eo seditiones provocantes Venedotos ad proelia. Convenient nemorum robora et cum saxis Gewisseorum con-
18 gredientur. Advolabit corvus cum miluis et corpora peremptorum devorabit. Super muros Claudiocestriae nidificabit bubo et in nido suo procreabitur asinus. Educabit eum serpens Malverniae et in plures dolos commovebit. Sumpto diademate transcendet excelsa et horrido rugitu populum
19 patriae terrebit. In diebus eius titubabunt montes Pachaii et provinciae nemoribus suis spoliabuntur. Superveniet namque vermis ignei anhelitus, qui emisso vapore comburet arbores. Egredientur ex eo septem leones capitibus hircorum turpati. Foetore narium mulieres corrumpent et proprias communes facient. Nesciet pater filium proprium, quia
20 more pecudum lascivient. Superveniet vero gigas nequitiae, qui oculorum acumine terrebit universos. Exsurget in illum

summons the wolf it will become like a horned bull against them. As soon as it has indulged its cruelty, it will devour their flesh and bones, but it will be burned upon the summit of Urian. The ashes of its funeral pyre will be changed into 16 swans, which will swim on dry ground as if in a river. They will devour fishes inside fishes and swallow up men inside men. But when old age comes upon them they will become pikes under water and devise underwater traps. They will sink ships and collect much silver. The Thames will flow 17 again and summoning the rivers together it will overflow the confines of its channel. It will cover the nearby cities and undermine the mountains that stand in its way. It will call the fountain of Galabes to itself, filled with wickedness and deceit. Rebellions will arise from it, provoking the Venedotians to war. The oaks of the forest will come together and attack the rocks of the Gewissae. A raven will 18 stoop down with the kites and devour the bodies of the slain. An owl will nest atop the walls of Gloucester and in its nest an ass will be born. The serpent of the Malvern will raise the ass and provoke it to many acts of treachery. After it takes the crown it will surpass the heights and it will terrify the people of the land with its horrible braying. In its 19 days the mountains of Pachius will totter and the provinces will be stripped of their forests. For a fire-breathing worm will arrive that will burn the trees with the steam it sends forth. Seven lions will emerge from it, disfigured with the heads of goats. They will corrupt women with the stench of their nostrils and turn faithful wives into common whores. The father will not know his own son, because they will rut like animals. The giant of wickedness will arrive, who will 20 terrify everyone with his piercing eyes. The dragon of

draco Wigorniae et eum exterminare conabitur. Facto autem congressu superabitur draco et nequitia victoris opprimetur. Ascendet namque draconem et exuta veste insidebit nudus. Feret illum ad sublimia draco erectaque cauda verberabit nudatum. Resumpto iterum vigore, gigas fauces illius cum gladio confringet. Implicabitur tandem sub cauda sua draco et venenatus interibit.

21   "Succedet post illum Totonesius aper et dira tyrannide opprimet populum. Eliminabit Claudiocestria leonem, qui diversis proeliis inquietabit saevientem. Conculcabit eum sub pedibus suis apertisque faucibus terrebit. Cum regno tandem litigabit leo et terga nobilium transcendet. Superveniet taurus litigio et leonem dextro pede percutiet. Expellet eum per regni diversoria, sed cornua sua in muros Exoniae 22 confringet. Vindicabit leonem vulpes Kaerdubali et totum dentibus suis consumet. Circumcinget eam Lindicolinus coluber praesentiamque suam draconibus multis horribili sibilo testabitur. Congredientur deinde dracones et alter alterum dilaniabit. Opprimet alatus carentem alis et ungues in genas venenatas configet. Ad certamen convenient alii et 23 alius alium interficiet. Succedet quintus interfectis; residuos diversis machinationibus confringet. Transcendet dorsum unius cum gladio et caput a corpore separabit. Exuta veste ascendet alium et dextram caudae laevamque iniciet.

Worcester will rise against him and try to drive him out. But after he attacks the dragon will be overcome and it will be crushed by the wickedness of the victor. For the giant will mount upon the dragon and casting off his clothes he will sit there naked. The dragon will carry him to the heights and beat the naked one with its upraised tail. Regaining his strength, the giant will smash its jaws with his sword. In the end the dragon will become entangled under its own tail and it will die of poison.

"After him the boar of Totnes will follow and it will op- 21 press the people with grievous tyranny. Gloucester will send out a lion, which will harass the savage boar in different battles. He will trample him beneath his feet and terrify him with open jaws. At last the lion will argue with the kingdom and climb over the backs of the nobles. A bull will join the argument and strike the lion with its right foot. It will drive him through all the byways of the kingdom, but it will break its horns against the walls of Exeter. The fox of Kaerdub- 22 alum will punish the lion and completely devour him with its teeth. The snake of Lincoln will encircle it and it will make its presence known to many dragons with a terrible hissing. The dragons will come together and tear each other to pieces. The winged dragon will oppress the one lacking wings and sink its talons into the poisoned cheeks. Others will join the contest and one will kill another. The fifth one 23 will follow those that are slain; it will destroy those that remain with different stratagems. It will climb upon the back of one with its sword and sever its head from its body. Shedding its garment, it will get upon another and grab the tail with its right hand and its left. It will overcome him naked,

Superabit eum nudus, cum nihil indutus proficeret. Ceteros tormentabit a dorso et in rotunditatem regni compellet.

24 "Superveniet leo rugiens, immani feritate timendus. Ter quinque portiones in unum reducet et solus possidebit populum. Splendebit gigas colore niveo ac candidum populum generabit. Deliciae principes enervabunt et subditi in beluas mutabuntur. Orietur in illis leo humano cruore turgidus. Supponetur ei in segete falcifer, qui, dum laborabit mente,
25 opprimetur ab illo. Sedabit illos Eboracensis auriga expulsoque domino in currum quem ducit ascendet. Abstracto gladio minabitur Orienti et rotarum suarum vestigia replebit sanguine. Fiet deinde piscis in aequore, qui sibilo serpentis revocatus coibit cum illo. Nascentur inde tres tauri fulgurantes qui consumptis pascuis convertentur in arbores.
26 Gestabit primus flagellum vipereum et a postgenito dorsum suum divertet. Nitetur ipse flagellum ei eripere, sed ab ultimo corripietur. Avertent mutuo a sese facies, donec venenatum scyphum proiecerint. Succedet ei colonus Albaniae, cui a dorso imminebit serpens. Vacabit ipse tellurem subvertere, ut patriae segetibus candeant. Laborabit serpens venenum diffundere, ne herbae in messes proveniant. Letali
27 clade deficiet populus et moenia urbium desolabuntur. Dabitur in remedium urbs Claudii, quae alumnam flagellantis interponet. Stateram namque medicinae gestabit et in brevi renovabitur insula. Deinde duo subsequentur sceptrum,

although it had accomplished nothing when clothed. It will torture the rest from behind and will drive them around the kingdom.

"A roaring lion will arrive, dreadful for its extreme feroc- 24 ity. It will reduce fifteen parts to one and hold the people by itself. The giant will shine with a snowy color and will beget a fair-skinned people. Pleasures will soften the princes and their subjects will be changed into beasts. A lion bloated with human gore will rise among them. A man with a scythe will be placed under him in the corn, but while he labors with his mind he will be crushed by the lion. The charioteer 25 of York will restrain them and after he drives out his lord he will mount the chariot he drives. He will threaten the east with his unsheathed sword and fill the tracks of his wheels with blood. Then he will become a fish in the sea, who will be called back by the hissing of the serpent and will mate with it. As a result three flashing bulls will be born that will eat up their pastures and be turned into trees. The first will 26 carry a flail made of vipers and turn its back on the eldest. He will try to snatch away the flail, but he will be seized by the last. They will turn their faces away from each other, until they cast aside the poisoned cup. The farmer of Albany will follow him, behind whom a snake will loom. He will busy himself in plowing the earth, so that the fields of the land will shine. The serpent will try to spread its poison, so that the plants do not come at harvest time. The people will disappear in this fatal disaster and the walls of the cities will be abandoned. The city of Claudius will be given as a rem- 27 edy, which will put forward the ward of the one with the flail. For she will carry a measure of medicine and in a short time the island will be restored. Then two men will hold the

quibus cornutus draco ministrabit. Adveniet alter in ferro et volantem equitabit serpentem. Nudato corpore insidebit dorso et dexteram caudae iniciet. Clamore ipsius excitabun-

28 tur maria et timorem secundo inicient. Secundus itaque sociabitur leoni et, exorta lite, congressum facient. Mutuis cladibus succumbent mutuo, sed feritas beluae praevalebit. Superveniet quidam in tympano et cithara et demulcebit leonis saevitiam. Pacificabuntur ergo nationes regni et leonem ad stateram provocabunt. Locata sede ad pensas studebit, sed palmas in Albaniam extendet. Tristabuntur igitur aquilonares provinciae et ostia templorum reserabunt.

29 Signifer lupus conducet turmas et Cornubiam cauda sua circumcinget. Resistet ei miles in curru, qui populum illum in aprum mutabit. Vastabit igitur aper provincias, sed in profundo Sabrinae occultabit caput. Amplexabitur homo leonem in vino et fulgor auri oculos intuentium excaecabit. Candebit argentum in circuitu et diversa torcularia vexabit.

[117] "Imposito vino inebriabuntur mortales postpositoque caelo in terram respicient. Ab eis vultus avertent sidera et solitum cursum confundent. Arebunt segetes his indignantibus et humor convexi negabitur. Radices et rami

2 vices mutabunt novitasque rei erit in miraculum. Splendor Solis electro Mercurii languebit et erit horror inspicientibus. Mutabit clipeum Stilbon Archadiae, vocabit Venerem

scepter in succession, whom the horned dragon will serve. One will come in armor and ride upon the flying serpent. He will sit upon its back with his naked body and grab its tail with his right hand. The seas will be aroused by his outcry and he will strike terror into the second. The second will 28 therefore make an alliance with the lion, and once an argument arises they will do battle. They will each suffer defeats from the other's hand, but the ferocity of the beast will prevail. A certain man will arrive with a drum and a lute and soothe the savagery of the lion. Then the peoples of the realm will be at peace and will lead the lion to the measure of medicine. Taking his seat, he will examine the scales, but will hold out his palms to Albany. The regions of the north will be saddened by this and they will open the gates of the temples. The standard-bearing wolf will lead the troops and 29 surround Cornwall with its tail. A soldier in a chariot will oppose it, who will transform that people into a boar. Then the boar will ravage the provinces, but it will hide its head in the depths of the Severn. A man will embrace a lion in wine and the blazing of gold will blind the eyes of the beholders. Silver will shine all around and trouble the different wine presses.

[117] "After the wine has been served mankind will become drunk and, ignoring the heavens, they will gaze upon the ground. The stars will turn their faces away from them and alter their accustomed orbit. Because of their anger the crops will wither and precipitation will be denied. Roots and branches will be interchanged, and the novelty of this will become a marvel. The brightness of the sun will fade before the amber of Mercury and it will cause dread to those who witness it. Stilbon of Arcadia will alter his shield, the

245

galea Martis. Galea Martis umbram conficiet, transibit terminos furor Mercurii. Nudabit ensem Orion ferreus, vexabit nubes Phoebus aequoreus. Exibit Iuppiter licitas semitas et Venus deseret statutas lineas. Saturni sideris livido corruet et falce recurva mortales perimet. Bis senus numerus domorum siderum deflebit hospites ita transcurrere. Omittent Gemini complexus solitos et Urnam in fontes provocabunt. Pensa Librae oblique pendebunt, donec Aries recurva cornua sua supponat. Cauda Scorpionis procreabit fulgura et Cancer cum Sole litigabit. Ascendet Virgo dorsum Sagittarii et flores virgineos obfuscabit. Currus Lunae turbabit Zodiacum et in fletum prorumpent Pleiades. Officia Iani nulla redibunt, sed clausa ianua in crepidinibus Adriannae delitebit. In ictu radii exsurgent aequora et pulvis veterum renovabitur. Confligent venti diro sufflamine et sonitum inter sidera conficient."

helmet of Mars will call to Venus. The helmet of Mars will cast a shadow, the fury of Mercury will exceed its bounds. Iron Orion will draw his sword, sea-born Phoebus will disturb the clouds. Jupiter will stray from his lawful paths and Venus will abandon her established lines. The spite of Saturn's star will fall down and will slay mankind with a curved sickle. The dozen houses of the stars will weep for the stray- 3 ing of their guests. The Gemini will abandon their accustomed embraces and will call forth Aquarius to the fountains. The scales of Libra will hang askew, until Aries supports them with his curved horns. The tail of Scorpio will beget lightning and Cancer will argue with the Sun. Virgo will mount upon the back of Sagittarius and stain her virginal flowers. The chariot of the Moon will disrupt the Zo- 4 diac and the Pleiades will burst into tears. All the duties of Janus will go unfulfilled; instead with his door closed he will hide in the bases of Ariadne. The seas will rise up in the twinkling of an eye and the dust of the ancients will be renewed. The winds will battle with a terrible blowing and they will make their noise among the stars."

BOOK EIGHT

Liber VIII

[118] Cum igitur haec et alia prophetasset Merlinus, ambiguitate verborum suorum astantes in admirationem commovit. Vortigernus vero prae ceteris admirans et sensum iuvenis et vaticinia collaudat. Neminem enim praesens aetas produxerat, qui ora sua in hunc modum coram ipso solvisset. Scire igitur volens modum exitus sui ex hac vita, rogavit iuvenem ut sibi indicaret quid intelligeret. Cui Merlinus:

2   "Ignem filiorum Constantini cave, si valueris. Iam naves parant, iam Armoricanum litus deserunt, iam vela per aequora pandunt. Petent Britanniam, invadent Saxonicam gentem, nefandum populum subiugabunt; sed prius te intra turrim inclusum comburent. Malo tuo patrem eorum prodidisti et Saxones contra eos invitasti. Invitasti eos tibi in

3 praesidium et ecce supervenerunt in tuum supplicium. Imminent tibi duo funera, nec est promptum quod prius vites. Hinc enim regnum tuum devastant Saxones et leto tuo incumbunt. Hinc autem applicant duo fratres, Aurelius et Uther, qui mortem fratris sui in te vindicare nitentur. Quaere tibi diffugium, si potes; cras Totonesium portum te-

4 nebunt. Rubebunt sanguine Saxonum facies et interfecto

Book 8

[118] When Merlin had prophesied about this and other things, he moved the bystanders to admiration with the obscurity of his words. Indeed Vortigern, admiring him more than the others, praised both the youth's thought and his prophecies. For the present age had produced no one who had spoken so freely this way in his presence. Therefore, wishing to know about the manner of his own death, he asked the youth to tell him what he knew. To this Merlin replied:

"Beware the passion of the sons of Constantine, if you 2 are able. Already they prepare their ships, already they leave the Armorican coast, already they spread their sails across the sea. They will aim at Britain, they will attack the Saxon race, they will subjugate the wicked people. But before that they will consume you with fire enclosed in your tower. In your evil you betrayed their father and invited the Saxons against them. You invited them as your protection and, behold, they came as your punishment. Two funerals threaten 3 you and it is not clear which you should avoid first. For on the one hand the Saxons lay waste to your kingdom and press for your death; on the other hand the two brothers draw near, Aurelius and Uther, who will strive to avenge the death of their brother on you. Seek refuge for yourself, if you can; tomorrow they will reach the port of Totnes. The 4 faces of the Saxons will be reddened with blood, and with

Hengisto Aurelius coronabitur. Pacificabit nationes, restaurabit ecclesias, sed veneno deficiet. Succedet ei germanus suus Utherpendragon cuius dies anticipabuntur veneno. Aderunt tantae proditioni posteri tui, quos aper Cornubiae devorabit."

[119] Nec mora, cum crastina dies illuxit, applicuerunt fratres in loco quo praedixerat Merlinus. Rumore itaque eorum divulgato, convenerunt Britones qui in tanta clade dispersi fuerant et, societate suorum roborati, hilariores efficiuntur. Moxque Aurelius in regem erectus est atque hostes persequi secum omnes cohortatur; sed prius Vorti-

2 gernum qui patrem et fratrem eius dolo extinxerat. Convertit ergo exercitum in Kambriam ad opidum Genoreu, quod situm erat in natione Herging, super fluvium Guaie in monte qui Cloartius nuncupatur. In quo forti munimento Vortigernus se receperat, ut ab hostibus suis se ibidem tueretur. Quo cum pervenisset Ambrosius cum exercitu, affatur Eldol, du-

3 cem Claudiocestriae, dicens: "Memento, dux nobilis, qualiter te et pater et frater meus dilexerint et honoraverint et de periuro isto et doloso, qui eos prodidit faciamus ultionem." Nec mora, diversis machinationibus incumbunt, murum diruere festinant. Postremo, igne adhibito, turris simul cum Vortigerno et omnibus qui cum eo aderant in cineres concremata est.

[120] His pro voto patratis, convertit rex exercitum persequi Saxones qui audita fama eorum trans Humbrum

Hengist dead Aurelius will be crowned. He will bring peace to the people, he will rebuild the churches; but he will be killed by poison. His own brother Utherpendragon will succeed him, whose days will be cut short by poison. Your descendants will be present at such treachery, whom the boar of Cornwall will devour."

[119] Without delay, when the next day began to dawn, the brothers landed in the place which Merlin had predicted. And so, news of their arrival having spread, the Britons who had been scattered in defeat came together and, strengthened by their alliance, they were more encouraged. And soon Aurelius was raised up as king, and exhorted them to take vengeance with him against all their enemies, but first against Vortigern, who had destroyed his father and his brother by treachery. He therefore turned the army toward 2 Wales, to the fort of Genoreu, which was situated in the country of Ergyng, on the River Wye, on the mountain which is known as Cloarcius. Vortigern had shut himself in that strong fortress, in order to protect himself there against his enemies. When Ambrosius had arrived there with his army, he spoke to Eldol, Duke of Gloucester, saying: "Remember, noble duke, how both my father and my brother loved and honored you, and let us take revenge on that lying and deceitful one who betrayed them." Without delay, they brought up various siege engines, and hurried to demolish the walls. After that, fire was applied and the tower was burned to ashes along with Vortigern and everyone who was there with him.

[120] Once these things were accomplished according to his vow, the king turned the army to pursue the Saxons who, having heard of his reputation, had fled across the Humber

diffugerant ut Scotia eis ad munimentum et defensionem pateret. Ducens itaque rex Aurelius Ambrosius exercitum per longum Britanniae post hostes in tanto itinere augmentum suscepit exercitus de Britonibus hinc inde confluentibus, ut arenae maris comparari posset. Sed cum praeteriret, urbes et castra et maxime ecclesias a gentilibus hostibus destructas indoluit, restaurationem promittens post triumphum.

[121] At Hengistus convocans in unum Saxones suos sic hortabatur eos, dicens: "Nolite terreri, fratres et commilitones mei, a supervenientibus pueris quorum audacia nullis adhuc populis nota, temerario se ausu in nos bellatores notissimos et exercitatissimos ingerere festinant. Nolite, inquam, timere eorum de diversis nationibus congregatam multitudinem, quorum in proeliis multotiens experti estis

2   imbellem invalitudinem. Mementote victores semper extitisse et de eis stragem non modicam cum paucis peregisse. Dux quoque eorum qui indoctum ducit exercitum necdum ad virilem pervenit aetatem, magis puerilibus exercitatus lusibus quam bellis. Faventibus ergo diis nostris invictissimis et fugari et prosterni necesse est illos, qui necdum arma ferre noverunt et quorum inbecillis est bellandi astutia."

3   Et cum omnes hoc modo animasset Hengistus, dato signo in hostes iter tendit ut subitum et furtivum impetum in illos faceret Britonesque incautos et inparatos occuparet. Sed quomodo posset imparatos reperire, qui semper in armis etiam noctis excubias in castris munierunt? Aurelius

so that Scotland would be available to them as a refuge and defense. Then, Aurelius Ambrosius led the army after his enemies through the length of Britain, and along the way the army was reinforced by so many Britons arriving from every side that they could be compared to the sands of the sea. But as he advanced, he grieved for the towns and camps and especially the churches destroyed by the pagan enemies, and promised their restoration after victory.

[121] But Hengist, calling his Saxons together, encouraged them in this way: "Do not allow yourselves to be terrified, my brothers and companions, by the approaching young men, whose boldness is still known to no people; with their reckless daring they hasten to throw themselves against us, the most famous and experienced fighters. Do not, I say, allow yourselves to be afraid of them, a crowd assembled from various nations, a great number of whom have been proven many times in battle to be weak and unfit for war. Remember you have always been victorious and have 2 accomplished a great slaughter of them with few men of your own. Also their leader, who leads the untrained army, has not yet reached the age of manhood, being more practiced in childish games than in battles. Because we are supported by our most unconquerable gods, they shall be put to flight and laid low who have not yet learned to bear arms and whose cleverness in fighting is feeble."

And when Hengist had inspired them all in this manner, 3 he gave the signal and headed toward the enemy to make a secret assault against the Britons and to catch them unaware and unprepared. But how could he find them unprepared, who always protected themselves with armed guards, even at night in their camps? Knowing the enemy to be near,

ergo sciens hostes prope adesse, dispositis turmis, prior campum adiit in quo bellum futurum sibi aptum existima-

4 vit. Tria milia ex Armoricanis equitibus iussit equis insidere. Ipse cum ceteris pedestri milite acies ordinavit et duxit. De-metas in collibus, Venedotos in prope sitis nemoribus loca-vit ea providentia ut, si hostes ad ea diffugerent, adessent qui exciperent.

[122] Interea accessit Eldol, dux Claudiocestriae, ad re-gem et ait: "Sola dies pro omnibus vitae meae diebus mihi sufficeret, si congredi cum Hengisto copiam mihi fortuna daret. Reminiscerer namque diei qua sine armis convenimus quasi pacem commissuri, in campo iuxta coenobium Am-brii, ubi proditor ille cum cultris repositis omnes interemit praeter me solum, qui reperto palo ad defensionem vix evasi. Iugulati sunt ea die quadringenti octoginta inter duces et consules ac proceres qui omnes convenerant ad pacem com-ponendam."

[123] Dum talia referret Eldol, ecce Hengistus cum suis partem campi non minimam occupavit. Dispositis ex utra-que parte cuneis congrediuntur atque mutuos ictus ingemi-nant. Hinc Britones, hinc Saxones vulnerati cadunt. Horta-tur Aurelius suos ut pro patria et libertate viriliter pugnent; monet Hengistus Saxones quatinus omni spe fugae post-posita fortiter feriant. Fit proelium anceps; nunc isti, nunc

2 illi superiores fiunt. Clamor ad sidera tollitur: Christiani Deum omnipotentem invocant, illi deos suos et deas sup-plices exorant. Dumque diu taliter decertarent, prevaluit Christianus exercitus atque Saxones fugere coegit. Hengis-tus igitur, ut vidit suos christianis cedere, confestim fugiens

Aurelius arranged his troops and preceded them to a field that he judged to be suitable for the coming battle. He ordered three thousand of the Armorican cavalry to mount their horses. He himself organized and led the vanguard along with the rest of the foot soldiers. He wisely positioned Demetians in the hills, and Venedotians in the nearby woods so that, if the enemies fled there, those would be present who could intercept them. 4

[122] Meanwhile Eldol, the Duke of Gloucester, approached the king and said: "This day alone would suffice for all the days of my life if Fortune gave me the opportunity to confront Hengist. For I remember the day when we assembled without arms as if to make peace in the field by the monastery of Ambrius, where that traitor killed everyone with hidden knives except me, who barely escaped after finding a staff to defend myself. Four hundred eighty among the dukes and earls and nobles had their throats cut that day, who all came together to make peace."

[123] While Eldol was recalling all of this, Hengist occupied much of the field with his men. After their forces were arrayed on either side, they joined in battle and increased their exchange of blows; here Britons, here Saxons fell wounded. Aurelius exhorted his men to fight manfully for their country and their freedom. Hengist admonished the Saxons, so that with all thought of retreat put behind them, they hit strongly. The battle went both ways; now this side, now that had the upper hand. The roar of battle rose to the stars: the Christians invoked God almighty, the others entreated their gods and goddesses. And while they were fighting like this, the Christian army prevailed and put the Saxons to flight. Then Hengist, as he saw his men killed by the 2

petivit oppidum Kaerconan, quod nunc Cunungeburg ap-
3 pellatur. Insequitur Aurelius et in itinere quoscumque reperit vel in interitum vel in servitutem redigit. Cumque
vidisset Hengistus quia insequeretur eum Aurelius, noluit
introire oppidum sed convocato in turmas populo iterum
proeliari disponit, malens vitam in gladio et hasta committere quam murorum tuitione. Adveniens itaque Aurelius,
conglomeratis simul aciebus suis coepit iterum pugnam re-
parare, Saxones econtra acriter resistere, quippe pro vita
tantum dimicantes nullum sibi existimabant diffugium pro-
4 venire. Et forte praevaluissent in illo proelio Saxones, nisi
equestris turma Armoricanorum supervenisset, quae consti-
tuta in priori proelio fuerat ad praesidium. Cesserunt igitur
Saxones confutati atque de statione sua pulsi dilapsique fugam arripiunt quidam, quidam fortiter resistentes cum Hengisto se defendebant.

[124] Tunc Eldol locum congrediendi cum Hengisto nactus, quod desiderabat opere complevit. Congressi namque
ipse et Hengistus, singulare certamen inierunt. Qui dum
mutuos enses alter in alterum inmitterent, excutiebantur ex
ictibus ignes ac si fulgura coruscarent. Dumque in hunc modum decertarent, supervenit Gorlois, dux Cornubiae, cum
2 suis quibus praeerat, turmas Saxonum infestans. Quem cum
aspexisset Eldol, securior factus, coepit Hengistum per na-
sale cassidis atque totis viribus utens, ipsum intra suorum
acies extraxit magnoque fluctuans gaudio voce clara dixit:
"Desiderium meum implevit Deus! Prosternite, viri, am-
brones, prosternite rabidum canem atque domini sui prodi-
torem. Vobis est in manu victoria Hengisto perempto."

Christians, suddenly fled and made for the town of Kaer- 3
conan, which is now called Conisbrough. Aurelius followed
and whomever he found along the way he killed or captured.
And when Hengist saw that Aurelius was pursuing him, he
did not want to enter the town but, calling his people into a
group, he positioned them to do battle again, preferring to
entrust his life to sword and spear rather than to the protection of walls. And so as Aurelius approached he too re-
formed his front lines, and began to renew the battle once
more, while the Saxons on the other hand began to oppose
them fiercely because fighting for their lives like this they
expected no way of escape to appear for them. And perhaps 4
the Saxons would have prevailed in that battle, if a troop of
Armorican cavalry had not arrived that had been be formed
as an escort before the battle. The Saxons therefore fell
back defeated and, driven from their stations and scattered,
some took flight while some defended themselves, bravely
making a stand with Hengist.

[124] Then Eldol found a place to confront Hengist and
finished the job he wanted to do. For once he and Hengist
came together, they engaged in single combat. While they
swung their swords against each other, flames were thrown
off by their blows and flashed like lightning. And as they
fought like this, Gorlois, the Duke of Cornwall, arrived with
the men he was leading and harassed the Saxon troops.
When Eldol saw this he became more confident, seized 2
Hengist by the nosepiece of his helmet and, using all his
strength, dragged him behind the front lines of his own
men. Overflowing with great joy, he said in a loud voice:
"God has fulfilled my wish! Strike down the thugs, men,
strike down the rabid dog and leader of the traitors. With
Hengist dead, victory is at hand."

3   Retento itaque eo ac vinculis mancipato, diffugerunt omnes complices sui quo quemque impetus duxit. Alii montana, alii nemora petebant tantum ut manus Britonum ferientium duriter evadere possent. Octa vero, filius Hengisti, cum parte Saxonum Eboracum adiit et Eosa, cognatus suus, urbemque munierunt.

    [125] Aurelius autem victor factus ad urbem supra memoratam Cunungesburg divertens, ibidem tribus diebus moratus est se et vulneratos suos quiete reficiens. Interea mortuos iussit sepeliri et fatigatos quiescere cibisque et potibus indulgere. Inter haec convocatis ducibus decernere iussit

2 quid de Hengisto ageretur. Aderat Eldadus Claudiocestrensis episcopus, frater Eldol, vir summae prudentiae et religionis. Hic cum Hengistum coram rege vinctum aspexisset, si-

3 lentio facto ait: "Etsi omnes istum liberare decernerent, ego sum qui Samuelem prophetam insequens hunc in frusta conciderem. Nam cum Agag, regem Amalech, vivum in Saulis potestate vidisset, iratus secuit eum in frusta dicens: 'Sicut fecisti matres sine liberis, sic faciam hodie matrem tuam sine liberis inter mulieres.' Sic igitur facite de isto qui alter Agag existit."

4   Accepit itaque Eldol gladium et extra urbem educto Hengisto capite privavit. At Aurelius, ut erat in cunctis modestus, iussit saepeliri corpus eius ac more pagano tumulari.

    [126] Post haec rex Eboracum ducens exercitum, Octam filium Hengisti et eos qui cum eo erant in civitate obsedit. Verum ille nil valens resistere processit de civitate obviam

With Hengist restrained and placed in chains, all his ac- 3
complices ran away whom he led to that battle. Some made
for the mountains, some for the forests, as many as could
escape the cruel blows of the British force. But Octa, the
son of Hengist, went to York with part of the Saxons and
Eosa, his kinsman, and they fortified the city.

[125] Aurelius, however, being the victor, turned toward
the city of Conisbrough mentioned above, and stayed there
for three days, quietly refreshing himself and his wounded.
Meanwhile he ordered the dead to be buried and the fa-
tigued to rest and enjoy food and drink. During this time, he
summoned his commanders and ordered them to decide
what should be done with Hengist. Eldad, the bishop of 2
Gloucester, brother of Eldol, was present, a man of the highest wisdom and piety. When he saw Hengist bound in fet-
ters before the king, he grew quiet and said: "Even if every- 3
one decided to free him, I am one who, following the
Prophet Samuel, would chop him to pieces. For when he
saw Agag, the king of Amalech, alive in Saul's custody, he
was enraged and sliced him to pieces, saying: 'As you have
made mothers childless, so today I will make your mother
childless among women.' Therefore you should do the same
with this man who has become another Agag."

And so Eldol took up his sword and, after Hengist was led 4
outside the city, he cut off his head. But Aurelius, because he
was moderate in everything, ordered his body to be buried
and to be covered with a mound after the pagan custom.

[126] Leading the army to York after this, the king besieged Octa, the son of Hengist, and those who were with
him inside the city. But Octa, lacking the strength to resist,
came forth from the city toward the king, bearing an iron

regi, catenam gestans ferream in manu, pulvere asperso ca-
2 pite et sese regi in haec verba praesentavit: "Victi sunt dii
mei Deumque vestrum regnare non haesito qui per vos tot
bellatores nos in armis devictos deditioni amissa libertate
coegit. Suscipiat ergo celsitudo nobilitatis tuae catenam istam et, nisi misericordiam adhibueris, habe nos vinctos ad
quodlibet supplicium vel, si magis placet, nos in servos ac-
cipe foederatos omni tempore."

3   Motus pietate Aurelius iussit adiudicari quid in illos agendum foret. Cum autem diversi diversa proferrent, surrexit
Eldadus praefatus episcopus et sententiam in eos hoc ser-
4 mone disseruit: "Gabaonitea ultro venerunt ad filios Israel
misericordiam petentes et impetraverunt. Erimus ergo
Christiani deteriores Iudeis misericordiam abnegantes? Misericordiam petunt; habeant illam. Ampla est Britannia et in
multis locis deserta. Foederatos itaque illos sinamus saltem
deserta inhabitare et nobis in sempiternum serviant." Acquievit ergo rex et omnis multitudo exercitus quae aderat
deditque eis rex mansionem iuxta Scotiam foedusque cum
eis firmavit obsidibus acceptis.

[127] Triumphatis itaque hostibus convocat rex in contione omnes proceres et seniores ac sapientiores terrae infra
Eboracum, consulens de restauratione ecclesiarum, quae
per gentem Saxonum destructae erant, de urbium quoque
reparatione atque totius regni status renovatione, ac primum ipsam metropolitanam Eboracensem sedem atque ceteros episcopatus provinciae illius ipse reaedificare coepit.
2 Emensis deinde quindecim diebus, cum operarios in diversis

chain in his hand, his head sprinkled with dust, and presented himself to the king with these words: "My gods are 2 conquered and I have no doubt that your God rules, who, through you, forced so many of our fighters to surrender, defeated in battle and deprived of liberty. Therefore, in the loftiness of your nobility you should accept this chain and, unless you will extend mercy, hold us bound to whatever punishment you please or, if you prefer, take us in servitude for all time."

Moved by pity, Aurelius ordered it to be decided what 3 should be done with them. But when different people offered different ideas, Eldad, the bishop mentioned before, rose and explained his opinion to them in these words: "The 4 Gibeonites came voluntarily to the sons of Israel seeking mercy and they obtained it. Shall we Christians then be worse than the Jews by denying mercy? They seek mercy, and they shall have it. Britain is large, and empty in many places. And so, after making a pact with them, we should let them inhabit at least the empty parts and serve us forever." The king therefore agreed, along with the whole army that was present, and the king gave them a home next to Scotland and confirmed a treaty with them and hostages were received.

[127] And so, having triumphed over his enemies, the king called all the nobles and elders and wiser men of the land to an assembly at York, consulting them about the restoration of the churches that had been destroyed by the Saxon people, and also about the repair of the towns and the renewal of the whole condition of the realm; but first he began to rebuild the metropolitan seat of York itself and the other bishoprics of that province. After fifteen days had 2

locis statuisset, adivit urbem Londoniae cui hostes nequaquam pepercerant. Cuius condolens excidio, revocat cives
undique dispersos et civitatem a concivibus restituit. Ibidem disponit de regno legesque sopitas revocat; maiorum
possessiones nepotibus distribuit quas in tanta calamitate
heredes amiserant. Tota itaque eius intentio versabatur circa
regni restitutionem, ecclesiae reformationem, pacis ac legis
3 renovationem et iustitiae compositionem. Exin petivit
Wintoniam ut eam sicut ceteras restitueret. Cumque haec
omnia peragrasset et in restauratione urbium et ecclesiarum
quae necessaria erant posuisset, monitu Eldadi episcopi monasterium Ambrii adiit, quod prope Kaercaradoc, quae nunc
Salesberia dicitur, situm consules et duces regni quos Hen-
4 gistus interfecerat in sepultura continet. Huius coenobii, ut
fertur, fundator exstiterat Ambrius quidam olim, de cuius
nomine locus appellatus est; in quo trecenti fratres Deo
famulabantur. Ubi cum sepulturas interemptorum circum-
spiceret, motus pietate in lacrimas resolutus est. Postea in
diversas cogitationes animum educens deliberabat apud se
qualiter locum faceret memorabilem.

[128] Convocatis itaque artificibus lapidum et lignorum,
praecepit totis ingeniis uti novamque ac mirabilem structuram adinvenire, quae in memoriam tantorum virorum in aevum constaret. Cumque omnes haesitarent ad praeceptum
regis et ignorarent quid agerent, surrexit Tremorinus, Urbis
2 Legionum archiepiscopus, et coram rege ait: "Si Merlinum

passed, when he had established workmen in various places, he went to the city of London, which the enemy had by no means spared. Lamenting the destruction, he recalled the widely scattered residents and restored the city to his fellow citizens. At the same time he organized his kingdom and revived the dormant laws; he distributed the properties of ancestors which had lost direct inheritors in the great disaster to other descendants. He focused all his attention on the rebuilding of the kingdom, the reformation of the church, the renewal of peace, and the arrangement of justice. After 3 that, he made for Winchester in order to restore it like the other cities. And when he had traveled everywhere and had specified what was necessary for the restoration of the towns and churches, on the advice of Bishop Eldad he went to the monastery of Ambrius, located near Kaercaradoc (which is now called Salisbury), which held the graves of the earls and dukes of the kingdom that Hengist had killed. The 4 founder of this monastery, it is said, had been a certain Ambrius, from whose name the place was called; there three hundred brothers were servants to God. Moved by pity when he surveyed the graves of the dead, he melted into tears. After that, his mind wandering over various thoughts, he deliberated internally how to preserve the memory of that place.

[128] And so, having called together craftsmen in stone and wood, he instructed them to use all their ingenuity to devise a glorious structure that would stand through the ages in memory of such men. And when they were all taken aback by the king's command and did not know what to do, Tremorinus, the archbishop of Caerleon, arose and said before the king: "If you ask Merlin the prophet to complete 2

vatem ad hoc opus quod disponis mirabile peragendum invitares, puto quia ipse prae ceteris omnibus qui advocati sunt solus ingeniosus erit ad tale opus insinuandum. Quippe in toto regno tuo non est similis eius, sive in futuris praedicendis sive in operationibus machinandis. Iube ergo illum venire ut ingenio suo innitaris."

3   Missis itaque nunciis in regionem Gewisseorum ad fontem Galabes, quem solitus fuerat frequentare, adductus est ad regem. Excepit illum rex cum honore, rogavitque ut de futuris aliqua praediceret sibi, quatinus quae ventura erant 4 in diebus suis praesagiret. Cui Merlinus, "Non sunt," inquit, "revelanda huiusmodi mysteria nisi cum summa necessitas incubuerit. Nam si ea in derisionem aut vanam iactantiam proferrem, taceret spiritus qui me docet nec per me valerem aliter loqui quam ceteri homines. De his ergo pro quibus huc adductus sum, si vultis, edicam consilium meum."

5   Cui rex, "Novo," ait, "et inaudito opere vellem decorare sepulturam virorum, qui pro pace constituenda hic tamquam oves iugulati sunt."

At Merlinus, "Si desideras," inquit, "quod dicis perfecte facere, pro Chorea Gigantum mittendum tibi est, quae est 6 in Killarao monte Hiberniae. Est etenim structura lapidum quam nemo huius aetatis construeret, nisi ingenium artem subvectaret. Grandes sunt lapides et importabiles, nec est aliquis cuius virtuti cedant nisi sit mechanica arte eruditus. Qui si eo modo quo ibidem positi sunt circa plateam hanc locabuntur, in aeternum stabunt."

[129] Ad verba haec solutus Aurelius in risum cum aliis qui

this extraordinary work you have ordered, I think that he alone, above all the others who were summoned, will be naturally suited to accomplish such work. For indeed there is no one comparable to him in your whole kingdom, whether in predicting the future or in devising operations. Therefore direct him to come so that you can rely upon his ingenuity."

Messengers were sent to the fountain of Galabes in the region of the Gewissae, which Merlin was in the habit of visiting, and he was brought to the king. The king received him with honor and asked whether he could predict something about the future for him, so that the king could foretell what would be coming in his days. To which Merlin replied: "Mysteries must not be revealed in this manner except when the greatest necessity demands it. For if I were to offer them in mockery or empty boasting, the spirit who teaches me would be silent, and I would not be able to speak any differently than other men. If you wish, therefore, I shall offer my counsel about those things for which I was brought here."

To which the king replied: "I want to adorn with some novel and unheard-of work the grave of the men who were butchered here like sheep while trying to establish peace."

But then Merlin said: "If you desire to do what you say perfectly, you must send for the Giant's Ring which is on Mount Killaraus in Ireland. It is a structure of stones which no one of this age could build unless he joined native talent with art. The stones are huge and immovable; and there is no one to whose strength they would yield unless he was schooled in mechanical science. If they are placed around this plot of land in the same way they were laid out there, they will stand for eternity."

[129] At these words Aurelius, dissolved in laughter along

aderant ait nequaquam intelligere se posse, qualiter id fieret ut tam grandes et inconpositi lapides ex tam longinquo veherentur, ac si Britannia lapidibus careret qui ad operatio-

2 nem sufficerent. Tunc Merlinus: "Ne movearis, rex, super his quae dixi neque falsum existimes, quia mystici sunt lapides illi de quibus nobis sermo est et ad diversa medicamenta sa-lubres. Gigantes asportaverunt olim eos ex ultimis finibus Africae et posuerunt illic dum Hiberniam inhabitarent. Erat autem causa ut balnea infra eos conficerent ad usus ho-

3 minum salubres. Lavati enim lapides et infra balnea ea aqua diffusa multorum generum infirmitates curabat, dum balne-arentur aegroti. Mixta cum herbarum succis vulnera quae-libet sanabat. Non est ibi lapis qui medicamento careat."

4 Cum igitur haec audissent qui aderant Britones, hortati sunt pro lapidibus mittere. Eligitur ergo Utherpendragon, frater regis, ad id negotium, licet ipse ultro se ingereret, ut regnum videlicet Hiberniae videret et populum. Eligitur et ipse Merlinus cuius ingenio et auxilio agenda tractentur. Pa-rato itaque navigio, cum quindecim milibus armatorum Hi-berniam adeunt ac prosperis velis litora intrant.

[130] Ea tempestate regnabat in Hibernia Gillomanius rex. Qui cum audisset Britones applicuisse in terra sua, col-lecto exercitu perrexit obviam eis. Et cum didicisset causam

2 adventus eorum, astantibus risit et ait: "Non est mirandum si ignavam gentem Britonum Saxones devastare potuerunt,

with the others who were present, said he could not understand at all how it should be that such huge and unformed
stones could be brought from such a distant place, as if Britain was lacking in stones that would suffice for the work.
Then Merlin said: "Do not be troubled, my king, about what   2
I said, nor suppose it to be false, because those stones of
which we speak are mystical and beneficial for various rem-
edies. Giants transported them long ago from the farthest
ends of Africa and placed them there while they lived in Ireland. The reason for this was so they could make baths beneath them for the use in human healing. For after the   3
stones were washed and that water was poured into the
baths, many types of illness were cured while the sick were
bathed in it. Mixed with the juice of herbs it healed wounds
of every kind. There is not a stone there that lacks healing
properties."

Accordingly, after the Britons who were present had   4
heard this, they were encouraged to send for the stones.
Utherpendragon, the brother of the king, was chosen for
this work, although he willingly volunteered himself in order to see the kingdom and people of Ireland. Merlin himself was also chosen, so that what had to be done could be
managed with his talent and assistance. Once the ships were
ready, they went to Ireland with fifteen thousand soldiers,
and with favorable winds they landed on the shore.

[130] At that time King Gillomanius was ruling in Ireland. When he heard the Britons had landed in his country,
he assembled his army and proceeded against them. And after he learned the reason for their arrival, he laughed and
said to those standing around him: "It is no wonder the Sax-   2
ons were able to slaughter the cowardly race of Britons,

cum Britones bruti sint et fatui. Quis enim fatuitatem eorum satis ammirari posset? Numquid meliora sunt saxa Hiberniae quam Britanniae ad quodlibet opus? Armate vos,
viri, et defendite patriam vestram ab ignavis et brutis anima-
libus, quia dum vita mihi inerit non auferent etiam minimum lapillum Choreae."

3   Uther igitur ut vidit illos ad proeliandum venire paratos,
agmen suorum dirigit in illos. Nec mora, praevaluerunt
Britones Hiberniensibusque laceratis atque devictis regem
suum Gillomanium in fugam coegerunt. Potiti victoria Kil-
laraum montem adeunt duce Merlino lapidumque structuram secundum quod coniector eorum Merlinus edixerat
reperiunt. Circumstantibus itaque cunctis, ait Merlinus:
4   "Utimini viribus vestris quantum potestis et videamus si lapides istos integros deponere valueritis."

Quod cum fecissent, nullo modo potuerunt saxa movere
vel minimum lapillum excidere. Deficientibus igitur cunctis, solutus in risum Merlinus ait: "Ut sciatis animi ingenium
praevalere fortitudini corporis, ecce lapidum haec structura,
quae vestris viribus non cessit, levius quam credi potest nostris iam machinationibus deponetur."

5   Et paulisper insusurrans motu labiorum tamquam ad orationem praecepit ut adhiberent manus et asportarent quo
vellent. Depositis itaque mox lapidibus ad naves leviter de-
latos intus locaverunt et sic cum gaudio et admiratione in
Britanniam revertuntur. Rex autem Aurelius eorum congratulans reditui, ex diversis regni sui partibus iussit clerum et

since the Britons are idiots and fools. Indeed, who could be sufficiently amazed at their stupidity? Surely it cannot be that Irish stones are better than British ones for any kind of work? Arm yourselves, men, and defend our country against these cowardly and brutish animals, for while there is any life in me they shall not carry away the smallest little stone from the ring."

When Uther saw them come prepared for battle, he directed his army against them. Without delay, the Britons prevailed and, with the Irish cut to pieces and defeated, the Britons forced their king Gillomanius to flee. Having achieved victory, the Britons were led by Merlin to Mount Killaraus and found the stone structure just as their soothsayer Merlin had declared. With everyone standing around the ring, Merlin said: "Use your strength as much as you can, and we will see if you are powerful enough to pull those stones down in one piece." 3

4

When they did this, they were not able to move the rocks in any way or to bring down the smallest little stone. After they were all defeated, therefore, Merlin dissolved in laughter and said: "So that you will understand that native ability of the spirit prevails over strength of the body, watch how this structure of stones, which did not yield to your strength, will now be brought down by our machinations more easily than you can imagine."

And whispering for a moment, moving his lips as if in prayer, he told them to use their hands and carry the stones where they wished. After the stones were soon pulled down and easily carried to the ships, they loaded them aboard and thus returned to Britain with joy and wonder. Indeed, King Aurelius, congratulating them on their return, ordered the 5

populum convenire, ut tantorum virorum celebrationem
6   honore summo perficeret. Ad edictum ergo eius conveniunt
pontifices et clerus populusque innumerabilis in monte
Ambrii. Et die Pentecostes rex, imposito capiti diademate,
festum regaliter tribus diebus ibidem celebravit functique
epulis cum gaudio et exultatione hymnorum omnes affue-
runt. Quarta autem die honores ecclesiasticos qui personis
carebant secundum auctoritatem canonicam distribuit.
Eboracensi ecclesiae, quae pastore carebat, Samsonem, il-
7   lustrem et religiosum virum, metropolitanum praefecit. Urbem vero Legionum et eius ecclesiam Dubricio nihilominus
prudenti viro, decoravit. Statutisque regni legibus atque
omnibus quae in tanta celebratione constituenda erant patratis compositis lapidibus a Merlino in sepulturam et circa
Choream, sicut in Hibernia prius fuerant, dimissa contione
omnes cum laetitia redierunt ad propria.

[131] Eodem tempore Pascentius, Vortigerni filius, qui in
Germaniam diffugerat, congregato undecumque exercitu
navigioque comparato applicuit in aquilonaribus Britanniae
partibus atque eas vastare coepit. Sed rex Aurelius, ut audivit, collecto exercitu ei obviam venit et commissa pugna devictus Pascentius fugit.

[132] Nec ultra ausus est redire in Germaniam, sed cum
paucis ad Gillomanium Hiberniae regem se contulit. Et cum
infortunium suum ei notificasset, miseratus Gillomanius
promisit se laturum auxilium, conquerens de iniuria Britonum, qui nuper Choream Gigantum de Hibernia asportave-
rant. Foedere itaque inter se facto, naves ingrediuntur cum

clergy and the people to assemble from various parts of his kingdom, to complete the celebration of such men with the highest honor. In response to his edict, therefore, innumer- 6 able bishops and clerics and people gathered at Mount Ambrius. And there on the day of Pentecost the king, having placed the crown on his head, celebrated a royal feast for three days and, after the banquets were performed, they all joined in hymns with joy and exultation. On the fourth day, according to canon law, he distributed the ecclesiastical honors that were vacant. For the church of York, which lacked a pastor, he made Samson the archbishop, a famous and religious man. He honored Caerleon and its church 7 with Dubricius, a no less worthy man. And after the laws of the realm were established and everything that had to be ordained in such a celebration was accomplished, and the stones were arranged at the grave and around the ring by Merlin just as they had been before in Ireland, the assembly was dismissed and everyone returned to their own homes with joy.

[131] At the same time Pascent, the son of Vortigern, who had fled to Germany, with an army assembled from every direction and his ships fully prepared, landed in the northern parts of Britain and began to lay waste to them. But when King Aurelius heard this, he gathered his army and attacked them. After the battle was fought, Pascent fled in defeat.

[132] He did not dare return to Germany again, but with a few men he took himself to King Gillomanius of Ireland. And after he had acquainted him with his misfortune, Gillomanius felt sorry for him and promised to bring help, while complaining about the offense of the Britons, who had recently carried the Giants' Ring away from Ireland. And so they made an alliance, boarded ships with their army,

2 suo exercitu et ad Meneviam urbem applicuerunt. Interea
rex Aurelius Wintoniae infirmatus lecto decubuit. Qui audiens Pascentium et Hibernienses applicuisse, misit Uther,
fratrem suum, cum exercitu valido in Kambriam contra illos
ut de regno suo disturbaret. Et dum iter faceret, exercitum
congregando moram fecit in itinere quod longum erat et
3 valde laboriosum. Accedens interim unus ex Saxonibus, nomine Eappa, qui linguam Britonum edidicerat, ad Pascentium ait se regem Aurelium cito perempturum si sibi daren-
tur argenti mille librae. Pactus est ei Pascentius quod
petebat et amplius si regni diadema per eum adquireret. Ille,
promissis ditatus, iter versus Wintoniam arripuit, ubi regem
4 Aurelium infirmatum audierat esse. Obiter minister fraudis
se dolo armavit, nam veste monachi se induit atque corona
capud falso coronavit sicque Wintoniam veniens, ad thalamum regis accessit et se medicum finxit. Quo intromisso
promisit statim, infra breve tempus, regi salutem si sibi se
committere vellet. Omnes qui aderant congratulati sunt et
magnam ei pecuniae mercedem promiserunt, si dictis facta
5 compensaret. Nec mora, potionem temperans venenatam
regi bibendam porrexit. Qua hausta iussus est a nequissimo
ambrone sabanis cooperiri et obdormire. Paruit ille atque
obdormivit, sperans salutem optatam consequi posse. At
priusquam nox incumberet, veneno intra viscera grassante
periit. Medicus autem dolosus ab oculis omnium lapsus evasit atque per fugam vitae reservatur.

and landed at the city of St. David's. Meanwhile, King Aure- 2
lius lay sick in bed at Winchester. Hearing that Pascent and
the Irish had landed, he sent his brother Uther with a strong
army to Wales against them, in order to dislodge them from
his kingdom. But when he set out to assemble his army,
he encountered a delay along his route, which was long and
very laborious. Meanwhile, one of the Saxons by the name 3
of Eappa, who had learned the language of the Britons, approached Pascent and said that he would quickly kill King
Aurelius if a thousand pounds of silver were given to him.
Pascent promised him what he asked for, and more if he
were to acquire the crown of the kingdom through him. After those promises were given, Eappa set out for Winchester,
where he had heard that Aurelius was lying ill. On the way 4
this agent of deceit equipped himself for treachery; for having clothed himself in the habit of a monk and crowned his
head with a false tonsure just as he was coming to Winchester, he approached the king's bedchamber and disguised
himself as a doctor. When he was ushered in, he immediately promised to restore the king's health in a short time if
the king would put himself in his hands. All who were present rejoiced, and they promised him a large reward of money
if that would pay for doing what he said. Without delay, mix- 5
ing a poisonous potion, he held it out to for the king to
drink. After the king swallowed it, the most wicked thug ordered him to cover himself with sheets and go to sleep. He
obeyed him and went to sleep hoping that the good health
he wanted would follow. But before night fell he died from
the poison flowing through his veins. The deceitful doctor,
however, dropped out of everyone's sight, sneaked away, and
by fleeing his life was spared.

[133] Haec dum Wintoniae agerentur, apparuit stella mirae magnitudinis et claritatis, quam cometam dicunt, uno contenta radio. A radio vero procedebat globus igneus in similitudinem draconis extensus, de cuius ore procedebant duo radii, quorum unus radiorum longitudinem ultra Gallicana regna videbatur extendere, alter vero versus Hibernicum mare vergens, in septem minores radios terminabatur.

2 Apparente itaque tali sidere, perculsi sunt omnes metu et admiratione qui viderunt. Uther igitur convocans Merlinum ad radium stellae interrogat vatem quid portendat tale signum. Mox ille, in fletum erumpens, spiritu coepit deficere prae dolore cordis. Reversus postea in se exclamavit et dicit:

3 "O damnum irrecuperabile! O populum orbatum Britanniae, defuncto Aurelio nobilissimo rege!"

Uther audiens fratris mortem tristis factus est valde et flevit amare. Merlinus autem dolorem eius delinire cupiens prosecutus ait: "Festina, dux nobilissime, festina hostes praesentes devincere; nam tibi debetur dominium totius

4 Britanniae. Victoria de his tibi parata est et multas tibi post hos subdes nationes. Te etenim sidus istud signat et igneus draco sub sidere. Radius autem qui versus Gallicanam plagam porrigitur filium tibi futurum portendit potentissimum, cuius potestas usque ad montes Alpium protendetur. Alter vero radius filiam designat nascituram, cuius filii et nepotes regnum Britanniae succedenter habebunt."

[134] Uther igitur nocte illa in castris quiescens, aurora illucescente exercitum legionibus ordinatis in hostes producit. Illi econtra copias suas obviam educunt atque invicem

[133] While this was being done at Winchester, a star of marvelous size and brightness appeared, which they call a comet, with one ray stretched out. A lengthy globe of fire extended from the ray in the likeness of a dragon, from whose mouth extended two rays, one of which seemed to extend beyond the length of the Gallic realm while the other, sloping down toward the Irish sea, ended in seven smaller rays. At the appearance of such a star, all who saw it 2 were struck with fear and wonder. Then Uther summoned Merlin and questioned the prophet about the ray of the star and what this sign portended. Merlin grew sick at heart and soon burst into tears. After that, returning to his senses, he exclaimed and said: "O the irreparable loss! O the bereaved 3 people of Britain, now that the most noble King Aurelius dead!"

Hearing of his brother's death, Uther became very sad and wept bitterly. Merlin, however, wishing to lessen his pain, followed him and said: "Make haste, most noble duke, make haste to defeat the enemies at hand; for the dominion of all Britain is destined to be yours. Victory over these men 4 awaits you, and you shall subdue many nations after that. Indeed that star, and the fiery dragon beneath the star, signifies you. The ray that extends across the Gallic sea, however, portends your most powerful future son, whose power shall reach as far as the mountains of the Alps. The other ray indicates your unborn daughter, whose sons and nephews will subsequently hold the kingdom of Britain."

[134] Therefore, after resting that night in his camp, when dawn began to break Uther led his army forth arranged in legions against the enemy. The enemy, on the other hand, drew their troops up in opposition, and both

congrediuntur. Gladiis extractis comminus res agitur consertoque proelio Uther, interfectis Gillomanio et Pascentio, triumpho potitur ut veritas coniectoris probaretur. Fugientibus igitur barbaris ad naves magna de eis strages antequam ad naves pervenirent a Britonibus facta est et innumeri trucidati sunt. Dux itaque victor retro iter agens, obvios habuit nuntios qui fratris casum indicaverunt ipsumque iam ab episcopis sepultum, iuxta coenobium Ambrii in Chorea Gigantum, cum ceteris terrae ducibus qui ibidem, sicut dictum est, sepulti fuerant. Ita enim rex, vivens adhuc, se sepeliri iusserat.

[135] Veniens ergo Uther Wintoniam, convocato clero et populo, omnibus expetentibus et acclamantibus illum regem fieri, suscepit diadema regni Britanniae et in regem sublimatus est. Reminiscens autem interpretationis Merlini quam de sidere fecerat, iussit fabricari duos dracones ex auro purissimo et unum in ecclesia episcopali Wintoniae obtulit, alterum sibi ad ferendum in proelia retinuit. Ab illo ergo tempore ipse appellatus est Utherpendragon, hoc est Britannice "capud draconis," sicut Merlinus eum per draconem in regem prophetaverat.

[136] Interea Octa filius Hengisti et Eosa cognatus suus, cum soluti essent a foedere quod Aurelio pepigerant, moliti sunt inquietudinem toti regno Britanniae inferre, associantes sibi Saxones quos Pascentius secum adduxerat, nuntiosque suos in Germaniam mittunt ut sibi auxilia invitarent.

armies met each other in battle. With swords drawn, the battle was conducted hand to hand, and having joined the fight Uther, once Gillomanius and Pascent were killed, obtained the triumph so that the accuracy of the soothsayer was proved. As the barbarians were fleeing toward their ships, a great slaughter of them was made by the Britons before they could reach their ships and countless were butchered. While the victorious duke was making his way back, he was met by messengers who told him about his brother's death and his burial by the bishops in the Giants' Ring next to the monastery of Ambrius with the rest of the leaders of the land who, as said before, had been buried in the same place. For while the king was still alive he had ordered that he should be buried there.

[135] Coming then to Winchester, after the clergy and the people were called together, with everyone demanding and acclaiming him to be made king, Uther received the crown of the kingdom of Britain and was raised up as king. Recalling, however, Merlin's interpretation of the star, he ordered two dragons to be made from the purest gold, and he presented one to the cathedral church of Winchester, while he kept the other for himself to be carried in battles. From that time on he was called Utherpendragon, which is "head of the dragon" in British, since Merlin had prophesied by means of the dragon that he would be king.

[136] Meanwhile Octa the son of Hengist and Eosa his kinsman, since they were freed from the treaty they had agreed to with Aurelius, labored to bring unrest to the whole kingdom of Britain, associating themselves with the Saxons whom Pascent had led, and they sent their messengers to Germany to summon help for themselves. Accompanied by

Maxima itaque multitudine stipati, omnes provincias ab Albania usque Eboracum occupant, ipsamque urbem Eboracum obsidione vallant. Superveniens autem rex Uther cum exercitu grandi obsidioni, congrediuntur Britones Saxonibus, quibus viriliter primo impetu restiterunt Saxones atque eorum irruptiones tolerantes tandem illos in fugam propulerunt. Saxones autem insecuti sunt eos cedentes usque ad montem Damen dum sol diem stare permitteret. Erat autem mons ille arduus in cacumine, coryletum habens circa radicem, in cacumine saxa praerupta, latebris ferarum habilia. Ascendentes vero montem Britones pro castris se munierunt in coryletis et rupibus et nocte ibidem quieverunt. A media autem nocte excitati convenerunt simul, ut consilium caperent qualiter hostes invaderent. Commiserunt igitur omnes Gorloi, duci Cornubiae, sententiam tractandam, qui et ipse consilii magni erat atque aetatis mature.

4   "Non est opus," inquit, "ambagibus vanis aut magnis circumlocutionibus. Dum adhuc noctis umbra involvimur, utendum est nobis audacia et fortitudine: necessitas haec belli non habet legem ut turmis dispositis et aciebus pugnemus. Quoquo modo liberemus animas nostras et precemur Deum omnipotentem, quem forte peccando offendimus, ut liberet nos ab imminentibus adversariis qui et ipsi inimici sunt Dei vivi, idolorum cultores. Confitentes itaque peccata nostra et emendationem promittentes, descendamus quiete et sine strepitu armorum ad eos et circumveniamus illos inopinate nihil tale de nobis timentes. Fugatis enim nobis et velut obsessis securiores dormiunt, exspectantes ut in luce

a vast multitude, they occupied all the provinces from Albany to York, and they surrounded that same city of York
with a blockade. King Uther arrived at the blockade with a   2
great army, and the Britons came against the Saxons, but the
Saxons boldly resisted their first attack and, tolerating their
continued assaults, finally drove them away. Moreover, while
daylight remained the Saxons pursued them as they retreated, all the way to Mount Damen. That mountain was
steep at its summit, with a hazel thicket around its base, and
jagged stones at the summit suitable as a refuge for wild
beasts. Ascending the mountain, for their camp the Britons   3
fortified themselves among the hazels and the rocks, and
they rested in that place for the night. However, being awakened in the middle of the night, they gathered together to
consider how they could attack the enemy. Then they all entrusted the decision to Gorlois, the Duke of Cornwall, who
was full of great judgment and mature in years.

"There is no need," he began, "for empty equivocation or   4
great circumlocution. While we are still wrapped in the
shadow of night, we must use boldness and courage: in this
battle necessity has no law that requires us to fight with our
troops and battle lines in formation. In this manner we may
free our spirits and we should pray to God almighty, whom
we perhaps offend by sinning, to free us from our threatening adversaries, who themselves are enemies of the living
God, and worshipers of idols. Therefore, confessing our sins   5
and promising amends, let us descend upon them quietly
and without the noise of arms, and encircle them unexpectedly while they are fearing no such thing from us. For they
sleep more securely with us put to flight and apparently besieged, expecting that they will capture us in daylight.

nos comprehendant. Paretur ergo unusquisque nostrum ocius et si qua sarcina est hic dimittatur ut postpositis omnibus tantum pro vita et libertate solliciti simus. Iam si fortiter egerimus, victoria in manibus nostris sita est; nam si Deus pro nobis, quis contra nos?"

6   Placuit regi simulque Christianis omnibus qui aderant consilium Gorlois et unanimiter se invicem cohortantes, invadunt hostes somno oppressos, feriunt praecordialiter, obtruncant, vulnerant et illidunt et tamquam leones in armenta saeviunt et fugam hesternam vindicant. Hostes vero attoniti nec arma capessere neque de loco cedere aliquo
7   pacto poterant. Sic Britones cedentes omni nisu instabant. Quotquot evasere periculum fugiendo noctis beneficio computaverunt. Captivi retenti sunt Octa et Eosa duces eorum et Saxones per virtutem Christi penitus dissipati.

[137] Post hanc victoriam animatus rex ulterius progressus est versus Scotiam venitque ad urbem Aldclud illique provinciae disposuit et pacem ubique renovavit. Circuivit etiam omnem Scotorum regionem rebellemque populum a sua feritate deposuit, tantam ubique iustitiam cum terrore et moderatione agens quantam alter ante se nemo fecerat. Denique, pacificatis omnibus, Londoniam reversus est Octa et Eosa prae se in vinculis mancipatis, quos in carcerem trudi praecepit donec adiudicaret quod supplicium de eis
2   sumeret. Festo igitur paschali superveniente ibidem rex suscepto diademate cum magno sumptuum apparatu sicut

Therefore each of us should quickly be prepared and whatever is a burden should be abandoned so that, with everything left behind, we will be concerned only about life and liberty. If we act courageously now, victory shall be in our hands; for if God is with us, who shall be against us?"

Gorlois's advice pleased the king, and likewise all the 6 Christians who were present, and exhorting each other as one they attacked the enemy as they lay asleep; they struck them heartily, cut down, wounded, and crushed them and, just like lions among a herd of cattle, they ravaged them and avenged the previous day's rout. The enemy being astonished, they could neither take up their arms nor escape from that place by any other means. Thus the Britons, striking 7 with all their power, pressed hard. However many escaped counted on the benefit of darkness to flee from danger. Their leaders Octa and Eosa were taken as captives and the Saxons, through the power of Jesus Christ, were thoroughly scattered.

[137] Refreshed after this victory, the king marched further toward Scotland, and when he came to the city of Dumbarton he arranged the affairs of that province and restored peace everywhere. He went around through the whole region of the Scots and put down the ferociousness of the rebellious people, dispensing a type of justice everywhere with fear and moderation as no one had done before him. Then, with everyone pacified, he returned to London with Octa and Eosa bound in chains before him, and he ordered them to be thrown in prison until he could decide what punishment to select for them. The feast of Easter arriving at that very time, the king put on his crown and with a great supply of food, as was fitting, after all the nobles of the 2

decebat, diem Paschae accitis omnibus regni proceribus cum suis uxoribus et familiis celebravit. Suscepit eos rex cum summo honore et epulati sunt cum gaudio magno et exsultatione regi congratulantes quod cum tanto honore eos invitasset. Sed quia in conviviis taetra solet esse libido insidiatrix et inimica laetitiae, nequaquam praeterire voluit

3 hostis humani generis quin huic interesset convivio. Aderat namque inter ceteras Gorlois ducis Cornubiae uxor, nomine Igerna, cuius pulchritudo omnes Britanniae mulieres superabat. Quam cum ex adverso respexisset rex, tamquam David in Bethsabee, subito Satana mediante incaluit et postpositis omnibus curam amoris sui totam in eam vertit atque fercula multimoda sibi gratulando dirigebat. Aurea quoque pocula familiaribus internuntiis cum salutationibus iocundis, sicut assolet inter amantes fieri, quandoque clam,

4 quandoque palam mittebat. Quod cum marito compertum esset—quis enim ignem celare potest, praesertim flamma estuante?—statim de curia absque regis licentia iratus abscedens, Cornubiam petit atque uxorem a conspectibus regis subtraxit, quam super omnia diligebat Gorlois. Iratus itaque rex misit post eum, praecipiens redire ut de illata iniuria sibi satisfaceret. Ille vero renuens iter suum peregit quo tende

5 bat. Indignatus itaque rex iureiurando asseruit se in illum omni nisu animadversurum et in omnem terram suam nisi ad praestitutam diem rediret et satisfaceret de iniuria et constituit diem. Transacto igitur die, collecto exercitu insecutus est iniurias ducis sui atque Cornubiam ferro ac

realm were summoned with their wives and families, he celebrated Easter day. The king received them with the highest honor and they feasted with great joy and exultation, rejoicing in a king who entertained them with such honor. But because foul lust, the ambusher and enemy of happiness, is always present at feasts, the enemy of mankind was in no way willing to pass up the chance to attend at this feast. For 3 there was present among the rest the wife of Duke Gorlois of Cornwall, named Igerna, whose beauty surpassed all the women of Britain. When the king gazed at her across from him, like David with Bathsheba, with Satan acting as the go-between, he was suddenly inflamed and, ignoring everyone else, turned all the attention of his love at her and, congratulating himself, he directed all manner of dishes to her. He also sent golden cups with his servants acting as messengers with friendly greetings, as often done between lovers, sometimes in secret, sometimes openly. When her husband became aware of this—for who can conceal a fire, especially 4 when the flame of love is burning?—departing immediately from the court without the king's leave, he made for Cornwall and carried his wife, whom Gorlois loved above all, away from the attentions of the king. Then the king was angry and sent after him, ordering him to come back and make amends to him for the insult that was inflicted. Refusing, however, Gorlois pressed on to where he was going. Indignant, therefore, the king swore an oath to use all his strength 5 to punish him and his entire land unless he came back on a prescribed date and made amends for the insult, and the king established the date. When that day had passed, he assembled his army, followed up against the insults of the duke, and rushed to waste Cornwall with sword and fire.

6 flammis vastare contendit. At Gorlois nullam habens copiam resistendi, castrum quoddam munivit ubi se cum
valida manu suorum inclusit et uxorem, pro qua magis time-
bat, in oppido Tintagol super litus maris sito et undique
vallibus praeruptis ac mari circumsepto cum custodibus re-
clusit. Adveniens igitur rex castro quo erat Gorlois, undique
obsedit eum ita ut a nulla parte posset ei provenire auxilium.

7 Considerat namque Gorlois ut ab Hibernia, si necesse foret,
subsidium haberet sicut per legatos suos quos illuc direxerat
rex ille pepigerat. Cumque per hebdomadam unam iam ob-
sidio durasset, rex Uther de amore Igernae pro qua totum
certamen erat reminiscens vocavit ad se quendam fidelem et
sibi familiarem, Ulfin nomine de Ridcaradoch, et revelavit

8 ei affectum et amorem suum, dicens: "Uror nimis amore
Igernae uxoris huius ducis quem obsedimus nec corporis
mei aut vitae periculum evadere existimo, nisi ea potitus
fuero. Tu igitur adhibe diligentiam, sicut me amas, ut ea
fruar aut scias me diu sustinere non posse quin mortis periculum incurram."

Ad haec Ulfin: "Nemo, mi domine, tibi melius consilium
dare valet ex omnibus qui terram tuam incolunt quam Merlinus vates, qui si operam dederit, poteris compos esse desi-
derii tui."

9 Credulus ille iussit Merlinum ad se venire: nam et ipse
cum ceteris ad obsidionem venerat. Et expositis angustia-
rum causis mox regem alacriorem reddidit, inquiens: "Ut
potiaris, rex, desiderio tuo necesse est novis artibus uti.

But Gorlois, lacking the resources to resist, fortified a cer- 6
tain castle where he enclosed himself with a strong band of
his men, and he shut his wife, for whom he was more afraid,
with guardians in the fortress of Tintagel, situated on the
coast and enclosed by steep ramparts on every side and also
surrounded by the sea. Coming to the castle where Gorlois
was, the king besieged him on all sides so that help could
not come to him from any direction. And so Gorlois thought 7
that if it became necessary he would get support from Ireland, because that king had agreed to provide it through the
ambassadors whom Gorlois had directed there. And when
the siege had already lasted for one week, King Uther, recalling the love of Igerna that was the cause of the whole dispute, called to himself a certain retainer and member of his
household named Ulfin of Ridcaradoch, and told him all
about his passion and his love, saying: "I burn too much with 8
love for Igerna, the wife of this duke whom we have besieged, and I do not think I can escape the danger to my
body or my life unless I obtain her. If you love me, then apply diligence so that I can enjoy her, or you should know
that I cannot hold myself back any longer without running
the risk of death."

To which Ulfin replied: "No one, my lord, can give you
better advice out of all who inhabit your land than the
prophet Merlin; if you will give him this job, you will be able
to have what you desire."

Believing this, the king ordered Merlin to come to him: 9
for Merlin had come to the siege with the others. And after
the reason for the king's difficulties was explained, Merlin
quickly revived his spirits, saying: "In order to obtain what
you desire, my king, it is necessary to use unusual skills. For

Nam castrum quo Igerna quam diligis retinetur adeo fortis munimenti est loci situ ut nullus introitus pateat alter quam angusta rupes, quae a tribus armatis prohiberi potest toti exercitui tuo. Verum quia in hac necessitate meum quaeris consilium et auxilium, studebo quantum potero ut arte mea
10 voluntatem tuam expleas. Novi medicaminibus meis mutare hominum figuras, ita ut per omnia is videatur similis eius cuius formam arte magica impressero. Si ergo parere vis, actibus meis faciam te per omnia similem Gorlois ut nihil differas ab eo vel facie vel incessu, eroque tecum quasi unus ex famulis Gorlois transmutatus; Ulfin quoque in Iordanum familiarem illius transformabo sicque tuto poteris adire oppidum Tintagol atque aditum habere."

11   Paruit itaque rex dictis et actibus Merlini commissaque familiaribus suis obsidione, crepusculo ingressus est castrum Tintagol tamquam esset Gorlois receptusque gratanter ab Igerna, post oscula desiderata collocatus est una in cubili atque desiderio suo satisfecit. Concepit eadem nocte Igerna celeberimum illum Arturum, qui postquam adultus est probitate sua toto orbe enituit.

    [138] Interea dum compertum esset in obsidione regem abesse, exercitus inconsulte agens oppidum adit, muros invadit et machinas muro apponere aggreditur. Dux obsessus videns se suosque nimis interius artari atque grandinem telorum desuper iactari, provocatus ad bellum, agmine ordi-
2 nato exivit et se hostibus parva manu inseruit. Qui mox

the castle in which Igerna, whom you love, is shut up, is so strongly fortified by its situation that no entrance lies open besides a narrow cliff, which could be denied to your entire army by three armed men. Truly because you ask for my advice and help in this difficulty, I will be as diligent as I can so that you achieve your wish by my art. I know how to change 10 a man's shape with my drugs in such a way that he appears similar in every way to him whose form I impose by the magical art. Therefore if you wish to appear so, through my actions I will make you similar in every way to Gorlois, so that you differ in nothing from him, either in your appearance or in your walk, and I will be with you, transformed as one of Gorlois's servants; Ulfin I will also transform into Jordanus, a member of his household, and thus you will be able to go safely to Tintagel Castle and gain entrance."

And so the king agreed with Merlin's words and actions 11 and, after he turned the siege over to his companions, he entered Tintagel Castle at dusk as if he were Gorlois and he was joyfully received by Igerna; after longed-for kisses he lay down in the marriage bed and satisfied his desire. The same night Igerna conceived that celebrated Arthur who, after he grew to manhood, shone throughout the whole world for his goodness.

[138] Meanwhile, when it was realized that the king was absent from the siege, acting rashly, the army went to the fort, attacked the walls, and siege engines were brought up to set before the wall. The besieged duke, seeing that he and his men were packed too closely inside and that a hail of spears was being thrown from above, was provoked to battle, and after arranging his troops he went out himself and engaged the enemy with a few of his men. He was soon 2

hostili multitudine circumventus, confossus cecidit et pars quaedam suorum secum, pars autem dissipata in fugam se dedit. Capto itaque oppido festinaverunt nuntii ad Igernam, qui et necem ducis et obsidionis eventum indicarent. Sed cum regem in specie Gorlois iuxta illam sedere vidissent, erubescentes admirabantur ipsum, quem in obsidione interfectum didicerant ita incolumem praevenisse. Uther autem rex tales deridens rumigerulos tamquam mendaces dicebat:

3 "Non equidem me ut mortuum dolere debetis, sed vivum, sicut nunc cernitis, congaudete, neque enim omni rumori credendum est. Doleo tamen oppidi mei captionem et meorum interfectionem: unde timendum est ne superveniat rex et nos inopinatos hic intercipiat. Ibo igitur obviam ei et pacificabo me si potero cum ipso, ne deterius quid contingat."

4 Amplexans itaque Igernam atque deosculans deliniensque egressus venit ad exercitum, exuta specie et forma Gorlois quam susceperat. Cumque rei eventum didicisset, de morte ducis sui subtristem se simulans, de Igerna a maritali copula soluta non modicum gaudens, reversus ad oppidum Tintagol, coepit illud et Igernam simul votoque suo potitus est. Nuptiis igitur legitime atque magnifice celebratis, commanserunt pariter rex et regina Igerna. Partusque tempore genuit illum Arturum famosum. Deinde concipiens peperit filiam nomine Annam.

surrounded by the hostile multitude, and he fell pierced with holes. Part of his men fell with him, but another part scattered and took flight. After the castle was taken, messengers hastened to Igerna and related both the death of the duke and the outcome of the siege. But when they saw the king in the guise of Gorlois sitting next to her, blushing, they were astonished to come upon him thus unharmed who they had said was killed in the siege. King Uther, however, mocking such rumormongers as if they were liars, said: "Certainly you must not grieve for me as dead, but rejoice 3 that I am alive, as you now can see; indeed not all rumors are to be believed. I grieve, nevertheless, for the capture of my castle and the killing of my men, because of which we must take care that the king does not arrive and catch us here when we least expect it. Therefore I will go to meet him and make peace with him if I can, so that something worse does not happen."

And so, embracing Igerna and also kissing her warmly 4 and soothing her, he departed and went to the army, putting aside the appearance and form of Gorlois that he had assumed. And when he had learned about the outcome of things, pretending to be saddened by the death of his duke, but rejoicing not a little about Igerna's release from her marital bond, he returned to Tintagel Castle, captured it and Igerna at the same time, and his desire was fulfilled. After their nuptials were lawfully and splendidly celebrated, the king and Queen Igerna lived together side by side. And at the time for her delivery she gave birth to that famous Arthur. Afterward, she conceived and brought forth a daughter, named Anna.

[139] Cumque dies multi et tempora praeterissent, occupavit infirmitas regem eumque pluribus diebus vexavit. Interim custodes carceris qui Octam et Eosam reclusos servabant, taedio affecti atque promissionibus illorum illecti in Germaniam cum eis diffugium fecerunt. Deinde minis et

2 terroribus totam Britanniam perculerunt. Venientes itaque in terram suam classem paraverunt non modicam atque cum magna armatorum manu redierunt quantocius in Albaniam ingressique regionem, ferro ac flammis vastabant terram.

3 Eligitur itaque dux Leil nomine de Lodonesia, cui rex Annam, filiam suam, locaverat nuptiali thalamo, eique committitur exercitus Britonum contra hostes deducendus regnique curam suscepit dum rex infirmitate teneretur. Hic in hostes progressus saepe ab eis repulsus, saepe superior factus ad naves usque diffugere coegit.

[140] Fuitque inter eos diu anceps bellum donec rex Uther, audita suorum segnitia, ipse feretro impositus, se ad exercitum deportari fecit.

[141] Perductus itaque Verolamium ad urbem, in qua Saxones se receperant propter eius adventum quem timebant, obsedit urbem et moenia cum machinis diruere coepit. Quod cum vidissent Saxones et se viliter inclusos sensissent, egredientes diluculo de civitate ad campestre proelium Bri-

2 tones provocaverunt. Nec mora, devictis Saxonibus, cessit victoria Britonibus et Octa et Eosa ibidem obtruncantur. Unde in tantam laetitiam rex Uther emersit ut feretro

[139] And when many days and seasons had passed, weakness overcame the king and plagued him for many days. Meanwhile the guards of the prison who kept Octa and Eosa shut up grew weary and, being enticed by their alluring promises, fled with them to Germany. Afterward they upset all of Britain with threats and alarms. Coming to their own 2 land, they prepared a large fleet and with a great band of armed men they returned as quickly as possible to Albany and after they invaded the region they devastated the land with sword and flames. Accordingly a duke named Leil of 3 Lothian was chosen, to whom the king had married his daughter Anna, and to him was entrusted the army of the Britons to be led against the enemy, and he took over the management of the kingdom while the king was overcome by weakness. After he advanced against the enemy, often they pushed him back while often he prevailed and forced them to flee all the way to their ships.

[140] For a long time the war between them was undecided, until King Uther, having learned of their weakness, placed himself in a wagon and had himself carried to the army.

[141] After he was conducted to the city of St. Albans, in which the Saxons had hidden themselves because they feared him and his approach, he besieged the city and began to demolish the fortifications with machines. When the Saxons saw this and realized they were poorly protected, marching forth at dawn from the city to the open field they challenged the Britons to battle. Without delay the Saxons 2 were defeated, victory fell to the Britons, and at the same time Octa and Eosa were killed. Thereupon King Uther arose with such joy that, jumping from the wagon, not

prosiliens nil sibi doloris de infirmitate contestans, in risum
solutus tamquam sanus ac validus factus, suos exhilarabat
atque insequi Saxones fugientes accelerabat, nisi hoc sui dis-
suasissent ne eum infirmitas gravior occuparet.

[142] Dimisso ergo exercitu ipse remansit cum paucis Verolamium, indulgens quieti et corporis refectioni. Sed nec
devicti et fugati Saxones ab iniquitate et malitia sua cessaverunt. Quod enim armis et iure belli exercere non poterant,
hoc veneficiis et proditione pessima agere machinati sunt.
2 Mittunt ergo in paupere cultu quosdam maleficos Verolamium qui, cum didicissent regem adhuc aegrotare nec perfecte convaluisse, explorantes aditum quo ad ipsum pertin-
gerent interficiendum, non invenientes deliberaverunt apud
se ut quoquo modo illum veneno extinguerent. Et cum mo-
rati essent ibidem aliquamdiu, didicerunt quia de fonte niti-
dissimo, qui prope aulam fluebat, solitus esset rex cottidie
3 potare. Quo comperto, inficiunt fontem veneno et abeuntes
rei eventum expectabant. Ut autem gustavit rex aquam,
festine mortuus est ut veritas Merlini coniectoris et eius
vaticinium compleretur. Multi etiam de fonte illo potantes
perierunt, donec comperta malitia cumulum terrae superap-
posuerunt. Delatum est autem corpus regis ad coenobium
Ambrii et ibi traditum sepulturae iuxta Aurelium fratrem
suum et infra Choream Gigantum.

Liber IX

[143] Convenientes igitur post mortem regis optimates totius terrae in civitatem Silcestriae, Dubricio Urbis Legionum archiepiscopo suggerente Arturum filium eius in regem sublimaverunt. Erat tunc Arturus quindecim annorum iuvenis, magnae virtutis et audaciae atque largitatis; unde populo ac principibus totius regni gratus et acceptus erat. Insignibus itaque regiis initiatus, mox Saxones invadere decrevit per quos et pater et patruus eius dolo perierant, per quos etiam tota terra turbata erat. Congregato igitur exercitu, Eboracum venit. Colgrinus autem, qui post Octam et Eosam Saxones regebat, ut audivit quia novus rex Britonum surrexerat, cum gravi multitudine Saxonum suorum et Scotorum et Pictorum obviam Arturo venit et iuxta flumen Duglas congressi utrorumque exercitus in magna parte cecidit, victoria tandem Britonibus favente et Colgrino dedecorose fugiente. Quem insequens Arturus festino pede infra Eboracum ingressum obsedit. Baldulfus, frater Colgrini, audita fratris fuga, cum sex milibus virorum Eboracum petit atque in spatio decem miliariorum ab urbe in nemore delituit, volens nocturnam et inopinatam irruptionem obsidioni inferre. Erat autem tunc ipse Baldulfus quando frater pugnaverat expectans adventum Cheldrici ducis Germanorum iuxta maritima; qui in auxilium eorum venturus erat.

Book 9

[143] Coming together in the city of Silchester after the death of the king, at the suggestion of Dubricius the archbishop of Caerleon the leading men of the whole kingdom raised up his son Arthur as king. Arthur was then fifteen years old, a youth of great strength and boldness and generosity; for that reason he was welcomed and accepted by the people and the leaders of the entire kingdom. After he was invested with the royal insignia, he soon decided to attack the Saxons, through whom both his father and his uncle had died by treachery, and through whom the whole land had been thrown into confusion. Therefore, after assembling his 2 army he went to York. But when Colgrin, who was ruling the Saxons after Octa and Eosa, heard that a new king of the Britons had arisen, he came against Arthur with a great multitude of his Saxons and Scots and Picts, and once they joined in battle next to the River Duglas, a large part of both their armies was struck down, with victory favoring the Britons in the end and Colgrin fleeing in disgrace. Following 3 swiftly on foot, Arthur besieged them after they entered York. When Baldulf, the brother of Colgrin, heard about his brother's retreat, he made for York with six thousand men and hid in the forest near the tenth milestone from the city, wanting to launch an unexpected nighttime assault against the siege. While his brother was fighting, Baldulf himself was by the coast, awaiting the arrival of Cheldric, Duke of the Germans, who was coming to their assistance.

4 At Arturus a metatoribus praemunitus quod in nemore de-
litescerent Saxones, misso Cadore duce Cornubiae cum
sescentis militibus et tribus milibus peditum, eadem nocte
supervenientes hostibus maiorem partem eorum interfecerunt et Baldulfum in fugam coegerunt. Qui cum suos amisis-
set et de auxilio quod fratri ferre speraverat se frustratum
vidisset, anxius quid faceret vel quomodo aut quo aditu ad
fratris colloquium pervenire posset, meditatus est apud se
quod habitum ioculatoris assumeret et capillis cum barba
semirasis in castra cantitando cum cithara coepit deambu-
5 lare et citharistam se finxit. Cumque nulli iam suspectus
esset, accessit paulatim ad murum civitatis et agnitum se
cum funibus infra trahi fecit et cum germano quod cupiebat
prolocutus est. Interea dum de egressione et fuga despe-
rarent—circumvallati enim undique obsidione fuerant—
rumor innotuit Cheldricum cum sescentis navibus in Albania applicuisse. Quod cum iam notum ac divulgatum per
omnes foret, suaserunt maiores natu in exercitu regi suo
obsidionem dimittere, ne tantae multitudini impares forte
resistere non praevalerent.

[144] Paruit igitur rex Arturus seniorum consilio et dimissa obsidione Londoniam adiit. Ibi convocato clero et
populo, qauerit consilium qualiter expugnare possit adve-
nientium multitudinem barbarorum. Communi tandem assensu cognatos suos Britones de Armorico tractu ad tantae
2 necessitatis auxilium ascire decreverunt. Erat autem tunc

But Arthur was forewarned by his advance men that the 4
Saxons were hidden in the forest, and Cador, Duke of Cornwall, was sent with six hundred knights and three thousand
foot soldiers, and coming upon the enemy that night they
killed the greater part of them and drove Baldulf into flight.
When he lost his men, and saw himself robbed of the help
that he was hoping to bring to his brother, Baldulf worried
about what he could do and in what way or by what approach he could come to talk with his brother. He thought
to himself that he would assume the costume of a jester and,
with half of his hair and beard shaved off, he began to walk
around the camp singing with a harp and pretended to be a
harper. Since he was still suspected by no one, he gradually 5
approached the wall of the city and, once he was recognized,
had himself pulled inside by a rope and talked with his
brother about what he wanted. Meanwhile, as they were giving up any hope of escape and flight—because they were
surrounded on every side by the siege—word came that
Cheldric had landed in Albany with six hundred ships.
When this became known and was revealed to them all, the
more senior men in the king's army recommended that he
abandon the siege in case it happened that, being unequal to
such a multitude, they should not have the superior strength
to oppose them.

[144] Accordingly, Arthur heeded the advice of his elders
and, after the siege was abandoned, he went to London.
There, once the clergy and the people were gathered, he
sought counsel about how he could overcome the multitude
of approaching barbarians. Finally, by common consent,
they decided to make an alliance with their kindred Britons
of the Armorican region for assistance in such need. At that 2

temporis Britonum illorum rex Hoelus, filius sororis Arturi,
ex Budicio rege Armoricanorum generatus. Unde audita necessitate fratrum navigium parant collectisque quindecim
milibus armatorum, proximo ventorum flatu ac prospero,
Hamonis Portum intrant. Excepti a rege Arturo, sicut decebat honorifice, [145] urbem Kaerliudcoit, quae Lindicolinia
nostra lingua dicitur, festinanter adeunt, quae ab hostibus
supra memoratis obsidebatur. Quo cum pervenissent, proelium ante urbem mox commissum est; in quo tanta caedes
Saxonum facta est quanta nec antea nec postea audita fuit.
Ceciderunt namque partim armis interfecti, partim fluminibus submersi fugientes relictaque obsidione omnes pariter
fugam arripiunt. Quos persequi non cessaverunt Britones
2 usque dum venirent in silvam Calidonis. Illuc ex fuga undique confluentes et suas cohortes reparantes silva tegente resistere Britonibus temptant. At Britones circumfusi, partem
silvae cedentes egressum eis ea parte prohibuerunt atque
tribus diebus ibidem obsidentes, fame coactos deditioni
coegerunt, conventione taliter facta ut relictis armis et sar-
cinis et omnibus quae habebant tantum cum vita et navibus
3 in terram suam redire sinerentur. Pacti sunt quoque se tributum omni anno de Germania daturos, obsides plures
transmittere, fide eorum mediante. Tunc rex Arturus,
sumpto festinanter consilio, petitioni eorum acquievit.

[146] Cumque illi iam in altum sulcarent aequora, re-
deuntes in se piguit pactionis patratae, retortisque velis

time the king of those Britons was Hoel, the son of Arthur's sister, who was fathered by Budicius, the king of the Armoricans. When he heard about his fellow Britons' need, he prepared a fleet and, after fifteen thousand armed soldiers were collected, with the next favorable breath of wind he entered the port of Southampton. After he was honorably received by King Arthur, as was fitting, [145] they promptly went to the town of Kaerliudcoit, called Lincoln in our language, which was besieged by the enemy. As soon as they arrived, a battle was fought outside the town, in which a slaughter of the Saxons was made the likes of which has not been witnessed before or since. Some fell slain by arms, others drowned in the river while fleeing, and the remnant all fled together from the siege. The Britons did not cease to pursue them until they came to the wood of Colidon. There, 2 coming back together from their flight in all directions and reassembling their cohorts, they sheltered in the wood and tried to make a stand against the Britons. But the Britons encircled them and, cutting down part of the forest, prevented their escape in that direction. Besieging them in that place for three days, they forced them, compelled by hunger, to surrender, and an agreement was made such that, with their arms and baggage and everything they owned left behind, they would be allowed to return to their own land with only their life and their ships. They also pledged to de- 3 liver tribute every year from Germany, and to send over several hostages as a token of their faith. Then King Arthur, after quickly taking counsel, agreed to their request.

[146] And when they were already plowing across the high seas, returning to Germany, they repented of the bargain they had made and, resetting their sails, they returned

redierunt in Britanniam atque Totonesium intrant portum. Exeuntes igitur in terram, totam patriam illam igne vastaverunt ex transverso usque Sabrinum mare, depopulantes colonos et armis suis privantes de quibus ipsos letiferis vulneri-

2 bus sauciabant. Inde arrepto itinere versus pagum Badonis, urbem obsident et regionem dissipare non cessant. Quod cum regi nuntiatum esset, qui adhuc Scotos et Pictos expugnare parabat, admirans perfidiam Saxonum, de eorum obsidibus mox supplicium sumit et relictis Scotis Saxones

3 persequi festinat. Sed magno dolore cruciatur quod Hoelum nepotem suum post se in civitate Aldclud dimittere morbo oppressum coactus est, accelerans obsidionem Saxonum dirimere. Quo cum pervenisset, armare militem iussit [147] ac seipsum armis suis munivit, loricam vestiens tanto rege dignam, auream galeam simulacro draconis insculptam capiti imponens, umeris clipeum vocabulo Pridwen, in quo sanctae Mariae imago impressa sui memoriam dabat. Accinctusque gladio nomine Caliburno, in insula Avallonis, ut aiunt, mira arte fabricato, dexteram munivit lancea nomine Ron:

2 haec erat rigida latoque ferro, hostium cladibus apta. Deinde dispositis catervis Saxones aggreditur expugnare. At illi sustinere non valentes eius impetum, proximum occupant montem in quo tamquam ex oppido se defendunt. Arturo itaque post eos montem viriliter ascendente atque suos magnanima voce inclamante montis cacumen post paululum adeptus est atque dextra laevaque hostium phalanges

to Britain and entered the port of Totnes. Disembarking on land, they devastated that whole country with fire, all the way across to the Severn Sea, exterminating the inhabitants and robbing them of their arms, with which they inflicted deadly wounds on them. Making their way from there to- 2 ward the district of Bath, they besieged the city and did not hesitate to destroy the region. When this was made known to the king, who until then was preparing to assault the Scots and the Picts, he was astonished by the faithlessness of the Saxons, immediately inflicted punishment on their hostages, and, abandoning the Scots, he rushed to attack the Saxons. But he was tormented with great sorrow be- 3 cause he was forced to leave his nephew Hoel behind him in the city of Dumbarton, overcome by illness, as he hurried to break up the siege of the Saxons. When he had arrived there, he gave orders for the soldiers to arm themselves, [147] and he also equipped himself with arms, donning a coat of mail worthy of such a king, putting on his head a golden helmet engraved with the likeness of a dragon, and on his shoulder the shield called Pridwen, on which the image of Saint Mary was imprinted to invoke her memory. And girded with the sword named Caliburn, which was made with great skill, they say, on the Island of Avalon, he took the spear named Ron in his right hand: this was of iron, hard and broad, fit for the slaughter of enemies. Then, with his 2 troops in order, he advanced to attack the Saxons. But they, unable to withstand his assault, seized a nearby mountain, on which they could defend themselves as if from a fortress. Boldly ascending the mountain after them, and shouting to his men with a loud voice, after a short while Arthur gained the summit of the mountain and scattered the enemy's

stravit. Plusquam quadringenti tam ab Arturo quam a suis illo primo impetu ceciderunt, inter quos Colgrinus et Baldulfus interfecti sunt et, caede peracta, multa milia ibi Saxonum perierunt. Cheldricus vix per fugam elapsus evasit atque versus naves suas redire conatur.

[148] Sed rex, mittens Cadorem ducem Cornubiae post eos cum decem milibus equitum persequi iussit, dum ipse rediens Albaniam de Scottis et Pictis triumpharet. Nuntiatum enim ei fuerat illos in urbe Aldclud Hoelum, nepotem suum, obsedisse qui ibi, ut dictum est, remanserat infirmitate gravatus. Dux autem Cornubiae cum decem milibus Cheldricum insequens, praeterire illum volens alia via prior ad portum navium descendit et naves manu armatorum pagensium Britonum munivit, ne accessum, si venirent, ad naves ulterius haberent. Ipse vero hostibus ex adverso obvians, per montes et colles et nemora dispersos persequitur, nec quievit donec perempto Cheldrico cum multis aliis, ceteros in deditionem coegit.

[149] Peractis igitur pro voto omnibus, dux Cornubiae post Arturum iter arripiens venit Aldclud, quam rex ab obsidione barbarica iam liberaverat, nepote suo Hoelo sano recepto. Deinde duxerat exercitum Mireif, civitatem Albaniae, ubi audierat hostes se recepisse. Quo cum perveniret, deserentes munitionem Scotti et Picti ingressi sunt stagnum Lumonoy atque insulas quae infra stagnum erant occupaverunt refugium quaerentes. Hoc stagnum sexaginta continebat insulas, sexaginta flumina a montibus Albaniae fluentia

formations right and left. More than four hundred fell in that first assault, as much from Arthur as from his men; among which Colgrin and Baldulf were killed and, once the slaughter was ended, many thousands of Saxons perished there. Cheldric, having barely escaped by flight, evaded them and attempted to go back toward his ships.

[148] But the king, sending Cador the Duke of Cornwall after them with ten thousand mounted soldiers, ordered him to overtake them, while he himself, returning to Albany, would conquer the Scots and the Picts. For it had been reported to him that they had besieged his nephew Hoel in the city of Dumbarton where he, as said before, had stayed behind stricken with illness. The Duke of Cornwall followed after Cheldric with ten thousand men, wishing to overtake him, and he descended on the ships' harbor before him by another route and guarded the ships with a band of the local British residents so that the Saxons would not have access to the ships if they came later. Going against the enemy himself, he pursued them through the mountains and valleys and forests and did not rest until, after killing Cheldric with many others, he forced the rest to surrender.

[149] Having accomplished everything according to his vow, the Duke of Cornwall took to the road after Arthur and came to Dumbarton. The king had already freed it from the barbarian siege, and his nephew Hoel had recovered his health. Then Arthur led the army to Moray, a city in Albany, where he had heard that the enemy were sheltering themselves. When he arrived there, abandoning the fortifications the Scots and Picts advanced to Lake Lumonoy and occupied the islands that were in the middle of the lake, seeking shelter. This lake contained sixty islands, with sixty rivers

recipiens nec ex tot fluminibus de stagno labitur in mare praeter unum. In insulis autem huius loci sexaginta rupes feruntur esse totidem aquilarum nidos continentes, quae singulis annis convenientes prodigium quod in regno futurum
3 esset celso clamore communiter edito notificabant. Ubi dum praedicti hostes presidio fruerentur, Arturus, collecto undecumque navigio, per flumina navigabilia stagnum intrat atque per quindecim dies eos obsidendo tanta afflixit fame ut milia morerentur. Dumque illos in hunc modum opprimeret, Gillamurius, rex Hiberniae, cum magna classe super-
4 venit ut eis auxilum ferret. Quo audito Arturus dimissis Scotis ad Hibernienses vertit arma, quos statim devictos ad naves fugere compulit et Hiberniam redire. Postea rediens ad stagnum quod dimiserat, perseveravit Scotos et Pictos infestare, donec episcopi omnes miserandae patriae cum omni clero suo, reliquias sanctorum et cruces in manibus ferentes, convenerunt atque regem nudis pedibus flexisque genibus adeuntes pro se populoque suo nimis afflicto misericordiam eius exorabant suppliciter, ut saltem ecclesiis et populo inbelli misericordiam praestaret atque arma ab interfectione gentis miserae contineret, adicientes se satis poenas luisse pro Saxonum superbia, quibus illi non consen-
5 serant nisi coacti. Nunc permitteret eius generosa nobilitas portiunculam gentis suae quae remanserat in Dei cultu perseverare, servitutis iugum perpetuae sub eius dominio ferre, et vectigalia qualiacumque foederatos reddere. Commotus

receiving the flow from the mountains of Albany, and out of so many rivers none drained from the lake to the sea except one. In the islands of this place, moreover, there were sixty cliffs containing just as many nests of eagles; coming together once a year, the eagles jointly announced with an elevated, rising clamor a prodigy that was about to occur in the kingdom. While the enemies mentioned before were enjoying protection there, Arthur collected a fleet from every direction, entered the lake via the navigable streams, and after they were blockaded for fifteen days so many were afflicted by hunger that thousands perished. And while he was oppressing them in this way, King Gillamurius of Ireland arrived with a great fleet to bring them help. After Arthur heard this, he abandoned the Scots and turned his arms against the Irish, whom he quickly defeated and forced to flee to their ships and return to Ireland. Returning afterward to the lake he had abandoned, he continued to harass the Scots and Picts until all the bishops of that miserable nation assembled with all their clerks, carrying the relics of their saints and crosses in their hands and approaching the king with bare feet and bended knees, and humbly begged his mercy for themselves and their people, at least to show mercy to the churches and the peace-loving people and to restrain his arms from the slaughter of the wretched nation, adding that sufficient penalty had been inflicted for the arrogance of the Saxons, which they would not have joined in unless they were coerced. Now his noble generosity should permit the small part of their people that remained to continue in the worship of God, to bear the yoke of perpetual servitude under his dominion, and to render whatever tribute had been agreed upon. Moved by pity for the shattered

ergo rex pietate super afflictos veniam donavit atque expugnationem eorum dimisit.

[150] Interim explorat Hoelus situm prefati stagni admiraturque tot flumina, tot insulas, tot rupes, tot aquilarum nidos numero adesse. Cumque id mirum duceret, respondit ei rex magis esse mirandum aliud stagnum quod in eadem provincia haud longe situm erat, longitudinem et latitudinem aeque habens viginti pedum, altitudinem quinque pedum. In quadrum sic sive hominum arte sive natura constitutum, quatuor genera piscium infra quatuor angulos continens, nec in aliqua partium pisces alterius partis repe-

2 riri. Adiecit etiam aliud stagnum esse in partibus Gualliarum prope Sabrinam, quod pagenses terrae Liliguan apellant, quod cum in ipsum mare refluctuat, recipitur in modum voraginis sorbendoque fluctus nullatenus repletur ut riparum margines operiat. At dum mare decrescit, eructat adinstar montis aquas absortas quibus demum ripas rigat et aspergit.

3 Interim si gens patriae eius facie versa prope accederet, recepta in vestibus undarum aspergine, vel vix vel numquam elabi valeret quin a stagno voraretur. Tergo autem verso non est retractio timenda etiam si in ripis astaret.

[151] His itaque gestis, rex sonitu bucinae suae atque lituorum toti exercitui signum donavit regressionis ad propria veniensque Eboracum festum natalis Domini instantis ibidem celebravit. Ubi visa sacrarum ecclesiarum desolatione atque templorum semiustorum totiusque urbis

people, the king pardoned them accordingly and abandoned the attack against them.

[150] Meanwhile Hoel explored the situation of the lake mentioned before and marveled at there being so many streams, so many islands and so many eagles' nests there. And when he thought this was amazing, the king responded to him that he would be even more amazed by another lake located not far away in that province, having an equal length and breadth of twenty feet and a depth of five feet. It was formed in a square, whether by human skill or by nature, containing four species of fish in the four corners, and the fish in one part were not found in the other parts. He added 2 that there was another lake in the region of Wales near the Severn which the inhabitants of that land called Liliguan, which, when the sea flows back into it, is swallowed up like a whirlpool, and once absorbed, the flow is in no way refilled to cover the edges of its banks. But when the sea shrinks back, the lake violently discharges the waters it absorbed in the likeness of a mountain, with which it finally wets and splashes the banks. Meanwhile, if the people of that country 3 come near it with their faces toward it, after they are drenched with the spray from the waves on their clothes they can scarcely or not at all escape without being devoured by the lake. However, with their backs turned they need not fear the receding waters even if they stand on the bank.

[151] After these things were done, by the sound of his horn and the war trumpets of the entire army the king gave the signal to return home, and, coming to York, he cele-brated there the impending feast of the Lord's birth. Then, after he saw the desolation of the sacred churches there and the destruction of the half-burned temples done by the

destructione a pagana gente facta, corde indoluit et de
2 reparatione civitatis et ecclesiarum cogitavit. Convocato
deinde clero et populo Piramum, capellanum suum, sedi illi
metropolitanum praefecit. Cui et ecclesiarum curam reno-
vandarum iniunxit. Viros ac mulieres civitatis indigenas per
Saxones in regiones longinquas expulsos, data pace, revocavit, quos patriis honoribus restituit.

[152] Inter quos inventi sunt tres fratres regali prosapia
orti, Loth videlicet atque Urianus et Auguselus, qui antequam Saxones in terra prevaluissent totius terrae illius ab
Albania usque Humbrum principatum tenebant. Hos igitur
ut ceteros paterno affectu suscipiens, reddidit Auguselo regiam potestatem Scotorum fratremque suum Urianum scep-
2 tro Murefensium insignivit. Loth autem, qui tempore Aure-
lii sororem ipsius duxerat, ex qua Walwanum et Modredum
genuerat, ad consulatum Lodonesiae ceterarumque provin-
ciarum quae ei pertinebant remisit. Denique cum in pristinam dignitatem reduxisset totius regni statum, Arturus ipse
duxit uxorem nomine Guenhauerham ex nobili genere Romanorum ortam, pulchram satis ac decoram, in thalamis
Cadoris ducis Cornubiae honeste educatam.

[153] Sequenti subinde aestate classem paravit atque Hiberniam adivit ut eam dominio suo subiugaret. Applicanti
ergo sibi Gillamanus rex praedictus cum gente sua obviam
venit quasi bello dimicaturus. Sed cum proeliari coepissent,
gens eius nuda et inermis non ferens telorum grandinem a
Britonibus missam, lacerata fugit et per nemora dispersa

pagan nation, he was sad of heart and gave thought to the restoration of the city and the churches. Once the clerics 2 and the people had been called together, he put his chaplain Pyramus in charge of the metropolitan see. He charged him with the duty of restoring the churches. With peace restored, he called back the native men and women of the city who were driven away to remote areas by the Saxons, and he restored their ancestral honors.

[152] Among them were found three brothers born of royal lineage, namely Loth and Urianus and Auguselus, who before the Saxons had taken over the land held control over all that land from Albany to the Humber. Therefore, supporting their ancestral rights, as he did for others, he restored the royal power of the Scots to Auguselus, and he honored his brother Urianus with the scepter of Moray. To 2 Loth, on the other hand, who in the time of Aurelius married his sister, by whom he fathered Gawain and Modred, Arthur returned the earldom of Lothian and other provinces that belonged to him. Finally, when he had restored the dignity of all the realm to its original state, Arthur himself took a wife named Guinevere, born of noble family of Romans, sufficiently beautiful and proper, decently educated in the court of Cador, Duke of Cornwall.

[153] The very next summer he prepared a fleet and sailed to Ireland in order to subject it to his dominion. After he landed, Gillamurius the king mentioned before came against him with his people as if to make war. But when they had begun to fight, that naked and defenseless people, unable to bear the hail of spears thrown by the Britons, fled wounded and, scattered through the woods, lay hidden in any place that was available as a refuge for them.

2 latuit quo ei refugii patuit locus. Nec mora captus est Gillamanus et regi Arturo adductus. Qui mox deditioni se tradens
datis obsidibus tributo ascripto suscepit Hiberniae regnum
sub Arturo possidendum. Subiugatis itaque Hiberniae partibus in Islandiam direxit navigium atque eam similiter po-
3 pulo debellato subiugavit. Interea divulgato rumore per ceteras insulas quod ei nemo in armis coequari vel resistere
posset, Doldavius rex Gothlandiae et Gunvasius rex Orchadum ultro venere ad eum, praecaventes eius expugnationem
superatis hostibus dampnosam promissoque vectigali et
facta subiectione obsidibusque datis quisque ad terram
suam abiit, ab Arturo rege ulterius possidendam. Reversus
deinde in Britanniam statum regni duodecim continuis annis semper meliorando confirmavit.

[154] Tunc ex generosi sui animi consilio et providentia,
invitatis quibusque ex longe positis regnis, familiam suam
coepit augmentare tantamque facetiam in curia sua habere,
ut emulationem eius longe lateque manentibus populis fama
celebris incuteret. Unde inclitus quisque incitatus ad famam
illius nihili pendebat seipsum nisi armis et indumentis ad
2 modum familiae Artur se ornaret. Fama quoque largitatis
eius omnes terrae principes superabat, unde quibusdam
amori, quibusdam timori erat, metuentes ne regna terrarum
Europae probitate sua et donorum largitate sibi subiugaret.
Arturus igitur de die in diem in melius proficiens, hanc
eandem sententiam et voluntatem quam timebant in animo

Without delay Gillamurius was captured and brought be- 2
fore King Arthur. Immediately surrendering himself, after
hostages were given and the amount of tribute was assigned,
he received the kingdom of Ireland to be held under Arthur.
And so, after the regions of Ireland were conquered, Arthur
directed his fleet to Iceland and conquered it in the same
way, with its people vanquished. Meanwhile, after word had 3
spread through other islands that no one could equal Arthur
in arms or stand against him, Doldavius the king of Gotland
and Gunuasius the king of the Orkneys came to him voluntarily, wishing to avert his ruinous assault against conquered
enemies, and after they promised tribute and did homage
and gave hostages, each of them left for his own land, to be
held under king Arthur from that point forward. He then
returned to Britain, and strengthened the condition of the
realm by constantly improving it for twelve consecutive
years.

[154] Then, out of the wisdom and foresight of his generous spirit, with everyone attracted from far off kingdoms,
he began to enlarge his household and to have such elegance
in his court that word of his celebrity instilled envy of him in
peoples living far and wide. Because of this each and every
famous person, prodded by Arthur's reputation, counted
himself as nothing unless he was equipped with arms and
robes in the manner of Arthur's household. The fame of his 2
generosity surpassed all the leaders of the land, so that he
was loved by some and feared by others, dreading that he
might conquer all the lands of Europe through his uprightness and the generosity of his gifts. Accordingly, while he
was accomplishing greater things day after day, Arthur had
already conceived in his own mind this same thought and

iam conceperat, ut scilicet extra Britanniam se et gentem suam dilataret et nomen suum cunctis gentibus manifesta-
3 ret et exaltaret. Et primum quidem parato navigio Norguegiam adit, ut ibi Loth sororium suum regni diademate investiret. Erat namque Sichelinus rex Norguegiae, nuper defunctus; cuius nepos iste Loth fuerat, regnumque suum eidem destinaverat. At Norguegenses indignati quod alienigenam regem sibi ingereret, quendam nomine Riculfum indigenam in regem iam erexerant munitisque urbibus Arturo
4 resistere parabant. Erat tunc Walwanus, filius Loth, fere quindecim annorum obsequio Sulpicii papae ab avunculo traditus, a quo arma recipiens vir factus est strenuus et miles audacissimus. Arturus itaque Norguegensi litore appulsus, eductis ad terram navibus, coepit patriam mox ferro et igne
5 vastare atque colonos ferreis vinculis mancipare. Quo adveniens Riculfus rex cum suis, proelium commissum est grande atque ex utraque parte multi ceciderunt. Praevaluerunt tandem Britones factoque congressu Riculfum cum multis peremerunt. Victoria itaque potitus Arturus regnum Norguegiae sibi subiugavit et Loth regendum tradidit; Daciamque mox adiens dominio suo subegit.

[155] Quibus subactis, navigavit ad Gallias et patriam infestare coepit. Erat tunc Gallia Romae subdita, sicut et cetera regna tribunoque Frolloni commissa qui eam sub Leone imperatore regebat. Qui cum adventum Arturi in Galliam comperisset, collegit omnem armatum militem qui potest

BOOK NINE

desire which they feared, namely to extend himself and his people beyond Britain and to make his name known and praised by all peoples. And indeed, after his fleet was ready, 3 he went first to Norway in order to invest his sister's husband Loth with the crown of the kingdom there. For Sichelinus the king of Norway had recently died, whose nephew this Loth had been, and he had arranged for his kingdom to go to him. But the Norwegians, indignant that a foreign king should be forced upon them, had already raised up a certain native by the name of Riculfus as king, and with their cities fortified they were preparing to make a stand against Arthur. At that time Gawain, the son of Loth, was 4 almost fifteen years old; he had been placed by his uncle in the service of Pope Sulpicius, and after receiving his arms from him he became a vigorous man and a most daring soldier. And so, after Arthur was driven to the Norwegian coast, with his ships drawn up on land he soon began to lay waste to the country with sword and fire, and to confine the inhabitants in iron chains. Riculfus arriving there with his 5 men, a great battle was fought and many died on either side. The Britons finally prevailed and, after they met in battle, they killed Riculfus with many of his men. Having achieved victory, Arthur made the kingdom of Norway subject to himself and turned it over to be ruled by Loth; and going next to Denmark he subjected it to his dominion.

[155] After these lands were conquered, Arthur sailed to Gaul and began to harass the country. At that time Gaul was subject to Rome and like other realms was entrusted to the tribune Frollo, who ruled them under Emperor Leo. When he had learned about the arrival of Arthur in Gaul, he collected all the armed soldiers who were subject to his

suae parebat et cum Arturo proeliatus mox primo congressu
2 confusus atque devictus fugae se dedit. Quippe Arturum
committabatur omnis electa iuventus terrarum et insularum
quas subegerat, praeter privatam familiam quae de praeelec-
tis erat bellatoribus; favebatque ei pars maxima Gallicanae
militiae quam sua munifica largitione sibi obnoxiam fecerat.
At Frollo fugiens, Parisius cum paucis devenit urbemque
munivit milite armato ac cibariis quantum potuit. Sed Arturus festinato gradu insequens illum in civitate obsedit sedi-
tque cum toto exercitu ibidem fere toto mense et sic civitatem undique vallavit milite ut nulla spes cibariorum inclusis
3 restaret. Cumque Frollo populum fame deditioni coactum
cerneret, malens se periculo opponi quam populum deditioni, misit nuntios regi Arturo ut ipse secum singulare certamen iniret et cui victoria proveniret alterius regnum et
populum optineret. Placuit Arturo ista legatio datoque ex
utraque parte foedere convenerunt in insulam Sequanae fluminis praeterfluentis, populo spectante a civitate et ab exer-
4 citu eventum rei. Ambo erant in armis decenter ornati, super equos mirae velocitatis residentes, nec erat promptum
agnoscere cui triumphus proveniret. Ut ergo erectis hastis
in adversis partibus steterunt, subdentes equis calcaria, invicem se magnis ictibus percusserunt. Arturus vitato Frollonis
ictu lanceam suam in summitate pectoris illius fixit et quantum hastae longitudo fuit ipsum Frollonem in terram prostravit. Extractoque mox ense festinabat eum ferire, cum

authority, and when he fought with Arthur, he was soon confused and defeated in their first encounter and abandoned
himself to flight. For in fact all the chosen youth of the lands   2
and islands that he had conquered joined with Arthur, in addition to his personal household, who were among the most
select warriors; the better part of the Gallic army also supported him, whom he had obligated to himself with his lavish giving. But after fleeing, Frollo arrived at Paris with a few
of his men, and strengthened the city with armed soldiers
and provisions as much as possible. Following at a rapid
pace, however, Arthur besieged him in the city and remained there with his whole army nearly the entire month,
and he surrounded the city with soldiery in such a way that
no hope of provisions remained for those inside. And when   3
Frollo saw the people forced into submission by hunger, preferring to expose himself to danger rather than the people
to submission, he sent messengers to King Arthur to say
that he would enter into single combat with him and whoever won the victory would obtain the kingdom and the
people of the other. This embassy pleased Arthur, and once
agreement was reached on either side, they came together
on an island in the Seine with the river flowing by, the people watching from the city and from the army to see the outcome. Both men were adorned with splendid arms, sitting   4
on horses of marvelous speed, and it was not easy to discern
who would triumph. Then they stood opposite each other
with spears erect, and, spurring their horses, they struck
each other with tremendous blows. After Arthur avoided
Frollo's blow, he fixed his lance high up in Frollo's chest and
knocked Frollo to the ground a spear's length away. Quickly
drawing his sword, he was rushing to kill him when Frollo,

Frollo velociter erectus praetensa lancea occurrit illatoque in pectore equi Arturi letali vulnere utrumque ad terram

5 ruere fecit. Britones ergo ut regem suum in terram prostratum viderunt, attoniti timuerunt et vix retineri potuerunt quin foedere rupto in Gallos unanimes irruerent; et dum foederis metas egredi meditarentur, erectus est ocius Arturus pretensoque clipeo imminentem sibi Frollonem ense excepit. Instant igitur cominus, mutuos ictus ingeminant,

6 alter alterius neci insistens. Denique Frollo reperto aditu percussit Arturum super frontem in casside atque collisione cassidis vulnus ei inflixit. Manante ergo sanguine cum Arturus loricam et clipeum rubere vidisset, ira succensus est vehementi erectoque ense Caliburno totis viribus per galeam in capud Frollonis impressit et in duas partes dissecuit. Cecidit Frollo terram calcaneis pulsans; nec mora spiritum in auras emisit. Occurrunt continuo cives apertisque portis civitatem Arturo tradiderunt.

7 Qui deinde exercitum suum in duo divisit, committens partem unam Hoelo duci ad expugnadum Guitardum Pictavensium ducem et partes Aquitanniae. Ipse vero cum reliqua parte exercitus ceteras Galliae provincias subiugandas suscepit. Hoelus ergo, Acquitanniam ingressus, urbes et castra subegit Gwitardumque pluribus proeliis devictum dedicioni coegit; Guasconiam quoque ferro et igne depopulans principes terrae sibi subiugavit.

arising swiftly, ran to meet him with his lance extended and, with Arthur's horse stabbed in its shoulder and lethally wounded, caused both of them to fall to the ground. When 5 they saw their king lying on the ground, the Britons were astonished and afraid, and they were barely able to hold back without breaking the agreement and dashing as a group against the Gauls; but while they were thinking about violating the terms of the agreement, Arthur suddenly arose and with his shield held before him he warded off the threat from Frollo with his own sword. Then they approached at close quarters and redoubled their exchange of blows, each one striving for the other's death. Finally Frollo found an 6 opening, struck Arthur on the brow of his helmet, and inflicted a wound on him from the smashing of the helmet. When Arthur saw his breastplate and shield turn red from the blood that was gushing forth, he was enraged and, raising his sword Caliburn, he smashed it down with all his strength through the helmet on Frollo's head and sliced him in two. Frollo died kicking the earth with his spurs; without delay he exhaled his spirit to the winds. The citizens immediately came running and, after the gates were flung wide, surrendered the city to Arthur.

He then divided his army in two, sending one part with 7 Duke Hoel to conquer Guitard, Duke of the Poitevins, and the regions of Aquitaine. He undertook to conquer the rest of the provinces of Gaul himself with the remaining part of the army. Once he entered Aquitaine, Hoel conquered the towns and castles and, after he defeated Guitard in many battles, he forced his surrender; wasting Gascony as well with sword and fire, he made the nobles of the land subject to himself.

8   Emensis interim novem annis, cum totius Galliae partes potestati suae submisisset, Arturus iterum Parisius venit festum Paschae celebraturus convocatoque clero et populo statum regni pace et legibus confirmavit. Tunc familiarium suorum fidele servitium et laborem diuturnum recompensans, Beduero pincernae suo Neustriam, quae nunc Normannia dicitur, donavit Keioque dapifero Andegavensem
9   provinciam. Pluribus quoque secundum meritum et generis dignitatem ceteros largitus est honores. Pacificatis itaque quibusque civitatibus et populis dispositisque omnibus incipiente vere in Britanniam reversus est.

[156] Ubi, cum sollemnitas Pentecostes adveniret, post tot triumphos Dei permissione sibi concessos magna exaestuans laetitia statuit festum magno conventu cleri et populi regioque diademate sollemniter decorare. Missis ergo nuntiis per omnes regiones terrarum proximas, invitavit quotquot erant in potestate sua regulos et duces ac ceteros regnorum proceres ad tantam sollemnitatem celebrandam.
2   Consilioque suorum locum delegit in Urbe Legionum coetum tantum congregare, tum quia civitas illa agris fertilibus et pratis silvisque undique vallata, tum quia palatiis regalibus prae ceteris Britanniae civitatibus praecellebat, ita ut aureis tectorum fastigiis Romam orbis dominam imitaretur. Est enim civitas haec sita in Glamorcantio territorio super Oscam fluvium non longe a Sabrino mari omnibus copiis
3   abundans. Praeterea duabus praefulgebat ecclesiis, quarum una in honore beati Aaron sanctissimi confessoris fuerat

Meanwhile, after nine years had passed, when he had re- 8
duced all the parts of Gaul to his power, Arthur went again
to Paris to celebrate the Paschal feast, and after he called together the clergy and the people he strengthened the condition of the realm in peace and law. Then, rewarding the
faithful service and lasting work of his household, he gave
Neustria, which is now called Normandy, to his butler Bedivere, and the province of Anjou to his steward Kay. He was 9
generous in giving other honors to many according to their
merit and dignity of birth. And so after all the cities and
peoples were pacified and everything was in order, at the beginning of spring he returned to Britain.

[156] There, as the feast of Pentecost was approaching,
swelling with great happiness after all the triumphs granted
to him by the permission of God, he decreed that a feast
should be held with a large gathering of clergy and people in
order to wear the royal crown in accordance with tradition.
He sent messengers through all the nearby regions of the
land, and summoned all the princes and dukes and other
nobles of the kingdom that were under his authority to celebrate so great a ceremony. And with the advice of his men 2
he picked Caerleon as the place to bring together so great an
assembly, not only because that city was surrounded on all
sides by fertile fields and meadows and forests but also because it surpassed all the other cities of Britain in royal palaces, as if by the golden peaks of its roofs it was imitating
Rome, the mistress of the world. This city is in fact located
in the territory of Glamorgan, on the River Usk, not far
from the Severn Sea, overflowing with all abundance. In ad- 3
dition, it was famous for its two churches, of which one had
been dedicated in honor of the blessed Aaron, a most holy

dedicata atque canonicorum conventu regulariter famulata tertiam sedem Britanniae metropolitanam continebat, altera in honore Iulii martiris fundata virgineo sanctimonialium choro fulgebat. Fuerat quoque tunc temporis civitas haec astrologorum atque omnium artium eruditorum celebris, qui diligenter cursus stellarum observantes futura veris 4 argumentis praedicebant. Tot igitur stemmatibus atque divitiarum copiis urbs praeclara festivitati praedictae disponitur. Nam et mare vicinum mercium diversarum abundantiam navigio advectans, dat deliciarum incrementum. Venerunt itaque ad festum regis celebrandum hii reges et duces subscripti: Auguselus rex Albaniae; Urianus rex Murefensium; Cadwallo Lauith rex Venedotorum; Stather rex 5 Demetorum; Cador dux Cornubiae. Venerunt et nobilium civitatum consules: Morvid consul Claudiocestriae; Mauron Wigorniensis; Anaraud Salesberiensis; Arthgal Kaergueirensis, quae nunc Warewic appellatur; Iugein ex Legecestria; Cursalem ex Kaicestria; Kimmare dux Doroberniae; Galluc Silcestriae; Urbgennius ex Badone; Ionathal Dorocestrensis; Boso Ridochensis, id est Oxinefordiae. Praeterea convenerunt magnae dignitatis heroes multi quos longum est enu- 6 merare vel nominare. Ex collateralibus insulis Gillamurius rex Hiberniae; Malvasius rex Hislandiae; Doldavius rex Gothlandiae; Gunvasius rex Orchadum; Loth rex Norguegiae; Aschillus rex Dacorum; Holdinus dux Rutenorum; Leodegarius consul Boloniae; Beduerus dux Neustriae; Borellus Cenomannensis; Keius dux Andegavensis; Guitardus Pictavensis; duodecim quoque pares Galliarum, quos Gerinus Carnotensis secum adduxit; Hoelus dux Armoricanorum Britonum cum heroibus sibi subditis qui tanto apparatu

martyr, and also contained the third metropolitan see of Britain, attended by a college of regular canons; the other, founded in honor of the martyr Julius, shined with a virginal choir of nuns. At that time the city had been famous for astrologers and also scholars of every art who, carefully observing the course of the stars, predicted the future with well-founded reasoning. Accordingly, with so many garlands 4 and such a wealth of riches, the splendid city was designated for the feast just mentioned. And because the nearby sea brings in an abundant diversity of goods by ship it contributes an increase of riches. The kings and dukes listed below came to celebrate the king's feast: Auguselus, king of Albany; Urianus, king of Moray; Cadwallo Lauith, king of the Venedotians; Stather, king of the Demetians; Cador, Duke of Cornwall. The earls of the important cities also came: 5 Morvid, Earl of Gloucester; Mauron of Worcester; Anaraud of Salisbury; Arthgal of Kaergueirensis, which is now called Warwick; Iugein of Chester; Cursalem of Chichester; Kimmare, Duke of Canterbury; Galluc of Silchester; Urbgennius of Bath; Ionathal of Dorchester; Boso Ridochensis, that is of Oxford. In addition there came heroes of great fame whom it would be tedious to enumerate or name. From the 6 nearby islands came Gillamurius, king of Ireland; Malvasius, king of Iceland; Doldavius, king of Gotland; Gunvasius, king of the Orkneys; Loth, king of Norway; Aschil, king of the Danes; Holdinus, Duke of the Flemings; Leodegarius, Earl of Boulogne; Bedivere, Duke of Neustria; Borellus of Le Mans; Kay, Duke of Anjou; Guitard of Poitiers; also twelve peers of Gaul whom Gerin of Chartres brought with him; Hoel, Duke of the Armorican Britons, with the heroes subordinate to him who marched with such a stock

et fastu ornamentorum, mularum et equorum incedebant,
7 quantum difficile est enarrare. Praeter hos non remansit
princeps terrae citra Hispaniam qui ad istud edictum non
veniret, etiam non invitatus; fama enim largitatis Arturi
longe lateque diffusa totum fere mundum perculerat.

[157] Omnibus ergo in Urbe Legionum congregatis die
sollemnitatis, regali diademate insignitus rex ducitur a me-
tropolitanis ad ecclesiam, clero psallente ac populo applau-
dente et quatuor regibus quatuor enses aureos ante ipsum
ferentibus. Ex alio latere regina, non minus pompose ab
episcopis laureata, deducebatur ad templum sanctimonialium, voce clara episcopis ac clero ante illam praecinentibus.
2 Quatuor quoque reginae regum predictorum quatuor albas
columbas ex more praeferebant. Uxoresque consulum ac
heroum quae aderant reginam sequentes magno tripudio
exsultabant. Peracta processione tot organa, tot cantus in
utrisque fiunt templis, ut prae mira consonantium vocum
dulcedine multi obdormirent et seipsos capere non pote-
3 rant, attoniti tanto gaudiorum strepitu. Divinis tandem obsequiis sollemniter celebratis, rex et regina cum omni heroum coetu domum regressi, regalibus ferculis epulati sunt.
Antiquam consuetudinem Troianorum servantes mares cum
maribus, mulieres cum mulieribus separatim discubuerunt.
Refecti denique sollemnibus dapibus, diversi diversos ludos
componunt et extra civitatem per campos et prata se dif-
4 fundunt. Alii caestibus, alii palaestra, alii aleis ac diversis lusibus diem illam iocunde consumpserunt sicque in hunc

of equipment, mules, and horses it is difficult to describe. Beyond these there did not remain any prince from the land 7 this side of Spain who did not come in response to this edict, even those who were not invited; for the fame and generosity of Arthur had spread far and wide and inspired nearly the whole world.

[157] With everyone gathered in the City of Legions on the day of the festivities, the king, adorned with the royal crown, was led to the church by the archbishops, with the clergy singing psalms and the people applauding and four kings carrying four golden swords in front of them. On the other side the queen, no less solemnly adorned with laurel by the bishops, was led to the holy temple, with the bishops and clergy singing in a clear voice in front of her. The four 2 queens of the kings just mentioned carried four white doves in front, according to custom. And the wives of the consuls and heroes who were there, following the queen, celebrated with a great triumphal dance. With the procession over, so many organs, so many chants were sounded in both temples that from the amazing sweetness of the concordant voices many could not catch themselves and fell asleep, made drowsy by so much joyful noise. Once the divine services 3 had been solemnly performed, and the king and queen with all the assembly of heroes had returned home, they dined sumptuously on royal dishes. Observing the ancient custom of the Trojans, the men sat apart with men, the women with women. Finally, refreshed by the ceremonial feast, various individuals organized various games and spread themselves over the fields and meadows outside the city. Some spent 4 that day pleasantly with boxing gloves, some with wooden swords, some with dice and various games, and in this way

modum tres reliquos dies sollemnes peregerunt. Quarta vero die dividuntur honores singulis quibusque pro merito famulatus sui et civitatum ecclesiis quibus deerant personae
5 episcopi eliguntur et abbatiae distribuuntur. Beatus autem Dubricius, heremiticam vitam eligens, de sede archipraesulatus se deposuit. In cuius loco sacratur David avunculus regis, vir religiosus ac timens Deum. In loco Samsonis Dolensis praesulis substituitur Theliaus, illustris presbiter Landaviae, annitente Hoelo duce Armoricanorum cui vita et boni mores testimonium dederant. Episcopatus quoque Silcestriae Magaunio, Wintoniae vero Duviano decernitur. Eledemio necnon religioso viro pontificalis infula donatur Aldclud.

[158] Dumque haec aguntur, ecce Romanorum legati, duodecim videlicet viri aetatis maturae, reverendi vultus, ramos olivae in signum legationis in dextris ferentes, moderatis passibus curiam ingrediuntur salutatoque rege chartam protulerunt et regi porrexerunt a parte Lucii Romanorum principis missam in haec verba:

2 "Lucius rei publicae procurator Arturo regi Britanniae quod meruit. Ammirans vehementer ammiror super tuae tyrannidis protervia. Ammiror, inquam, et iniuriam quam Romae intulisti recolligens, indignor quod extra te egressus eam non agnoscas nec animadvertere festinas quid sit iniustis actibus senatum Romanum offendisse, cui totum orbem famulari non ignoras. Etenim tributum quod Gaius Iulius ceterique post eum principes Romani a gente Britonum susceperunt, necglecto senatus imperio, iam per plurimos

the three remaining days of the festivities were finished. On the fourth day, honors were distributed to each one of them according to value of their service, and bishops were elected to the churches of the cities which lacked prelates and abbacies were distributed. Blessed Dubricius, however, choosing 5 a life of solitude, resigned from his archiepiscopal see. The king's uncle David, a religious and god-fearing man, was consecrated in his place. In the place of Bishop Samson of Dol was substituted Teilo the illustrious priest of Llandaff, with the support of Hoel, Duke of the Armoricans, to whom his life and good character had borne witness. Magaunius was also settled as bishop of Silchester, and Duvianus of Winchester. To the pious man Eledemius was given the episcopal robe of Dumbarton.

[158] While this was being done, legates from Rome unexpectedly entered the court with measured steps, namely twelve men of mature years and venerable countenance, carrying olive branches in their right hands to show they were members of an embassy, and after they saluted the king they brought forth a letter sent on behalf of Lucius, leader of the Romans, and presented it to the king with these words:

"Lucius, procurator of the republic, sends greetings to 2 Arthur, king of Britain, as he deserves. I am greatly astonished by the impudence of your tyrannical rule; astonished, I say, and thinking about the insult that you inflict on Rome I am indignant that you have risen above yourself and neither acknowledge nor hasten to amend that which is offensive to the Roman Senate, to which the whole world is a servant, as you know. For indeed, ignoring the authority of the Senate, you have presumed to withhold the tribute that Gaius Julius and the rest of the Roman emperors after him

3 annos retinere praesumpsisti. Eripuisti quoque Galliam, eripuisti nobis Allobrogum provinciam omnesque Oceani insulas quarum reges potestati Romanae subditi vectigalia antecessoribus nostris ad supplementum aerarii persolvebant.
Quia igitur de tantis iniuriarum excessibus Romanam dignitatem lacescere non timuisti, calumniatur te senatus atque
ut reum maiestatis Romanae vocat et invitat, quatinus mediante Augusto proximi anni Romae satisfacias senatui de
4 his omnibus quibus accusaris. Sin autem ego cum exercitu
Romano a senatu missus trans Alpes, partes quas nobis eripuisse gloriaris adibo atque eas te invito Romanae potestati
restituam. Deinde te ipsum quocumque loco latitantem re-
periam, vinculis mancipatum mecum Romea adducam."

5 Hiis itaque perlectis et auditis, murmur in tanta heroum
turba non minimum surrexit et de tributi mentione legatos
iniuriarum ac minarum conviciis afficiebant. Verum rex, sedato strepitu suorum, in giganteam turrim secessit, de his
tractaturus cum senioribus gentis suae. Et cum circa regem
tamquam in corona omnes consedissent, Cador dux Cornubiae prior in verba prorumpens silentium rupit et ait:
6 "Hucusque in timore fueram ne Britones armis semper assuetos, paci nunc redditos, segniores et ignavos quies longa
redderet laudemque et famam probitatis qua ceteris gentibus clariores censentur amitterent. Quippe ubi armorum
usus videtur abesse, merito aleae et mulierum contubernia

received from the British people. You also seized Gaul by 3
force, you seized our province of the Allobroges and all the
islands of the sea whose kings, subject to the power of
Rome, paid tribute to fill the treasury for our predecessors.
Therefore, because you do not fear to provoke the dignity
of Rome by such an excess of offenses, the Senate accuses
you and calls you as a defendant before the majesty of Rome
and summons you so that, in the middle of August next year,
you may answer to the Roman Senate for these and all the
other things of which you are accused. However, if I am sent 4
by the Senate across the Alps with the Roman army, I will
come and take possession of the regions that you pride
yourself in having seized and restore them to Roman authority against your will. Then I will find you yourself in
whatever place you are hidden and take you bound in chains
back to Rome with me."

After these things were read out loud and understood, no 5
little grumbling arose among the great crowd of heroes, and
at the mention of tribute they assailed the ambassadors
with a shouts of insults and threats. But the king, after calm-
ing their outcry, withdrew to a gigantic tower, to discuss all
this with the elders of his race. And when everyone had settled in a circle around the king, Cador the Duke of Cornwall, who was the first to speak up, broke the silence and
said: "Up until now I had been afraid that the long period of 6
inactivity would cause the Britons, always accustomed to
warfare but now returned to peace, to become slothful and
lazy, and that they would lose the glory and reputation for
uprightness for which they are more famous than other nations. The reason is that when the use of arms is absent, and
the love of dice and companionship of women and other

ceteraque oblectamenta adesse, dubium non est ut id quod erat virtutis, quod audaciae, quod honoris, quod famae, ignavia et socordia occupet. Deus igitur et eius providentia ut nos liberet segnitia, Romanos in hanc sententiam induxit, quatinus ad pristinum statum nostra reducatur probitas quae quasi semisepulta convivendo obdormivit."

[159] Haec et his similia illo prosequente, rex silentium petens ait: "Consocii prosperitatis et adversitatis, quorum virtute hactenus contumaciam regum ac ducum proximorum superavi et quorum in dandis consiliis et militiis agendis expertus sum diligentiam, advertite, si quid de vobis merui, advertite nunc quanta nobis omnibus inferuntur obprobria. Audistis Romanorum superbam legationem, audistis quoque in eorum petitionibus nostram depressionem. Quidquid ergo a sapiente diligenter praevidetur, cum ad rem agendam ventum fuerit, facilius superatur atque decernitur. Facilius itaque Lucii huius inquietationem tolerare poterimus, si communi studio praemeditati, quibus modis illam debilitare possimus, praevideamus. Tributum exigit a nobis sibi dari debere, quod vi a Iulio Caesare ceterisque regibus Romanis extortum a gente nostra atque violentia surreptum dudum fuisse testatur. Quod autem violentia a populo libero surreptum est, licet aliquando redintegrari et ad pristinum statum duci. Enimvero si id quod iniustum est et vi sublatum a nobis praesumunt exigere Romani, consimili ratione et nos expetamus ab illis vectigal quia antecessores nostri Romam quondam subegerunt et in servitutem redegerunt.

pleasures is present, there is no doubt that whatever there was of virtue, boldness, honor, and fame will be overcome by laziness and inaction. In order to free us from slothfulness, God and his providence encouraged the Romans to issue this condemnation, so that our uprightness, which slept as if to live half buried, would be restored to its former condition."

[159] As he was explaining these and other thoughts similar to these, the king called for silence and said: "My companions in prosperity and adversity, with whose strength I hitherto overcame the disobedience of nearby kings and dukes, and whose diligence I have put to the test in giving counsel and in waging war, listen, if I deserve anything from you, listen now to how much shame is brought upon us all. You heard the arrogance of the Roman embassy; you also heard our oppression in their claims. Whatever can be care- 2 fully foreseen with wisdom is more easily battled and overcome when the time for action arrives. And so we will be able to withstand the disruption of this Lucius more easily if, having thought it through together, we consider in advance the means by which we can disable him. He claims that tribute must be paid from us to him, because he swears it was formerly extorted from our people by force and also stolen away by violence by Julius Caesar and the rest of the Roman kings. But what is stolen away by violence from a 3 free people, it is lawful to make whole again and restore to its original condition at any time. Certainly, if the Romans presume to demand that which is unjust and was taken from us by force, by the same reasoning we too may demand a tax from them, because our ancestors once conquered the Romans and reduced them to servitude. Should I recount what

Quid enim Belini tempore et Brennio duce Romanis factum fuisse a nostris Britonibus recenseam? Etsi illis excidit, omnibus tamen nota fuerunt qui usque Romam terras incolue-

4 runt. Annon Constantinus nostrae Helenae filius ac nobis propinquus Britanniae sceptro insignitus, Maximianus quoque, alter post alterum imperii Romani fastigium adepti sunt? Eia, si subacti sunt Romani, sicut verum est, a nostris, non habent iustiorem causam a nobis exigere tributum quam nos ab ipsis. Facessant ergo exhinc calumnias liberis Britonibus inferre donec iterum ferro subactos—quod Deus avertat—in servitutem redigant. De Gallia autem sive insulis collateralibus non est illis respondendum, cum eas defendere a nobis vel nollent vel nequirent."

[162a] Haec et his similia rege prosequente, placuit omnibus qui aderant et collaudaverunt eius sententiam. Reversique ad Romanorum legatos responderunt eis quae in contione, rege dictante, collata fuerant atque scripto mandaverunt; chartisque signatis Romam quantocius regrediuntur, narrantes Britonum constantem audaciam atque regis Arturi modestam per omnia responsionem, virorum quoque bellatorum incomparabilem dignitatem atque divitiarum ammirabilem copiam.

[163] Lucius igitur, consul Romanus, agnita per legatos Arturi responsione indignatus mox senatus consultu misit per totum Orientem legationem regibus et principibus Romanae potestati parentibus, ut quisque cum exercitu

was done to the Romans by our Britons in the time of Belinus and Brennius the duke? Even if it is forgotten by them, nevertheless it was known to everyone who inhabited the lands up to Rome. Is it not true that Constantine, the son of 4 our Helen and our relative, after he was honored with the scepter of Britain, and also Maximian, arrived one after the other at the summit of the Roman empire? Indeed, if the Romans were conquered by our people, as is true, they do not have any more lawful reason to demand tribute from us than we do from them. After this, then, they move to bring false charges against free Britons, until at last, conquered again by the sword—God forbid!—they would reduce us to servitude. But we need not answer to them for Gaul or the neighboring islands, since they were either unwilling or unable to defend them from us."

[162a] After these and other things like them were explained by the king, it pleased all who were there and they praised his decision. When they returned to the Roman ambassadors, they delivered the response which, after the king had spoken, had been debated in council and also committed to writing; once the document was sealed, the ambassadors returned to Rome as soon as possible, where they described the steadfast courage of the Britons and the measured response of King Arthur in everything, the incomparable dignity of the warlike men and the astonishing abundance of riches.

[163] When he was made aware of Arthur's response by the ambassadors, Lucius, the Roman consul, was indignant, and with the consent of the Senate he immediately sent an embassy throughout the East to the kings and princes subject to Roman authority, that every one collected from ev-

undecumque comparato Romam properarent et Idibus Iulii servata maiestate Romanae dignitatis, omnes in urbe Roma

2 convenirent. Ad edictum itaque tantae potestatis convenerunt ocius Epystrophus rex Graecorum; Mustensar rex Affricorum; Aliphatima rex Hispaniae; Hirtacius rex Parthorum; Boccus rex Medorum; Sertorius Libiae; Xerses Mircorum; Pandrasus Aegypti; Micipsa rex Babiloniae; Politetes dux Bithiniae; Teucer Phrygiae; Evander Syriae; Echion Boetiae; Ypolitus Cretae, cum principibus sibi sub-

3 ditis. Ex senatorio ordine Lucius Catellus; Marius Lepidus; Gaius Metellus Cocta; Quintus Milvius Catulus; Quintus Caritius. Tot etiam confluxerunt quod ducenta octoginta milia armatorum computati essent.

[164a] Dispositis ergo quibusque ad iter necessariis incipientibus Kalendis Iulii Britanniam adire coeperunt ut contumatiam Britonum Romanae potestati resistentium confutarent et vectigali reddendo iterum assuescerent.

erywhere should hurry to Rome equipped with an army and should all convene in the city of Rome on the fifteenth day of July, in service to the majesty of Roman authority. Accordingly, in response to an edict of such force, they came together quickly: Epystrophus, king of the Greeks; Mustensar, king of the Africans; Alifatima, king of Spain; Hirtacius, king of the Parthians; Boccus, king of the Medes; Sertorius of Libya; Xerses of the Myreans; Pandrasus of Egypt; Micipsa, king of Babylon; Politetes, Duke of Bithynia; Teucer of Phrygia; Evander of Syria; Echion of Boeotia; Ypolitus of Crete; along with the princes who were under them. From the senatorial rank came Lucius Catellus; Marius Lepidus; Gaius Metellus Cocta; Quintus Milvius Catulus; Quintus Caritius. Indeed, so many assembled together that one hundred eighty thousand armed soldiers could be counted.

[164a] Then, after everything necessary for the journey had been arranged, on the fourteenth day of June they began to approach Britain, so they could suppress the stubborn resistance of the Britons to Roman authority and accustom them to the rendering of tribute again.

BOOK TEN

Liber X

[161] Interea Arturus rex suos affatus poscit ab omnibus auxilia congregandi exercitus atque Romanorum superbiae obviare. Promiserunt ei mox gratanter omnes sui suorumque famulatum fidelem in obsequium suum quocumque eos ducere vellet, quatinus nomen suum in omnes terras celebraretur. Et primum Auguselus, rex Albaniae, eius necessitati operam dare quantam posset spopondit, dicens:

2 "Nunc opus est, ut omnes quotquot dicioni tuae subicimur, totis viribus et animis paremur ad maiestatis tuae dignitatem exaltandam et amplificandam. Nihil enim mihi ante hoc facilius persuaderi potuit quam cum Romanis congressum, quod nisi ultro oblatum foret omnibus nobis optandum esset. Quis enim contumaciam eorum atque iugum servitutis liberis hominibus impositum ferre umquam sine invidia potuit, cum tam despecta gens et ignava multitudo tot viros, fortes robore atque bellicis rebus assuetos, suis exposcant sisti tribunalibus atque rationem de vectigalibus antiquis reddi, quae si umquam praedecessoribus data sunt, violentia quadam et iniusta exactione a nostris, tunc forte resistere non valentibus, magis extorta quam suscepta sunt? Aggrediamur ergo semiviros istos, ut et nobis et ceteris gentibus libertatem comparemus et eorum opibus, quibus

340

Book 10

[161] Meanwhile, after he addressed his men, King Arthur asked them all for help in assembling an army to confront the arrogance of the Romans. Immediately they all gladly promised faithful service in obedience to him on behalf of themselves and their men, wherever he wished to lead them, so that his name would be celebrated in all lands. And first Auguselus, king of Albany, pledged as much aid as possible in his need, saying:

"Right now there is need for however many of us are un- 2 der your authority to prepare with all our strength and spirit to exalt and magnify the honor of your majesty. For nothing before this could have more readily won me over than a confrontation with the Romans, which if it had not been voluntarily offered, would have been wished for by us all. Indeed, 3 who could ever endure without hatred their arrogance and the yoke of servitude imposed on free men, when such a despicable race and cowardly rabble demand that so many men, strong in military power and accustomed to warlike behavior, be summoned before their tribunals and that an accounting be rendered for old taxes which, if they were ever paid by our predecessors, were more extorted than received, by a certain violence and unjust exaction from our people who, as it happened, were not then strong enough to resist. Therefore let us attack these half-men, so that we may secure liberty for ourselves and other peoples and, after we

4 superflue abundant et unde tam petulantes existunt, victoria potiti perfruamur. Ut autem noveris, domine mi rex, me verbis operam accommodare, duobus milibus armatorum equitum exceptis peditibus, qui sub numero facile non veniunt, expeditionem tuam stipabo atque Romanis aquilis prior, si placuerit, occurram. Cumque devictis Romanis eorum copiis fuerimus ditati, Germanos adhuc rebelles necesse est invadamus quatinus tota terra Cisalpina conspectui tuo pareat."

[162b] His dictis, omnes quotquot aderant reges, duces ac principes ad expeditionem parandam contra Romanos animati sunt et promiserunt singuli auxilium ferre quantum famulatui suo iusta descriptione debebant aut eo amplius exhibere. Hoelus, Armoricanorum dux, decem milia armatorum fortium promittit. Et ne longum foret omnium partes singulas describere, reges insularum adiacentium, videlicet Hiberniae, Islandiae, Gothlandiae, Orchadum, Norguegiae atque Daciae, centum viginti milia ad augmentum regis exercitus promittunt. Ex Galliarum vero ducatibus, Rutenorum, Portinensium, Neustriensium, Cenomannorum, Andegavensium, Pictavensium, octoginta milia equitum annumerati sunt. Ex ipsa Britannia sexaginta milia equitum praeter pedites connumerati sunt.

[164b] Dispositis itaque omnibus quae ad tantam expeditionem competebant, rex Arturus Modredo nepoti suo atque Gwenneware regine regnum Britanniae conservandum dimittens cum exercitu suo Portum Hamonis petit et parato navigio vento flante prospero mare ingreditur navigandum.

achieve victory, we may thoroughly enjoy their riches, the overabundance of which makes them so insolent. So that 4 you will know, my lord king, that my actions conform to my words, I will accompany your campaign with two thousand cavalry, excluding the foot soldiers who are not easily counted, and if it pleases you I will lead the attack against the Roman eagles. And after the Romans are defeated and we have been enriched with their wealth, we must attack the still-rebellious Germans, to the point where the whole Cisalpine region shall lay open before you."

[162b] After these things were said, all the kings, dukes, and leaders who were present were roused to prepare for the campaign against the Romans, and each of them promised to bring such help as he owed according to the lawful terms of his service to him, or to furnish even more than that. Hoel, the Duke of the Armoricans, promised ten thousand powerful men in arms. And without taking time to describe 2 all their contingents one by one, the kings of the neighboring islands, namely Ireland, Iceland, Gotland, the Orkneys, Norway, and Denmark, pledged a hundred and twenty thousand to augment the king's army. From the Gallic provinces of Flanders, Ponthieu, Neustria, Maine, Anjou, and Poitiers, eighty thousand cavalry were added in. From Britain itself sixty thousand cavalry in addition to foot soldiers were included in the total.

[164b] Once everything was arranged that was sufficient for such a campaign, leaving the kingdom of Britain to be protected by his nephew Modred and Queen Guinevere, King Arthur made for Southampton with his army and, once his fleet was prepared and a favorable wind was blowing, he put to sea. Then while they were already plowing

Dum igitur altum iam pelagus sulcarent, quasi media noctis hora rex somno pressus obdormivit viditque per somnum quasi quendam ursum in aere volantem, cuius murmure litora tota infremebant; terribilem quoque ex adverso draconem ab occidente advolare cuius oculorum tamquam stellarum splendore tota Neustriae provincia refulgebat; alterum vero alteri occurrentem miram inire pugnam, sed draconem sibi saepius irruentem ursum foedo et urente anhelitu suo ad terram prosternere. Expergefactus igitur rex circumsedentibus somnium narrat et hinc atque illinc, aliis sic, aliis vero sic somnii significationem conicere temptabant. Verum Arturus se et somnium Deo committens spe bona fretus in meliorem partem eius significatum convertebat. Rubente itaque aurora litora Neustriae conspiciunt atque in Portum Barbae fluvii applicuerunt tentoriaque figentes exercitus augmentum e diversis partibus confluentis prestolabantur.

[165] Interea nuntiatur Arturo quendam mirae magnitudinis gigantem ex partibus Hispaniarum advenisse et Helenam neptem Hoeli ducis Armoricanorum custodibus vi eripuisse et in cacumine montis qui nunc dicitur archangeli Michaelis illam detulisse, milites autem regionis illius insecutos nihil adversus gigantem profecisse. Audito hoc, rex nocte sequenti assumpto Keio dapifero et familiari suo et Beduero pincerna cum armigeris tantum suis, clam tentoria egressus ad montem praefatum tendit et, cum monti appropinquaret, in modum rogi ardere ignem super montem cernit, aliumque super minorem montem qui non longe ab

through the open sea, around the middle of the night, the
king, who had become drowsy, fell asleep and in his sleep he
saw what appeared to be a certain bear flying in the air, with
whose growls all the shores resounded; he also saw a terrible
dragon flying against him from the east, whose eyes flashed
over the whole province of Neustria like the brilliance of the
stars; with one rushing at the other they entered into a marvelous battle, but the dragon rushing against it repeatedly
drove the bear to the ground with his foul and burning
breath. After the king awakened, he described the dream to   2
those sitting around him, and here and there, some this way,
others that way, tried to guess the meaning of the dream.
But Arthur, entrusting both himself and the dream to God
and hoping for the best, turned their interpretations in a
better direction. Then, as the dawn became tinged with red,
they saw the shores of Neustria and landed in the port of
Barfleur; pitching their tents they waited for the growth of
the army coming together from various directions.

[165] Meanwhile, it was announced to Arthur that a certain giant of marvelous size had come from the parts of
Spain and had snatched Helen, the niece of Hoel, Duke of
the Armoricans, from her guards by force and had carried
her off to the summit of the mountain that is now called
Archangel Michael's: the knights of that region had followed but accomplished nothing against the giant. After he
heard this, the next night the king, after selecting his steward Kay with his household and his butler Bedivere with all
his squires and quietly leaving the tents, headed for the
mountain just mentioned and, when he approached the
mountain he saw a fire burning on top of the mountain in
the form of a funeral pyre, and another on top of a smaller

2 altero distat. Dubitans autem super quem illorum montium habitaret gigas Beduerum praemisit ut rem certius exploraret. At ille, inventa navicula, navigavit ad minorem montem qui infra mare situs fuerat et propior illis advenientibus erat. Cuius dum cacumen ascendisset, audito ululatu femineo primum inhorruit. Deinde propius accedens mulierem reperit lacrimantem iuxta tumbam cadaveris nuper humati. Erat autem mulier haec anus, puellae altrix, quam asportaverat gigas ex finibus Armoricanorum, ut suprafatum est. Quae ut conspexit Beduerum ad se venientem, timuit ne a

3 gigante perciperetur. Exclamans ait: "O infelix homo, quod infortunium te huc adduxit miseret me tui. Nam nocte hac si nefandum monstrum te hic offenderit, membris omnibus discerptis morte turpissima morieris. Iste est sceleratissimus ille qui nuper neptim ducis Hoeli puellam pulcherrimam—proh nefas—meque cum illa simul advexit et cum illa concumbere temptans pondere magnitudinis suae illam oppressit atque morti addixit et hic tumulatam reliquit. Fuge ergo quisquis es et quantum potes fugiendo salva te ipsum."

4 At ille, festinum promittens ei auxilium, ad Arturum reversus est narrans ea quae audierat et viderat. Rex ergo casum ingemiscens puellae, tendit ad alium montem et dimissis equis cum armigeris pedes ascendit montem armatus. Ipseque praecedens socios inventum aggreditur monstrum qui ad rogum igne succensum illitus ora tabo sedebat; semesorum porcorum partes verubus infixas suppositis prunis

5 torrebat. Qui ut respexit in regem, mox festinavit ut clavam

mountain that stood not far from the first one. However, 2
since he was not sure on which of those mountains the giant
was dwelling, he sent Bedivere ahead to make certain. Having found a little boat, Bedivere sailed to the smaller mountain, which was located in the sea and was closer for them
coming this way. When he had ascended to its summit, hearing a woman's scream, at first he shuddered. Then, drawing
closer, he found a woman crying next to the tomb of a recently buried body. This woman was old, the nurse of the
girl that the giant had carried away from the country of the
Armoricans, as related earlier. When she saw Bedivere coming toward her, she was afraid he might be noticed by the giant. Exclaiming, she said: "O unlucky man, because misfor- 3
tune brought you here I pity you. For if the wicked monster
finds you here tonight, you will die a shameful death, with
all your limbs torn to pieces. He is that accursed being who
recently brought the niece of Duke Hoel, a beautiful girl—
how awful!—and me along with her, and, while he was trying
to lie with her, he crushed her with the weight of his great
bulk, killed her, left her buried here. Flee, therefore, whoever you are, and save yourself by fleeing as best you can."

But he, promising quick help to her, returned to Arthur, 4
relating everything that he had seen and heard. Then the
king, crying with anguish over the death of the girl, headed
for the other mountain, and leaving the horses behind, together with his squires he climbed up the mountain armed
and on foot. Going ahead of his comrades by himself, he
proceeded to find the monster, who sat before a burning
pyre with his mouth covered in gore; he was roasting half-
eaten pieces of pork that were fixed on spits placed under
glowing coals. When he saw the king, the giant immediately 5

assumeret suam magni ponderis et in regem dirigeret. At ille, praetenso clipeo, evaginato gladio ut illum prius feriat quantum potest celeri cursu properat. Verum gigas festinato ictu clavam librat regemque interposito clipeo tanto conamine ferit quod sonitu ictus et litora maris replevit et aures

6 eius fere hebetavit. Arturus ergo, ira accensus, erecto ense in frontem illius vulnus intulit non modicum, unde sanguinis rivi per totam faciem copiose fluentes, aciem oculorum illius turbaverunt. Percussus tamen acrior insurgit et velut aper in venatorem per venabulum, ita per gladium, caecus factus, ruit in regem et complectens illum bracchiis vi et

7 pondere suo humi fere geniculando eum stravit. At rex sentiens monstri illius molem suis bracchiis non esse tractandam, elabitur in parte altera et, sublato in sublime ense, totis viribus in cervicem gigantis pressit, ita ut vix ensis cum cerebro extraheretur. Mox ille, mugitum magnum cum dolore emittens, corruit et spiritum exhalavit. Beduerus tunc

8 praecepto regis oboediens, amputato eius capite detulit secum ad castra ut spectaculum foret intuentibus. Testatus est rex se non repperisse tantae virtutis alium, praeter Rithonem gigantem in Aravio monte, quem similiter interfecerat. Iste gigas ex barbis regum quos congrediendo interfecerat pelles in testimonium virtutis suae et triumphi ad induendum composuerat et mandaverat Arturo ut suam diligenter excoriatam transmitteret: nam quemadmodum ipse ceteris praeerat regibus, ita in honore ceteris barbis suam

rushed to pick up a club of great weight and aim it at the king. But Arthur, with his shield extended and his sword drawn, hurried as fast as possible in order to strike him first with a swift advance. However the giant, with a rapid blow, swung his club and struck the king on the shield he had raised with such effort that he filled the shores of the sea and nearly deafened the king's ears with the noise of the blow. Then Arthur, inflamed with anger, raised his sword 6 and inflicted no small wound on the giant's forehead, from which the rivers of blood flowing copiously over his whole face blurred his eyesight. Stunned, he nevertheless rose up more fiercely and being blinded, like a wild boar runs toward the hunter along a hunting spear, he ran toward the king along the sword and, embracing him with his arms, forced him almost kneeling to the ground with his strength and weight. But the king, realizing that the mass of that monster 7 could not be managed with his arms, slipped away to the other side and, raising his sword on high, thrust it with all his strength into the neck of the giant so that the sword could scarcely be drawn out along with his brain. Immediately uttering a great anguished bellow, he collapsed and breathed out his soul. Then Bedivere, following the king's 8 command, cut off his head and carried it to the camp so that it would be a wonder for everyone to behold. The king swore that he could not recall another of such power except the giant Ritho at Mount Aravius, whom he had killed in the same way. That giant had made himself furs from the beards of kings that he had killed in battle, to wear as a testament to his strength and his victory, and he had ordered Arthur to send his own carefully skinned: for in the same way that he was above the other kings, the giant would put his beard in

9 superponeret. Sin autem ad singulare certamen invitabat eum et cui sors victoriam daret pelles et barbam devicti tolleret. Inito itaque certamine fortior apparuit Arturus et eo interfecto barbam et spolium tulit sicut gigas ille ante prolocutus fuerat. Hoelus vero, audito neptis suae infortunio, ob memoriam ipsius fecit basilicam aedificari super corpus illius in eodem monte quo tumulata fuerat; qui mons postea nomen traxit ex sepultura puellae Tumba Helenae usque in hodiernum diem.

[166] Francorum igitur exercitu atque regum quos praestolatus est Arturus insimul collecto, dirigit iter versus Alpes contra Romanos. Qui cum ad Albam fluvium in Burgundia usque progressus esset, nuntiatur Romanus exercitus circa Augustudunum castra posuisse et tanto incedere commi-

2 tatu, ut vix eos terrae illius solum caperet. Ut autem trans flumen castra sua metatus est rex Arturus, ex communi consilio suorum legavit tres viros ad imperatorem Romanum, Bosonem videlicet, consulem de Vado Boum, et Gerinum Carnotensem et nepotem suum Walwanum, mandavitque ei ut a finibus Galliae quantocius recederet, quae dominio suo iure belli subdita erat quemadmodum antea Romanis fuerat. Sin autem sciret se armis eam velle tueri quoad viveret atque hos quos secum adduxerat. Pergentes itaque legati nuntiave-

3 runt Romanis quae eis a rege iniuncta fuerant. Qui dum responderet quod non deberet recedere, immo ad regendam illam accedere, interfuit Gaius Quintilianus eiusdem nepos,

the place of honor above the others. If he did not do this, 9
however, the giant invited him to single combat and whoever happened to win would take the furs and the beard
from the loser. And so, once the fight began, Arthur proved
to be stronger and after he killed the giant he took the beard
and the spoils just as the giant had specified beforehand.
Now Hoel, after he heard about his niece's misfortune,
caused a church to be built in her memory, over her body on
the same mountain where she had been buried; which
mountain afterward carried the name "Helen's Tomb" from
the girl's grave, up to the present day.

[166] Then after the army of Franks and other kings
whom Arthur was awaiting had gathered together, he directed their march toward the Alps and against the Romans.
When he had reached the River Alba in Burgundy, it was announced that the Roman army had pitched camp near Autun and had advanced with so great a company that the land
of that region could barely contain them. But as soon as 2
King Arthur had pitched his camp across the river, by the
common consent of his men he sent three men as envoys to
the Roman emperor, namely Boso the Earl of Oxford, Gerin
of Chartres, and his nephew Gawain, and he ordered the
emperor to withdraw as quickly as possible beyond the borders of Gaul, which Arthur had subjected to his dominion
by right of war just as the Romans had done before him: if
not the emperor should know that he would defend it and
those he brought with him by force as long as he lived. Pro-
ceeding in this way, the legates conveyed to the Romans
what the king had told them to say. Even as the emperor re- 3
sponded that he was not obliged to withdraw but rather to
come forward to rule them, his nephew Gaius Quintilianus

inquiens Britones magis iactantia et minis abundare quam audacia et probitate. Indignatus illico Walwanus, extracto ense quo accinctus erat irruit in eum et amputato eius capite ad equos qui secus stabant se cum sociis recepit atque simul redire coeperunt. Turbato igitur per Walwanum Romanorum exercitu, partim pede, partim equis insidentes ad vin-

4 dicandum mortuum suum accelerant. Insequentibus itaque illis iamiamque approximantibus, Gerinus Carnotensis, in quendam illorum qui prae ceteris equo admisso celerius festinabat, lanceam direxit et de equo quantum hasta longa erat prostravit. Boso quoque de Vado Boum retorquens equum suum similiter alium ex apropinquatoribus equo deiecit. Marcellius autem Mutius, nobilis decurio Romanus, Walwano iam imminens a tergo manus in eum inicere gestiens ut Quintilianum vindicaret, repente gladium Walwani in vertice capitis sui sensit et letaliter percussus, equo ca-

5 dens, expiravit. Walwanus in verba facetiae prorumpens praecepit ut Quintiliano socio suo in infernum renuntiaret Britones armis et audacia magis valere quam minis et iactantia. Romanis deinde usque insequentibus, quandoque lanceis, quandoque gladiis a tergo infestabant; sed nec retinere quemquam illorum praevalebant nec equo deicere. Dum autem apropinquarent nemori quod erat inter se et exercitum suum, prosiliunt subito de nemore sex milia Britonum in armis fulgentibus qui ad explorandum venerant et in eodem loco nemoroso delituerant ut, si opus esset, suis auxilium

6 ferrent. Qui ut conspexerunt Romanos pluribus catervis

interrupted, saying that Britons are more full of boasts and threats than of courage and honesty. Enraged, Gawain instantly rushed against him, with the sword he was wearing drawn from its sheath, and after he cut off his head he took himself with his comrades to the horses that stood nearby and they started back together. Thrown into confusion by Gawain, the army of Romans, some on foot, some mounted on horses, rushed to avenge the death of their comrade. Just 4 as they were drawing close behind him, Gerin of Chartres aimed his lance at a certain one of them, who had urged his horse ahead of the others and was rushing forward more quickly, and knocked him down a spear's length from his horse. Turning his horse around, Boso of Oxford also threw another of the pursuers from his horse. On the other hand, Marcellius Mutius, a noble Roman decurion, who was already threatening Gawain from behind and was reaching out seize him in order to avenge Quintilianus, suddenly felt the sword of Gawain on the top of his head and, lethally wounded, he fell from his horse and died. Erupting with sar- 5 casm, Gawain told him to report to his comrade Quintillian in hell that Britons have more strength in arms and courage than in threats and boasts. Still following after that, the Romans harassed them from behind, sometimes with lances, sometimes with swords; but they lacked the power either to hold any of them back or to dislodge them from their horses. However, as they were drawing near to the wood that was between them and their army, six thousand Britons in shining arms suddenly rushed forward out of the wood, who had come to reconnoiter and had hidden themselves in that wooded place so that, if the need arose, they could bring help to their comrades. When they saw the Romans 6

suos insequentes, subductis calcaribus equis ac clipeis prae-
tensis, clamore signi sui aera complentes, Romanis obviant
et in fugam compellunt. Persequentes a tergo feriunt et
quosdam vulneratos prosternunt, quosdam interficiunt.
Quod cum Petreio senatori nuntiatum esset, decem milibus
commitatus suis subvenire festinat, et progressus coegit Bri-
7 tones ad silvam, ex qua fuerant egressi, iterum redire. Quibus hoc modo cedentibus, Hiderius filius Nu cum quinque
milibus advenit ut auxilium Britonibus ferret. Redeunt ergo
audacter in campum et Romanis resistentibus fit pugna valida et prosternuntur utrimque. Cumque in hunc modum
contenderent, Boso callens suorum audacem temeritatem
quosdam seiunxit a ceteris et eos hoc modo affatus est:
8 "Quoniam nesciente rege nostro congredimur Romanis,
cavendum nobis est valde ne in deteriorem partem incepti
nostri fortuna decidat. Nam si contigerit nos inferiores esse,
et nostrorum damnum incurremus et regem offendemus.
Quia ergo incaute et absque ducis nostri provisione ad certamen hoc devenimus, elaboremus quantum possumus, ut
cum honore ad castra regrediamur et insidiemur Petreio
huic Romanorum duci ut vel vivum vel mortuum regi nostro
presentemus."
9   Sumentes itaque omnes qui aderant ex verbis eius audaciam, pari impetu in hostes ruunt turmasque penetrant usque ad locum quo Petreius similiter suos hortabatur. In
quem Boso irruens amplectitur illum sicut praemeditatus
fuerat et secum in terram corruit. Concurrunt igitur Romani

chasing their comrades with many troops, putting spurs to their horses and holding forth their shields, filling the air with their battle cry, they attacked the Romans and drove them away in flight. Pursuing them, they hit them from behind and some they struck down wounded, some they killed outright. When this was reported to Petreius the senator, he hastened to bring help with ten thousand of his troops, and after he came forward, he forced the Britons to go back into the forest from which they had emerged. As they were withdrawing in this way, Hider the son of Nu came with five thousand men to help the Britons. Then they boldly returned to the battlefield and, with the Romans resisting them, a strong battle ensued, and both sides suffered casualties. And while they were fighting in this way, Boso, knowing the daring rashness of his men, called some of them aside from the rest and addressed them in this fashion: "Because our king does not know that we are joined in battle with the Romans, we must take care that fortune does not turn our efforts against us. For if it should happen that we are the losers, we would both suffer our own defeat and give offense to our king. Therefore, since we came to this battle unexpectedly and without the knowledge of our leaders, we must exert as much effort as we can so that we return to our camp with honor, and ambush this Petreius, the leader of Romans, so that we can present him to our king either alive or dead."

Accordingly, with all who were present drawing courage from his words, charging together they rushed upon the enemy and broke through their troops all the way to the spot in which Petreius was exhorting his men in the same way. Dashing up to him Boso threw his arms around him just as he had planned and fell with him to the ground. Then the

7

8

9

ut eum eripiant, concurrunt et Britones ut eum abducant; et fit utrimque clamor et caedes de Romanis, praevalentibus

10 Britonibus. Extrahentes autem Petreium de medio suorum, duxerunt usque in fortitudinem proelii sui ac revertentes ad Romanos, multos straverunt, quamplures retinuerunt, et cum Petreio ad castra deduxerunt. Venientes itaque ante regem, rationem de legatione sua reddiderunt et Petreium cum sociis suis captivos praesentaverunt. Quibus rex congratulans, honorum et possessionum augmentationes, si tri-

11 umphum de Romanis obtineret, promisit. Captivos autem custodibus tradens, consilium accepit ut eos Parisius in crastinum mitteret ne, si in castris servarentur, casu aliquo accideret quo eos amitteret. Tradidit ergo eos ducendos Cadori duci Bedueroque necnon Borello et Richero, ut cum suis familiis eos conducerent, donec venirent eo quo minime timerent Romanorum irruptionem.

[167] At Romani per exploratores suos quos in exercitu Arturi habebant, agnoscentes haec fieri, miserunt Vulteium Catellum cum decem milibus armatis et Quintum Caritium senatorem, Evandrum quoque regem Syriae et Sertorium Libiae qui iter eorum nocte illa praecederent atque suos liberarent. Nacti ergo locum latibulis aptum delituerunt, donec Britones cum captivis iter agentes super Romanorum

2 insidias devenerunt. Prosilientes mox ex insidiis, circumvenire Britones imparatos aestimaverunt atque captivos de manibus eorum eripere. Verum per catervas distributi

Romans ran forward to rescue him, and the Britons ran forward to carry him away; and on both sides there was noise and slaughter of the Romans, with the Britons prevailing. Extracting Petreius from the middle of his men, the Britons led him all the way to the main body of their troops, and then, turning back against the Romans, they scattered many, captured even more, and escorted them along with Petreius back to their camp. Coming then before the king, they rendered an account of their embassy, and presented Petreius with his captive companions. Pleased with this, the king promised an increase in their honors and estates if they should obtain victory over the Romans. Handing the captives over to the guards, he accepted the advice that they should be sent to Paris the next day so that some accident would not occur by which he might lose them if they were kept under guard in the camp. Therefore he handed them to be escorted by Duke Cador and Bedivere and also Borellus and Richerius, so that they might accompany them with their retainers until they reached a point where they would have little fear of attack by the Romans.

[167] But the Romans, learning this was to be done through the spies they had in Arthur's army, sent Vulteius Catellus with ten thousand armed soldiers and Quintus Caritius the senator, and also Evander the king of Syria and Sertorius of Libya to get in front of them that night along their route and rescue their men. After they found a place suitable for hiding, they concealed themselves until the Britons following the route with their captives came upon the Romans' ambush. Immediately leaping forth from their ambush, they expected to surround the unprepared Britons and to snatch the captives from their hands. Distributed in

357

praecedebant agmen Cador dux Cornubiae cum suis atque Borellus. Post illos vero ducebantur captivi, vinctis manibus post terga, cum quingentis armatis quibus praeerant Richerus et Beduerus. Qui ut Romanorum insidias persenserunt, tamquam in acie pugnaturi, audacter eos susceperunt, di-

3 missis in tuto loco captivis cum paucis. Romani ergo sine ordine erumpentes non curabant suos per turmas disponere neque cum Britonibus congredi; immo diffusi huc illucque captivos quaerebant quoquo modo eripere et sic ad castra redire. At Britones nulli parcentes stragem magnam de Romanis primo fecere. Deinde rex Syriae Evander et Sertorius in unum convocantes fusas suorum cohortes, Britones invadere acriter coeperunt et, quia maior eorum numerus ac fortior erat, mox omnes eorum turmas penetraverunt et quassaverunt; ac omnino, illis prostratis, captivos abduxissent, nisi Guitardus Pictavensis dux comperto dolo Romanorum cum tribus milibus virorum bellatorum supervenisset atque

4 ab instanti periculo liberasset. Revocatis itaque suis Britones, in hostes acrius saeviunt et omni nisu eos debellare intendunt. Illi congressum eorum non ferentes reliquerunt campum castra sua petentes. Britones insequentes sternunt, obtruncant, retinent captos, et suos vindicant. Ceciderunt illic Vulteius Catellus et Evander rex Syriae cum ceteris in-

5 numerabilibus; ceteri fuga dissipati sunt. Cumque redissent

companies, the troop with Cador, Duke of Cornwall, and his men and also Borellus marched in front. After them the captives were led with their hands bound behind them with five hundred soldiers who were commanded by Richerus and Bedivere. When they spotted the Romans' ambush, in order to fight in the vanguard, they confronted them fearlessly, leaving the captives behind in a secure spot with a few men. The Romans, bursting forth without order, took no 3 care to arrange their men in squadrons or to engage the Britons; scattered instead, they searched about here and there for the captives in order to snatch them by one means or another and thus return to their camp. The Britons, however, with no one holding back, at first made a great slaughter of the Romans. Then the king of Syria, Evander, and Sertorius, calling their scattered troops together into a unified force, began to attack the Britons fiercely and, because the number of Romans was larger and stronger, they soon broke through and weakened all the British squadrons; and having overthrown them, they would have carried the captives away if Duke Guitard of Poitiers, after learning of the Romans' cunning, had not come up with three thousand warlike men and rescued them from the impending danger. Af- 4 ter they recalled their men, the Britons vented their rage more fiercely on the enemy and strove with all their might to finish them off. Unable to withstand the Britons' attack, the Romans abandoned the field, making for their camp. Following, the Britons scattered them, cut them down, took captives, and avenged their comrades. In that place fell Vulteius Catellus and Evander the king of Syria with innumerable others; the rest were scattered in flight. And when the 5

Britones ad campum quo strages suorum facta est, invenerunt inter peremptos illum inclitum Borellum Cenomanen-
sem ultimum spiritum exhalantem, lancea fixum per gulam,
sanguine cruentatum, et de nominatis viris ac strenuis quatuor, Hirelglas de Perirum, Mauricum Cardorcanensem,
Aliduc de Tintagol, et filium Hider. Traditis igitur illis sepulturae cum immenso fletu et planctu, miserunt captivos cum
his quos noviter ceperunt Parisius, ad regem Arturum repe-
dantes et spem futurae victoriae promittentes, cum admo-
dum pauci de tot hostium milibus triumphassent.

[168] At Lucius Hiberus, Romanorum dux, tales casus
moleste ferens, animum diversis cruciatum cogitationibus
nunc hoc, nunc illud revolvens, haesitabat an incepta proelia
cum Arturo perficiat, an auxilium Leonis imperatoris ex-
spectet intra Augustudunum receptus. Formidans itaque
bellum, nocte insequente civitatem praefatam aditurus,
2 Lengrias cum exercitibus suis ingreditur. Quod ut Arturo
compertum est, iter illius eadem nocte praecedere decrevit,
relictaque a laeva civitate quandam occupat vallem quae Siesia vocabatur, quam Lucius cum exercitu transgressurus
erat. Commilitones igitur suos per acies iure belli disponens,
legionem unam, cui praefecerat Hoelum ducem, ordinavit
post se in equis adesse ut, si opus accidisset, quasi ad castra
sese ibi recipere posset vel, si hostes fugae operam darent,
3 illi post eos, admissis equis, insequerentur fugientes. Catervas itaque septenas distribuens, in unaquaque quinquies

Britons had returned to the field in which their men had been slaughtered, they found among the dead that celebrated warrior Borellus of Le Mans, breathing his last, his throat pierced by a lance, stained with blood, and also four of their famous and vigorous men, Hirelglas of Peritum, Mauricus of Cahors, Aliduc of Tintagel, and the son of Hider. After these men were buried with tremendous wailing and lamentation, the Britons sent the prisoners along with those they had just captured to Paris, and they returned to King Arthur promising the hope of future victory, since so very few of them had triumphed over so many thousands of the enemy.

[168] But Lucius Hiberus, leader of the Romans, was distressed by so many casualties, and going over one thing after another, his mind tormented by various thoughts, he could not decide whether to finish the battles he had begun with Arthur or to wait for the help of Emperor Leo after retreating to Autun. And so, afraid of war, in order to approach the city just mentioned on the following night, he entered Langres with his army. As soon as this was made known to Arthur, he decided to go ahead along their route that same night; and after he went around the city on his left he occupied a certain valley that was called Siesia, which Lucius would be passing through with his army. Distributing his fellow soldiers in battle lines according to the custom of war, he ordered one legion, which he had placed under the command of Duke Hoel, to be present behind him on horses so that, if the need should arise, he himself could regroup there as if in a fortress or, if the enemy tried to escape, they could charge forth with the cavalry and pursue them as they fled. Making a sevenfold division of his forces, he put five 3

mille et quingentos et quinquaginta quinque viros omnibus armis instructos collocavit. Erant autem acies Britannico more cum dextro et sinistro cornu in quadrum statutae: quibus Auguselus rex Albaniae et Cador dux Cornubiae, unus in dextro et alius in sinistro cornu, praeficiuntur; secundae autem turmae, quae post eos incedebat, duo insignes consules, Gerinus videlicet Carnotensis et Boso de Ridechen, id est Oxinefordiae, praestituuntur; tertiae vero Aschil rex Dacorum atque Loth Norguegensium; quartae Walwanus cum duobus comitibus praefertur. Post has autem fuerunt aliae quatuor a dorso constitutae: quarum uni praeponitur Keius dapifer et Beduerus pincerna; alii praeficiuntur Holdinus, dux Rutenorum, et Guitardus Pictavensis; tertiae Iugenis de Legecestria et Ionathal Dorocestrensis; quartae Cursalem de Kaycestria atque Urbgennius de Badone. Ipse rex post hos locum quendam eminentiorem nactus, cum vexillo aureo draconis legionem habebat fortium virorum, in qua sex milia sescentios sexaginta sex numero erant.

[169] Dispositis itaque omnibus bellicis rebus, hos qui circa se aderant sic affatus est:

"Commilitones mei domestici, quorum virtute semper et ubique triumphavi, qui Britanniam nobilem insulam ceterorum regnorum fecistis dominam, vestrae congratulor probitati quam nullatenus deficere, immo magis ac magis vigere considero. Duos mihi iam de Romanis attulistis triumphos; tertius adhuc restat quem haud segniter per iuventutis vestrae robur et innatam audaciam tamquam futurorum praesagus Deo in omnibus opitulante hodie accumulari confido

thousand five hundred and fifty-five men equipped with all types of weapons in each resulting unit. The battle lines were set up, according to the British custom, in a square with a right and left wing: Auguselus, king of Albany and Cador, Duke of Cornwall were placed in charge, one on the right and the other on the left wing; two distinguished earls, namely Gerin of Chartres and Boso of Ridechen—that is Oxford—were appointed for the second company that marched behind them; for the third Aschil, king of the Danes, and Loth of Norway; for the fourth Gawain was given the lead along with two counts. After these another four were also set up behind: Kay the steward was placed in command of one along with Bedivere the butler; Holdinus, Duke of the Flemings, was put in charge of the second with Guitard of Poitiers; Iugenis of Chester and Ionathal of Dorchester in the third; in the fourth Cursalem of Chichester and Urbgenius of Bath. Having found a certain spot of high ground behind them, the king himself with the golden banner of a dragon held a legion of strong men, which was six thousand six hundred and sixty-six in number.

[169] And so, after all these matters of war were arranged, he addressed those who were around him in this way:

"My personal comrades, by whose strength I have triumphed always and everywhere, you who made the noble island Britain the mistress of all other kingdoms, I rejoice in your worthiness, which I do not expect to falter in any way, but rather to flourish more and more. You bring word to me of two triumphs over the Romans; a third still remains that I believe without any doubt will today be added to the others, through the strength and innate boldness of your youth, like a sign of things to come, with God providing help in all.

2 ceteris. Sane orientalium gentium segnitiam in nobis esse existimabant Romani, dum patriam nostram facere tributariam et nosmet ipsos sibi subiugare volebant. Numcquid noverunt quae bella Dacis, quae Norguegensibus, quae Gallorum ducibus et ceteris gentibus vestra virtute peregimus atque triumphavimus? Qui igitur adversus tam fortes et bellatores populos prevaluimus, his semiviris et effeminatis 3 fortiores esse non desperemus? Ecce iam tota victoria in manus nostras se contulit, si hodierna die tantum patienter ac viriliter stemus."

Haec eo vociferante, omnes uno clamore assentiunt parati mortem subire potius quam ipso vivente campum belli deserere.

[170] At Lucius Hiberus, compertis his quae ab Arturo rege sibi parabantur, noluit ut prius cogitarat, nec potuit absque dedecore belli instantis congressum vitare neque sine rei publicae detrimento diffugium facere. Convocatis itaque ad se in unum separatim locum regibus ac ducibus imperii Romani sic affatur eos, dicens:

2 "Patres invictissimi, totius orbis triumphatores ac Romani nominis propagatores et defensores, videtis mecum belli huius instantem necessitatem, videtis hostes inter locum illum, quo proponebamus ire, et nos acies suas ordinasse. Non aliunde nobis patet iter ad praesidia civitatis nostrae quam per vallem istam quae ab adversariis praeclusa 3 est. Sumite animos, sumite arma et veterum vestrorum memores et hostium iniuriam Romanae maiestati illatam recolentes armorum discrimine cum multa sanguinis effusione,

Truly, the Romans expected the weakness of the eastern 2
races to be in us when they sought to make our country a
source of tribute and to subject us ourselves to their dominion. Is it possible they know what wars we waged with your
strength against the Danes, the Norwegians, the leaders of
Gaul, and other races, and how we triumphed? Having prevailed against such strong and warlike peoples, should we
despair of being stronger than these eunuchs and effemi-
nate ones? Total victory has placed itself in our hands if we 3
can only stand patiently and boldly on this day."

After these things were said, everyone agreed with a
unanimous outcry, prepared to suffer death rather than to
abandon the field of battle so long as Arthur was alive.

[170] But Lucius Hiberus, having learned these things
that were being prepared for him by King Arthur, decided
not to do as he had previously planned, because he could not
avoid the impending battle without disgrace in war, and he
could not retreat without harm to the republic. After he
called upon the kings and commanders of the Roman Empire to join him separately in one location, he addressed
them in this way, saying:

"Most invincible fathers, conquerors of the whole world 2
and spreaders and defenders of the Roman name, you see
with me the present necessity for this war, you see the enemy has arranged their battle lines between us and that
place where we were proposing to go. No other route to the
protection of our city lies open for us than through that valley which is blocked by our adversaries. Summon your cour- 3
age, gather your arms, and, recalling the memory of your
ancestors and the injury inflicted on Roman authority, clear
this route with distinction of arms and much spilling of

si oportet, viam hanc patefacite et eam libertatem et audaciam qua usi semper estis bellorum militiis, hodie necesse
est ad memoriam revocetis et ut inprobos istos, qui tamquam latrunculi et iter vestrum obcludere praesumunt, dissipare et eorum robur confutare, omnes unanimiter inten-
damus ut, si perstiterint incepto, triumphati atque devicti
Romanae subdantur potestati: si fugae se dederint, viles et
abiecti terras et urbes quas se nobis surripuisse gloriantur
amittant et in perpetuum nobis servientes vectigalia aerario
cum ceteris gentibus dependant."

4 Ut igitur finem dicendi fecit, uno omnes assensu faventes,
socias manus iureiurando promittunt et ad armandum sese
festinant. Armati tandem dispositis turmis ad vallem praedictam accedunt; hostes intuentur totam vallem dextra laevaque obsidentes.

[171] Postquam autem in adversa parte hinc Britones, illinc Romani erectis steterunt signis, lituis insonantibus,
conveniunt et grandine sagittarum et omnium genere telorum primas belli partes lacessunt. Deinde cominus gladiis et
2 lanceis sese invicem obviant atque vulnerant. Et sic diu se ex
utraque parte verentes contendunt ut dubium esset quis eorum praevaleret, donec Beduerus et Keius, agmine suo Romanos penetrantes, seipsos cum magna audacia periculo
dederunt atque sanguine multo Romanorum fuso, a turmis
hostilibus circumventi, undique confossi sunt. Beduerus
peremptus cecidit, Keius letaliter vulneratus vix evasit
corpore Bedueri secum sublato. In agmine enim Medorum

blood, if necessary; today you must recall to memory that
freedom and boldness in the service of war to which you are
always accustomed. In order to destroy and restrain the
force of those shameless ones, who just like brigands dare to
block your way, let us all strive as one so that, if they persist
in this undertaking, they shall be placed under Roman authority, conquered, and defeated. If they should take flight,
they shall lose the worthless and humble lands and cities
that they boast about seizing away from us, and in perpetual
servitude to us they shall pay their tribute to the treasury
like other races."

As soon as he finished speaking, they all supported him 4
by common consent, pledged their allied forces to him under oath, and hastened to arm themselves. Once they were
armed and had their troops in order, they approached the
valley mentioned before; there they stared at the enemy oc-
cupying the whole valley to the left and right.

[171] After that they stood on opposite sides, the Britons
here, the Romans there, with their battle standards raised;
after they sounded their trumpets they came together and
assailed the front lines with a hail of arrows and spears of every kind. Then they came against each other in hand to hand
combat with swords and lances and wounded each other in
turn. And thus they competed for a long time, each fearing 2
the other side, so that it was uncertain which of them would
prevail, until Bedivere and Kay, penetrating the Romans
with their company, threw themselves into danger with
great boldness, and after spilling much Roman blood they
were surrounded by enemy troops and stabbed from every
side. Bedivere fell dead and Kay, lethally wounded, barely escaped, taking the body of Bedivere with him. For they had

pariter inciderant et a rege Bocco lancea pectori medio fixus
Beduerus interiit.

[172] Hirelglas autem, nepos Bedueri, ob mortem
avunculi sui dolore simul et ira commotus, ad vindicandum
illum vehementer exarsit et cum trecentis suorum per
hostiles catervas, veluti aper inter canes, dextra laevaque
sternens ac dissipans quantum robur equorum sibi et suis
vires augebant ad vexillum regis Medorum pervenit, nihil
verens quid sibi contingere posset, dum avunculum suum
2 vindicaret. Extracto itaque gladio, regem ipsum peremit
peremptumque ad socios suos detraxit, suis undique defen-
dentibus ac viam patefacientibus et iuxta corpus Bedueri
avunculi sui totum dilaniatum et in frusta concisum dimisit.
Deinde magno clamore in hostes ruens, stragem non modi-
3 cam de eis fecit. Signum Britonum saepius inclamando suos
exhortabatur quasi furore plenus ut fortiter ferirent et sine
pietate obtruncarent. Gentiles enim inimici Dei cum Christianis erant mixti et idcirco nec ipsis Christianis parcen-
dum. Illo tunc impetu corruerunt in parte Romanorum Alifatima, rex Hispaniae, et Micipsa Babiloniensis; Quintus
quoque Milvius et Marius Lepidus senatores. Ceciderunt et
in parte Britonum Holdinus, dux Ruthenorum, et Leodegarius Boloniensis; tres etiam consules Britanniae, Cursalem
Caicestrensis, Anaraud Salesberiensis, et Urbgennius de Badone.

[173] Turmae autem quas isti regebant quassatae, amissis
ducibus, retro cesserunt, donec venirent ad aciem Armoricanorum Britonum, quam Hoelus et Walwanus tuebantur.

happened together upon the army of the Medes, and Bedivere perished with the middle of his chest pierced by King Bocco's lance.

[172] Bedivere's nephew Hirelglas, however, moved by sorrow and anger at the same time over the death of his uncle, was violently provoked to avenge him, and moving through the hostile troops with three hundred of his men, like a wild boar among dogs, throwing and scattering them left and right with all the power that the strength of the horses lent to him and his men, he reached the banner of the king of the Medes, fearing nothing that might happen to himself as long as he could avenge his uncle. And so, drawing 2 his sword, he killed the king himself, and after he killed him he dragged him back to his companions, with his men opening the way and guarding him on all sides, and dumped him completely torn apart and chopped to pieces next to the body of his uncle Bedivere. Next he ran at the enemy and with a great battle cry he slaughtered them without restraint. Frequently invoking the battle standard of the Brit- 3 ons, as if filled with madness he incited his men to strike more boldly and kill without mercy: pagans hateful to God were mixed with Christians and on that account even those Christians must not be spared. In that assault there died on the Roman side Alifatima, the king of Spain, and Micipsa of Babylon; also the senators Quintus Milvius and Marius Lepidus. And on the British side fell Holdinus, Duke of the Flemings, and Leodegarius of Boulogne; and also three of the earls of Britain, Cursalem of Chichester, Anaraud of Salisbury, and Urbgenius of Bath.

[173] But the troops which they commanded, having lost their leaders, retreated until they came to the front line of the Armorican Britons, which Hoel and Gawain directed.

Ut ergo viderunt hi duo duces socios prae se peremptos, magis ac magis in iram accensi hostibus instant et dextra laevaque caedunt donec ad turmam imperatoris, ubi signum
2 aquilae tenebatur, pervenirent. Hic renovatur proelium et Romani, sicut recentes leones in defessos canes, ruunt sine lege et sine lege utrobique pereunt. At Walwanus, recenti semper vigens vigore, aditum congrediendi cum Lucio quaerebat sternens quosque sibi obvios habebat Romanorum. Hoelus quoque non inferior ex alia parte fulminabat, socios exhortans ut acriter ferirent; hostium ictus haud timidus suscipiens et econtra repercutiens multos solus ense suo vita privavit, quia non erat tempus vacuum quin aut percutere-
3 tur aut percuteret. Non erat facile agnosci quis eorum alterum audacia excederet: quibus ante saecula meliores non genuerunt. Tandem Walwanus, acies Romanas cedendo penetrans, pervenit ad ipsum Lucium imperatorem, quem valde siciebat invenire. Lucius quoque non segnis, ab Hispania oriundus, prima virtute florens multum audaciae, mul-
4 tum vigoris, multum probitatis habebat. Congressus itaque cum Walwano mire laetatur et gloriatur quod cum viro, de quo tanta fama fuerat, singulare certamen iniret commissoque diutius inter se agone, dant ictus validos et scuta galeasque ensibus detruncant. Et dum acriter in hunc modum decertant, ecce Romani subito recuperantes impetum in Armoricanos faciunt et imperatori suo subveniunt; Hoelum et Walwanum cum suis caedentes retro ad cohortes suas paulisper coegerunt.

When they saw two of their fellow leaders lie slain before them, they approached the enemy more and more incensed with anger and killed them left and right, until they came to the squadron of the emperor, where the standard of the eagle was kept. Here the battle was renewed, and the Romans, 2 like rested lions among worn-out dogs, charged without restraint and men died without restraint on both sides. But Gawain, constantly flourishing with renewed vigor, searched for an opening to meet with Lucius, scattering any of the Romans he found in his way. Hoel too, no less than he, struck like lightning on the other side, urging his companions to attack more fiercely; enduring the enemies' blows fearlessly and striking against them in return, he took many of their lives with his sword alone, because there was not an empty moment in which he was not either striking or being struck. It was not easy to tell which of them exceeded the 3 other in boldness: better men than these were never born before this time. Eventually Gawain, penetrating the Roman lines by cutting his way through, came to the Emperor Lucius himself, whom he thirsted greatly to find. Lucius, too, was eager; born in Spain, he was flourishing in his prime and had great boldness, great vigor, and great virtue. After 4 he came together with Gawain he rejoiced greatly and swelled with pride to engage in single combat with a man of such great fame, and as they battled a while longer among themselves, they exchanged mighty blows and cut pieces from their shields and helmets with their swords. And while they struggled fiercely in this way, behold, the Romans, suddenly recovering, charged at the Armoricans and came to the rescue of their emperor; for a short while they forced Hoel and Gawain to withdraw with their men back toward their retinue.

[174] Quibus mox rex ipse Arturus cum agmine suo, adhuc recenti in auxilium festinus occurrens, extracto Caliburno ense celsa voce se testatur adesse atque retro cedentes his verbis hortatur, dicens: "Utquid fugitis? Quid pertimescitis? Ne abscedat ullus vestrum! Ecce dux vester, qui ad certamen vos adduxi, paratus, si forte contingat, pro vobis occumbere; nec, dum vita comes fuerit, vos vel campum hunc relinquam donec triumpho potitus hostes fugae aut

2 deditioni hodie compellam. Mementote dextrarum vestrarum quae tot proeliis exercitatae omnibus adversariis usque modo prevaluerunt. Mementote libertatis vestrae quam sibi subdere affectant semiviri isti."

Haec cum vociferatus esset, irruit in hostes, caedit, prosternit et tamquam leo famelicus in animalia saevit. Nemo ei obvius esse ausus est. Diffugiunt omnes et latere magis

3 quam pugnare quaerunt. Quippe nullus evadere poterat eorum quem cruento ense summotenus tangebat: ita erat mortiferum vulnus illius gladii. Hic duos orientales reges obvios sibi infortunium dedit quos abscisis capitibus ad tartara misit. Viso igitur rege suo Britones in hunc modum decertare, animosiores effecti, adversarios unanimiter invadunt et catervatim sternunt; resistunt Romani quantum possunt.

[175] Dumque sic omnibus viribus invicem decertant, ecce Morvid, consul Claudiocestriae, cum legione equitum de nemorosis collibus, ubi ad praesidium dimissus fuerat, prosiliens a dorso supervenit hostibus, et eos nil tale

[174] Soon King Arthur himself, along with his column, which was still rested, quickly ran up to help, and, drawing his sword Caliburn, he announced his presence with a loud voice and encouraged those who were retreating with these words, saying: "Why do you run away? What are you afraid of? Do not withdraw, any of you! Here is your leader, who led you to the battle, ready to die for you, should that happen; while life is with me, will not I abandon you or this field of battle until, once victory is achieved, this day I drive the enemy to flight or surrender. Be mindful of your right hands 2 which, tested in so many battles, have up to now prevailed against all adversaries. Be mindful of your liberty, which these eunuchs aim to make subject to themselves."

After shouting these things, he rushed against the enemy, cut them, struck them down, and vented his fury on them like a starving lion on other beasts. No one dared to stand against him. Everyone fled and sought to hide rather than to fight. Of course none was able to escape among those whom 3 he struck with the end of his bloodstained sword: the wounds of that sword were deadly in this way. Here misfortune sent two eastern kings against him, whom he sent to the lowest region of hell with their heads cut off. After seeing their king fight in this way, the Britons, inspired to greater courage, attacked their adversaries as one and laid them out in large numbers; the Romans resisted as much as they could.

[175] And while they fought against each other with all their might, Morvid the Earl of Gloucester suddenly appeared with a legion of horsemen, leaping out from the wooded valley where he had been sent as a precaution, and came upon the enemy from behind; and catching them by

verentes caedunt et obtruncant et disturbatos a fronte et a
2 tergo in fugam compellunt. Tunc multa milia orientalium
pariter ac Romanorum, aliis alios urgentibus, stipatis catervis ceciderunt; quidam vestigiis fugientium pressi et calcati
occumbunt, quidam armis propriis iugulantur, maior pars
hostium gladiis intereunt. In turbine illo Lucius ille praeoc-
3 cupatus cuiusdam lancea confossus occubuit. Britones igitur usque insistentes victoriam de Romanis, omnibus saecu-
lis celebrem, adepti sunt. Ut autem insequendo et caedendo
exsaturati sunt, revertentes spolia diripiunt et armis et spoliis Romanorum ea die ditati sunt.

[176] Rex itaque Arturus, tanto triumpho glorificatus,
corpora suorum ab hostium cadaveribus separans quaedam
ibidem sepulta reliquit, quaedam ad comprovinciales abbatias deferri fecit et honorifice sepeliri. Corpus autem
Bedueri, dilecti sui, ad Neustriam civitatem Baiocas a
Neustriensibus suis delatum sepulturae egregiae tradi praecepit. Ibi in cimiterio ecclesiae, quae tunc erat in australi
parte civitatis iuxta murum, honorifice cum magnis lamen-
2 tis suorum positus est. Keius vero ad Camum oppidum,
quod ipse construxerat graviter vulneratus asportatur ac
paulo post eodem ex vulnere defunctus ad cenobium eremi-
tarum in quodam nemore non longe ab oppido delatus, ut
decuit Andegavensium ducem, sepultus est. Holdinus, dux
Ruthenorum, Flandrias vectus in Tervana civititate sua in-
humatus iacet. Ceteri autem consules et proceres prout

surprise he and his men cut them down and killed them and forced them into flight, thrown into disorder from both the front and the rear. Then, urging each other on, they killed 2 many thousands of those from the east and an equal number of Romans, whose army was surrounded. Some of those fleeing met their deaths pursued and trampled in their tracks, some had their throats cut with their own weapons, but most of the enemy perished by the sword. In that whirlwind Lucius lay dead, after being caught and pierced by someone's lance. Accordingly the Britons, always pressing 3 ahead, won from the Romans a victory that was celebrated throughout the ages. But when they were finally sated with chasing and killing, they turned back to grab the spoils, and that day they were enriched with the arms and spoils of the Romans.

[176] And so King Arthur, his glory increased by such a triumph, separated the bodies of his men from the corpses of the enemy, left some to be buried there, and had some carried to the neighboring abbeys to be buried with dignity. But he ordered the body of his beloved Bedivere to be given a distinguished burial after his own Neustrian men carried it to the Neustrian city of Bayeux. There in the cemetery of the church, which was then in the southern part of the city, next to the wall, he was placed with honor amid great lamentation by his men. Kay, however, was carried gravely 2 wounded to the city of Chinon which he had built himself, and shortly thereafter, having died from his wounds, he was buried as befits a Duke of Anjou in a convent of hermits in a certain forest not far from the city. Holdinus, Duke of the Flemings, after being sent to Flanders, lies buried in his city of Thérouanne. Other earls and nobles were carried to their

quisque civitate aut praedio in vita sua floruit ad propria de-
3 lati sunt. Hostes quoque rex miseratus praecepit indigenis
sepelire, corpus quoque Lucii Romae ad senatum deferre,
mandans non debere aliud tributum ex Britannia reddi.
Postea vero subsequente hieme in partibus illis moratus est
et civitates Allobrogum subiugare vacavit. Adveniente aestate, dum Romam petere et Alpes transcendere cogitaret,
nuntiatur ei Modredum, nepotem suum, cuius tutelae per-
miserat Britanniam, eiusdem diademate per tyrannidem et
proditionem usurpatum esse reginamque Gwennewaram,
violato iure priorum nuptiarum, eidem nefando thalamo
copulatam.

own people, according to the city or estate where each one had been prominent during his life. With pity for the enemy 3 as well, the king ordered the local inhabitants to bury them and also to carry the body of Lucius to the Senate in Rome, sending word that no other tribute was owed from Britain. After that he stayed the following winter in those parts, and took time to conquer the cities of the Allobroges. With the arrival of spring, as he planned to make for Rome and pass over the Alps, it was announced to him that his nephew Mo-dred, under whose protection he had left Britain, had usurped the crown through tyranny and treachery, and that Queen Guinevere had joined with him in a wicked union, in violation of her earlier wedding vows.

BOOK ELEVEN

Liber XI

[177] Rex Arturus audita fama, immo infamia, Modredi nepotis sui continuo dimissa inquietatione quam Romanis adhuc cogitarat inferre, Hoelo duci Armoricanorum exercitum Gallorum relinquens ad pacificandas partes Allobrogum, ipse cum insulanis regibus eorumque exercitibus atque obiter associatis sibi pluribus Britanniam rediit. Praedictus autem proditor ille Modredus Cheldricum, Saxonum suorum ducem, Germaniam direxerat ut inde exercitum copiosum compararet, spondens se illi hoc pacto daturum illam partem Britanniae quae a flumine Humbri usque in Scotiam porrigitur et simul quicquid in Cantia tempore Vortigerni

2 Horsus et Hengistus possederant. At ille, peracta legatione, cum octingentis navibus bellatorum Saxonum plenis rediens applicuit et, foedere dato, huic tamquam regi suo parebat. Associaverat quoque Scotos, Pictos, Hibernienses et quoscumque sciebat ante habuisse avunculum suum odio. Erant autem omnes numero quasi octoginta milia tam paganorum quam Christianorum, quorum multitudine vallatus, Arturo in Rutupi Portu applicanti obviam venit et commisso proe-

3 lio, magnam stragem applicantibus intulit. In quo loco Auguselus, rex Albaniae, et Walwanus, nepos Arturi, cum innumerabilibus corruerunt. Tandem exercitus Arturi bello

Book 11

[177] After King Arthur heard the news, or rather the scandal, about his nephew Modred, he abandoned the further harassment of the Romans that he had been planning to inflict, and leaving the army of the Gauls to Hoel, the Duke of the Armoricans, in order to pacify the regions of the Allobroges, he returned to Britain himself with the island kings and their armies, and he also gathered more men to himself along the way. But Modred, that traitor just mentioned, had sent Cheldric, the leader of his Saxons, to Germany in order to collect from there a vast army, promising by this compact to give him that part of Britain which stretched from the River Humber to Scotland, along with that part which Horsa and Hengist had possessed in Kent in the time of Vortigern. Having completed that mission, Cheldric returned and landed with eight hundred ships full of Saxon fighters, and after a formal alliance was made, he became subject to Modred as if to his own king. Modred also allied with Scots, Picts, Irishmen, and whoever else he knew to have been hostile toward his uncle in the past. There were about eighty thousand in all, as many pagans as Christians, and with their help he attacked Arthur as he was landing in Richborough and, engaging in battle, inflicted great slaughter on those who were landing. In that place died Auguselus, king of Albany, and Gawain, the nephew of Arthur, along with innumerable others. Eventually Arthur's army, being

2

3

381

magis assuetus, post mutuam cladem Modredum et exercitum eius in fugam coegerunt. Periurus igitur ille atque proditor infandus sequenti nocte fugiens Wintoniam ingressus
est cum paucis. Quo Arturus adveniens civitatem obsedit et,
cum exercitum suum per turmas in obsidionem disponeret,
ille agminibus suorum ac civium Wintoniensium in unam
coniurationem provocatis, tamquam proeliaturus egreditur
atque inito certamine fugae praecipitem se dedit fugiensque
Hamonis Portum petit ac cito remige evectus Cornubiam
4 devenit. Interea Iwenus, filius Uriani fratris Auguseli, in regnum Albaniae succedens, rex Albanorum creatus est; qui
postea in decertationibus huiuscemodi multis probitatibus
praeclaruit. Gwennewara autem regina, auditis de tanto
eventu bellorum nuntiis, confestim desperans ab Eboraco
ad Urbem Legionum diffugit atque in templo Iulii martyris
inter monachas vitam professa monachalem delituit.

[178] Arturus itaque interno dolore cruciatus, quoniam
totiens manus suas evasisset proditor suus, congregans
quantum potuit exercitum illum usque in Cornubiam prose-
quitur. Modredus autem, copiis interim terra marique comparatis, ad fluvium Cambula Arturo proeliaturus occurrit.
Tradens fortunae rei eventum atque diem extremum vitae
suae, si contingat, cum triumpho compensans, maluit cum
avunculo suo Arturo constanter dimicare atque finem rebus
2 dubiis inponere quam totiens turpiter cedere. Inito igitur
certamine committitur durissima pugna, in qua fere omnes
duces qui ex utraque parte affuerant cum suis catervis

more accustomed to battle, after mutual casualties, forced
Modred and his army into flight. The oath-breaking and un-
speakable traitor fled that night and entered into Winchester with a few of his men. When Arthur arrived there,
he besieged the city and, after he had arranged his army in
squadrons for the siege, Modred came out as if to do battle,
with his own columns of men and the citizens of Winchester
assembled in one band of conspirators; but as soon as the
fighting began, he threw himself headlong into flight,
headed for Southampton, and then conveyed by oarsmen he
speedily arrived in Cornwall. Meanwhile Ywain, the son of 4
Urian the brother of Auguselus, succeeded to the kingdom
of Albany and was made king of the Albans; afterward he became famous for his great prowess in actions of this kind.
On the other hand, once Queen Guinevere heard the reports about the outcome of the war she suddenly gave up
hope, fled from York to Caerleon and, having professed the
monastic life, went into seclusion among the nuns in the
temple of Julius the Martyr.

[178] And so Arthur, tormented by inner anguish that his
betrayer had so often slipped through his hands, gathered
together as large an army as possible, and pursued him all
the way to Cornwall. Modred, however, having raised many
troops by land and sea, ran to meet Arthur in battle at the
River Camlan. Entrusting the outcome to chance, and also
balancing the final day of his life, if it came to that, against
the chance of triumph, he preferred to fight resolutely
against his uncle Arthur rather than to withdraw disgrace-
fully so many times. Therefore, once the fighting began, he 2
engaged in a most bitter struggle, in which nearly all of the
leaders who were present on either side, along with their

mutuis vulneribus occubuerunt. Cecidit ea die Modredus cum suis ducibus, Cheldrico, Elasio, Egbricto, Brunnigo cum omnibus eorum Saxonibus, necnon et Gillapatric, Gillamor, Gillasel, Gillaruum Hiberniensibus, Scoti etiam et
3 Picti cum omnibus quibus dominabantur. In parte autem Arturi Odbericus, rex Norguegiae; Aschillus, rex Daciae; Cador Limenic; Cassibellaunus cum multis milibus suorum tam Britonum quam ceterarum gentium quas secum adduxerat. Omnes hi eadem die perierunt iuxta flumen Cambula. Sed et inclitus ille Arturus letaliter vulneratus est; qui illinc ad sananda vulnera sua in insulam Avallonis evectus, Constantino cognato suo et filio Cadoris Cornubiae Britanniam regendam dimisit, anno ab incarnatione Domini quingentesimo quadragesimo secundo.

[179/180] Postea duo filii Modredi cum Saxonibus qui remanserant, alter Londoniam, alter vero Wintoniam ingressi, contra Constantinum munire coeperunt. At Constantinus, cum armata manu Britonum civitatibus adveniens, Saxones potestati suae subiugavit et alterum iuvenem Wintoniae in ecclesia sancti Amphibali delitescentem trucidavit, alterum vero Londoniis in quodam coenobio absconditum crudeli
2 morte multavit. Tunc temporis sanctus Daniel, Bangornensis ecclesiae religiosus antistes, migravit ad Dominum. Tunc quoque obiit sanctus David, Urbis Legionum archiepiscopus, sepultusque est in Menevia civitate infra monasterium suum, quod prae ceteris suae dioceseos dilexerat, pro eo quod beatus Patricius, qui nativitatem eius prophetaverat,

armies, lay dead from the wounds they had inflicted on each other. That day Modred fell with his leaders Cheldric, Elasius, Egbrictus, and Brunigus, along with all their Saxons; and also the Irishmen Gillapatric, Gillamor, Gillasel, and Gillarum; as well as the Scots and Picts with all of those who ruled over them. On Arthur's side fell Odberic the king of 3 Norway, Aschil the king of Denmark, Cador Limenic, and Cassibellaunus, with many thousands of their men, as many thousands of Britons as of the other nations he had brought with him. All of these perished that same day beside the River Camlan. But that famous Arthur was mortally wounded; when he was carried from there for his wounds to be healed on the Island of Avalon, he left the kingdom to be ruled by Constantine, his relative and the son of Cador of Cornwall, in the five hundred and forty-second year after the incarnation of the Lord.

[179/180] Afterward the two sons of Modred, along with the Saxons that still remained, with one having gone to London, the other to Winchester, began to fortify against Constantine. But Constantine, coming to those cities with an armed band of Britons, brought the Saxons under his power, and he butchered one of the youths as he took refuge in the church of Saint Amphibalus at Winchester; the other he punished with a cruel death as he hid within a certain cloister in London. At that time Saint Daniel, the pious head of 2 the church of Bangor, went to the Lord. Then too Saint David died, archbishop of Carleon, and he was buried in the city of St. David's in his own monastery, which he loved more than the others in his diocese because the blessed Patrick himself, who had prophesied his birth, had founded

3 ipsum fundavit. Subrogatur sedi illius Kinnocus, Lampaternensis ecclesiae antistes, et ad altiorem dignitatem in metropolitanum promovetur. Cum autem duobus annis regnasset Constantinus, tertio anno interfectus est a Conano suo consanguineo et infra structuram lapidum, quae Saxonica lingua Stanheng nuncupatur, iuxta cenobium Ambrii sepelitur.

[181] Conanus vero regni diademate insignitus, dignus laude si non foret civilis belli amator, post multa facinora ab illo perpetrata secundo regni sui anno obiit.

[182] Cui successit Vortiporius, in quem insurrexerunt Saxones de Germania educentes magno navigio exercitum. Sed superatis his monarchiam totius regni adeptus est, populum gubernans annis quatuor cum diligentia et pace.

[183] Huic successit Malgo, omnium fere ducum Britanniae pulcherrimus et probitate praeclarus, nisi sodomitica esset peste foedatus et sic Deo sese invisum exhibuisset, multorum tamen tyrannorum depulsor, robustus armis, largior ceteris. Hic totam Britanniam sibi subiugavit, adiacentes quoque insulas, Hiberniam videlicet atque Islandiam, Gothlandiam, Orcades, necnon Norguegiam et Daciam, durissimis proeliis suae potestati adiecit.

[184/186] Successit Malgoni Caretius, amator civilium bellorum, invisus Deo et Britonibus Saxonibusque, cuius inconstantiam atque saevitiam Saxones ferre non valentes, miserunt nuntios ad Godmundum, regem Affricanorum, in Hiberniam quam magno navigio advectus sibi subiugaverat

it. Kinnoc, the head of the church of Llanbadarn, was ³
appointed to the see at Caerleon and promoted to metropolitan status. And when Constantine had ruled for two
years, in the third year he was killed by Conan, his relative,
and was buried next to the monastery of Ambrius, under the
structure of stones which is known as Stonehenge in the
Saxon language.

[181] Then Conan was honored with the crown of the
kingdom, worthy of praise if he had not been a lover of civil
war, and after perpetrating many crimes he died in the second year of his reign.

[182] He was succeeded by Vortipor, against whom the
Saxons rose up, bringing over an army with a large fleet from
Germany. But after he overcame them he obtained the monarchy of the whole kingdom, governing the people with diligence and in peace for four years.

[183] Malgo succeeded him, who was the most handsome
of almost all the leaders of the Britons and renowned for his
virtue, except that he was defiled by the curse of sodomy
and had thus rendered himself hateful to God; nevertheless
he was the scourge of many tyrants, powerful in arms, more
generous than all the rest. He brought all of Britain under
his control, and also the adjacent islands, namely Ireland,
Iceland, Gotland, and the Orkneys, not to mention Norway
and Denmark, which he brought under his authority
through the fiercest battles.

[184/186] Caretius succeeded Malgo, a lover of civil war,
detested by God and the Britons as well as the Saxons; unable to bear his fickleness and cruelty the Saxons sent messengers to Godmund, king of the Africans, in Ireland, which
he had conquered after he landed there with a large fleet,

et adduxerunt eum in Britanniam cum centum sexaginta milibus Affricanorum bellatorum. Inito igitur foedere Godmundus cum Saxonibus oppugnavit Caretium regem Britonum et post plurima proelia fugere coegit et persequens eum de civitate in civitatem tandem in Cicestria ob-
2 sedit eum. Dum autem ibi moram faceret, venit ad eum de Francia Ysembertus, nepos Ludovici regis Francorum, navigio advectus et cum eo iniit foedus amicitiae, rogans ut se vindicaret de avunculo suo, rege Francorum, qui, ut aiebat, vi et iniuste illum de Francia expulerat et ut ei facilius acquiesceret de Christiano factus est paganus et sacrificiis idolorum se commaculavit. Capta deinde civitate illa quam obsederat, fugae iterum se dedit Caretius et pertransiens totam Britanniam usque ultra Sabrinam non cessavit fugere,
3 donec pervenit in Guallias. At Godmundus, dimisso illo, agros depopulatus est et succendit igni urbes et municipia, vicos et castra necnon et monasteria et omnes regionis ecclesias depredatus est et ferro et igne ad terram diruit colonosque cum mulierculis partim necavit, partim abduxit; nec quievit donec omnem terrae superficiem fere a mari usque ad mare exussit. Fugiunt episcopi de sedibus suis et presbyteri simul reliquias sanctorum secum asportantes, monachi et moniales et universi quotquot Affricanorum gladium evadere potuerunt, et desolata est terra ab omni specie sua, maxime Loegria quae pars Britanniae melior exstiterat.

[186/187] Postquam infaustus ille tyrannus totam re-

and they brought him to Britain with one hundred sixty thousand African warriors. Having made an alliance with the Saxons, Godmund fought against King Caretius of the Britons and after many battles he forced him to flee, and pursuing him from city to city he finally besieged him in Cirencester. But while he waited there, Ysembertus the 2 nephew of Ludovicus, king of the Franks, came to him with a fleet from France, and entered into an alliance of friendship with him, asking Godmund to take revenge for him against his uncle the king of the Franks, who, it was said, had expelled him from France wrongfully and by force; and so that Godmund would more readily agree, he converted from a Christian to a pagan and defiled himself with sacrifices to idols. Then, once they captured that city that Godmund had besieged, Caretius once again took flight and, crossing over the whole of Britain all the way beyond the Severn, he did not cease to flee until he came to Wales. But 3 Godmund let him go and laid waste to the fields and set fire to the cities and towns, villages and camps; he also plundered both the monasteries and all the churches of the region, and razed them to the ground with sword and fire. Some of the farmers he put to death with their wives, some he carried away; and he did not rest until he completely burned the surface of the land almost from sea to sea. The bishops fled from their sees together with the priests, carrying away with them the relics of the saints, and as many of the monks and the nuns and all the people as could escape the sword of the Africans; and the land was emptied of all its splendor, especially Loegria, which had stood out as the better part of Britain.

[186/187] After that ill-omened tyrant devastated that

gionem illam devastavit, Saxonibus tenendam dimisit atque ad Gallias cum Ysembarto transivit. Hinc Saxones Angli vocati sunt qui Loegriam possederunt et ab eis Anglia terra postmodum dicta est. Britonibus enim fugatis atque dispersis, amisit terra nomen Britanniae sicque Angli in ea super reliquias Britonum regnare coeperunt et Britones regni diadema amiserunt nec postea pristinam dignitatem nisi post

2 longum tempus recuperare potuerunt. Secesserant itaque eorum reliquiae partim in Cornubiam, partim in Guallias, ubi nemoribus obtecti in montibus et speluncis cum feris degentes longo tempore delituerunt, donec revocata audacia irruptiones in Anglos Saxones crebras facere conati sunt et sic diu perseveravere ut nec Saxones in illos, nec illi in

3 Saxones praevalerent. Creati sunt interea plurimi reges Anglorum Saxonum qui in diversis partibus Loegriae regnaverunt. Inter quos fuit Athelbrictus rex Cantiae, vir illustris et magnae pietatis, [188] cuius temporibus missus est beatus Augustinus a beato Gregorio papa Romano in Angliam ut Anglis verbum vitae praedicaret, qui fugatis Britonibus Christianis adhuc in errore gentilitatis perseverabant. Veniens itaque Augustinus in Cantiam susceptus est a rege Athelbricto gratanter et, eo permittente et concedente, verbum Dei genti Anglorum praedicavit et signo fidei eos insignivit. Deinde non multo post Athelbrictus rex ipse cum

2 ceteris baptismatis sacramentum consecutus est. Suscepta igitur ab Anglis in Cantia Christianitate, diffusa est per totam Loegriam fides Iesu Christi usque ad fines Britonum. Quo perveniens beatus Augustinus invenit in provincia

region, he left it to be held by the Saxons and crossed over to Gaul with Ysembertus. Henceforth the Saxons were called English who possessed Loegria, and from them the land was afterward called England. The Britons having fled and dispersed, the land lost the name of Britain and thus the English in it began to rule over the remnants of the Britons, and the Britons lost the crown of the kingdom, nor were they able to regain it for a long time afterward. Thus the remnants of them had withdrawn partly into Cornwall, partly into Wales, where they hid for a long while, passing their time among the wild beasts, concealed among the mountains in forests and caves until, recalling their courage, they attempted to make repeated attacks against the Anglo-Saxons; and they continued like this for a long while, so that neither could the Saxons prevail over them nor they over the Saxons. Meanwhile many kings of the Anglo-Saxons were created, who reigned in different parts of Loegria. Among them was Ethelbert the king of Kent, a famous man and one of great piety, [188] in whose time the blessed Augustine was sent to England by the blessed Roman Pope Gregory to preach the word of life to the English, who were driven away by the Christian British and still persisted in their pagan ways. Coming then to Kent, Augustine was graciously received by King Ethelbert and, with his permission and consent, preached the word of God to the English people and marked them with the sign of the faith. Not long after that, King Ethelbert himself, along with others, followed in the sacrament of baptism. Once Christianity had been accepted by the English in Kent, the faith of Jesus Christ was spread all the way to the borders of the Britons. Arriving there, Augustine found in the province which the

Britonum, quam tunc possidebant, septem episcopatus et unum archiepiscopatum et abbatias quam plures, in quibus grex Domini ordinem ecclesiasticum tenebat. Inter quos erat abbas, Dinoot nomine, liberalibus artibus eruditus, in Bangor civitate praesidens bis mille fere monachis, qui per diversas mansiones divisi labore manuum victum sibi adquirebant et in septem portiones dividebant prout singulis quibusque opus erat; sed et nulla portionum minus continebat

3 quam trecentos monachos. Augustino itaque petenti subiectionem ab eis sibi debere fieri, utpote metropolitano et totius regni primati, et communem evangelizandi laborem secum susciperent in gentem Anglorum, renuerunt omnes pariter et episcopi et abbates, dicentes nullam ei subiectionem debere facere nec inimicis suis communicare pro eo quod et regno et lingua et sacerdotio et consuetudinibus omnino divisi essent, praesertim cum gens illa maledicta illis foret exosa, utpote quae de propriis sedibus illos violen-

4 ter eiecerat, et adhuc eis vim inferre perseverarent. Neque enim aiebant Anglis magis quam canibus communicare velle; praeterea ipsi proprium metropolitanum tamquam primatem et regem cum regni sui diademate sibi praefecerant, quibus potius oboedire secundum legem Dei satagebant et, quia ipsi priores baptismi gratiam consecuti fuerant, indignum videbatur et contra morem ecclesiasticum fieri ut posteris et barbaris inimicis ullatenus subderentur.

[189] Athelbrictus ergo, rex Cantiorum, ut audivit Britones indignantes subiectionem facere Augustino et praedicationem eius spernere, graviter ferens misit ad regem Edelfridum Nordamhumbrorum et ceteros subregulos

Britons held at that time seven bishoprics and one archbishopric and many abbeys in which the Lord's flock held
holy orders. Among them was an abbot named Dinoot, educated in the liberal arts, governing almost two thousand
monks in the city of Bangor. Divided among various houses,
they acquired their sustenance through the labor of their
own hands, and divided it in seven parts according to each
one's need, and no part contained less than three hundred
monks. When Augustine insisted that they ought to submit 3
themselves to him, as the bishop and primate of the whole
realm, and should join with him in the common task of converting the English people, they all refused, bishops and ab-
bots alike, stating that they owed him no submission, and
did not wish to speak with their enemies for him, because
their kingdom and language and priesthood and customs
were entirely different; especially since that accursed nation
was hateful to them, inasmuch as it had violently expelled
them from their proper home, and still continued to use
force against them. Indeed, they said, they did not wish to 4
communicate with the English any more than with dogs.
Moreover, they had put their own archbishop and primate
in command, and a king with the crown of his kingdom,
whom they preferred to obey according to the law of God.
Finally, because they had received the grace of baptism earlier, it seemed unworthy and would be against the custom of
the church for them to be made subordinate in any way to
late-coming and uncivilized enemies.

[189] When Ethelbert, the king of Kent, heard that the
Britons refused to submit to Augustine and spurned his
preaching, he took it very badly and sent to King Ethelfrith
of the Northumbrians and other petty kings of the Saxons,

Saxonum rogans ut, collecto exercitu, in civitatem Bangor abbatem Dinoot cum ceteris Augustini praedicationem

2 spernentibus perditum irent. Qui mox regis praeceptis acquiescentes, exercitum magnum producunt et provinciam Britonum petentes venerunt Legecestriam, ubi Brochinail, consul urbis eiusdem, cum exercitu suo adventum eorum praestolabatur ut dimicaret cum eis. Qui pauciori militum numero resistens, Anglis insistentibus attrociter in fugam versus est amisso exercitu. Edelfrido itaque, civitate capta, occurrerunt cives obviam et populi, qui terrore suo se intra

3 incluserant, ut pro salute sua supplicarent. Venerant quoque ad eandem civitatem monachi et eremitae, viri religiosi quamplures ex diversis Britonum provinciis et maxime de Bangor, ut pro salute populi sui intercederent apud regem Edelfridum et ceteros regulos. Quos diri et funesti barbari, cum intellexissent causam quare advenissent, tamquam ovium greges in caulas usque ad duo milia et ducentos trucidaverunt absque misericordia et de confessoribus martyres

4 fecerunt. Cumque ulterius progrederentur ut civitatem Bangornensium adirent atque caedem inceptam peragerent, Britonum duces, audita eorum insania, in unum convenerunt, Bledricus videlicet, dux Cornubiae, et Margadud, rex Demetorum, Cadvanus quoque, rex Venedotorum, et conserto proelio ipsum Edelfridum vulneratum Dei auxilio in fugam propulerunt et totum fere eius exercitum extinxerunt. In parte quoque Britonum cecidit Bledricus dux.

[190] Post haec convenerunt principes Britonum in urbem Legecestriae communemque assensum simul

asking them to gather an army and come to the city of Bangor to destroy Abbot Dinoot along with the rest of those who scorned the preaching of Augustine. Quickly obeying 2
the orders of the king, they led forward a great army and, making for the province of the Britons, they came to Chester, where Brochmail, the commander of that city, was waiting for their arrival with his own army. Opposing them with a smaller number of soldiers, as the English savagely pressed forward he lost his army and turned to flight. And so, after the city was captured by Ethelfrith, the citizens and the commoners who had shut themselves inside because of their fear came running out to beg for their safety. Monks 3
and hermits also came to that city, very many religious men from the various provinces of the Britons and mostly from Bangor, to intercede for the safety of their people in the presence of King Ethelfrith and the other lesser kings. When the terrible and deadly barbarians understood why they had come, just like herds of sheep in their pens they slaughtered as many as two thousand two hundred of them without mercy, and made martyrs of the faithful. When they 4
advanced farther in order to attack the city of Bangor and complete the ongoing massacre, the leaders of the Britons heard of their madness and came together as one, namely Bledric the Duke of Cornwall and Margadud the king of the Demetians, and also Cadvan, king of the Venedotians. After they joined in battle, with God's help they drove that same Ethelfrith away in flight, wounded, and wiped out nearly his whole army. On the side of the Britons Duke Bledric was also killed.

[190] After this the leaders of the Britons came together in the city of Chester and by common consent they all

habuerunt ut Cadvanum sibi regem facerent eoque duce Edelfridum ultra Humbrum insequerentur. Cumque id nuntiatum esset Edelfrido, associavit sibi omnes reges Saxonum obviusque Cadvano perrexit. Qui cum catervas suas ex utraque parte statuissent ad bellum, intervenerunt amici eorum pacemque inter eos tali pacto fecerunt ut Edelfridus trans Humbrum, Cadvanus vero citra Humbrum Britanniam possideret. Cum autem Deo praeside conventionem huiusmodi iureiurando atque obsidibus datis comfirmassent, orta est tanta amicitia inter eos ut omnia sua communia haberent. Elapso deinde tempore natus est Cadvano ex propria coniuge filius nomine Cadwallo. Sub eodem quoque tempore peperit uxor Edelfridi filium nomine Edwinum.

[191/192] Hi post mortem parentum diademate insigniti susceperunt curam regnorum agendam secundum antecessorum institutionem et amicitiam quam prius patres eorum tenuerant inter se ipsi statuere tenendam. Emenso deinde biennio, rogavit Edwinus Cadwallonem ut sibi diadema liceret habere celebraretque statutas sollemnitates in partibus Nordamhumbrorum quemadmodum ipse citra Humbrum antiquo more consueverat. Cumque inde iuxta fluvium Duglas colloquium haberent, disponentibus sapientioribus et antiquioribus qua ratione id melius fieri posset, Cadwallone in altera parte fluminis existente consilio Briani nepotis sui, qui forte secum aderat, paenituit eum inceptae pactionis mandavitque Edwino quod nullatenus a consiliariis suis impetrare poterat, quatinus permisissent eum petitioni eius

agreed to make Cadvan their king, and to pursue Ethelfrith beyond the Humber under his command. And when this was reported to Ethelfrith, he formed an alliance with all the kings of the Saxons and proceeded against Cadvan. When their troops had been arranged for battle on either side, their friends intervened and made peace between them with the understanding that Ethelfrith would be master of Britain across the Humber, and Cadvan on the near side of the Humber. But after they had confirmed this agreement 2 before God by swearing oaths and giving hostages, such friendship arose between them that they held all their possessions in common. Then, with the passage of time, a son named Cadwallon was born to Cadvan by his own wife. At the same time the wife of Ethelfrith gave birth to a son named Edwin.

[191/192] After the death of their parents, once they were crowned they began to manage their kingdoms in accordance with the arrangement of their predecessors, and decided to maintain between themselves the friendship that their fathers had previously maintained. After two years had passed, Edwin asked Cadwallon that he be allowed to have a crown and to observe the established ceremonies in the regions of the Northumbrians, just as Cadwallon was accustomed to do in accordance with ancient tradition on the near side of the Humber. And while they were holding a 2 conference next to the River Duglas, with their counselors and elders trying to decide the best way to proceed, Cadwallon, who was standing on the far side of the river, regretted the agreement they had established, with the counsel of his nephew Brian, who happened to be with him, and he sent word to Edwin that there was no way he could persuade his

3 acquiescere. Aiebant enim contra ius veterumque traditio-
nem esse regnum unius coronae duobus coronatis summitti
debere. Iratus itaque Edwinus, dimisso colloquio reversus
est in Nordamhumbriam, asserens se sine licentia Cadwallonis regali diademate initiaturum. Quod cum Cadwalloni
esset nuntiatum, intimavit ei per legatos se amputaturum
caput eius sub diademate si infra regnum Britanniae coro-
nari praesumeret.

[193] Orta igitur inter eos discordia, cum utrorumque
homines magis bellum quam pacem affectantes sese plurimis decertationibus inquietassent, convenerunt ambo iuxta
Humbrum factoque congressu amisit Cadwallo multa milia
sociorum et in fugam versus est. Arreptoque per Albaniam
2 itinere transfretavit in Hiberniam. At Edwinus, ut triumpho
potitus fuit, duxit exercitum suum per provincias Britonum
combustisque civitatibus cives et colonos pluribus affecit
tormentis. Dum ergo sic saeviret in Britones, conabatur
Cadwallo clam reverti et in aliquo portu applicare; nec poterat quia per magum quendam qui venerat ad Edwinum de
Hispania, adventum illius praesciebat et, quocumque portu
3 applicare destinabat, armato milite illi obvius erat. Nomen
magi Pellitus dicebatur et volatu avium cursuque stellarum
praedicebat regi omnia quae ei accidere poterant: unde
valde ei erat carus. Interea consilium quaerit Cadwallo quid
inter haec agendum sit et tandem deliberavit apud se ut

counselors to let him agree to his request. For they said that 3
it would be against the law and ancient tradition that an island with one crown should be obliged to be subject to two
crowned heads. And so Edwin became angry, abandoned the
meeting, and returned to Northumbria, stating that he
would be crowned with the royal diadem without permission from Cadwallon. When this was reported to Cadwallon, he sent word through his ambassadors that he would
cut off the head beneath his diadem if he dared to be
crowned within the kingdom of Britain.

[193] Hostilities therefore broke out between them, and
after each one's men, desiring war more than peace, had harassed each other with many battles, the two of them came
together beside the Humber and, once they met in battle,
Cadwallon lost many thousands of his comrades and turned
away in flight. After he marched through Albany, he crossed
over to Ireland. But as soon as Edwin had achieved victory, 2
he led his army through the provinces of the Britons and,
after burning the cities, he afflicted the citizens and farmers
with many torments. While he vented his rage against the
Britons in this way, Cadwallon was secretly making an effort
to return and make a landing in some harbor; but he could
not because Edwin learned about his coming in advance
through a certain magician who had come to him from
Spain, and attacked Cadwallon with armed men wherever
he tried to land. The name of this magician was Pellitus, and 3
by the flight of birds and the orbit of stars he predicted to
the king everything that might happen to him; for this reason he was highly valued by him. Meanwhile Cadwallon
sought counsel as to what should be done in these circum-
stances, and eventually he decided to seek out his kinsman

regem Armoricanorum Salomonem cognatum suum peteret, quatinus consilio eius et auxilio in regnum suum restitueretur.

[194/195] Pandens itaque vela, iter flexit versus Armoricum regnum et transfretavit et applicuit in portum Kidale-
tae urbis veniensque ad regem Salomonem gratanter ab illo
et honorifice susceptus est. Cumque causam adventus eius
didicisset, mox sibi ferre auxilium quantum praevaleret spopondit. Sed quia hiemis tempus instabat et opus erat maiori
consilio ad tantam rem peragendam, hiemandum illi secum
erat, ut post hiemem collecto exercitu navibusque paratis
hostes Saxonicos viriliter invaderent.

[196] Interea consilium ineunt ut magus ille Pellitus aliquo modo perimeretur, ne machinationes eorum et adventus eorum in Britanniam detegantur. Praemiserunt Brianum
Cadwallonis nepotem, ut curam eius rei ageret, quatinus
clam ex insidiis prorumpens magum interimeret et a presti-
giis suis et maleficiis arte diabolica comparatis Britanniam
2 liberaret. Navigans ergo ille applicuit in Portum Hamonis et
exiens in terram de navi finxit sese pauperculum vilibus
pannis obsitum fecitque sibi fieri baculum in summitate fer-
reum et acutum valde, tamquam peregrinus de longa pere-
grinatione advectus esset. Deinde perrexit Eboracum, quo
audierat degere regem Edwinum et, cum ingrederetur civitatem, associavit se pauperibus qui regis eleemosynam pete-
3 bant. Eunte autem illo et redeunte ac deambulante cum
ceteris, egressa est soror eius de triclinio reginae, baiulans

Salomon, king of the Armoricans, so that with his advice and help he could be restored to his kingdom.

[194/195] And so, spreading his sails, he turned his course toward the kingdom of Armorica and passed over the sea and landed in the port of the town of Quidalet, and coming to King Salomon he was graciously and honorably received by him. And when Salomon had learned from him the reason for his coming, he soon promised to give him as much help as he needed to prevail. But because the time of winter was approaching and there was need for greater deliberation to accomplish such a task, he had to spend the winter with him so that after the winter, with their army assembled and their ships prepared, they could boldly attack their Saxon enemies.

[196] Meanwhile they considered in what manner that magician Pellitus might somehow be killed, so that their schemes and their coming into Britain would not be revealed. They sent Cadwallon's nephew Brian ahead to manage that task, so that by secretly rushing forth from an ambush, he could kill the magician and free Britain from his magic and the sorcery prepared by his diabolical art. He 2 sailed to Southampton and as he disembarked he transformed his appearance by covering himself with worthless rags like a pauper, and he made himself a staff with a very sharp iron tip, such as a pilgrim would have carried back from a long pilgrimage. Then he proceeded to York where he had heard that Edwin spent his time and, when he entered the city, mingled with the paupers who were seeking alms from the king. But as he went back and forth and wan- 3 dered about with the others, his sister emerged from the queen's dining chamber, carrying a bowl in her hand to draw

pelvim in manu ut de fonte proximo aquam hauriret. Illam enim rapuerat Edwinus ex urbe Wigorniensium dum post fugam Cadwallonis in provincias Britonum desaeviret. Cum ergo ante Brianum praeteriret, agnovit eam Brianus et in fle-
4 tum solutus eam voce dimissa vocavit. Quae cum illius faciem propius intueretur, agnito fratre in lacrimas collapsa est atque osculis praelibatis familiaribus collocuti sunt invicem sermonibus. At illa indicavit breviter fratri, quasi aliud loquens, statum regni et magum quem quaerebat, qui forte tunc inter pauperes deambulabat, digito demonstravit et
5 agnoscere fecit. Qui mox dimissa sorore intromisit se infra turbam pauperum. Et cum aditum feriendi reperisset, erexit burdonem et infixit in pectore magi; cadensque in terram magus mortuus est. Mox proiecto Brianus in terram baculo, inter pauperes pannosos, pannosus ipse delituit nulli astan-
6 tium suspectus. Dehinc egressus cum ceteris, propero gradu relinquens civitatem et totam regionem illam Exoniam usque pervenit, ubi convocatis Britonibus de Cornubia et de finitimis locis, notificavit Cadwallonis adventum fore in proximum cum grandi exercitu ad eorum omnium liberationem et palmam civitatesque et oppida munirent et sibi conservarent, misitque citam legationem ad Cadwallonem. Divulgato itaque hoc rumore, Peanda, Merciorum rex, cum magna multitudine Saxonum ab Edwino missus, venit Exoniam et obsedit eam.

[197] Interea applicuit Cadwallo ad portum Totonesium cum decem milibus militum bellatorum quos ei rex

water from a nearby fountain. For Edwin had carried her off from the city of Worcester while he was venting his rage against the provinces of the Britons after the flight of Cadwallon. As she passed in front of him, Brian recognized her, uttered a sob, and called to her in a quiet voice. When she looked at his face nearby, recognizing her brother, she collapsed in tears, and they spoke together with kisses to the cheek and talk of family matters. But then in a few words she revealed to her brother the state of the realm, as if speaking of other things, and she pointed with her finger and identified the magician he was looking for, who happened at that time to be wandering among the paupers. He soon left his sister and plunged into the crowd of paupers. And once he had found an opening to strike him, he raised his staff and drove it into the magician's chest, and, falling to the ground, the magician died. Quickly throwing the staff to the ground, Brian hid among the paupers dressed in rags, being dressed in rags himself, and none of the bystanders suspected him. Departing with the others, leaving behind the city and that entire region behind at a speedy pace, he came all the way to Exeter where, after he summoned the Britons of Cornwall and neighboring areas, he told them that because Cadwallon was coming soon with a great army to liberate them all and win the palm of victory they should fortify their cities and towns and keep themselves safe; and he sent a swift ambassador to Cadwallon. When news of this had spread, Penda, king of the Mercians, who was sent by Edwin with a great multitude of Saxons, came to Exeter and besieged it.

[197] Meanwhile Cadwallon landed at the port of Totnes with ten thousand armed warriors that his kinsman King

Salomon, cognatus suus, tradiderat petivitque celeriter Exoniam. Ut ergo comminus vidit exercitum Peandae circa civitatem, divisit milites suos in quatuor partes et sic per turmas hostes undique invasit. Consertoque proelio, captus

2 est Peanda et exercitus eius peremptus. Cumque ille aditum alium non haberet, subdidit se Cadwalloni fide sua et adiuratione promittens datisque obsidibus sese cum illo Saxones inquietaturum. Convocavit itaque Cadwallo proceres suos multo tempore a se delapsos et desolatos atque verbis consolatoriis eos exhortans, congregavit quantum potuit exercitum atque in Nordamhumbriam contra Edwinum regem duxit; patriamque totam in transitu suo non cessavit vastare ferroque et igne trucidare atque cremare quoscumque ho-

3 stes invenit. Audiens autem hoc Edwinus rex, convocavit omnes sibi subditos Anglorum regulos cum exercitibus eorum et in campo qui Hedfeld appellatur obviam veniens Britonibus bellum commisit sibi suisque cruentum. In quo bello interficitur ipse et totus fere populus cum regulis qui cum eo venerant necnon et filius eius Osfridus cum Godbaldo, rege Orcadum, qui in auxilium eorum venerat.

[198] Confecto itaque proelio et victoria patrata, universas Cadwallo provincias Saxonum perlustrans ita in totum Anglorum Saxonum genus debacchatus est et omnis exercitus eius, ut ne quidem sexui muliebri vel parvulorum aetati parceret, multos inauditis tormentis afficiens, ceteros diversis mortibus puniens. Post haec commisit proelium cum Osrico, qui Edwino successerat, et interfecit eum et duos

Salomon had sent to him, and he went quickly to Exeter. When he saw the army of Penda close at hand around the city, he divided his soldiers into four parts and advanced through the hostile troops on every side. Once the battle was joined, Penda was captured and his army was destroyed. And since he had no other way out, he gave himself up to Cadwallon, and he promised on his faith and by swearing oaths and giving hostages to harass the Saxons himself together with Cadwallon. And so Cadwallon called his long-abandoned and forsaken nobles together, and, encouraging them with words of consolation, he put together as large an army as he could, and led them against King Edwin in Northumbria; and along his way he continued to lay waste to the whole country with sword and fire and to slaughter and burn alive whatever enemies he came upon. Hearing this, however, King Edwin called together all the lesser kings of the English who were subordinate to him together with their armies, and, coming against the British in a field called Hatfield, he and his men engaged in a bloody battle. In that battle he himself was killed and nearly the whole multitude together with the lesser kings who had come with him, and also his son Osfrith along with Godbald, king of the Orkneys, who had come to help them.

[198] Once the battle was over and victory was achieved, traversing through all the provinces of the Saxons, Cadwallon vented his fury against the whole Anglo-Saxon race and all of its armies in such a way that he spared not even the female sex or the very young in age, afflicting many with unheard-of torments, punishing others with various deaths. After this, he engaged in battle with Osric, who had succeeded Edwin, and killed him and two of his nephews who

nepotes eius quos post illum regnare sperabat sed et Eada-
num, regem Scotorum, qui eis in auxilium venerat.

[199] His itaque omnibus interemptis, successit Oswaldus in regnum Nordamhumbrorum, quem rex Cadwallo,
mox ut audivit, cum grandi exercitu invasit atque fugavit
usque ad murum quem Severus imperator olim inter Britanniam Scotiamque construxerat. Ut ergo vidit illum in re-
motas partes fugientem, noluit vexare seipsum et totum
exercitum suum insequendo eum, sed misit Peandam, Merciorum regem, cum quadam sui exercitus parte ut eum de-
2 bellaret. Quo comperto, Oswaldus noluit diutius fugere sed
mansit in loco qui dicitur *Hevenfeld,* id est "celestis campus,"
expectans Peandam insequentem ibique erexit Dominicam
crucem et indixit commilitonibus suis ut orationem ad
Deum facerent in haec verba: "Flectamus genua omnes et
Deum omnipotentem, unum ac verum, in commune depre-
cemur ut nos ab exercitu superbo Britannici regis et eius
nefandi ducis defendat. Scit enim ipse quia iusta pro salute
gentis nostrae bella suscepimus."

3 Fecerunt ergo omnes ut iusserat et sic, diluculo in hostes
progressi, secundum fidei suae meritum victoria potiti sunt.
Fugiens ergo Peanda venit ad Cadwallonem, dolens quod sic
ab Oswaldo devictus esset et fugatus. At Cadwallo, acri
insurgens ira, collecto exercitu Oswaldum persecutus est et
conserto cum illo proelio in loco qui Burne vocatur irruit in
eum Peanda et interfecit.

[200] Oswaldo itaque perempto et martyre effecto,

were hoping to rule after him, and also Aidan, king of the Scots, who had come to help them.

[199] And so, after all these men were killed, Oswald succeeded to the kingdom of the Northumbrians. As soon as he heard this, King Cadwallon invaded with a great army and drove him all the way to the wall that the Emperor Severus had long ago constructed between Britain and Scotland. Then, when Cadwallon saw him fleeing to remote regions, he did not want to harass him himself and follow after him with his whole army, and instead he sent Penda, the king of the Mercians, with a certain part of his army to vanquish him. When he learned this, Oswald did not want to flee any 2 longer, and instead he waited in the place that is called *Heavenfield*, that is "heavenly field," expecting Penda to come after him, and there he raised the Lord's cross and declared to his comrades that they should pray to God in these words: "Let us all bend our knees and together entreat the one and true almighty God to protect us from the proud army of the British king and his wicked commander. For he knows himself that we have undertaken a just war for the safety of our people."

Then everyone did as he commanded and thus, when 3 they marched forth at dawn against the enemy, they achieved victory as the due reward for their faith. Fleeing, therefore, Penda came to Cadwallon, lamenting that he had been defeated in this way and put to flight by Oswald. But Cadwallon, rising up with bitter anger, gathered his army, chased after Oswald and, after engaging him in battle in the place called Burne, Penda charged against him and killed him.

[200] After Oswald was killed and became a martyr, his

successit ei in regnum Oswi, frater eius, qui cum Cadwallone pacem constituens multa donaria auri et argenti dedit et amicitiam cum eo confirmavit et se sibi subdidit et sic ex tunc toti Britanniae imperavit rex Cadwallo. Nec mora insurrexerunt in Oswi Alfridus filius eius et Oiwald filius fratris eius. Sed cum praevalere ei nequissent, secesserunt

2 ad Peandam regem implorantes auxilium contra Oswi. At Peanda, timens pacem a rege Cadwallone constitutam infringere, distulit inquietationem Oswi sine licentia regis inferre, donec illum aliquo modo incitaret, quatinus vel ipse in Oswi insurgeret vel sibi copiam cum eo congrediendi concederet. Quadam igitur sollemnitate Pentecostes cum rex Cadwallo in Badonia civitate festum celebraret et omnes Anglorum reges et Britonum duces praeter Oswi adessent, adivit Peanda regem et quaesivit ab eo cur Oswi solus abes-

3 set a coetu baronum suorum. Cui rex cum responderet infirmitatis causa interveniente eum detineri posse, adiecit Peanda dicens nequaquam sic esse, sed illum propter Saxones misisse in Germaniam, ut fratrem suum Oswaldum in se et in ceteros vindicaret. Addidit quoque illum pacem contra ius suum infregisse, utpote qui Alfridum et Oiwald bello inquietatos a propria patria expulerit. Petivit ergo licentiam ut illum vel interficeret vel de regno fugaret. Rex

4 itaque Cadwallo haec audiens, emisit Peandam et familiares suos atque optimates convocans quaesivit ab eis quid super his esset agendum. Tacentibus ergo aliis, Margadud, rex Demetorum, pro ceteris respondit:

brother Oswiu succeeded him and, making peace with Cadwallon, he gave him many gifts of gold and silver and confirmed his friendship with him and made himself subject to
him, and so from that time on King Cadwallon ruled as high
king over all of Britain. Not long after that Oswiu's son Alhfrith and Oethelwald, the son of his brother, rose against
him. However, since they were unable to prevail over him,
they withdrew to King Penda, begging for help against Oswiu. But Penda, afraid to break the peace established by 2
King Cadwallon, was reluctant to bring any trouble against
Oswiu without the king's permission, until such time as he
could arouse him to the point where he would either rise up
against Oswiu himself or grant Penda the opportunity to
confront him. Then at a certain Pentecostal feast, when
King Cadwallon was celebrating the holiday in the city of
Bath and all the English kings and British leaders except Oswiu were present, Penda approached the king and asked him
why Oswiu alone was absent from the assembly of his barons. When the king answered that he might be detained be- 3
cause of an unexpected illness, Penda interrupted, saying it
was not that at all, but rather because Oswiu had sent to
Germany for Saxons in order to take revenge upon him and
others for his brother Oswald. He also added that Oswiu
had broken the peace in violation of his law, inasmuch as he
had driven Alhfrith and Oethelwald, harassed by war, from
their own country. Then Penda asked for permission either
to kill him or to drive him out of the kingdom. Hearing this, 4
King Cadwallon sent Penda and his retainers forth, and calling his nobles together he asked them what should be done
about all this. When the others remained silent, Margadud,
king of the Demetians, responded for the rest:

"Domine mi rex, quoniam omne genus Anglorum tibi infestum semper fuisse novimus et propter eius perfidiam te ex finibus Britanniae illud expulsurum proposuisti, cur pa-
5 cem eos inter nos habere pateris? Eia ergo permitte saltem ut ipsimet inter se ipsos oppugnantes se consumant et mutuis cladibus affecti universi a regno exterminentur. Peanda iste de illis est et eandem perfidiam quam in genus suum machinatur, ne dubites quin in te ipsum tuosque exerceat, si locum et tempus innatae proditionis habuerit. Da igitur ei licentiam ut in Oswi insurgat et debacchari invicem permitte, ut sic civili discordia exorta alter alterum perimens omnes a patria deleantur."

6 His itaque dictis, omnis procerum contio consensit et rex Peandae petitionem fieri concessit. Ille vero laetus discedens, collecto exercitu transivit Humbrum super Oswi et ferro et igne terram eiusdem vastare coepit. Cumque immaniter atque crudeliter superbia elatus in Oswi desaeviret, mandavit ei Oswi ut sibi parceret et donaria auri et argenti
7 multa daret. Cum autem nec sic a proposito Peanda cessare vellet, nec precibus nec muneribus eius acquiesceret, rex Oswi divinum expetens auxilium cum Peanda decrevit pugnare et convenientes iuxta fluvium Winied proelium inierunt. Sed licet Oswi minorem numero habuisset exercitum, superior tamen Deo auxiliante factus est, et Peanda
8 cum triginta ducibus perempto, victoriam adeptus est. Post Peandam Wlfridus, filius eius, donante Cadwallone successit ei in regnum Merciorum. Qui consociatis sibi Eba et Edberto ducibus rebellavit adversum Oswi. Sed iubente ac

"My lord king, since we know the whole race of the English was always hostile to you, and because of its treachery you proposed to drive it out from the land of Britain, why do you allow them to live in peace among us? Come now! At ₅ least allow them to exhaust each other fighting among themselves and be expelled from the entire kingdom after they are weakened by mutual slaughter. This Penda is one of them, and have no doubt but that he would exercise the same treachery against you and your men, if he had the time and place for his inborn treachery. Therefore, give him permission to rise up against Oswiu and let them vent their fury on each other, so that when civil war breaks out, with one killing the other, they are all erased from our native land."

After these things were said, the whole assembly of no- ₆ bles agreed and the king granted Penda's request. Penda marched away happy, and after he gathered his army he crossed over the Humber against Oswiu and began to lay waste to his land with sword and iron. And as he, swollen with pride, was raging brutally and savagely against Oswiu, Oswiu sent word to him that he would give many gifts of gold and silver if Penda would spare him. But when Penda ₇ would neither abandon his objective nor assent to Oswiu's request or his offer of gifts, asking for divine assistance King Oswiu decided to fight with Penda and, coming together by the river Winwaed, they engaged in battle. Even though Oswiu had a smaller army, nevertheless with God's help he gained the advantage and, after killing Penda and thirty of his leaders, he won the victory. After Penda, his son Wul- ₈ fred, with Cadwallon's approval, succeeded him to the kingdom of the Mercians. After making an alliance with the dukes Eba and Edbert, he rebelled against Oswiu. But at

prohibente tandem Cadwallone rege pacem habuerunt inter se ad invicem.

[201] Completis postea quadraginta octo annis, Cadwallo infirmitate gravatus quindecimo Kalendis Decembris obiit. Cuius corpus Britones balsamo et aromatibus conditum in aenea statua posuerunt atque super aeneum equum ipsam statuam, armis decoratam, collocaverunt. Deinde super occidentalem portam Londonie erexerunt in signum victoriae ad terrorem Saxonum. Sed et ecclesiam subtus in honore beati Martini aedificaverunt, in qua pro ipso et fidelibus omnibus defunctis divina celebrarentur obsequia.

[202] Successit Cadwalloni in regnum filius suus Cadwalladrus, cuius temporibus civile discidium inter Britones ortum est. Mater namque eius soror Peande fuerat, ex nobili quidem Gewisseorum genere edita, eamque Cadwallo post factam cum fratre concordiam in societatem tori acceperat et inde Cadwalladrum genuerat. Dum ergo regnaret Cadwalladrus et se omnibus amabilem praestaret, decidit in lectum et languore corripitur magno.

[203] Quo languente discordia, ut dictum est, afficiuntur Britones et opulentam patriam dissensione detestabili destruere totis viribus conantur. Accessit interea aliud infortunium: fames videlicet dira insipientem affecit populum adeo ut praeter venationem et herbarum surculos deficerent eis ciborum solatia. Quam famem continuo pestifera mortis lues subsecuta est, quae in brevi tantam populi stragem

length they were commanded and restrained by Cadwallon, and each of them made peace between themselves and King Oswiu.

[201] After forty-two years had passed, weighed down by illness Cadwallon died on the seventeenth day of November. The Britons placed his body, preserved with balsam and spices, in a bronze statue and then set that statue, adorned with arms, atop a bronze horse. Then they raised it up above the western gate of London as a sign of victory and an object of terror for the Saxons. And below it they built a church in honor of Saint Martin, in which divine services were performed for him and all the faithful who had died.

[202] Cadwallon's son Cadwallader succeeded him as king. In his time civil discord arose between the Britons. For his mother was the sister of Penda, descended from the noble race of the Gewissae. After making peace with her brother, Cadwallon had taken her to his bed and thus he fathered Cadwallader. Then, while Cadwallader was ruling and surpassing everyone in the degree to which he was loved, he was suddenly confined to his bed and overcome with great weakness.

[203] As he languished, the Britons were afflicted by discord, as mentioned before, and with their detestable quarreling they tried with all their might to destroy their wealthy land. Meanwhile another misfortune arrived: namely an awful famine that afflicted the foolish people to the point that they were lacking in sustenance other than game from hunting and sprouts of grasses. A deadly pestilential plague immediately followed the famine, which in a short while produced such carnage among the people that the living were

2 fecit, ut vivi mortuos vix sepelire possent. Ad cuius mortali-
tatis excidium—miserabile ac pavendum spectaculum—
multi sive in domo sive in agro attoniti passim moriebantur
sine aegrotatione, aeris tantum, ut ferebatur, corruptione.
Nonulli quoque stantes et loquentes, edentes et bibentes
subito exspirabant. Unde reliqui stupefacti transmarinam
fugam quam plurimi inierunt. Ipse quoque rex Cadwalladrus ad Armoricam cum paucis navigio effugit et inter navigandum fertur has lugubres voces ad Deum protulisse:

3 “Vae nobis miseris et peccatoribus, qui ob immania scelera nostra, quibus Deum offendimus, hanc tribulationem et
dispersionem patimur; gentem et patriam amittimus. Timendum est valde nobis ne post hanc caelestem patriam
perdamus et eterna hereditate privemur. Domine, miserere
nobis; tempus et locum paenitentiae misericorditer permitte. Ne irascaris nimis ut, si vel terrena caremus ac praesenti hereditate, illa omnino non frustremur ad quam boni

4 omnes quos in hac vita elegisti laborant pervenire. Extermi-
nat nos de terra nostra potestas ultionis tuae, quos nec olim
Romani vel quaelibet gens robustior eradicare potuit. Vere
peccavimus ultra modum coram te et angelis tuis, qui digni
non sumus, ut conversi ad paenitentiam terras quas coluimus inhabitemus. Expellimur flagello iracundiae tuae quia
servi nequissimi sprevimus, dum licuit, veniam misericordie

5 tue. Experimur nunc severitatem iudicantis qui, dum tempus habuimus, noluimus flectere lumina ad paternitatem
vocantis. Frustra patriam nostram adversus hostes, te

scarcely able to bury the dead. In this ruination of mortal- 2
ity—a wretched and frightening spectacle—many people
were struck with terror and died everywhere, whether at
home or in the field, without sickness, it was said, and only
from corruption of the air. Some actually fell dead while
they were standing and talking, eating and drinking. For this
reason very many of those who remained were stunned and
fled across the sea. King Cadwallader himself also escaped
by ship to Armorica with a few men, and it is said that during the voyage he offered up these mournful words to God:

"Woe to us wretches and sinners, who suffer this tribula- 3
tion and dispersion because of our tremendous sins, by
which we offended God; we have lost both our people and
our country. After this we must be very anxious not to lose
our heavenly country and be deprived of our eternal inheritance. Lord, take pity on us; allow us time and place for re-
pentance. Do not become exceedingly angry so that, if indeed we lose our earthly and immediate inheritance, we
shall not be completely deprived of that which all good men
you chose in this life strive to attain. The power of your ven- 4
geance banishes us from our country, we whom neither the
Romans of old nor any stronger race could root out. Truly
we have sinned beyond measure before you and your angels,
and are unworthy that we should, once we turn to repen-
tance, inhabit the lands that we lived in. We are banished by
the lash of your anger because we, your most worthless servants, scorned the indulgence of your mercy when it was allowed. Now we experience the severity of judgment who, 5
when we had time, did not want to turn our eyes to our pa-
ternity when called. In vain did we so often, with your help,
fight against the enemy for our land and so often, with your

adiuvante, totiens expugnavimus, totiens expulsi te donante recuperavimus, si sic olim decreveras universum genus nostrum extirpare de terra viventium. Sed placabilis esto, quaesumus, super malitiam nostram et converte luctum nostrum in gaudium ut, de periculo mortis erepti, viventes tibi Domino Deo nostro, cuius servi esse debemus, in perpetuum

6 famulemur. Redeant ergo Romani, redeant Scoti et Picti, redeant Saxones perfidi et ceteri, quibus patet Britannia, ira Dei deserta, quam illi desertam facere nequiverunt. Non nos fortitudo illorum expellit, sed summi regis indignatio et potentia."

[204] Ut igitur hos et alios gemitus rex Cadwalladrus navigando explevit, in Armorico litore appulsus est. Veniensque ad Alanum, regem Salomonis nepotem, susceptus est benigne cum omnibus suis mansitque cum eo quamdiu voluit. Britannia igitur civibus suis viduata ac desolata, per undecim annos ab incolis, exceptis paucis Britonibus, horrenda et inculta fuit; Saxonibus quoque Anglis eadem tempestate ingrata, quia in illa sine intermissione extingue-

2 bantur. Quorum residui, cum feralis illa lues cessasset, miserunt in Germaniam propter concives suos ut desolationem suam aliis civibus supplerent. Illi vero nihil haesitantes, ut audierunt terram ab incolis orbatam, festinato itinere cum innumerabili multitudine virorum ac mulierum navigantes applicuerunt in partibus Nordamhumbriae et ab Albania us-

3 que in Cornubiam universam terram occupaverunt. Nec enim supererat quisquam qui prohiberet vel commaneret in locis desertis, praeter paucas reliquias Britonum qui superfuerunt et de praefata mortalitate evaserunt vel postea nati sunt. Illi abdita nemorum inhabitant in Gualiis tantum

permission, regain it after being expelled, if you had long ago decided in this way to extirpate our entire race from the land of the living. But be appeased, we beg you, about our evil, and turn our sorrow into joy so that, snatched from the peril of death, living for you our Lord God, whose servants we must be, we shall serve forever. The Romans shall return, 6 the Scots and the Picts shall return, the faithless Saxons and others shall return, to whom Britain shall lie open, the island which they cannot empty being emptied by the wrath of God. The strength of those others does not banish us, but the anger and power of the highest king."

[204] As soon as King Cadwallader while sailing completed those and other laments, he was driven to the coast of Armorica. Coming to King Alan, the nephew of Salomon, he was received courteously along with his men and stayed with him as long as he wished. For Britain, bereft and deserted by its citizens, was overgrown and uncultivated for eleven years by its inhabitants, except for a few Britons; at the same time it was unpleasant for the Saxons and also the Angles, because they were dying in it without pause. After 2 that deadly plague had ceased, those who remained sent to Germany for their fellow countrymen in order to fill up their desolation with other citizens. Without hesitation, as soon as they heard the land was deprived of its inhabitants, sailing by the quickest route with a countless multitude of men and women, they landed in the region of Northumbria and occupied the entire land from Albany to Cornwall. Nor 3 was anyone left who might hinder them, or abide in that empty place except a few remnants of the Britons, who either survived and escaped the plague just mentioned, or were born afterward. They inhabited the hidden recesses of

et in Cornubia commanentes. Ab illo ergo tempore potestas Britonum cessavit et Angli in totum regnum regnare coepe-

4 runt. Adestano rege facto, qui primus inter eos diadema portavit, pacem et concordiam tamquam fratres inter se habentes, agros coluerunt, civitates et oppida reaedificaverunt et magistratus et potestates in urbibus constituentes leges quas de terra sua advexerant, subiectis populis tradiderunt servandas; ducatus et honores prout Britones ante habuerant inter se dividentes, summa pace et tranquillitate terram desiderabilem incoluerunt.

[205] Cumque magnum temporis spatium emensum esset et populus Anglorum, sicut dictum est, in Britannia roboratus et augmentatus fuisset, recordatus Cadwalladrus regni sui amissi, iam a praefata colluvione purificati, quaesivit maerens ab Alano, cognato suo, consilium et auxilium ut potestati pristinae restitueretur. Quod cum ab illo impetrasset, intonuit ei vox divina, dum classem pararet, ut coeptis

2 suis desisteret. Praeviderat enim Deus Britones in Britannia, quae tunc Anglis tradita erat, amplius non regnare donec tempus illud veniret quod Merlinus prophetaverat. Praecepit etiam illi ut Romam ad Sergium papam properaret ubi, peracta paenitentia, inter beatos reciperetur. Dicebat etiam populum Britonum per meritum suae fidei in posterum Britanniam fore adepturum, cum fatale tempus

3 compleretur. Nec id tamen antea futurum quam Britones, reliquiis corporis sui potiti, illas in Britanniam a Roma asportarent. Tunc demum, revelatis sanctorum quorundam

the woods, abiding only in Wales and in Cornwall. From that time the power of the Britons ceased and the English began to rule the whole kingdom. After Athelstan was made 4 king, the first among them who wore the crown, maintaining peace and concord among themselves like brothers, they cultivated the fields, rebuilt the cities and towns, and, appointing magistrates and rulers in the cities, they handed down the laws they had brought from their own land to be followed by their subjects; dividing up the dukedoms and honors among themselves exactly as the Britons had held them before, they lived in that desirable land with the greatest peace and security.

[205] And since a great length of time had passed and the English people, as we said, had been strengthened and increased, when Cadwallader remembered his lost kingdom, now cleansed of the contamination mentioned before, he grew sad and sought advice and help from his kinsman Alan, in order to be restored to his former power. But after he had obtained that from him, while he was preparing his fleet a divine voice thundered at him to stop what he had begun. For God had foreseen that the Britons would not reign any 2 more in Britain, which had then been given over to the English, until that time came which Merlin had predicted. It also instructed that he should hurry to Pope Sergius in Rome where, after doing penance, he would be received among the blessed. It also said the people of the Britons, according to the merit of their faith, would secure Britain in future generations, when the fated time should be completed. Nor would this time come before the Britons, after 3 they obtained the remains of his body, carried them from Rome to Britain. Then, after the remains of certain saints

reliquiis, quae propter paganorum terrorem dudum abscondite fuerant, amissum regnum recuperarent. Quod cum auribus beati viri intimatum fuisset, tamquam in extasi ex visione turbatus venit ad Alanum regem et indicavit ei quod ei caelitus indicatum fuerat.

[206] Tunc Alanus, sumptis de armariis libris et convocatis sapientioribus terrae suae philosophis, coepit per eos scrutari quae de prophetiis aquilae quae Sestoniae prophetaverat, quae de carminibus Sibyllae ac Merlini in scriptis suis reperissent sibi exponendo notificarent, ut videret

2 an revelatio Cadwalladri oraculis eorum concordaret. Et cum omnia haec perscrutasset et nullam discrepantiam eorum reperisset, suggessit Cadwalladro ut divinae providentiae pareret, et quod ei caelitus indicatum fuerat perficeret, filium autem suum Ivorum vel nepotem ad regendas Britonum reliquias in Britanniam dirigeret, ne gens eorum omnino interiret aut libertatem barbarica irruptione amitteret.

3 Mox ergo Cadwalladrus abrenuntians saecularibus pompis, recto itinere venit Romam, ubi a Sergio papa honorifice susceptus et criminum suorum omnium coram ipso confessione puro corde facta, languore inopino correptus duodecimo die Kalendarum Maiarum, anno ab Incarnatione Domini sescentesimo octogesimo nono, a carnis contagione solutus, caelestis curiae ianuam coronandus ingressus est.

[207] Ivor autem cum duodecim navibus in Kambriam venit et convocatis Britonum reliquiis ex cavernis et nemoribus cum multitudine quam secum adduxerat, Saxones

were revealed which had been hidden long ago out of fear of the pagans, they would regain their lost kingdom. Once the blessed man had heard this he came to King Alan as if thrown into a trance by his vision, and shared what had been revealed to him from heaven.

[206] Then, after he selected books from his cupboards and summoned the wiser philosophers of his land, Alan began with their help to examine what they had found in their writings about the prophecies of the Eagle that had prophesied at Shaftesbury, and about the verses of the Sibyl and Merlin, while they explained what they meant, in order to see whether the revelation of Cadwallader was in harmony with their oracles. And when he had examined all of these 2 things and had found no disagreement, he suggested to Cadwallader that, in order to comply with divine providence and bring to fulfillment what had been revealed to him from heaven, he should direct his son Ivor or his nephew into Britain to govern the remnants of the Britons, so that their race would not altogether perish or lose its freedom through barbarian attacks. Soon, therefore, Cadwallader, renounc- 3 ing all worldly displays, came directly to Rome, where after he was honorably received by Pope Sergius and confessed all his sins with a pure heart in his presence, he was overcome with an unexpected weakness, and on the twentieth of April, in the six hundred eighty-ninth year after the incarnation of the Lord, released from the contagion of the flesh, he entered through the gate of the heavenly court to be crowned.

[207] Ivor, however, came to Wales with twelve ships and, after he assembled the remnants of the Britons from the caves and the forests, along with the multitude that he had

invadere mox decrevit et eos viriliter per quadraginta octo annos oppugnavit. Sed Ivor de hac vita discedente, Britones propter civile discidium nullo modo Saxonibus resistere po-
2 tuerunt. Nam ultio divina in tantum exsecuta est Britones, ut de omnibus bellis victi discederent. Tunc autem Britones sunt appellati Gwalenses, sive a Gwalone duce eorum sive a Galaes regina sive a barbarie vocabulum trahentes. Sed illi Britones qui in parte boreali Angliae remanserunt, a lingua Britannica degenerati, numquam Loegriam vel ceteras australes partes recuperaverunt.

[208] Regum autem acta qui ab illo tempore in Gwaliis successerunt et fortunas successoribus meis scribendas dimitto ego, Galfridus Arturus Monemutensis, qui hanc historiam Britonum de eorum lingua in nostram transferre curavi.

brought with him, he immediately ordered that the Saxons should be attacked, and he fought against them vigorously for forty-eight years. But after Ivor departed from this life, because of their internal strife the Britons could not resist the Saxons in any way. For divine retribution was visited 2 upon the Britons to such a degree that they abandoned all their battles in defeat. At that time, however, the Britons were called the Welsh, taking the word either from their leader Gwalonus, or from Queen Galaes, or from their barbarism. But those Britons who stayed behind in the northern part of England, having degenerated from the British tongue, never recovered Loegria or the other parts in the south.

[208] But I, Geoffrey Arthur of Monmouth, who took pains to translate this history of the Britons from their language into ours, leave the deeds and fortunes of the kings who succeeded in Wales from that time on to be written by my successors.

Abbreviations

CM = Bede, *Chronica Maiora,* ed. Mommsen, vol. 3, pp. 223–333

Curley = Michael J. Curley, *Geoffrey of Monmouth* (New York, 1994)

Faral = Edmond Faral, *La légende arthurienne, études et documents: Des origines à Geoffroy de Monmouth* (Paris, 1929)

Gildas = *Gildae Sapientis de excidio et conquestu Britanniae,* ed. Mommsen, vol. 3, pp. 1–85

GRA = William of Malmesbury, *Gesta Regum Anglorum,* ed. and trans. R. A. B. Mynors, R. M. Thomson, and M. Winterbottom (Oxford, 1998)

HA = Henry of Huntingdon, *Historia Anglorum: The History of the English People,* ed. and trans. Diana Greenway (Oxford, 1996)

Hammer = Jacob Hammer, ed., *Historia Regum Britanniae: A Variant Version Edited from Manuscripts* (Cambridge, Mass., 1951)

HE = Bede, *Historia Ecclesiastica,* ed. Bertram Colgrave and R. A. B. Mynors, *Bede's Ecclesiastical History of the English People* (Oxford, 1969)

Jerome = Rudolf Helm, ed., *Eusebius Werke 7: Die Chronik des Hieronymus,* Die griechischen christlichen Schriftsteller der ersten Jahrhunderte, 47 (Berlin, 1956)

Landolfus = Amedeo Crivellucci, ed., *Landolfi Sagacis Historia romana,* Fonti per la Storia d'Italia, 49–50 (Rome, 1912–1913)

Mommsen = Theodor Mommsen, ed., *Chronica minora saec. IV. V. VI.*

VII., Monumenta Germaniae Historica, Auctores Antiquissimi, 9, 11, 12 (Berlin, 1892–1898)

Nennius = *Historia Brittonum cum additamenti Nennii,* ed. Mommsen, vol. 3, pp. 111–222

Reeve = Michael D. Reeve, ed., and Neil Wright, trans., *The History of the Kings of Britain: An Edition and Translation of* De gestis Britonum (Historia regum Britanniae) (Woodbridge, 2009)

Tatlock = J. S. P. Tatlock, *The Legendary History of Britain, Geoffrey of Monmouth's Historia Regum Britanniae and Its Early Vernacular Versions* (Berkeley, 1950)

TYP = Rachel Bromwich, ed., *Trioedd Ynys Prydein: The Triads of the Island of Britain* (Cardiff, 2006)

WCD = Peter C. Bartrum, *A Welsh Classical Dictionary: People in History and Legend up to about A.D. 1000* (Aberystwyth, 1993)

Wright = Neil Wright, ed., *Historia Regum Britannie of Geoffrey of Monmouth II: The First Variant Version: A Critical Edition* (Woodbridge, 1988)

Note on the Text

The text of the Variant has been preserved in six complete manuscripts, one small fragment, and a set of excerpts copied during the eighteenth century. Two more manuscripts contain later redactions that combine the Variant with other versions: *a* with the Second Variant, and *c* with the Vulgate. The following list uses Wright's *sigla,* adding *L* and *T* for two newly identified witnesses.

a = Aberystwyth, National Library of Wales, MS 13210 (13th century)

c = Cardiff, South Glamorgan Central Library, MS 2.611 (13th–14th century)

D = Dublin, Trinity College, MS 515 (E.5.12) (13th–14th century)

E = Exeter, Cathedral Library, MS 3514, Wales (13th century)

H = London, British Library, MS Harley 6358 (13th century)

L = Lawrence, Kans., Kenneth Spencer Research Library, MS 9/1 A:22 (12th century)

P = Aberystwyth, NLW, MS 2005 (Panton 37) (18th-century excerpts from *T*)

R = Paris, Bibliothèque de l'Arsenal, MS 982 (7.H.L.) (14th century)

S = Edinburgh, National Library of Scotland, MS Adv. 18.4.5 (13th–14th century)

T = Dublin, Trinity College, MS 11500 (14th century)

After it was written, chapters 108 to 178 of the hybrid text in *c* were lost and the omission was later supplied from a copy of the Vulgate. *H* is a composite in which an incomplete exemplar of the Variant was copied through the middle of chapter 149, and the Vulgate was used from there to the end. There is a lacuna in *a* resulting from the loss of four leaves between chapters 186/187 and 203. Three folios containing most of Book 7 were excised from *S* after the Prophecies of Merlin were proscribed by the church in 1564.[1]

The Variant has been edited critically twice, first by Jacob Hammer (from manuscripts *cDEHP*) and later by Neil Wright (from manuscripts *acDEHSPR*). Hammer based his edition from chapter 5 through the first sentence of 119 on the hybrid text of *c*, so that the strictly Variant text of *DEHP* can be reconstructed only by reference to his apparatus. From that point to the end, he printed two separate versions: the text of *c* (with the Vulgate portion of *H* after the middle of chapter 149), followed by the text of *DEP* (with the Variant portion of *H* up to 149). In this last section Hammer based his edition on *E* because he felt that it preserved the oldest and best text of the Variant. Wright, having identified three more manuscripts, determined that the available witnesses fell into two principal groups, *aHR* and *DES,* with *c* and *P* agreeing sometimes with one and sometimes with the other. He proposed a stemma with two main branches, with *aHR* in the first and *DES* in the second. He assigned *c* to the second branch, although it does not share any of the errors that define that group and agrees just as often with *aHR,* because it contains the same nonstandard version of Dares Phrygius that appears in *DES*. He concluded, provisionally, that the excerpts in *P* could be explained only as resulting from the conflation of a *DES*-type text with a manuscript similar to *H* and placed its lost exemplar at the bottom of his stemma by rejoining the two main branches at that point. Believing the Variant to be a later redaction of the Vulgate, Wright argued that *aHR* must be closer to the original since they often agree with the Vulgate text against *DES*. He chose manuscript *R* (the only complete member of this group) as the basis for his edition, although it is the only manuscript of continental origin (Italy or Southern France) and the furthest removed in date (late fourteenth century) from the composition of the Variant. The result is a text with very peculiar orthography, as well as some unique readings that probably reflect later correction against the Vulgate. In chapter 200, for example, *R* is the only Variant manuscript that agrees with the Vulgate by placing Cadwallon's Easter feast in London rather than Bath.

Since Wright's edition was published, two more witnesses to the Variant have come to light. *L* is a fragment of one twelfth-century leaf.[2] Its text is closely related to *aH* since it agrees with them (against both *R* and *DES*) in more than a dozen readings. This confirms Wright's treatment of *aH* and *R* as separate offshoots of his first branch. Manuscript *T* is the long-missing exemplar of the excerpts in *P*, which resurfaced in 2014.[3] In the choice of individual words and arrangement of phrases, *T* sometimes agrees with *aHR* and sometimes with *DES*. These changes in allegiance do not correspond with visible transitions in scribal hands or disruptions in foliation. Moreover, they are so frequent (occurring multiple times within individual paragraphs) that they cannot be explained simply by the use of different exemplars for different sections of the text. *T* does not share any of the errors or omissions that define *aHR* or *DES* as groups. I would therefore assign *T* to its own branch in the stemma rather than treating it as a contaminated text resulting from conflation of the two groups.

The text presented here is based on Wright's edition, but I have not felt bound by his preference for the readings of *aHR* over those in *DES*. There is ample evidence that the original reading might be preserved in either group. In chapters 112 to 117, for example, where the Prophecies were copied from the Vulgate into the common ancestor of all the surviving Variant manuscripts, departures from the original text are about evenly divided between the two groups. As in the case of *T*, I would assign *c* to a separate branch of the stemma, since it does not share the defining errors of either group and shows equally frequent agreement with both. The version of Dares it contains is irrelevant, because we have no idea whether that was present in the Variant manuscript used by the author of the hybrid text in *c*. I therefore adopt some readings from *DES* when they agree with *c* or *T* (or both). Each of those readings was also followed by Hammer. In two important passages (describing the parentage of Brutus in chapter 6 and the Britons' loss of dominion in 186/187), *DES* have the better text because in both cases they agree with Wace. His *Roman de Brut,* completed in 1155, provides an earlier witness to the original content of the Variant than any of the surviving manuscripts. In two other passages (describing the persecution under Diocletian in 77 and the two castles of Gorlois in 137), *aHR* agree with Wace, and their text is followed here. The Notes to the Text record all substantive departures from Wright's edition. Since the text printed here is normalized, purely orthographical variants of the same word noted by Wright are treated as a single reading. I have incorporated the readings of *L, T,* and the excerpt in Spelman, but dispensed with the now-superseded readings of *P.*

Book Divisions are handled differently in the surviving manuscripts. Manuscripts *aHR* have rubrics using the formula *incipit . . . explicit* and numbering each book (though not all at the same locations); *DS* begin each book with large capitals; and *E* has spaces for large capitals, with later-added marginal numbers for some books. *T* assigns numbers to Books 2 to 6 and has unnumbered rubrics at the head of Books 7 to 9; it marks no division at Book 10 and labels Book 11 as 9. The divisions adopted here occur in the majority of manuscripts, from both groups.

The manuscripts show no consistency in marking individual paragraphs or chapters of the text. Wright adapted the 208 numbered chapters used in Edmond Faral's 1939 edition of the Vulgate. These divisions sometimes apply awkwardly to the Variant text, in some cases resulting in chapters only a few sentences long and in others the combination of two chapters into one (191/192 and 194/195). They also involve the rearrangement and renumbering of partial chapters where the organization of the narrative in the Variant differs significantly from the Vulgate (160–64 and 179–87). Nevertheless, they are followed here because they greatly facilitate comparison between the two versions.[4]

Notes

1 In addition to these ten manuscripts, a portion of chapter 72 was printed from an unknown First Variant manuscript in Henry Spelman's *Concilia* of 1639, vol. 1, pp. 12–13. It was relegated to the Appendix in Wilkins' ex-

panded version of the *Concilia* in 1737, vol. 4, p. 693, and replaced with Vulgate text from the 1587 Heidelberg edition of the *Historia.*

2 This fragment was part of a "paleographical teaching set" donated by Professor William D. Paden to the Kenneth Spencer Research Library at the University of Kansas in the 1970s. The library dates the fragment to the second half of the twelfth century. Jaakko Tahkokallio, "Update to the List of Manuscripts of Geoffrey of Monmouth's *Historia Regum Britanniae*," *Arthurian Literature* 32 (1915): 187–203, dates it to the first half of the thirteenth century.

3 The manuscript belonged to Dr. Treadway Nash in 1773. His heirs brought it to Eastnor Castle in Herefordshire, where it remained in the muniment room until it was sold in 2014. For a description of its contents, see the catalog for Christie's Sale 1568, *Valuable Manuscripts and Printed Books* (London, November 19, 2014); and Bernard Meehan, "A Fourteenth-Century Historical Compilation from St Mary's Cistercian Abbey, Dublin," *Medieval Dublin* 15 (2016): 264–76.

4 Wright's adaptation of Faral's chapter numbers to the Variant was careful and needs refinement only at the beginnings of chapters 66, 89, and 145, which occur midsentence in the Variant.

Notes to the Text

turmis *cDEST*: catervis *aHR and Wright*

21.1   contis *aDEST (followed by Wace)*: concis *c*; conchis *HR and Wright*

BOOK 2

24.2   fuit *cDEST*: fuerat *aHR and Wright*

26.1   duxit uxorem et *cHT (followed by Wace)*: uxore *aDERS and Wright*

27.2   civitatem *cDEST*: civitas *aHR and Wright*

27.4   Angues *aHR and Wright*: Agnes *cDEST*

        Stadiald *a*: Stadralis *cDES*; Stadralus *T*; Stadialis *R and Wright*

29.1   civitatem *cDEST*: urbem *aHR and Wright*

        Egypti *DES*: Egipti *cT*; Epiti *aR*; Epyti filius *H*; *Wright emends to*
        Epit<us>

31.1   Goronilla *EST and Wright*: Gonorilla *aDH*

        Regau *aHRT and Wright*: Ragau *cDES*

31.4   Regau *aHRT and Wright*: Ragau *DES*

31.5   ut *acDEHRST*: sicut *R and Wright*

31.7   ad regem *cDEST*: regi *aHR and Wright*

31.8   intimatum esset *cDEST*: regi intimatum fuisset *aHR and Wright*

31.9   praedictas *cDEST*: priores *aHR and Wright*

31.19   Soram *cDELST*: Sora *aHR and Wright*

32.1   Cunedagio *DERST and Wright*: Conedagio *acHL*

32.4   Osee *acHR and Wright*: Iosue *DES*

33.2   Suhardi *DEHST*: Suardi *acR and Wright*

34.3   dixit *DEHLST*: indixit *aR and Wright*; ait *c*

BOOK 3

35.1   eius *cDEST*; eius duo *aHR and Wright*

35.2   iunior *cDEST*; minor *aHR and Wright*

35.4   consilio *cDEST*: consiliis *aHLR and Wright*

37.1   uxor *cDEST*: sponsa *aHR and Wright*

38.1   fidei iuramento *cDEST*: foedere iuramenti *aR and Wright*

39.3   praeceperit *cDES*: statuerit *aHRT and Wright*

41.1   totam *cDEST*: omnem *aHR and Wright*

43.6   scilicet *DEST*: et *c*; *omitted in aHR and Wright*

46.4   fluminibus *cDEST*: fluminibus rivisque *aHR and Wright*

BOOK 5

48.3   miserabiliter *cDES*: misere *aHRT and Wright*
48.4   pisciculum *cDES*: pisciculum belua *aHRT and Wright*
51.1   fratrem suum primogenitum *cDES*: primogenitum fratrem *aHRT and Wright*
52.1   Ennianus *c*; Enmanus *H*; Emmanus *DEST*; Enimaunus *a*; Eumanius *R and Wright*
52.2   Catellus *cDES*: Catullus *aRT and Wright*
        Eldaldus *cDES*: Eldadus *R and Wright*; Eldanus *aH*; Elbanus *T*
53.1   Heli *acHRT and Wright*: Beli *DES*
53.4   extrema *cDES*: externa *aHRT and Wright*

Book 4

54.2   Britanniam *cDES*: Britanniam insulam *aHRT and Wright*
56.2   scilicet *cDES*: videlicet *aHRT and Wright*
        Cridious *D*: Cridionus *c*; Eridious *E*: Eridionis *aT and Wright*; Eridionus *S;* Eridioris *R;* Eridion *H*
58.1   illis *DES*: *omitted in acHRT and Wright*
58.3   non solum *aDEHT*: non solum ipsum *c*; non solum non *RS and Wright*
62.8   noster *DEST*: vester *acHR and Wright*
63.3   Gallias *cDES*: Galliam *aHRT and Wright*
66.2   catervis *cDES*: cuneis *aHRT and Wright*
66.3   regis *cDES*: regis Arviragus *aHRT and Wright*
66.4   divisi sunt *cDES*: dividuntur *aHRT and Wright*
72.6   dicaverunt *acDEHT and Spelman*: dedicaverunt *RS and Wright*

Book 5

75.2   natus *cDES*: creatus *aHRT and Wright*
75.4   ad *cDES*: *omitted in aHRT and Wright*
78.1   Kaercolim *cDES*: Kaercolim id est Colecestrie *aHT and Wright* (*also in the Vulgate*)
78.2   pro *cDES*: de *aHRT and Wright*
78.3   insignitus *cDES*: potitus *aHRT and Wright*
81.1   filiam . . . laudarent *cDES*: laudarent filiam locare alicui nobilium Romanorum *aHRT and Wright*

86.2   perempto *cDEST*: interempto *aHR and Wright*
86.3   factus *cDEST*: creatus *aHR and Wright*
88.4   praedicti *cDEST*: praefati *aHR and Wright*
88.5   Praefati *cDEST*: Praedicti *aHR and Wright*
91.4   funerum genera *DEST (see Gildas §20 and Bede, HE 1.13)*: generum
         funera *acHR and Wright*
94.1   dux *cDEST*: consul *aHR and Wright*
95.1   cessisset *cDEST*: cederet *aHR and Wright*
95.8   est *cDEST*: *omitted in aHR and Wright*
96.1   ergo in *cDEST*: itaque *aHR and Wright*
96.3   Budicius *acD*: Buditius *Wright*; Gudicius *H*; Hudicius *ERST*

Book 6

98.1   Erat *aDEST*: Eratque *cHR and Wright*
         esset *cDEST*: fuisset *aHR and Wright*
98.6   in *cDES*: infra *aHRT and Wright*
99.6   vel Twangcastre *DEST*: vel Dwanceastre *c*; *omitted in aHR and*
         Wright
100.6   Genuerat *cDEST*: Generaverat *aHR and Wright*
101.1   consiliarius *cDEST*: consiliator *aHR and Wright*
101.3   iussitque *cDEST*: concessitque *aHR and Wright*
101.6   Episford *c*; Epiford *H*; Episfrod *aDERST and Wright*
102.2   Arianum vel Pelagianum *cDEST*; Arianum *aH*: Pelagianum *R*
         and Wright
102.4   Convocans itaque Vortimerius *DEST*: Convocans ergo *c*; Con-
         vocans *H*; Qui convocans *R and Wright*

Book 7

112.6   fruticosos *DE (and Vulgate)*: fructuosos *aHRST and Wright*
         After redibunt *all manuscripts of the Variant omit one sentence found*
         in the Vulgate: Exsurget iterum albus draco et filiam Germaniae
         invitabit.
115.5   Annae *aHR and Wright (and Vulgate)*: Amne *DET*
116.4   excitabit *H (and Vulgate)*: excaecabit *aDERT and Wright*

116.7 sua *aH (and Vulgate)*: *omitted in DERT and Wright*

116.9 Galabes *aDET (and some Vulgate manuscripts)*: Galahes *HR and Wright*

116.10 illa *DER (and Vulgate)*: illam *aHT and Wright*

116.11 dumque *H*: dum *aDERT and Wright*; et dum *in Vulgate*

116.13 ipsum *aHT (and Vulgate)*: *omitted in DER and Wright*

116.17 Galabes *aDET (and some Vulgate manuscripts)*: Galahes *HR and Wright*

116.18 rugitu *DERT and Wright*: rechanatu *aH (and Vulgate; see discussion in Wright, p. xcv)*

116.23 dorsum unius *(Vulgate)*: dorsum vivus *a*; vivus *HR and Wright*; unus *DET*

116.24 gigas *(Vulgate)*: *missing in all manuscripts of the Variant and omitted by Wright*

117.4 Officia Iani *DH (and Vulgate)*: Officio iam *ERS and Wright*; Officia iam *aT*

121.1 festinant *DEHRST*: festinat *a and Wright*

125.2 Eldadus *aHR and Wright*: Eldaldus *DEST*

125.3 in *DEST*: per *aHR and Wright*
fecisti *DES*: fecisti tu *aHRT and Wright*

128.3 Galabes *aDEHST (Labanes in Wace)*: Galahes *R and Wright*

130.6 Samsonem *aE*: Sansonem *H*; Sampsonem *DRST and Wright*

132.2 Uther *aHS and Wright*: Utherpendragon *DERT*

135.2 ipse *DE*: *omitted in aHRST and Wright*

136.5 ocius *aHT*: citius *R and Wright*; onus *DES*

136.6 aderant *DES*: aderant Britonibus *R and Wright*; aderant baronibus *aHT*

136.7 Christi *ES*: Iesu Christi *R and Wright*; Christi Iesu *aHT*

137.2 gaudio magno *DES*: magna laetitia *R and Wright*; laetitia magna *H*; summa laetitia *aT*

137.10 eius *aDES*: esse *R and Wright*; esse eius *T*

142.3 cumulum *DES*: tumulum *aHRT and Wright*

BOOK 9

143.1	sublimaverunt *DEST*: consecraverunt *aHR and Wright*
	Erat *DEST*: Et erat *aHR and Wright*
143.4	eorum *DES*: *omitted in aHRT and Wright*
145.1	Calidonis *DRST*: Colidonis *aE and Wright*; Kolidonis *H*
146.1	Exeuntes *DES*: Euntes *aT and Wright*; Errantes *R*; *omitted in H*
149.3	undecumque *DES*: undique *R and Wright*; *omitted in T*
150.3	retractio *ES*: irroratio *aRT and Wright*; retractatio *D (with ir-roratio in margin)*
153.3	Doldavius *aRT and Wright*: Doldanius *DES*
155.1	Gallia *DES*: Gallia provincia *aRT and Wright*
156.4	Demetorum *DES*: Demetorum id est Suthgualensium *aRT and Wright*
156.5	Morvid *S*: Morwid *aDET and Wright*; Mordwit *R*
	Arthgal *DES*: Archgal *RT and Wright*: Artgal *a*
	Legecestria *aR and Wright*: Leicestria *DEST*
163.3	ducenta *DES*: centum *aR and Wright*; *omitted in T*

BOOK 10

161.1	Auguselus *aDEST*: Anguselus *R and Wright*
162b.2	foret *DEST*: esset *R and Wright*
	promittunt *DEST*: spondent *R and Wright*
165.8	oboediens *DEST*: accedens *aR and Wright*
166.4	celerius *DEST*: armatus *aR and Wright*
	manus *DEST*: manus iam *aR and Wright*
166.7	affatus est *DEST*: affatur *R and Wright*
167.5	Hirelglas *DES*: Hirelgas *aRT and Wright*
168.1	hoc, nunc illud *aDERST*: *Wright emends to* h<u>c, nunc illu<c> *as in the Vulgate*
	incepta *DEST*: coepta *a and Wright* (and Vulgate); capta *R*
169.1	ceterorum *DES*: terdenorum *aT and Wright*; edenorum *R*
169.2	nostram *DES*: vestram *aRT and Wright*
170.2	Non *aDEST*: nec *R and Wright*
171.1	lanceis *DEST*: sicis *R and Wright*; cesi *a*
176.3	corpus quoque *DEST*: corpusque *R and Wright*

BOOK II

178.3   Odberictus *cDET*: Odbericus *a*; Obictus *S*; Obericus *R and Wright*

179/180.3 suo consanguineo *DEST*: omitted in *aR and Wright*

183.1   esset *DEST*: *omitted in aR and Wright*
         et sic *DES*: sic *T*; *omitted in aR and Wright*

184/186.1 Caretius *aDES*: Carecius *R and Wright*; Caresius *T*
         amator *DEST*: amator idem *aR and Wright*

186/187.1 Saxones Angli *DEST*: Angli Saxones *R and Wright*
         atque *DEST*: ac *aR and Wright*
         amiserunt *DEST*: in perpetuum amiserunt *aR and Wright*
         nisi post longum tempus *DEST*: *omitted in aR and Wright*

186/187.3 Athelbrictus *DES*; Athelbertus *T*; Edelbertus *R and Wright*

188.2   eruditus *DEST*: inbutus *R and Wright*

189.1   indignantes *DEST*: dedignantes *R and Wright*
         graviter *DEST*: gravissime *R and Wright*

189.2   magnum *DEST*: grandem *R and Wright*
         Legecestriam *RST and Wright*: Legrecestram *DE*; Leyrcestram *in margin of D*

189.3   et *DEST*: *omitted in R and Wright*

189.4   civitatem *DEST*: urbem *R and Wright*
         Cadvanus *DEST*: *Cadwanus R and Wright*
         ipsum *DEST*: ipsum regem *R and Wright*

190.1   urbem *DEST*: civitatem *R and Wright*

190.2   Elapso deinde *DES*: Lapso itaque *R and Wright*; Elapso itaque *T*
         peperit *DEST*: peperit et *R and Wright*

191/192.3 caput eius *DEST*: ei caput *R and Wright*

196.1   Interea *DEST*: Interim *R and Wright*

196.2   in Portu *DEST*: ad Portum *R and Wright*
         regni *DEST*: curiae *R and Wright (and Vulgate)*

197.2   datisque *DEST*: datis *R and Wright*
         Godbaldo *DEST*: Golboldo *R and Wright*

198.1   Anglorum Saxonum *DEST*: Saxonum Anglorum *R and Wright*

200.2   Badonia *DEST*: Londonia *R and Wright*:

200.8   Wlfridus *DEST*: Wilfridus *R and Wright*

203.4   coluimus *DEST*: incoluimus *ac and Wright*; incolimus *R*

205.2   veniret *DES*: compleretur *aRT and Wright*
         Merlinus *DES*: Merlinus antea *a*; Merlinus Arturo *RT and Wright*
205.3   Tunc *DES*: Tum *RT and Wright*
         indicatum *DES*: revelatum *a*T: relevatum *R and Wright*
206.2   indicatum *DES*: revelatum *aRT and Wright*
         Ivorum vel *DES*: Ivor Ayni *a*; Ivor et Aini *T*; Inor Ayni *R*; *Wright*
            emends to Ivor a<c>Yni
         nepotem *DES*: nepotem suum *aRT and Wright*
207.2   Sed ille Britones *DEST*: Degenerati autem a Brittanica nobili-
            tate Gualenses *aR and Wright*
         a lingua Britannica degenerati *DEST*: *omitted in aR and Wright*
         numquam *DEST*: numquam postea *aR and Wright*
208.1   acta *DEST*: eorum acta *aR and Wright*
Explicit *DE*; Explicit historia Britonum correcta et abbreviata *a*; Explicit
tractatus *c*; Explicit historia Britonum a magistro Galfrido Monemutensi
in Latinum translata *T*; Explicit historia Britonum a Galfrido Arthuro de
Britannico in Latinum translata *R*

Notes to the Translation

PROLOGUE

5.1   The Variant's description of Britain is taken almost entirely from
       that in Bede, *HE* 1.1, though abbreviated and reworded. The
       Vulgate version combines the descriptions from Gildas, Nen-
       nius, and Bede.

5.3   The Vulgate lists five races, adding the Saxons and the Normans.

BOOK 1

6.1   The first part of this chapter comes almost verbatim from
       Landolfus Sagax, *Historia Romana,* 1.2. The birth of Ascanius,
       his alternative name, the founding of Lavinium, and the trans-
       fer of the ancestral gods to Alba Longa are omitted from
       the Vulgate version. Landolfus assigns thirty-eight years to
       the reign of Ascanius (as does Jerome), Nennius thirty-seven
       (thirty-three in the Vatican recension). The idea that Daunus,
       father of Turnus, was king of the Tuscans appears only in Lan-
       dolfus Sagax, 1.2, and Paulus Diaconus, *Historia Romana* 1.1. The
       Vulgate does not mention Daunus, and says that Turnus was
       king of the Rutulians (as he is in Virgil and Livy).

6.4   This sentence is missing in manuscript group *acHR,* but its
       equivalent appears in Wace. Wright, *First Variant Version,* xcix–
       ci and cvii–cix, argued that it was not part of the original text
       of the Variant, because he thought it contradicted the state-
       ment in Variant 54 that Brutus was the "son of Silvius Aeneas."
       He assumed this "Silvius Aeneas" to be the same as Silvius Po-
       stumus, third king of the Latins, who is called "Silvius Aeneas,
       son of Aeneas" in chapter 22 of both versions. But Silvius the

son of Ascanius was given the same name as his uncle, and it is more likely that he is the individual referred to in Variant 54, which would be consistent with the statement in Vulgate 54 that Brutus was fathered by "Silvius, son of Ascanius the son of Aeneas." Moreover, the Silvius Aeneas of chapter 22 cannot be the father of Brutus, since he is still reigning in Italy when Brutus founds London in that chapter, while the father of Brutus had already been killed in chapter 6 of both versions.

6.5   The remainder of the chapter is a paraphrase of Nennius 10, which was the source of the legend that Brutus, descendant of the Trojan Aeneas, was the first king of Britain. The various recensions of Nennius offer differing accounts of his parentage. The genealogy in the Harleian recension is Aeneas > Silvius > Brutus. In the Vatican recension it is Aeneas > Ascanius > Brutus. The Gildasian and Nennian recensions both have the genealogy given here: Aeneas > Ascanius > Silvius > Brutus. In the first three (pre-Geoffrey) editions of the *Historia Anglorum* 1.9, Henry of Huntingdon followed the Vatican recension of Nennius in making Brutus the son of Ascanius. After discovering Geoffrey's book at Bec in 1139, he revised his fourth edition to make Brutus the son of Silvius, and grandson of Ascanius. See *HA,* ed. Greenway, 25n40.

6.6   *unexpected blow*: The characterization of the arrow's blow as "unexpected" *(inopino)* occurs only in the so-called "Nennian" recension of the *Historia Brittonum* (Mommsen, vol. 3, p. 152).

7.1   Pyrrus and Helenus appear in the *Aeneid* 3.295–96; apart from Priam and Achilles, the names of the remaining Greeks and Trojans in this section are invented. See Tatlock, 116–17.

16.3   The following verses appear in identical form in both the Variant and Vulgate versions. It has been suggested that they predate Geoffrey of Monmouth and were taken from a (now lost) work by "Gildas the Poet." See A. H. W. Smith, "Gildas the Poet," *Arthurian Literature* 10 (1990): 1–10.

17.1   The itinerary of the Trojans across the Mediterranean is borrowed from chapter 15 of Nennius, but there it was the route taken by the Scythians who escaped from Egypt and wandered for forty-two years through Africa before visiting Spain and then settling in Ireland. Nennius took most of the locations from Orosius. See Faral, vol. 1, pp. 204–5; Orosius, *Historiae adversus paganos* 1.2.

17.2   *Trojan exiles*: Tatlock, 117, suggests that this idea was derived from Strabo, *Geographica* 3.4.157, where it is noted that certain companions of Antenor settled in Cantabria (northern Spain). According to Virgil, *Aeneid* 1.242–49, and Livy, *Ab urbe condita* 1.1, Antenor himself settled in Italy and founded the city of Padua at the northern end of the Adriatic Sea.

19.3   The idea that Brutus built the city of Tours does not, of course, come from Homer. Nennius 10 states that when he came to Gaul, Brutus "founded the city of the *Turones,* which is called Tours."

20.5   *From his name the city of Tours took its title*: The statement that Brutus called the city Tours "after the name of a certain one of his soldiers, who was called Turnus," is found only in the Nennian recension of the *Historia Brittonum* (Mommsen, vol. 3, p. 152).

21.3   *named after his fall*: In the Vulgate it is given the proper name *Saltus Goemagag* (Goemagog's Leap).

22.2   Beginning with the founding of London by Brutus, and continuing through the next twelve kings of Britain, the author specifies the number of years they ruled and synchronizes their reigns with other events in world history, including the pre-Roman kings of the Latins. Geoffrey's handling of these synchronisms has been discussed by John J. Parry, "The Chronology of Geoffrey of Monmouth's *Historia,* Books I and II," *Speculum* 4 (1929): 316–22; Faral, vol. 2, pp. 113–15; Tatlock, 117–18; and Molly Miller, "Geoffrey's Early Royal Synchronisms," *Bulletin of the Board of Celtic Studies* 28 (1979): 373–89. Each concluded that Geoffrey used different sources (Jerome's translation of Eusebius or the later, derivative chronicles by Prosper of Aquitaine, Isidore of Seville, and Bede), but all agreed that his calculations were hopelessly muddled. However, if it is assumed that Brutus began his reign with the building of London in the same year the Ark was captured by the Philistines (an "absolute" date that Jerome ascribes to 1117 BCE), and that the reign of Cunedagius ends in the same year that Rome was founded (another absolute date placed by Jerome, in 755 BCE), the *total* of the reign lengths from Brutus through Cunedagius given in the Variant version matches Jerome's calculations exactly: 363 years. The internal subtotals of the thirteen reigns in each version cannot be reconciled with the intervening synchronisms, although the Vulgate has two additional synchronisms (drawn from Bede rather than Jerome), which partially offset the internal displacements. With regard to the synchronisms in this section, the dates assigned by Jerome are the prophet Eli (forty years, from 1156 to 1117 BCE); the sons of Hector (1154 BCE); and Silvius Postumus (*Sylvius Aeneae filius,* "Silvius son of Aeneas," twenty-nine years, from 1137 to 1109 BCE). Prosper does not have the sons of Hector, Isidore does not have the Latin kings, and Bede does not have the Ark, so it is clear that Jerome was the source used here.

uncle of Brutus: Bernhard ten Brink, "Wace und Galfrid von Monmouth," *Jahrbuch für romanische und englische Literatur* 9 (1868): 241–70, at 265, suggested that the word *avunculus* is used here as the equivalent of *avunculus magnus,* "great-uncle." Most manuscripts of Nennius state that Brutus was the "brother" *(frater)* of Silvius Postumus; only one states that he was his "nephew" or "grandnephew" *(nepos);* Mommsen, vol. 3, p. 153. The reading *nepos* is found in both the pre- and the post-Geoffrey editions of Henry of Huntingdon; see *HA,* ed. Greenway, 26.

third of the Latins: Most commentators assume that this passage was derived from chapter 11 of Nennius. However, the statement that Silvius Aeneas was "third of the Latins" shows that it was either based on, or supplemented by, Jerome's translation of Eusebius, which numbers each of the Latin kings in order and refers to this one as *Latinorum III, Silvius Aeneae filius* (Silvius son of Aeneas, third of the Latins).

BOOK 2

24.1   *Huns*: The Huns were unknown to European history before the fourth century and are introduced here merely to provide an eponym for the River Humber. See Tatlock, 110. Both Livy, *Ab urbe condita* 1.3, and Landolfus, 1.3, report that the River Tiber got its name when Tiberinus drowned in it (see Faral, vol. 2, p. 94, and Tatlock, 126). If that story was the model for this one, it is worth noting that the Variant is slightly closer to Landolfus, who says the king died by "falling" *(decidens)* in the river, while the Vulgate echoes Livy in stating that he was "submerged" *(submersus)* in the stream.

25.3   *At that time . . . his fame*: Jerome assigns a combined period of forty years to Samuel and Saul (1116–1077 BCE). Bede, whose chronology is based on the Vulgate rather than the Septuagint version of the Bible, assigns separate reigns to Samuel (twelve years, from 1116 to 1105 BCE) and Saul (twenty years, from 1104 to 1085 BCE). As suggested by Miller, "Early Royal Synchronisms," the statement that Silvius Aeneas "was still alive" probably means that he is the same king mentioned as "third of the Latins," above. If it is Aeneas Silvius, fourth of the Latins (son of Silvius Postumus), then his reign would cover the thirty-one years from 1108 to 1078 BCE. Jerome first mentions Homer at 1104 BCE. Prosper of Aquitaine assigns Homer to a later period, and Bede does not mention him at all.

26.2   *At that time . . . in Sparta*: See the preceding note for Saul; Jerome gives Eurystheus a reign of forty-two years, from 1101 through 1060 BCE.

27.1   *Ebraucus*: The Variant specifies the length of Ebraucus's reign only here, with the best manuscripts reading sixty years. The Vulgate provides two reign lengths, one before and one after the birth of his children. There is considerable variation among the Vulgate manuscripts in the number of years assigned to each, and it is not clear whether they are overlapping, cumulative, or simply a mistake. See Griscom, *Historia Regum Britanniae* 258–59; Faral, vol. 3, pp. 96–97; and Reeve, 34–35.

27.2   *City of Ebraucus*: *Eboracum* was the Latin name for York.

   Aldclud: Dumbarton was known to the Britons as Aldclud, capital of the early medieval kingdom of Strathclyde.

   Mount Agned: "Mount Agned" was the location of Arthur's eleventh battle in all recensions of Nennius except the Vatican version. Its equation with Edinburgh in later Welsh and Latin sources may have originated with the alternative name given to it here, since the "Castle of the Maidens" was a common name for Edinburgh in the twelfth century. See Tatlock, 12–14. Early editors and translators of the Vulgate assumed that the "Dolorous Mount" was another name for Mount Agned. However, it has since been noted that since it is in the accusative case it must be a separate, fourth city (either Melrose or Stirling).

27.3   *And at that time . . . in Israel*: According to Jerome, David ruled from 1076 to 1037 BCE; Latinus Silvius ruled from 1077 to 1028 BCE; and Gad, Nathan, and Asaph began to prophesy in 1070 BCE.

    names of his sons: Apart from those with obvious classical origins, most of these names are drawn from British sources, particularly the *Harleian Genealogies*. See Faral, vol. 2, pp. 99–100; Stuart Piggott, "The Sources of Geoffrey of Monmouth: I. The 'Pre-Roman' King-List," *Antiquity* 15 (1941): 269–86; and Arthur E. Hutson, *British Personal Names in the Historia Regum Britanniae* (Berkeley, 1940), 11–24 and 90–91.

27.5   *Silvius Alba*: According to Jerome, Alba Silvius ruled from 1027 to 989 BCE.

29.2   *the Eagle*: On the Eagle of Shaftesbury, see Tatlock, 44, and Crick, *Dissemination,* 65. Alan of Britanny consults a written account of its prophecies in chapter 206 below.

    Solomon began to build the temple of the Lord: Jerome reports that Solomon began to build the temple in 1033 BCE, the fourth year of his forty-year reign.

    Ahias, Amos, Jehu, Joel, and Azarias: The prophets listed by Jerome at 975 BCE include *Achia, Samaeus, Ieu, Ioed,* and *Azarias.* Prosper of Aquitaine's *Epitoma Chronicon* gives the same names (Mommsen, vol. 3, p. 392). The list found here is closer to that in the *Chronica Maiora* of Isidore of Seville: *Achias* (var. *Agias, Ageas, Aggeus, Ageus*), *Amos, Ieu, Ioel,* and *Azarias* (Mommsen, vol. 3, p. 441). Isidore replaces *Samaeas* with *Amos,* and uses the *Septuagint* spelling "Ioel" for the prophet Iaddo (Addo) of 2 Chronicles 9:29. The *Achia(s)* mentioned by Jerome and Isidore is "Ahias the Silonite" in 1 Kings 11:29 and should not be confused with the prophet Haggai (*Aggeus*), who lived four centuries later.

Silvius the son of Aegyptus: The translation assumes that Capis Silvius, son of Aegyptus Silvius, is intended here (as in Vulgate 29) and that the Variant has skipped over his father, who appears as Silvius "Epitus" in Vulgate 28 (with the spelling borrowed from Ovid, *Fasti* 4.44 or *Metamorphoses* 14.613). According to Jerome, Capis Silvius succeeded his father, Aegyptus Silvius, in 964 BCE, during the time of the prophets listed in the previous sentence. Wright emends the text of the Variant to read "Silvius Epit<us>," assuming that he is the son of Alba Silvius, but all manuscripts of the Variant have *Egipti* or *Epiti* in the genitive. The Vulgate avoids this confusion by referring to each king separately and adding two additional synchronisms derived from the *Chronica Maiora* of Bede (the Queen of Sheba in chapter 28 and the prophet Elijah in 30).

30.1   *hot baths*: The description of the hot baths with inextinguishable fires is taken almost verbatim from Solinus, *De Mirabilibus* 22.10.

31.15   *Karitia*: This location has not been identified. Wace, *Brut* (line 1976), translates as *Chauz* (Pays de Caux in Normandy). The Welsh *Bruts* substitute Paris. "Kaer-Itia" has been proposed as a hypothetical Welsh version of *Portus Itius*, the location from which Caesar launched his first invasion of Britain (Griscom, *Historia Regum Britanniae* 539). Tatlock, 92–93, suggests a pun on *caritia* (dear, beloved).

31.19   *a certain underground tomb*: The underground temple, crypt, or tomb (*subterraneum*) is said here to be "on or near" the River Soar (*supra fluvium Soram*). The Vulgate describes it as *sub Sora fluvio*, which has always been translated as "beneath" or "under" the river, even though *sub* can also mean "at, by, or near." Our text probably refers to the imposing Roman ruin in Leicester, located between the River Soar and the church of Saint Nicholas, with the tops of its arches reaching just above the floor level of the church. It was certainly visible in the twelfth century, when its stones were used in the Norman improvements to the church. In 1107 the church was given to the college of secular canons established in Leicester Castle by Robert de Beaumont, Count of Meulan, father of the Waleran addressed in one version of Geoffrey's dedication.

32.4 *a district of Wales*: The author of the hybrid text in manuscript *c* equates this district with the entire region of Glamorgan (Welsh *Morgannwg*), while the Vulgate appears to refer to the specific location where Margam Abbey was built. See Hammer, 51; Tatlock, 68.

Rome was founded: The eleventh day before the Kalends of May is April 21. Jerome places the founding of Rome at 755 BCE; he lists the prophets Isaiah and Hosea twice, first at 765 BCE and later at 739 BCE.

34.1 *Dunwallo Molmutius*: A *Dumngual Moilmut* appears as a fifth-century king in the *Harleian Genealogies*. The use of the name for a legendary ancient lawgiver, known as *Dyfnwal Moelmud* in subsequent Welsh literature, may have originated here. See Bartrum, *WCD* 214–15.

34.3 *the whole land grew quiet before him*: Compare 1 Maccabees 1:3, *et siluit terra in conspectu eius* (and the earth was quiet before him), describing the conquests of Alexander the Great.

34.4 *took sanctuary*: Compare the "cities of refuge" in Joshua 20:3, *ut confugiat ad eas quicumque animam percusserit nescius* (That whosoever shall kill a person unawares may flee to them).

Book 3

35.1 *Belinus and Brennius*: Brennius is based in part on the historical figure Brennus, who led the sack of Rome by the Gauls in the fourth century BCE. The name of Belinus may be derived from Bellovesus, who invaded Italy in the previous century, while his brother Segovesus went into Germany (see Livy, *Ab urbe condita* 5.34). Alternatively, it may recall the name of Belgius, who invaded Greece in the third century BCE together with a second Brennus. That event immediately follows the sack of Rome in

Justinus, *Epitoma historiarum Philippicarum* 24.4–6, and the two invasions are conflated in Paulus Diaconus, *Historia Langobardorum* 2.23, and Landolfus, 1.24. Henry of Huntingdon treats them as the same event in his "Letter to Warinus" (see *HA*, ed. Greenway, 568n5).

35.2   *makers of lies*: Compare Job 13:4, *fabricatores mendacii* (forgers of lies).

39.2   This description of the Four Roads deliberately contradicts that given by Henry of Huntingdon, *HA* 1.7. Henry's list included Icknield Way (running east/west), Ermine Street (south/north), Watling Street (southeast/northwest), and Fosse Way (southwest/northeast). See *HA*, ed. Greenway, 24n35. Here the list begins with the Fosse Way (running south/north), then introduces an entirely new road running west/east from St. David's to Southampton.

40.2   *Allobroges*: The Allobroges were a Gallic tribe located south of Lake Geneva and east of the Rhône, in modern Savoy.

41.3   *Remember, my son . . . did not exist*: Compare Luke 11:27, *beatus venter qui te portavit et ubera quae suxisti* (blessed is the womb that bore thee and the paps that gave thee suck).

43.1   Rome was sacked by the Senones, a tribe of Gauls led by Brennus, in 390 BCE (391 according to Jerome). The principle narrative sources are Livy, *Ab urbe condita* 5.35–49; Florus, *Epitome of Roman History* 1.7.13; and Orosius, *Historiae adversus paganos* 2.19. Shorter accounts appear in Eutropius, Paulus Diaconus, and Landolfus. The narrative here follows none of those sources directly, and freely invents details not found in any of them (the ambush in the Alps, the prolonged siege of Rome, and the hanging of hostages before the gates). The Variant consistently refers to Brennius as leader of the Allobroges, while the Vulgate has a single, incongruous reference to the Senones in chapter 43.

Gabius and Porsenna: There were no Roman consuls named Gabius or Porsenna. At this time Rome was governed by six consular tribunes, including three members of the *gens Fabia* who were sent as ambassadors to the Gauls (Livy, *Ab urbe con-*

dita 5.35). Several authorities, however, simply state that a consul named Fabius opposed the Gauls (Florus, *Epitome of Roman History* 1.7; Orosius, *Historiae adversus paganos* 2.19; Landolfus, 1.24). Porsenna was an Etruscan king whose name appears a few pages earlier in those sources.

44.1   *Roman History*: The "Roman History" may refer to the *Historia Romana* of Landolfus Sagax, or to the similarly titled works of his precursors Eutropius and Paulus Diaconus. The Vulgate refers to "histories" in the plural. All sources agree that the Gauls did not stay in Rome, but were soon defeated and driven away.

44.3   *In his days . . . later age experienced*: This sentence is borrowed from Gildas 21, and here the Variant is closer than the Vulgate to the wording of the source: *tantis abundantiarum copiis insula affluebat ut nulla habere tales retro aetas meminisset* (the island abounded in such abundance of goods as no age had recalled having before). The Vulgate replaces the Variant's *terram* (the land) with *populum* (the people), and *meminit* (recalled) with *testetur* (bears witness).

45.1   *His son*: This name appears in the *Harleian Genealogies* (no. 18) as *Guurgint Barmbtruch*, as do the names of roughly half the succeeding kings up through Heli. See Faral, vol. 2, pp. 137–38.

47.1   *the law which the Britons call Marcian*: "Mercian Law" was recognized in the twelfth century as one of the three divisions of English law (along with that of Wessex and the Danelaw), in Simeon of Durham, the *Leis Willelme*, and other sources. Some critics have argued that its attribution to Queen Marcia was intended as parody, but Tatlock, 283, sees it as consistent with the author's use of eponymy to hint (without directly stating) that Marcia was the founder of Mercia.

48.1   *Danius's mistress*: She is named Tangustela in the Vulgate version.

52.1   *his nephew*: This nephew is not named in any manuscript of the Variant, and he is also nameless in Wace. The name "Regin" is supplied in some manuscripts of the Vulgate. See Faral, vol. 3, p. 124.

52.3   *Capenronius*: All manuscripts of the Variant treat this individual as one king, while the Vulgate breaks the name into two separate kings, "Cap" and "Oenus." One manuscript of Wace, Corpus Christi College Cambridge MS 50, fol. 28v, has the single name "Caponeus," but the rest have two names as in the Vulgate.

53.1 *Heli*: "Heli" is the name found in the Vulgate and most manuscripts of the Variant. It is translated as "Beli Mawr" in the Welsh *Bruts,* reflecting a later Welsh tradition that regarded Beli as the father of Lludd, Nynniaw, and Caswallon. The spelling "Beli" found in manuscript group *DES* is probably a correction made by someone with knowledge of this tradition rather than the original reading here. Three late manuscripts of Wace have "Beli," but the rest read "Heli."

Lud: Although Lludd was well known in later Welsh folklore, it is not certain whether there was a tradition involving his name prior to Geoffrey of Monmouth. See Bartrum, *WCD* 416. Tatlock, 121, suggests the name was invented as an eponym for Ludgate. The appearance of his name (as "Luid") in the third edition of Henry of Huntingdon, *HA* 1.12, was due to Geoffrey; the earlier editions, following Nennius, had called him "Minocannus." See Tatlock, 31n121; *HA,* ed. Greenway, 32n60.

53.3 *Androgeus and Tenuantius*: Androgeus, leader of the Trinovantes in Bede, *HE* 1.2, is called "Androgorius" or "Mandubragius" in Orosius, *Historiae adversus paganos* 6.9.8, and is the same individual described as "Mandubracius" in Caesar, *De Bello Gallico* 5.20 and 22. Tenuantius does not appear in any classical or medieval source, but it is known from numismatic evidence that Tasciovanus, king of the Catuvellauni, was the father of Cunobelin (the Kimbelinus of chapter 64 below). See Philip P. Graves, "Tasciovanus of Verulam," *St. Albans and Hertfordshire Architectural and Archaeological Society Transactions 1934* (St. Albans, 1935): 143–65.

Book 4

54.1 *Thus it is written . . . passenger ships*: This sentence, which does not appear in the Vulgate, combines language from Bede, *HE* 1.2

and 5.24. Bede took the year 693 AUC (that is, *ab urbe condita*, or from the foundation of Rome) from Orosius, *Historiae adversus paganos* 6.7, where it refers to the beginning of Caesar's five-year governorship of Gaul. The actual date of Caesar's first expedition to Britain was 699 AUC (55 BCE).

54.2 *Ruteni*: According to Bede, *HE* 1.2, Caesar crossed to Britain from the province of the Morini in Flanders. Tatlock, 94–96, explains that the Ruteni were regarded as synonymous with the Flemings in the twelfth century, as attested by the popular eleventh-century Latin dictionary of Papias.

55.2 The speech by Cassibellaunus borrows from Pseudo-Hegesippus, *Historia* 2.9, the statement that the Britons were *extra orbem positos* (placed beyond the edge of the world) and *quid esset servitus ignorabant* (did not know the meaning of servitude). See Jacob Hammer, "Les sources de Geoffrey de Monmouth *Historia Regum Britanniae, IV, 2*," *Latomus* 5 (1946): 79–82. The Variant is closer to the wording of Hegesippus than the Vulgate is.

56.1 *to Dorobernum*: Nennius 19 says that Caesar fought *apud Dolabellum* (with Dolabellus), but our author took *apud* to mean "at" and the name to be a place rather than a person. *Dorobernum* was the medieval Latin name for Canterbury (see chapters 62, 98, 112 below), built on the site of the pre-Roman capital of Kent *(Durovernum Cantiaci)*. The Vulgate has *Dorobellum* here, a spelling found in one manuscript of Nennius for the person, but otherwise unknown as a place.

not at all reluctant: All manuscripts except *H* have the word *non* before *impiger.* The translation assumes that *non* before the negative prefix *im-* is intensive or emphatic. Compare the phrase *non immemor* (not at all mindful) in 89.2 below.

56.2 *Belinus*: A reference in Suetonius, *Vita Caesarum* 4.44, to *Adminius Cynobellini Britannorum regis filius* (Adminius the son of Cunobelin, the king of the Britons) was corrupted in Orosius, *Historiae adversus paganos* 7.5, to *Minocynobellinus Britannorum regis filius* (Minocunobellinus, the son of the king of the Britons), then further garbled and misplaced in Nennius 19, where a king named Bellinus the son of Minocannus confronts Caesar. Here, Caesar's opponent is correctly identified as Cassibellaunus (as in Orosius, 6.9, and Bede, *HE* 1.2) and is made the son of Lud, while Belinus becomes his general. The first version of Henry of Huntingdon, *HA* 1.2, called Belinus the son of Minocannus, as in Nennius, but the third version makes him the son of Lud and the brother of Cassibellanus.

56.6   *Labienus*: The tribune killed in Britain was actually Quintus Laberius Durus (Caesar, *De Bello Gallico* 5.15), but Orosius, *Historiae adversus paganos* 6.9 (followed by Bede, *HE* 1.2) confused his name with that of Titus Labienus, Caesar's second in command during the Gallic wars.

58.1   *the Gauls mounted a rebellion*: As Tatlock points out, 118–19, this rebellion is not mentioned in Orosius or Bede, but it does appear in Caesar, *De Bello Gallico* 4.37–38. There, it is immediately suppressed by the Romans. Here, Caesar is forced to offer gifts and promises for the Gauls' support. The Vulgate further underscores his humiliation.

59.1   *ships of both types*: Transport and cargo. The description of the number and type of Caesar's ships is taken directly from Bede, *HE* 1.2 (or his source, Orosius, *Historiae adversus paganos* 6.9), and does not appear in the Vulgate.

60.2   *as their rampart*: Hammer cites 1 Samuel 25:16, *pro muro erant nobis* (they were a wall unto us), but a more likely source is Sallust, *Bellum Catilinae,* 58.17, *audaciam pro muro* (boldness for a breastwork).

61.2   *burned offerings*: See 2 Chronicles 29:32.

62.8   *not returning evil for evil*: Compare 1 Peter 3:9.

66.5   *Hamo's Port*: Southampton.

68.1   *his daughter, named Genuissa*: Her name is spelled "Genuissa" in all manuscripts of the Variant and in the three Vulgate manuscripts reported by Griscom. However, the letters *uu* and *nu* were easily confused; both Faral and Reeve adopt the spelling "Gewissa" without comment in their editions of the Vulgate. If that was the original reading, her name may have been invented to provide an eponym for the Gewissae, mentioned below in chapters 80, 94, 128, and 202 (see Faral, vol. 2, p. 160; Hutson, *British Personal Names,* 49; and Tatlock, 120n20).

68.2   *Kaerglou*: William of Malmesbury states in the *Gesta pontificum*

4.153, that Gloucester was thought to have been named after Claudius because its British name was *Cairclau,* and he paraphrases Seneca the Younger, *Apocolocyntosis* 8.3, to the effect that "barbarians in Britain worship him as a god and are building a city in his honor." Henry of Huntingdon, *HA* 1.3, calls it *Kair Glou* or *Gloueceastria.* The alternative etymology is adapted from Nennius 49, where the city is built by Gloiu, greatgrandfather of Vortigern, and called *Cair Gloiu* in the British tongue or *Gloecester* in the Saxon. The Latin name *Claudiocestria* is used here; it is *Gloucestria* at this point in the Vulgate.

at that time: This synchronism is derived from the entry in Jerome under 42 CE. The Vulgate adds additional language taken from Bede, *CM* 4007 (p. 283).

70.1   *an inscription*: The source is generally assumed to be William of Malmesbury, who suggested in *Gesta pontificum* 3.99 that the inscription on this monument in Carlisle might commemorate the victory of the Roman general Marius over the Cimbri (described as a crushing defeat of the Gauls in Florus, *Epitome of Roman History* 1.38; Orosius, *Historiae adversus paganos* 5.16; and Jerome, at 102 BCE). Our author deliberately rejects this view, making it a tribute to the victory of the British king Marius over the Picts and thus providing an appropriate eponym for Westmorland *(Westmaria).*

72.1   The story of the introduction of Christianity under Lucius is mentioned by Bede in *CM* 4132 (p. 331), *HE* 1.4, and *HE* 5.24; and also in Nennius 22. It was used to different ends by several writers in the twelfth century: (1) to support the claims of Llandaff for metropolitan status in the *Liber Landavensis* (ca. 1124–1130); (2) to support the claims of St. David's in a letter from the chapter of St. David's to Pope Honorius II (ca. 1124–1130), preserved in Gerald of Wales, *De invectibus* 2.10; and (3) to support Glastonbury in William of Malmesbury's *De antiquitate ecclesiae Glastoniensis* (ca. 1129–1135). On the relative dating of these accounts, see Brooke, "The Archbishops," 201–42; and John Reuben Davies, *The Book of Llandaff and the Norman Church in Wales* (Woodbridge: Boydell, 2003), 110. For our author's description of British ecclesiastical institutions in general, see Flint, "Parody and Its Purpose," 460–62.

72.2   *their sound had gone forth*: Psalms 18:5. This quotation is omitted in the Vulgate.

72.3   *glory to God on high*: The opening line of the Greater Doxology (based on Luke 2:14); it is omitted in the Vulgate.

   Fagan and Duvian: The names of the missionaries do not appear in Bede or Nennius, but they are mentioned in the twelfth-century accounts from St. David's and Llandaff. Curiously, William of Malmesbury states in the revised edition of *GRA* 1.19, that "their work shall endure for ever, although many years' oblivion has devoured their names." This appears to reflect a conscious rivalry between William and our author on this point, but which of them wrote first has been the subject of much debate. See Faral, vol. 2, pp. 170–71; Tatlock, 230–35; and Flint, "Parody and Its Purpose," 453–54.

72.4   *the people of many nations*: Nennius 22 states that Lucius was baptized "with all the petty kings of the entire British people."

72.5   *they consecrated bishops . . . archpriests*: The idea that bishops and archbishops were ordained in place of pagan flamens and archflamens was long thought to be a fantasy concocted by Geoffrey of Monmouth. See Faral, vol. 2, p. 174; and Tatlock, 260. But Ernest Jones, "Geoffrey of Monmouth's Account of the Establishment of Episcopacy in Britain," *Journal of English and Germanic Philology*, 40 (1941): 360–63, showed that the idea came from the ninth-century forged decretals of Pseudo-Isidore. Schafer Williams, "Geoffrey of Monmouth and the Canon Law," *Speculum* 27 (1952): 184–90, identified the specific source as the *Collectio canonum* of Anselm of Lucca (ca. 1083).

72.6   *City of Legions*: Placing the third archbishopric in Caerleon avoids taking sides in the active rivalry between the bishops of St. David's and Llandaff over the primacy of Wales. It is likely that Bernard of St. David's and Urban of Llandaff were both personal acquaintances of Archdeacon Walter and Geoffrey of Monmouth. For background on the dispute, see J. E. Lloyd, *History of Wales* (London, 1912), vol. 2, p. 486; Brooke, "Geoffrey of Monmouth as a Historian;" and Flint, "Parody and Its Purpose," 460–62.

BOOK 5

73.2   *cathedral church*: Literally, "the church of the first see." The same phrase appears in the Vulgate, where it has been translated as "the church of the Archdiocese" (Thorpe), "the chief metropolitan church" (Wright), or "the archdiocesan church" (Michael Faletra). However, as noted by James Ussher, *Antiquitates* (London, 1687), p. 73, the phrase cannot refer to the metropolitan church of an archdiocese (which chapter 72 places only in London, York, and Carleon) but simply to the cathedral church of a bishop. Gloucester was not the seat of a bishopric under the Saxons or the Normans, but the Variant gives it one bishop under the Britons (Eldad) in chapter 125, and the Vulgate adds another (Theonus) in chapter 179.

74.1   *senator Severus*: Septimius Severus was emperor of Rome from 193 to 211 CE. He came to Britain with his sons Caracalla and Geta in 208 CE, where he invaded Caledonia and refurbished the Antonine Wall, before falling ill and dying at York. The Variant and the Vulgate refer to him, inconsistently, as both "senator" and "emperor."

74.3   According to Bede, *HE* 1.5 (following Orosius, *Historiae adversus paganos* 7.17), after building the wall Severus fell ill and died at York. Henry of Huntingdon, *HA* 1.31, follows Bede. Most versions of Nennius 23 (Mommsen, vol. 3, p. 165) state that he died *(moritur)* in Britain; only the Nennian recension says that he was killed at York, along with his commanders *(apud Eboracum cum suis ducibus occiditur)*.

75.1   *two sons*: See Bede, *HE* 1.5. The idea, invented here, that Bassianus (Caracalla) had a British mother may have been suggested by the late Roman tradition that he was the son of Severus's first wife, Marcia; see the *Historia Augusta* (Severus 20.2, Caracalla 10.1, and Geta 7.3); and Aurelius Victor, *De Caesaribus* 21.3.

75.2   *Carausius*: See Bede, *HE* 1.6.

76.2   *Asclepiodotus:* Asclepiodotus was the praetorian prefect and general sent by Constantius to defeat Allectus. See Eutropius, *Breviarium historiae Romanae* 9.22; Orosius, *Historiae adversus paganos* 7.25; Aurelius Victor, *De Caesaribus* 39. He is transformed here into a British patriot and Duke of Cornwall, who kills the Roman tyrant Allectus and reigns over Britain for ten years. The idea may have come from Bede, *HE* 1.6, which says that Asclepiodotus overthrew Allectus "and after ten years he regained possession of Britain" *(Brittaniamque post decem annos recepit).*

77.2   *In those days . . . imperial edicts:* The details in this sentence do not appear in the Vulgate, and they are not derived from Bede's account of the Diocletian persecution in *HE* 1.6. The idea that Diocletian sent Maximianus into Gaul *(misit . . . in Gallias)* appears in Orosius, *Historiae adversus paganos* 7.25; that he was sent to enforce the imperial edicts *(edicta principis)* against Christianity is in Rufinus's translation of the *Ecclesiastical History* of Eusebius. Maximianus's passage over the Alps is related in several accounts of the martyrdom of the Theban Legion, including the *Passio S. Mauritii,* the *Vita Babolini,* and the *Passio Acaunensium martyrum.*

77.3   *Julius and Aaron:* See Bede, *HE* 1.6–7. At this point the Vulgate inserts an account of the martyrdom of Saint Alban and invents the name "Amphibalus" (based on a misreading of Gildas 28) for the saint's unnamed confessor in Bede, *HE* 1.7, and Gildas 10–11. The name appears later, without explanation, in Variant 93 and 179/180.

78.1   *Kaercolim (Colchester):* Variant manuscripts *cDES* give only the Welsh name for Colchester, as do most manuscripts of Wace. The gloss *id est Colcestrie* (that is Colchester) appears in the Vulgate text and in Variant manuscripts *a* and *H.*

78.3   *Helena:* The legend that Constantine's mother, Helena, was daughter of the British king Coel is found earlier in Henry of Huntingdon, *HA* 1.37. William of Malmesbury, *GRA* 4.355, says only that Constantine was born in Britain. For background see Tatlock, 236; Bartrum, *WCD* 411–12; Winifred Joy Mulligan, "The British Constantine: An English Historical Myth," *The Journal of Medieval and Renaissance Studies* 8 (1978): 257–79; and Antonia Harbus, *Helena of Britain in Medieval Legend* (Cambridge: D. S. Brewer, 2002), 64–81.

80.1   *Gewissae*: According to Bede, *HE* 3.7, *Gewissae* was the original name of the West Saxons. He is followed in this usage by William of Malmesbury, *GRA* 2.129, and Henry of Huntingdon, *HA* 3.37. There has been much debate whether the name is actually British rather than English in origin. See W. H. Stevenson, "The Beginnings of Wessex," *English Historical Review* 14 (1899): 32–46; H. E. Walker, "Bede and the Gewissae: The Political Evolution of the Heptarchy and Its Nomenclature," *Cambridge Historical Journal* 12 (1956): 174–86; Richard Coates, "On Some Controversy Surrounding *Gewissae/Gewissei, Cerdic* and *Ceawlin,*" *Nomina* 13 (1989–1990): 1–11. Here the *Gewissae* are clearly regarded as a British tribe, as they are in chapters 94 (Vortigern is *consul Gewisseorum*) and 202 (Cadwaladr's mother is from "the noble race of the Gewissae").

81.2   *Conan Meriadoc*: Unknown to Gildas, Bede, and Nennius, the name of Conan Meriadoc first appears in the fragmentary eleventh-century *Life of Saint Goeznovius*. His role as the first king of Brittany and progenitor of a dynasty of Breton kings is generally dismissed as fabulous, but the legend clearly existed in some form before it was further developed here. See Bartrum, *WCD* 164–66; Bromwich, *TYP* 320–21.

        Maximian: Maximian is the name used in Nennius 26–27 for the historical Roman emperor Magnus Maximus (383–388 CE). The principal sources used here include Nennius; Gildas 13–14; and Bede, *HE* 1.9. But he was also a prominent figure in Welsh tradition, regarded as the ancester of several royal dynasties. See Bartrum, *WCD* 433–34; Bromwich, *TYP* 441–44. In particular, the legend of his marriage to Elen, daughter of Octavius and sister or cousin to Conan, is independently attested in the later twelfth-century Welsh tale of the *Dream of Macsen Wledig.* The idea that he was born in Britain appears in the Anglo-Saxon Chronicle, the Chronicle of Aethelweard, and in Henry of Huntingdon, *HA* 1.42.

82.1   The Vulgate adds several pages in which Mauricius has to per-
        suade Maximian to leave Rome; as they travel through Gaul,
        Maximian conquers all the cities of the Franks, amassing a for-
        tune and attracting a large army. When they arrive in Britain,
        Octavius is alarmed and tells Conan to oppose the invasion;
        Mauricius debates with Maximian and Conan, before they
        agree to peace; and Caradoc persuades Octavius to make Max-
        imian his heir.

86.2   *setting up the throne of his empire in Trier*: Here the Variant may be
        following Gregory of Tours, *Decem libri historiarum* 1.43 *(in urbe
        Treverica sedem insitutens),* while the Vulgate in this and the fol-
        lowing sentence quotes nearly verbatim from Gildas 13.

86.3   *the three hundred and seventy-seventh year*: Bede, *HE* 1.9, says that
        Gratian, the fortieth emperor, ruled the empire alone for six
        years after the death of Valens in 377 CE (an error for 376).
        Bede notes that Maximus was elected emperor by the army in
        Britain "at that time" *(ea tempestate)*, but the actual date was
        later (383 CE).

        he killed Maximian near Aquileia: In Orosius, *Historiae adversus
        paganos* 7.34, it is Theodosius who kills Maximus; in Bede he is
        killed by both Valentinian and Theodosius *(ab eis);* here it is
        by Valentinian alone. All of the available sources agreed that
        Magnus Maximus was killed at or near Aquileia; the phrase
        apud Aquileiam appears in Gildas 1.3. This conflicts with the
        statement at the end of chapter 88 that Maximus was killed at
        Rome by friends of Gratian. The Vulgate eliminates the con-
        tradiction by omitting the information given here and retain-
        ing the latter (historically incorrect) version of events.

87.2   *Dionotus, the Duke of Cornwall*: In the Vulgate, Dionotus is not
        duke but "king" of Cornwall and is said to have succeeded his
        brother Caradoc in that kingship. Neither version makes them
        kings of Britain, as suggested by Thorpe, *History of the Kings of
        Britain,* 141.

87.3   *Ursula*: The legend of Saint Ursula arose as early as the tenth
        century and was extensively developed thereafter. See Tatlock,
        236–41; Bartrum, *WCD* 728–29.

88.6   *the citizen Gratian*: The idea that Gratian *municeps* was sent to

Britain by Magnus Maximus involves a significant anachronism, noted by Ussher, *Antiquitates,* p. 309. The principal sources agree that Gratian *municeps* arose after the death of Magnus Maximus. See Orosius, *Historiae adversus paganos* 7.40; Bede, *HE* 1.11; Paulus Diaconus, *Historia Romana* 12.17; Landolfus, 13.30. It is possible that our author was confused by the mention in some chronicles of a second usurper named Maximus who was made emperor in Spain in 409 CE and was still alive in 417. In Sigebert he appears in the same entry with Gratian *municeps,* under the year 414 CE. In Paulus Diaconus, *Historia Romana* 13.1 and Landolfus, 14.1, his death is mentioned in the chapter immediately following that of Gratian *municeps.* He was probably the same Maximus who is killed at Ravenna in Paulus Diaconus, *Historia Romana* 13.5 and Landulfus, 14.4; his death is placed in 422 by Marcellinus Comes and the Gallic Chronicle of 452.

88.7   I have found no source for the statement that Magnus Maximus was killed at Rome. In his paper for the 1957 Bangor conference, Caldwell suggested that the idea arose from confusion with the death of Petronius Maximus, who was killed during the Vandal sack of Rome in 455 CE (mentioned in Landolfus, 15.13). However, it is more likely that Magnus Maximus is confounded here with the usurper Maximus who appears in Landolfus, 14.1 and 14.4.

89.2   *not at all mindful*: The Vulgate follows Gildas in stating that the Romans were "unmindful" *(immemor)* of past offenses. All manuscripts of the Variant except *c* have the phrase *non immemor.* The translation assumes that *non* is used intensively here, as it is in the phrase *non impiger* in 56.1 above.

89.3   *massive rampart with a wall*: Variant 89–91 is a loose and abbreviated paraphrase of Gildas 14–20. Where the Variant states that the Britons built a "massive rampart with a wall" *(vallum cum muro immensum),* Gildas mentions only a "wall" *(murum)* but explains that the Romans ordered them to build it as a terror to the enemy. Throughout chapters 89 to 91, the Vulgate quotes Gildas nearly verbatim and at much greater length.

90.1   At the end of chapter 90 the Vulgate adds a lengthy speech by Guizelinus urging the Britons to defend themselves.

91.1   *encouraging them*: As noted by Hammer, 101n414, the word *suadentes* (encouraging, persuading) comes directly from Gildas. It does not appear in the Vulgate, which shows that the author of the Variant used Gildas directly.

92.1   *Aldroenus*: Aldroenus is generally regarded as fictional, but the fact that he is referred to as "fourth after Conan" suggests the existence of some Breton genealogical source similar to the Welsh genealogies used elsewhere in the work. Later Breton chroniclers inserted the names of Gradlon and Salomon as the second and third kings; see Bartrum, *WCD* 333–34 (Grallo), and 656 (Salomon I).

92.2   *Aldroenus received him with honor*: At this point the Vulgate inserts a lengthy speech in which Guizelinus offers the kingdom of Britain to Aldroenus, followed by another in which Aldroenus declines the crown but offers his brother Constantine instead, a man "skilled in military affairs and well endowed with other virtues." Constantine is based on the late Roman usurper Constantine III (who ruled Britain and Gaul from 407–411), but here he is moved later in time and represented as a member of the royal dynasty of Brittany. This is a marked departure from Bede, *HE* 1.11, who said that "Constantine, a worthless soldier of the lowest rank, was elected in Britain solely on account of the promise of his name and with no virtue to recommend him." Bede's negative view was echoed by Henry of Huntingdon, *HA* 1.45, and William of Malmesbury, *GRA* 1.2.

93.1   *Silchester*: The site of the former Roman city of Calleva Atrebatum, between Oxford and Winchester. Not mentioned by any previous historian, here it is the seat of a bishopric, held by Magaunius, and the location where both Constantine and Arthur are crowned. See Tatlock, 49–50. In the twelfth century, Silchester was held by the Bloet family, relatives of Robert Bloet, the bishop under whom Walter began his career as archdeacon. Their manor house and chapel were located just inside the eastern gate of the still-impressive Roman walls.

93.2   *Christ conquers . . . commands*: The opening words of the *Laudes Regiae* (Royal Acclamations), adopted by Charlemagne for his coronation in 800 CE and used in praise of the Norman dukes and English kings during the eleventh and twelfth centuries.

93.3   *three sons*: It is characteristic of the author to invent a direct family connection among these three kings (as he does with the five post-Arthurian monarchs taken from Gildas). Constans is based on the historical son of the British usurper Constantine III. Ambrosius Aurelianus was also a historical figure, but not related to Constans and removed by several decades in time. He was prominent in Welsh folklore under the name of "Emrys Wledig."

94.1   *Constans*: The historical Constans, son of Constantine III, was made Caesar by his father, even though he was a monk. Bede, *HE* 1.11, says that he was subsequently betrayed and killed by his own general, Gerontius. Here the role of Gerontius is assigned to Vortigern. The parallels are discussed in Sharon Turner, *History of the Anglo-Saxons,* (London, 1820), vol. 1, p. 203.

96.1   Bede, *HE* 1.11 (followed by Henry of Huntingdon, *HA* 1.45), says that Constans "was put to death at Vienne by Gerontius, his own officer."

96.3   *King Budicius*: Budicius is generally regarded as fictitious, but Breton princes with that name appear in the *Life of Saint Melor* (from the Cartulary of Quimperlé); in the *Life of Saint Oudoceus* (from the Book of Llandaff); and in Gregory of Tours, *Historia Francorum* 5.16. See Bartrum, *WCD* 68–69.

Book 6

98.1   *three keels*: See Nennius 31, and Bede, *HE* 1.15.

99.2   *brothers unknown to me*: In the Vulgate, Hengist refers to Ambrosius by name.

99.6   *Twangcaster*: This alternate spelling, found only in the Variant, suggests familiarity with the Old and Middle English word *þwang,* meaning a thong or narrow strip of land. The location is usually identified as Caistor in Lindsey; Tatlock, 24.

100.1   *Ronwen*: Hengist's daughter is mentioned in Nennius 37, William of Malmesbury, *GRA* 1.7, and Henry of Huntingdon, *HA* 2.1, but her name does not appear in any known source before this. See Tatlock, 146. On the wide variation among the manuscripts in the spelling of her name, see Jacob Hammer, "Note on Geoffrey of Monmouth's *Historia Regum Britanniae* VI.12 and VI.15," *Modern Language Notes* 49 (1934): 94–95.

100.2   *golden goblet*: Only the Irish version of Nennius mentions that Ronwen served the wine in "cups of gold and silver"; see Mommsen, vol. 3, pp. 141 and 178n2.

100.5   *prompting by Satan*: The Variant here follows the "Vatican version" of Nennius 37, (using the present participle *instigante*); the Vulgate is closer to the other recensions, which all state that Satan "entered into his heart" *(intravit . . . in corde)*. See Mommsen, vol. 3, p. 178.

      bride-price: The legal term *dos* (dower) normally refers to the property a bride receives from her husband at the time of their marriage. In chapter 31 above it was used in reference to the dowry or marriage portion provided by the father of the bride (Lear). Here it refers to the payment made by the husband to the family of the bride. The term never appears in the Vulgate.

100.6   *three sons*: The statement that Vortigern had three sons indicates a connection between the Variant and the so-called *tres filios* group of Vulgate manuscripts, on which see Crick, *Dissemination,* 162–64, and Reeve, "Transmission," 162–63. Reeve situated the *tres filios* group within his larger manuscript family *Φ,* which shares a number of readings with both the Variant and Henry of Huntingdon's *Letter to Warinus* (a summary of the Vulgate made in 1139). These include the statements that Constantine was killed by Conan in the third year of his reign, instead of being struck down by God in the fourth (chapter 180); that Aurelius Conanus died in the second year of his reign, instead of the third (181); and that Vortipor ruled for four years, instead of the unspecified period of time found in other Vulgate manuscripts (182).

101.1   *Ebissa*: Ebissa, the younger brother of Octa, comes from Nennius 38. He is not mentioned again, and he appears in no other historical source. A "kinsman" of Octa named Eosa appears later in 124–41, and some have suggested that Ebissa and Eosa should be regarded as the same individual. See Fletcher, *Arthurian Material,* 25 and 158; Faral, vol. 2, p. 237n4; and Reeve, 290–91 (index entries for Ebissa and Eosa). The two are confused at one point by Wace (*Brut,* line 7830); they are both mentioned together in Layamon (*Brut,* lines 9100 and 9735). See note on Eosa in chapter 124 below.

101.3   *Cherdich*: Cherdich, who is not mentioned again, is the first of several individuals with names that may recall that of the Saxon king Cerdic of Wessex, including Cheldric in chapters 143–48 and a second Cheldric in 177–78. None of them, however, offers a close parallel with the Cerdic prominently described as founder of the royal house of Wessex in William of Malmesbury, *GRA* 1.16, and Henry of Huntingdon, *HA* 2.16. Since Cerdic of Wessex landed fifty years after Hengest, this Cherdich was more likely suggested by the Cerdic who serves as an interpreter between Vortigern and the Saxons in Nennius 37.

101.6   The source for Vortimer's campaign against the Saxons is Nennius 43–44, but there the Saxons are besieged on Thanet before, rather than after, the four battles with Vortimer.

102.2   *Arian or Pelagian*: Germanus appears earlier in the Vulgate, at chapter 100, where only the Pelagian heresy is mentioned (as in Bede, *HE* 1.17). Wright adopts manuscript *R*'s reference to the Pelagian heresy alone, rejecting the reference to the Arian heresy in manuscripts *aH* and to both heresies in manuscripts *cDES*. However, Bede mentions the impact of both heresies within a few pages of each other, in *HE* 1.8 and 1.10. The two are directly conflated by Jocelin of Furness, *Life of Saint Kentigern* 27, who says that both heresies were cast down and conquered by Saint Germanus. Though historically inaccurate, the reading in *cDES* is probably correct.

102.3   *Gildas*: The reference is to Nennius 32–35, 39, and 47, where two separate missions by Saint Germanus are related in great detail. Only the first visit is mentioned here. The Vulgate places this mission earlier, at the beginning of chapter 101.

102.5   All versions of Nennius say that Vortimer's instructions were ignored; the "Nennian" recension states that he was buried at Lincoln. See Mommsen, vol. 3, p. 188.

104.1   *Nimat ore saxas*: "Grab your knives!" The Saxon command and other details of the story come from Nennius 46. Reeve, p. lviii, notes that the form of the command given here is closest to that found in the so-called "Nennian" recension.

107.4   *as Apuleius holds*: This information is not found in Apuleius, but was derived either from Augustine, *De civitate Dei* 3.5, 8.14, and 15.23, or from William of Conches, *De philosophia mundi* 1.22.

BOOK 7

111.2   *Ambrosius Merlinus*: In Nennius 42 the prophetic youth is called Ambrosius and explicitly identified with the Ambrosius who is king of the Britons in chapters 31 and 48. See Bartrum, *WCD* 281 and 564, on this conflation. The Variant distinguishes between the two by naming the prophet Merlin and stating here that his *cognomen* (an additional personal name) was Ambrosius. The Vulgate introduces the clarification earlier, in chapter 108, by explaining that Merlin "was also called Ambrosius" *(qui et Ambrosius dicebatur)*.

112.1–17.4   *Woe to the red dragon . . . among the stars*: Unlike the rest of the Variant, the Prophecies of Merlin were unquestionably written by Geoffrey of Monmouth. They circulated independently as a separate *Libellus Merlini* (Book of Merlin) before the death of Henry I in 1135, but comparison with the variants listed by Reeve, pp. xxix–xxxi, as characteristic of this separate text (his manuscript group *Π*) shows that the version inserted into the common ancestor of all Variant manuscripts was copied later, from a manuscript of the Vulgate. Structurally, the Prophecies fall into three main sections. Those in chapter 112 deal with events that take place within the *Historia*. Those in 113 concern the later history of Britain, down to the author's own time. The prophecies in 114–17 relate entirely to the future. Curley, 53–73, provides a concise summary of the meanings of the prophecies in chapters 112–13.

112.3   *Six of his successors*: The Variant lists only five successors to Ar-
          thur before the arrival of Godmund: Constantine, Conan, Vor-
          tipor, Malgo, and Caretius. The Vulgate adds an unnamed sec-
          ond uncle of Conan who was thrown into prison and whose
          sons were killed before Conan took the throne. See note to
          chapter 181 below. This uncle is counted among the six suc-
          cessors to Arthur in the commentary formerly attributed to
          Alain of Lille; see *Prophetia Anglicana Merlini Ambrosii Britanni*
          (Frankfurt, 1603), p. 23.

          location of the metropolitan sees: See Curley, 55–60, for a full dis-
          cussion of the prophecies concerning the relocation of various
          metropolitan sees in relation to the ongoing twelfth-century
          controversies over primacy. Flint, "Parody and Its Purpose,"
          460–62, discusses Geoffrey's handling of British ecclesiastical
          institutions in general.

113.1   *one hundred and fifty years*: Derived from Gildas 23, which relates
          a prophecy that the Saxons would remain in Britain for 300
          years and cause frequent devastation for half that time, 150
          years.

113.3   *one of which will be killed by the sting of envy*: Orderic Vitalis, *Histo-
          ria ecclesiastica* 12.47, recognized this as a reference to the death
          of William Rufus, killed by an arrow in the New Forest in 1100.
          He interprets the rest of the sentence as a reference to the
          death of Robert Curthose in prison at Cardiff in 1134.

113.4   *Those who curl their hair*: This alludes to the practice of wearing
          long, curled hair among the courtiers of Henry I, which is de-
          scribed in some detail by Orderic Vitalis, *Historia ecclesiastica*
          11.11, and William of Malmesbury, *Historia novella* 1.4. See Cur-
          ley, 66.

          the half will be rounded: A reference to Henry I's promise, made
          in 1108, to create a separate round coin for the halfpence in or-
          der to eliminate the common practice of breaking pennies in
          half. See Tatlock, 404, and Curley, 65.

113.5   *The cubs of the lion*: This alludes to the drowning of Henry's chil-
          dren in the White Ship disaster of 1120. The rest of the sen-
          tence probably refers to Henry's conquest of Venedotia in 1121.
          See Tatlock, 64–65.

house of Corineus: Sometime prior to 1130, Frewin, the sheriff of Cornwall, was involved with six other Cornishmen in an infamous feud that ended with the slaying of six sons of a Norman named Toki. See Curley, 67. This is the last of the prophecies relating to past events.

provoked to all things: At the end of chapter 113 some manuscripts of the Vulgate insert another prophecy, beginning *Vae tibi Neustria* (Woe to you Normandy), which alludes to the death of Henry I in 1135. It does not appear in any manuscript of the Variant.

115.5   *source of the Anna*: Possibly the Valley of Annuc or *Pant Annwg* that is mentioned in the *Liber Landavensis* as the boundary between Chepstow and St. Kinmark's. See Tatlock, 75n324.

116.16   *pikes*: Reeve, 155n215, construes the word *luces* as a variant of the nominative plural *lucii*, from medieval latin *lucius*, a pike (resulting from confusion of third declension ending *-es* with second declension *-ii*). All manuscripts of the Variant read *luces*, but Hammer, 131, found the word to be "meaningless" and adopted the reading *lynces* (lynxes) found in some manuscripts of the Vulgate. Faral reads *lynces*, while recording the variants *luces, duces*, and *lupi vel linces*. Aaron Thompson, J. A. Giles, and Thorpe translate as "sea wolves."

117.1–4   This disordering of the cosmos was inspired by the portents of civil war described in Lucan, *Pharsalia* 1.639–72. See the discussion in Tatlock, 405–6.

BOOK 8

118.3   *to avenge the death of their brother*: The Vulgate refers to vengeance for the death of their father, while manuscripts of the Variant are split between vengeance for their brother *(DEST)* or their father *(acHR)*. Vortigern does not appear in the narrative until after Constantine is dead (chapter 74), but in 119 and 143 he is said to be responsible for the deaths of both Constantine and his son. It has been suggested there was some independent tradition that Vortigern had caused Constantine's murder. The commentary on the Prophecies attributed to

Alain of Lille (Frankfurt, 1603), p. 10, says that Vortigern treacherously arranged for him to be killed *(dolo fecit occidi)*.

118.4   *your descendants . . . boar of Cornwall*: Vortigern's son Pascent arranges the poisoning of Ambrosius in chapter 132, but he is dead before the poisoning of Uther by nameless Saxons in 142. The "boar of Cornwall" is Arthur, as in chapter 112 of the Prophecies. Since Pascent is killed by Uther in 134, the "descendants" whom Arthur will devour must refer in general to the progeny of the Saxons invited over from Germany by Vortigern and his son.

119.1   *the brothers landed*: All manuscripts of the Variant report both brothers' arrival. The Vulgate manuscripts diverge at this point, with groups Σ and Φ mentioning only Ambrosius, but Δ stating that he landed with his brother and ten thousand knights (Reeve, 161).

119.2   *Genoreu*: According to Nennius 42, Vortigern had built a city in the region called "Guunnessi" ("Gueneri" in the Vatican recension).

        Cloarcius: Here the narrative departs from Nennius, who had placed Vortigern's tower in the west of Wales, on the river Teifi. Cloarcius is usually identified with the hillfort at Little Doward Hill near Monmouth. Tatlock, 72; Curley, 1.

119.3   *burned to ashes . . . with him*: The statement that Vortigern was burned along with those who were with him appears in all versions of Nennius 47 except the Vatican recension.

120.1   *his reputation*: At this point the Vulgate adds several sentences describing Ambrosius's bravery, generosity, and skill in warfare, as well as Hengist's fear of meeting him in battle.

        sands of the sea: Genesis 41:49; 2 Samuel 17:11; 1 Kings 4:20; Isaiah 10:22; Hosea 1:10; Romans 9:27. This biblical simile, often used to describe the population of Israel, does not appear in the Vulgate version of Geoffrey's text.

121.1   In the Vulgate, which merely summarizes this speech, Hengist says the enemy should not be feared because they have only a few "Armorican Britons" and the "insular Britons" are worthless and easily defeated.

121.3　*a field that he judged to be suitable*: The field is called *Maisbeli* in the Vulgate, and it is Hengist rather than Ambrosius who chooses it as the appropriate spot for an ambush.

124.3　*Eosa, his kinsman*: The genealogy of the Kentish kings in Nennius 58 makes Ossa the son of Octha and grandson of Hengist. There is significant disagreement among the sources regarding the descendants of Hengist. See Tatlock, 146. According to Bede, *HE* 2.5, William of Malmesbury 1.8, and Henry of Huntingdon, *HA* 2.40, Oisc/Esc/Eisc/Aesc was the son of Hengist and the father of Octa. The *Anglo-Saxon Chronicle,* under 455 CE, makes Aesc the son of Hengist but does not mention Octa. Here Eosa is described as a "relative" of Octa, perhaps to avoid the conflict between the genealogy in Nennius and the other sources. In the Variant he goes to York with Octa, but in the Vulgate he proceeds separately to Dumbarton.

125.2　*Eldad, the bishop of Gloucester*: Saint Eldad or Aldate, thought by some to be fictitious, although there were churches dedicated to him in Gloucester and Oxford. See Tatlock, 242–43; Bartrum, *WCD* 264. Saint Aldate's church in Oxford appears in a charter issued by the empress Matilda in 1141. It was "devoted to worship of the holy bishop Aldate" according to the *Historia Ecclesie Abbendonensis,* edited by John Hudson (Oxford, 2002), vol. 2, pp. 254–55.

125.3　*As you have made . . . childless among women*: The quotation is from 1 Samuel 15:33.

126.4　*Gibeonites*: See Joshua 9:3–27.

128.1　*Tremorinus*: The name of Tremorinus may have been suggested by the eleventh-century bishop of Glasbury in Powys named Tryferyn *(Tremerin, Tramerin, Tremerig),* who appears (as bishop of St. David's) in Gerald of Wales, *Itinerarium Kambriae* 2.1, and under the year 1055 in both the *Anglo-Saxon Chronicle* and the *Chronicle* of John of Worcester. Bede, *HE* 3.24, lists Trumhere, "an Englishman, but educated and consecrated by the Irish," as the third bishop of Mercia; he may be the same as the bishop of Lichfield listed in William of Malmesbury, *Gesta pontificum* 4.172 (ca. 658–662).

128.3   *Galabes*: Tatlock, 74–75, identified the fountain of Galabes as the brook or valley of the Galles or Gall, a tributary of the Monnow located a few miles west of Monmouth.

128.5   *Mount Killaraus*: Almost certainly a reference to the Hill of Uisneach near Killare in Ireland, but the source of the author's knowledge of this ancient megalithic site is unknown. See Tatlock, 81–82.

130.5   *moving his lips as if in prayer*: Compare Judith 13:6 ("praying with the motion of her lips"). Here Merlin appears to move the stones by magic; in the Vulgate the Britons try ropes, cables, and ladders, before Merlin employs his own *machinationes* (an ambiguous term that could mean engines, machines, or some other form of device, contrivance, or artifice).

130.6   *Samson*: On the historical Samson, bishop of Dol, see Bartrum, *WCD* 657–61. There has been much debate whether this archbishop of York is the same person as the bishop of Dol mentioned in chapter 157. Vulgate 151 says that Samson was expelled from York by the Saxons and Arthur appointed Pyramus in his place. It is unlikely that there were two different Samsons who were contemporary with Arthur and Dubricius. See Tatlock, 243–44.

130.7   *Dubricius*: Saint Dubricius was the teacher of Samson and Teilo. His death is recorded in the *Annales Cambriae* under the year 612. He was bishop over the region of Ergyng, Glamorgan, and Gwent but is called bishop of Llandaff in twelfth-century sources such as the *Book of Llandaff* and the *Life of Saint Illtud*. See Tatlock, 245–46, and Bartrum, *WCD* 244–46.

131.1   *Pascent*: Pascent is mentioned only once in Nennius 48, where Ambrosius allows him to rule the provinces of Builth and Gwrtheyrnion after his father's death. Here he is an adversary of the Britons and is killed in chapter 134.

134.1   *so that the accuracy of the soothsayer was proved*: Compare Genesis 40:22 ("that the truth of the interpreter might be shown").

136.4   *necessity has no law*: A maxim commonly used in twelfth-century canon law.

136.5   *if God is with us*: Romans 8:31.

137.3   *like David with Bathsheba*: See 2 Samuel 11:2–3. The comparison
          with David and Bathsheba is not found in the Vulgate version;
          see Hammer, 10, and Wright, pp. xlviii and l.

137.6   *a certain castle*: In manuscripts *DES* Gorlois and his wife both
          take refuge in Tintagel, but in manuscripts *aHRT* and the Vul-
          gate he puts his wife in Tintagel and prepares a separate castle
          for himself and his men. Wace follows the version of events
          in *aHRT,* and the story would make little sense if Gorlois and
          his wife were in the same castle. See discussion in Wright,
          pp. xcviii–xcix. Geoffrey adds both an explanation and a name
          for the second castle: Dimilioc. A couplet with the name of the
          castle is inserted between lines 8636 and 8637 in three man-
          uscripts of Wace (Arnold, *Brut,* vol. 2, p. 454). Although the
          story is fabulous, the landscape was real and obviously known
          to the author. See Tatlock, 58–60.

138.2   *rumormongers*: The uncommon word *rumigerulos* (rumormon-
          gers) does not appear in the Vulgate, where the king merely
          laughs at the "rumors" rather than deriding those who spread
          them as liars.

139.3   *Leil of Lothian*: The name appears as Leil in all manuscripts of
          the Variant (except *a,* which follows the Vulgate at this point),
          but he is clearly meant to be the same person that other
          sources (notably the tenth-century *Life of Saint Kentigern*) refer
          to as Loth. All manuscripts of Wace appear to read "Loth" (Ar-
          nold, *Brut,* vol. 1, p. 465, line 8850). In the Vulgate, he is called
          "Loth of Lothian," but in the next sentence he is also said to be
          the Earl of Carlisle *(consul Leil)*. This additional sentence looks
          like a gloss inserted by Geoffrey to fix the apparent confusion
          over his name.

BOOK 9

143.1   *decided to attack the Saxons*: Here Arthur's principal motivation
          for attacking the Saxons is revenge; in the Vulgate it is the de-
          sire to use the spoils of battle to reward his followers with
          courtly largesse.

143.2   *River Duglas*: The only written source for Arthur's battles in Books 9 and 10 is the list contained in Nennius 56. The list was repeated by Henry of Huntingdon in *HA* 2.18, who says that "all of these places are now unknown." In Nennius the River Duglas is in the region of Lindsey, but here it is not far from York, and in chapters 161–62 it is somewhere near the border of Northumbria.

143.3   *Cheldric*: See the note on Cherdich above, 101.3.

143.4   *Cador*: Cador is called Duke of Cornwall throughout the Variant and in all but one reference in the Vulgate (see note to 157.1 below). In 178 he is named as the father of Constantine, who is said to be Arthur's relative *(cognato suo)* without further explanation. In later sources, including the *Book of Basingwerk,* Cador is the son of Gorlois, and thus Constantine is Arthur's nephew. See Bartrum, *WCD* 96–97; Bromwich, *TYP* 302–3.

        costume of a jester: The partially shaved head and beard are consistent with twelfth-century depictions of a fool or jester, such as the disguise of Tristan in the Oxford *Folie Tristan.* The word *semirasus* (half-shaved) is not in the Vulgate, but is translated by Wace (*Brut,* lines 9105–9).

144.2   *Hoel*: Arthur's nephew Hoel appears to be the author's invention, though his father, Budicius, may be based on the historical fifth-century Breton king Budic. See Bartrum, *WCD* 77–78. Hoel was, of course, a prominent name among the dukes and counts of Brittany in the tenth, eleventh, and twelfth centuries.

145.1   *the wood of Colidon*: Arthur's seventh battle according to Nennius 56 was fought in the forest of Calidon, and known as "Cat Coit Celidon" in Welsh. Faral, vol. 2, pp. 160–61, suggested that the author associated the name with "Cair Luyt Coit," last of the twenty-eight cities in Nennius; hence this fight with the Saxons begins near Lincoln but ends in the wood of Colidon. The "Cair Luyt Coit" of Nennius has been identified by modern scholars as the town of Wall, near Lichfield (Roman *Letocetum*), but our author clearly thought it was Lincoln, as did Henry of Huntingdon, *HA* 1.3.

146.2   *Bath*: Arthur's twelfth and final battle with the Saxons in Nennius 56 was at Mount Badon *(in monte Badonis)*. The location of this battle, famously described in Gildas 26 as the "siege of Mount Badon" *(obsessio Badonici montis)* has been the subject of much debate, but here it is clearly identified with the city of Bath.

147.2   *More than four hundred fell*: Most manuscripts of Nennius 56 report that 960 men fell in Arthur's first attack; the Variant puts the number at 400, and the Vulgate at 470. The Variant's statement that they died in Arthur's first assault *(primo impetu)* resembles the single assault *(uno impetu)* of Arthur in Nennius. However, the Vulgate's statement that Arthur killed them with Caliburn alone *(solo Caliburno gladio)* is closer to the observation in Nennius that they were killed by Arthur himself *(ipse solus)*.

148.2   *the ships' harbor*: The harbor is presumably Totnes (in Devon), where the Saxons had landed in chapter 146. The Variant does not say where Cador confronts the Saxons. In the Vulgate he follows them all the way across Britain to the Isle of Thanet before killing Cheldric and forcing the rest to surrender. Wace apparently understood the Variant to imply a less spectacular pursuit and has Cador intercept the Saxons at the River Teign (in Devon, northeast of Totnes) and kill Cheldric on a hill near Teignmouth.

149.1   *Moray*: Moray (Latin *Moravia,* British *Mureif*) was not a city but a region in northeast Scotland. By the twelfth century, however, it was the seat of a bishopric, centered on the cathedral at Elgin. See Tatlock, 11–12.

149.2   *Lake Lumonoy*: The first of the "Marvels of Britain" in Nennius 67 is the *fontem Lumenoi,* usually translated as Loch Lomond, though John Morris prefers Loch Leven. Either way, it is on the opposite side of Scotland from Moray. See Tatlock, 11.

150.1   *another lake*: This is the "Fount of Gorheli" *(Finnaun Guur Helic)* from Nennius 70, where it is in *regione Cinlipluc.* Morris translates the name of the region as "Cynllibiwg." The name was known in the eleventh to twelfth centuries as part of the re-

473

gion of Wales between the Severn and the Wye, so it was not "in the same province" as the first marvel.

150.2   *Liliguan*: Lake Lliwan *(Linn Liuan)* is described in Nennius 69. The phrase "swallowed up like a whirlpool," included here, is missing from all manuscripts of the Gildasian recension (see Reeve, p. lviii).

152.2   *in the time of Aurelius*: An anachronism, since Ambrosius Aurelianus was already dead before Arthur and his sister were born.

        beautiful and proper: One cannot help noticing the ambiguity in this tepid praise for Guinevere. Geoffrey omits the adverb *honeste* (decently) and says that she "surpassed all the women of the island in her beauty."

154.4   *Gawain*: Gawain was well established in Arthurian legend. See Bartrum, *WCD* 343–46; Bromwich, *TYP* 367–71. He was known to William of Malmesbury, *GRA* 3.287. The Vulgate says that Gawain was twelve years old and omits the statement that he had become a vigorous man and a daring soldier.

        Pope Sulpicius: The name of Sulpicius is taken from Pope Simplicius (468–483), who appears in chapter 49 of the *Liber Pontificalis* and is also mentioned as having been pope during the reign of Leo I in the chronicles of Hydatius, Marcelinus Comes, and Victor of Tunnuna (see Mommsen, vol. 2, pp. 35, 89, 188).

155.1   *Frollo*: It is tempting to connect the tribune Frollo with Tonantius Ferreolus, praetorian prefect of Gaul from 451 to 453, or to his son of the same name, who was a prominent Gallo-Roman senator during the reign of Leo I. Both are mentioned by Sidonius Apollinaris in the fifth century, and a descendant who was bishop of Limoges in the sixth was known to Gregory of Tours. However, I am aware of no source that would have brought Ferreolus to the attention of an author writing in the twelfth century.

        Emperor Leo: Leo I, eastern Roman emperor from 457 to 474, during which time there were a series of puppet emperors in the west, including Libius Severus, from 461 to 465, and Glycerius, from 473 to 474. Either of those may have provided the name for "Lucius Hiberius," who appears below in chapters 158–76.

155.8   *he gave Neustria . . . steward Kay*: Bedivere and Kay were prominent companions of Arthur in early legend. See Bartrum, *WCD* 40–41 and 102–6; Bromwich, *TYP* 286–87 and 308–11. The "steward" *(dapifer)* and "butler" *(pincerna)* were among the most important officials of the royal court during the eleventh and twelfth centuries. See J. H. Round, *The King's Serjeants and Officers of State* (London, 1911).

156.4   *Cadwallo Lauith*: Cadwallon Lawhir was a historical fifth-century king of Gwynedd in north Wales. He appears in several genealogies as the grandson of Cunedda and the father of Maelgwn Gwynedd. See Bartrum, *WCD* 94.

   Cador: After Cador, Duke of Cornwall, the Vulgate inserts the archbishops of London, York, and Caerleon, and states that Dubricius was both primate of Britain and papal legate.

156.5   *Anaraud of Salisbury*: Anaraud of Salisbury appears in all manuscripts of the Variant, as well as in Wace and Layamon. Most manuscripts of the Vulgate have him here, but Reeve, 211, drops his name altogether because it appears to conflict with the Vulgate's assignment of Salisbury to Galluc here and in chapter 172. E. K. Chambers discusses the textual variants and scribal confusion involving Anaraud and Galluc in "The Date of Geoffrey of Monmouth's History," *Review of English Studies* 1 (1925): 431–36. The Variant assigns Salisbury to Anaraud, and Silchester to Galluc. This arrangement is followed by Wace and Layamon.

   Iugein of Chester: Iugein's city is spelled *Legecestria* in manuscripts *aH* and *Leicestria* in *DEST*. There is extensive variation in spelling among the Vulgate manuscripts. The name is translated as "Leicester" by Thompson, Sebastian Evans, Thorpe, Faletra, and Wright. Nevertheless, it more likely refers to Chester here, as it certainly does in chapters 189 and 190. The name is rendered as *Kaer Lleon* in the Dingestow, Llanstephan, and Red Book of Hergest versions of the Welsh *Brut*. As Bede explains in *HE* 2.2, the City of Legions (Chester) was called *Legacaestir* by the English and *Carlegion* by the British.

   Chichester: The Latin *Kaicestria* is left as "Kaicester" in Thompson and Giles; it is rendered as "Caistor" by Evans and Thorpe, and translated as "Chester" by Faletra and Wright. However, it almost certainly refers to Chichester. Henry of Huntingdon, *HA* 2.2, refers to *Cair Ceim* (the thirtieth city listed in the Vatican version of Nennius 66a) as "Keir Cei, that is Chichester" *(Kair Cei, id est Cicestria)*. Unlike Caistor, a relatively insignificant town, Chichester was the seat of a bishopric in the twelfth century and the site of a castle built by the Earl of Shrewsbury and forfeited to the crown after 1104. Chichester was *Cicestre* in the Domesday Book; the usual twelfth-century spelling was *Cicestria.*

Galluc of Silchester: Galluc is assigned to Silchester in all manuscripts of the Variant, which is followed by Wace and Layamon. The Vulgate manuscripts substitute either Salisbury or Winchester. The Welsh *Bruts* have Salisbury or Shrewsbury.

heroes of great fame: In the middle of this sentence the Vulgate inserts a list of fourteen additional names drawn seemingly at random from the Old Welsh genealogies, most of them including the Welsh patronymic formula *map* . . . ("son of . . ."). For the sources of these names in the *Harleian Genealogies,* see Faral, vol. 2, p. 276.

157.1   *four kings*: The Vulgate identifies the four kings with golden swords as the kings of Albany, Cornwall, Demetia, and Venedotia. This is inconsistent with the list in chapter 156, where the second king (in both versions) is Urian of Moray. The explanation for this is that Vulgate 156 incorrectly listed Cador of Cornwall as a fifth king, rather than as a duke (which he is in Variant 156 and everywhere else in both versions). Wace, who was consulting both versions at this point, recognized the inconsistency and expanded the statement in chapter 157 to explain that Cador carried the fourth golden sword "as if he was royalty." See Arnold, *Brut,* vol. 2, p. 544, line 10380 (with variant readings "as if he was crowned king" or "of royal rank").

157.5   *The king's uncle David . . . in his place*: Having David follow Dubricius as archbishop of Caerleon again avoids involvement in the rival claims of Llandaff and St. David's for the primacy of Wales. See note to chapter 72.1 above. The idea that David was the uncle of Arthur seems to have been invented here. See Bartrum, *WCD* 219–23. Nevertheless, it was accepted by Gerald of Wales in his *Life of Saint David* 1.

Samson of Dol: Samson is here called "bishop" of Dol, while the Vulgate makes him "archbishop." The change may reflect Geoffrey's awareness of (and even support for) the longstanding efforts by the bishops of Dol to win independence from the archdiocese of Tours by claiming that Samson was an archbishop. See J. A. Everard, *Brittany and the Angevins: Province and Empire 1158–1203* (Cambridge, 2004), pp. 69–73.

Teilo: Teilo was bishop of Llandaff, but during the twelfth-century rivalry with St. David's, it was claimed that he succeeded Dubricius as archbishop there. Here again the author sidesteps that debate by referring to him as an "illustrious priest" at Llandaff who succeeds Samson as bishop of Dol. The twelfth-century life of Teilo in the *Book of Llandaff* says that he visited Samson at Dol, but not that he remained there as bishop. See Bartrum, *WCD* 693–95.

Magaunius . . . robe of Dumbarton: The bishops of Silchester, Winchester, and Dumbarton are fictional, but our author did not invent their names. See Tatlock, 247–48. Mauganius is derived from the Cornish saint Mawgan (see Bartrum, *WCD* 523–24); Eledemius from the Welsh saint Elidan (*WCD* 265). Duvianus recalls the missionary sent in response to the request from King Lucius in chapter 72.

163.1 Owing to reorganization of the text at this point, the Vulgate makes this section the beginning of Book 10.

163.2 *Xerses of the Myreans*: Xerses of the Myreans is called Serses king of the Itureans in Vulgate chapters 163 and 170. My translation assumes that the nonce-word *Mircorum* found in all Variant manuscripts is a mistake for *Myreorum* (a variant reading in Vulgate 170 reported by Griscom, *Historia Regum Britanniae*, 487, from the "Harlech" manuscript). Myra was a city in Lycia well known in the twelfth century as the home of Saint Nicholas and a stop on the pilgrimage route to Jerusalem; it is mentioned by Orderic Vitalis, *Historia ecclesiastica* 2.3 and 11.2. Ituria was a region in the Levant.

164a.1 The order of events in chapters 159 through 164 is significantly different in the Variant and Vulgate texts. Wright, pp. xxvi–xxvii and lvii–lix, provides an outline. In the Variant, the catalog of Roman forces appears first, in chapter 163, and the catalog of British forces comes later, in 162b. The Roman force consists of 180,000 armed soldiers (280,000 "besides the Romans" in manuscripts *DES*). The British forces appear to outnumber the Romans, with 272,000 soldiers, not including the additional infantry provided by Auguselus and from Britain itself. In the Vulgate, the catalogs are reversed and the numbers are significantly altered. Vulgate 162 explains that the 120,000 men from the islands are merely infantry *(pedites),* because the island kings do not have armed soldiers *(milites).* This reduces the British force to 152,000, plus infantry. The Roman force, on the other hand, is increased to a total of 400,160 (or 460,100, depending on the translation), outnumbering the Britons and increasing suspense over the outcome.

fourteenth day of June: There is a contradiction here. Whether the beginning of the Kalends of July is counted as July 1 or, more correctly, as the sixteenth day before that, the Roman forces leave for Britain several weeks before they were told to assemble in Rome. The Vulgate avoids this confusion: the date when they assemble in Rome is not specified, and in chapter 164 they depart for Britain at the beginning of the Kalends of August (properly July 16, though often translated as August 1).

BOOK 10

162b.2   See Tatlock, 91–95, for explanation of the Latin names used for the Gallic provinces listed here.

164b.2   In the Vulgate two different interpretations of the dream are offered: his men see the dragon as Arthur and the bear as some giant he will fight; Arthur sees the dragon as himself and the bear as the Roman emperor.

165.8   *Mount Aravius*: The story of the giant Ritho was associated with Mount Snowdon and greatly elaborated in later Welsh folklore. See Tatlock, 64–65, and Bartrum, *WCD* 634–35 for details.

478

165.9   *Helen's Tomb*: This story displays knowledge of the landscape around Mont Saint-Michel, either direct or secondhand. See Tatlock, 87–89. The name of the smaller mountain, *Tombelaine,* was long established, but it is uncertain whether the etymology was invented here or derived from a previously existing legend.

167.1   *ten thousand armed soldiers*: The Vulgate changes the number of Roman soldiers here to fifteen thousand.

167.5   *Hirelglas of Peritum*: Hirelglas of Peritum is unknown; he is different from Hirelglas the nephew of Bedivere. In the *Stanzas of the Graves,* the grave of Gawain is in "Peryddon," a name also used for several rivers in Wales, including the Dee.

        Mauricus of Cahors: Mauricus of Cahors may be associated with Cahors *(Cadurcum)* in southwest France. The Cotton Cleopatra *Brut* calls him "Meurig ap Cadwr" (Bartrum, *WCD* 523).

        the son of Hider: Since the first name is missing, one suspects a corruption here, and the name intended might have been that of *Hiderus filius Nu* from chapter 166. The legendary Welsh hero Edern ap Nudd is well attested in other sources; see Bartrum, *WCD* 252–53. At this point the Vulgate has the name *Er filius Hider,* who is otherwise unknown, and may have been invented to fix the lacuna in the Variant. His name appears as *Er le fiz Yder* in at least one manuscript of Wace, *Brut* line 12183, but in others only *le fiz Yder* is present, as in the Variant.

168.2   *Siesia*: Siesia is Val Suzon in Burgundy, northwest of Dijon, about midway between Langres and Autun. See William Matthews, "Where was Siesia-Sessoyne?," *Speculum* 49 (1974): 680–86, and Hans E. Keller, "Two Toponymical Problems in Geoffrey of Monmouth and Wace: Estrusia and Siesia," *Speculum* 49 (1974): 687–98. The location was previously identified by Antoine Le Roux de Lincy in his edition of Wace (Rouen, 1838), p. 357, and by William Hardy in his edition of Jehan de Waurin (London, 1864), p. 594. A few miles to the north was the Benedictine abbey of Saint-Seine, one of the richest and most powerful in Burgundy.

        Duke Hoel: In most manuscripts of the Vulgate it is Earl Morvid who is placed in command of this reserve. The choice of Hoel in the Variant is inconsistent with chapter 175 below, where Morvid leads the rear guard at the climax of the battle. Wace, *Brut* line 12319, follows the Vulgate and avoids the inconsistency by placing Morvid here, although one manuscript (see Arnold, *Brut,* vol. 2, p. 641) refers to him simply as *uns cuens* (a count) with no name. He is called Hoel in Vulgate manuscripts of the *tres filios* group.

168.3   *sevenfold division*: This is the only time the distributive number *septenas* (sevenfold) is used in either version. Previous translators have regarded it as equivalent to the cardinal number and rendered *catenas septenas* as "seven" parts, battalions, divisions, or bodies. Thorpe, *History of the Kings of Britain,* 247n2, assumes there is an error in the text, since it goes on to describe eight separate divisions. But there is no discrepancy: if you slice a loaf seven times, the result is eight pieces of bread.

   along with two counts: In the Vulgate, Hoel is placed in charge of the fourth division along with Gawain, and the two nameless counts disappear. Wace, *Brut* line 12367, follows the Vulgate here. The Vulgate's pairing of Hoel and Gawain at this point looks like a deliberate revision to explain why they later appear together in chapter 173.

169.1   *sign of things to come*: Compare Genesis 41:11, *somnium praesagum futurorum* (a dream forboding things to come).

173.1   *the Armorican Britons*: The Vulgate greatly expands this chapter, describing the valor of the Armorican troops and the death of their leader Chinmarcocus, Earl of Tréguier, along with two thousand of his troops and three Breton nobles: Richomarcus, Bloccovius, and Iagvivius of Bodloan.

174.1   *while life is with me*: Compare 2 Kings 4:16, *si vita comes fuerit* (while life remains).

176.2   *convent of hermits*: Probably a reference to the hermitage and monastery built to the east of the town in the fifth century by Saint Maximus of Chinon, a disciple of Saint Martin; see Gregory of Tours, *Gloria martyrorum* 22. It became the principal religious foundation in the city and a destination for pilgrimage in the twelfth century. The cell of the Breton hermit John of Chinon, spiritual advisor to Saint Radegund, was nearby. Gregory of Tours, *Gloria martyrorum* 23; Baudonivia, *Vita Radegundis* 4.

BOOK II

177.1   *Cheldric*: Not to be confused with the Cheldric killed by Cador in chapter 148. See note to 101.3.

177.3   *threw himself headlong*: Hammer compares the wording to Horace, *Satires* 1.2.41: *Hic se praecipitum tecto dedit* (referring to adulterers throwing themselves headlong from a roof to avoid punishment). The phrase does not appear in the Vulgate.

177.4   In the Vulgate, Guinevere goes to Caerleon earlier, as soon as she hears that Modred has fled to Winchester.

178.3   *five hundred and forty-second year after the incarnation*: Both versions give 542 CE as the date when Arthur went to Avalon, which is clearly at odds with the idea that Arthur fought with the Romans during the reign of Leo I (457–474 CE). The *Annales Cambriae* place the date of the Battle of Camlan at 537 or 539 CE.

179/180.1 *Saint Amphibalus*: In Gildas 28, Constantine kills the children who are hiding in the church "under the cloak of a holy abbot" (*sub sancte abbatis amphibalo*). Here the rare word *amphibalum* (the chasuble or sleeveless mantle worn over the alb and stole by a priest at Mass) is transformed into the name of the church's patron saint. The Vulgate carries this one step further, by assigning that name to the confessor of Saint Alban in chapter 77 above, thus giving birth to the imaginary saint whose cult was celebrated at St. Alban's from the twelfth century on.

179/180.2 After Daniel of Bangor, some manuscripts of the Vulgate (Reeve's group *Φ*) state that Theonus, bishop of Gloucester, was promoted to archbishop of London; the name is omitted in group *Δ*, and there is no mention of this bishop at all in manuscripts *UA* (of the *Σ* group). Bartrum, *WCD* 702, regards Theonus as fictitious, but he notes Phillimore's suggestion that the name may have been derived from Saint Tydiwg of Dixton (near Monmouth), who is called *Sanctus Tadeocus* in at least one twelfth-century document (*WCD* 717).

179/180.3 *Kinnoc*: Cynog, bishop of Llanbadarn and Mynyw, is listed as the second bishop at St. David's in Gerald of Wales, *Itinerarium Kambriae* 2.1, and his death is recorded in the *Annales Cambriae* under 606 CE.

in the third year he was killed by Conan: The reading of the Variant is also found in Reeve's Vulgate family Φ (which includes the *tres filios* group), as well as in Henry of Huntingdon's *Letter to Warinus*. Reeve's group Δ says that Constantine was struck down by the judgment of God in the fourth year of his reign; and group Σ says it was in his twentieth year.

181.1 *in the second year of his reign*: Again, the reading of the Variant is followed in Φ, the *tres filios* group, and the *Letter to Warinus*. The Δ group says that it was in the third year of his reign, and Σ says it was the thirtieth. All the Vulgate manuscripts add that Conan became king by attacking an unnamed uncle who should have reigned after Constantine, throwing him in prison, and killing his two sons.

183.1 *Malgo*: Malgo is the historical king Maelgwyn Gwynedd, who stands at the head of the royal line of Venedotia (north Wales), which Cadwallon describes in chapter 195 of the Vulgate. His negative qualities are derived from Gildas 33. He is also mentioned in Nennius 62, and his death is recorded under 547 CE in the *Annales Cambriae*.

184/186.1 *Caretius*: Caretius may recall the British king Cerdic of Elmet, mentioned in Bede, *HE* 4.23, and said in Nennius 63 to have been driven out of Elmet by Edwin. His death is recorded in the *Annales Cambriae* at 616 CE.

Godmund: The story of Gormund and Isembart was known from the eleventh- or twelfth-century chanson de geste of that name. But the name of the African king is spelled "Godmundus" here (and in most manuscripts of the Vulgate), "Ludowicus" is king of the Franks, and events are moved from ninth-

century France to sixth-century Britain and associated with
the Britons' loss of sovereignty. Sigebert of Gembloux mentions *Gothamundus rex in Africa* as a contemporary of *Ludowicus
rex . . . Francorum* immediately after the entry describing the
Britons' loss of sovereignty to the English (*Sigeberti Gemblac-
ensis Chronographia*, ed. Ludwig Bethmann, Monumenta Germaniae Historica, Scriptores, 6 [Hannover, 1844], p. 313 [at 491
CE]). Gunthamund was king of the Vandals from 484 to 496
CE; Clovis, called *Ludowicus* by Sigebert, was king of the
Franks from 481 to 511 CE.

184/186.3 *The bishops fled . . . part of Britain*: In the Vulgate this sentence is
reworded and moved to the end of chapter 186. Vulgate 185
contains a lengthy authorial aside in which Geoffrey (borrowing extensively from Gildas) upbraids the Britons for having
destroyed their own kingdom through civil discord.

186/187.3 *Ethelbert*: Ethelbert was king of Kent from about 560 to 616; he
received the mission of Saint Augustine in 597.

188.2 *according to each one's need*: Paraphrasing Acts 2:45 and 4:35 (they
divided their goods "according as every one had need").

188.3 The Variant follows Bede, *HE* 2.2, in having the Britons respond
collectively to Augustine's demands. In the Vulgate it is Dinoot
alone who answers.

189.1 *King Ethelfrith of the Northumbrians*: Ethelfrith was king of the
Bernicians from 592 to 616 and also of the Deirans from 604 to
616.

189.2 *Chester*: Chester is spelled *Legecestriam* in manuscripts *RS*, and
Legrecestram in *DE*. Further variations occur among manuscripts of the Vulgate, and translators have disagreed over the
meaning (Thompson and Giles leave it as "Legecester," Evans
and Wright have "Leicester," Thorpe and Faletra have "Chester"). Tatlock, 25–26, thought that Geoffrey used the word to
mean Leicester both here and in chapter 31, and that he was
ignorant about its location. This can hardly be true, since
Geoffrey (and the author of the Variant) was following Bede's
description of the battle in *HE* 2.2, where the location is iden-

tified as "the City of Legions, which is called *Legaecaistir* by the English and *Caerlegion* by the British." Henry of Huntington, *HA* 3.16, quotes Bede word for word. William of Malmesbury also knew the location, *GRA* 1.47, and he personally visited the ruins of Bangor Abbey (*Gesta pontificum* 4.185).

turned to flight: Here Brochmail fights the English and flees only after his army is lost. In Bede, *HE* 2.2, Brochmail and his men "turned their backs on those whom they should have defended, leaving them unarmed and helpless before the swords of their foes."

189.3   *like herds of sheep in their pens*: Compare Numbers 32:18; Deuteronomy 28:4; 2 Chronicles 14:15. The Vulgate omits this simile.

two thousand two hundred: The Vulgate follows Bede in putting the number slain at 1,200. All manuscripts of Wace, *Brut,* line 13921, agree with the Variant.

made martyrs of the faithful: The Vulgate says that the British martyrs "won their place in the kingdom of heaven." Both versions contradict Bede, who calls the British "impious" *(nefandae)* and "perfidious" *(perfidi)* and says that it was Augustine who was "taken up into the kingdom of heaven."

189.4   Blederic and Margadud are fictitious. Cadvan was king of Gwynedd; his father's death is recorded in the *Annales Cambriae* at 613 CE.

190.2   *Cadwallon*: Cadwallon was king of Gwynedd from about 625 until his death in battle, around 634. He invaded and conquered Northumbria, killing its king, Edwin, prior to his own death in battle against Oswald of Bernicia.

Edwin: Edwin was king of Deira and Bernicia (later Northumbria) from 616 until 633. Historically, he was not the son of Ethelfrith (king of Bernicia), but of Aelle (king of Deira). The Vulgate adds a detailed account of how Ethelfrith banished his first wife while she was pregnant. She went to live with Cadvan, where her son Edwin was born and raised together with Cadwallon. The two boys were then sent to King Salomon in Brittany for training in the art of war.

191/192.2 *Humber*: Tatlock, 22, assumes this to be the same river mentioned as the site of Arthur's battle with Colgrin in chapter 143.

194/195.1 *Quidalet*: Alet or Quidalet is the modern Saint-Servan near Saint Malo; see Tatlock, 98.

he needed to prevail: After the second sentence of this chapter, the Vulgate adds lengthy speeches by Salomon and Cadwallon, and Cadwallon explains how they are related by descent from the two sons of King Malgo, Ennianus and Run. He gives their genealogy as: (1) Ennianus > Belin > Iago > Cadvan > Cadwallon; and (2) Run > daughter (wife of Hoel II) > Alan > Hoel III > Salomon.

197.3 The Battle of Hatfield Chase ended in the defeat and death of Edwin and his son Osfrith. See Bede, *HE* 2.20.

198.1 *Cadwallon vented his fury . . . various deaths*: This language describing the savage character of Cadwalla is taken from Bede, *HE* 2.20.

Osric: For Osric of Deira, see Bede, *HE* 3.1. Bede also mentions Aedan, "king of the Irish living in Britain," in *HE* 1.34, but he died many years before the events related here.

199.1 *Oswald*: Oswald, king of Northumbria from 634 to 642, venerated as a martyr and one of the most important of all Anglo-Saxon saints. His miraculously uncorrupted arm was kept in a reliquary at Peterborough, where Archdeacon Walter was dispatched by Henry I during the three-year vacancy following the death of its abbot in 1125. The Variant states in chapter 200 that he became a martyr, but the Vulgate deletes that phrase.

199.2 *Let us all bend . . . our people*: Oswald's speech is taken directly from Bede, *HE* 3.2.

199.3 Oswald was killed by Penda at the Battle of Maserfield in 641 or 642 (the *Annales Cambriae* give the date as 644). Here his death is said to occur in an earlier battle, described by Bede, *HE* 3.1, as taking place at *Denisesburne* immediately following the Battle of Heavenfield. According to Bede, as well as the *Annales Cambriae* and other sources, it was Cadwallon who was killed by Oswald at that time. In the *Historia*, Cadwallon lives to old age and dies of an illness after a reign of forty-eight years. Faral, vol. 2, pp. 331–37, shows that these modifications of key historical events described by Bede were systematic and deliberate.

200.1   *gave him many gifts*: According to Bede, *HE* 3.24, Oswiu was forced to give gifts and treasures to buy peace with Penda (not Oswald, who was dead at this point). Oswiu's gifts to Penda are described separately below.

Cadwallon ruled as high king over all of Britain: This is a significant rewriting of history. According to Bede, *HE* 3.6, it was Oswald who obtained control over all the kingdoms and peoples of Britain (British, Pictish, Irish, and English). The word *imperium* is used by Bede to describe this overlordship in *HE* 2.5, and Oswald is listed as the sixth to hold it. The exact phrase used in the Variant does not appear in Bede, but it may reflect (and intentionally contradict) the statement in Adomnan's *Life of Columba* that after the Battle of Heavenfield Oswald became "high king of all Britain" *(totius Britanniae imperator)*. In chapter 204 below, it is Athelstan who is said to be the first among the English to wear the crown.

Alhfrith and Oethelwald: Alhfrith was son of Oswiu by his first marriage (Bede, *HE* 3.14). Oethelwald, son of Oswald and king of Deira from 651 to 655, was allied with Penda at the Battle of Winwaed (Bede, *HE* 3.24).

200.2   *in the city of Bath*: The Vulgate locates this event in London. All manuscripts of the Variant except *R* place it in Bath. The location is not specified in Wace, although an additional couplet found in three manuscripts (*Brut,* lines 14537–38) puts it in London.

200.6   *gifts of gold and silver*: The Vulgate describes Oswiu's gifts in more detail, borrowing additional language from Bede, *HE* 3.24.

200.8   *Wulfred*: According to Bede, *HE* 3.24, Oswiu gave the kingdom of Mercia to Penda's son Peada, but after Peada was murdered, the Mercian aldermen Immin, Eafa, and Eadberht rebelled against Oswiu and raised Penda's younger son Wulfhere as king. Here it is by grant of Cadwallon that Wulfhere (called "Wulfred" in both versions) becomes king.

202.1   *Cadwallader*: Cadwallader, king of Gwynedd, died in the plague of 664 (Nennius 64) or 682 *(Annales Cambriae)*. He is paired with Conan as a messianic figure in Welsh historical tradition (see *Armes Prydain* 163–64), as reflected here in chapter 115 and in Geoffrey's *Life of Merlin,* lines 967–68. For background see Bartrum, *WCD* 80–81; Bromwich, *TYP* 298–99; and Roberts, "Geoffrey of Monmouth and the Welsh Historical Tradition," 29–40. The Vulgate inserts a gloss at this point, stating that Bede "called him the youth *Chedwalla.*" This alludes to *HE* 4.15, where Bede says the Saxon king Caedwalla of Wessex was "a most vigorous youth from the royal family of the *Gewissae.*" Faral, vol. 2, p. 336, thought that Geoffrey misread Bede as referring to a Caedwalla "the Younger." Tatlock, 251–53, assumed that Geoffrey had somehow confused this Caedwalla with Bede's earlier reference to Caedwallon of Gwynedd in *HE* 3.1. But there was no confusion; both Geoffrey and the author of the Variant believed that it was Bede who had made the mistake by transforming Cadwallader into a Saxon king.

203.1   The description of internal discord, famine, and plague borrows language from chapters 17 and 22 of Gildas, which described conditions in the fifth rather than the seventh century.

203.3   The lengthy speech or prayer by Cadwallader contains a patchwork of biblical phrases and echoes (identified by Hammer, 205n552 [text of *C*] and 261n370 [text of *DE*] and supplemented by Wright, p. xxxii n. 41). The Vulgate shortens this speech significantly and inserts a separate, collective lament by all of the exiles that is taken directly from chapter 25 of Gildas.

204.4   *Athelstan*: Athelstan was king of Wessex from 924 to 927 and known as king of the English from 927 to 939. The Variant is here projecting into the future, not *(pace* Leckie and Wright) erroneously making Athelstan a contemporary of Cadwallader. Bede, *HE* 2.5, had famously listed seven English kings who held the *imperium* before Athelstan; the *Anglo-Saxon Chronicle* added an eighth (Egbert), and Henry of Huntingdon, *HA* 2.13, added a ninth (Alfred) and a tenth (Edgar). A few historians who did not incorporate Bede's list regarded Alfred as the first to obtain dominion over all the provinces of England (Aethelweard, *Chronicon* 4.3, and Orderic Vitalis, *Historia ecclesiastica* 4.17), but no one before this had assigned that role to a king so late in time as Athelstan. The twelfth-century marginalia to the Winchester Chronicle stating that he was first to rule the whole kingdom of England may actually have been influenced by Geoffrey of Monmouth. See Cyril Hart, "The Early Section of the Worcester Chronicle," *Journal of Medieval History* 9 (1983): 251–315, at 308.

205.1   *a great length of time had passed*: In chapter 204 a period of eleven years passed before the Saxons returned to Britain. It is followed here by a "a great length of time" *(magnum temporis spatium)* in which they strengthen and increase before Cadwallader makes his pilgrimage to Rome. The Vulgate describes it as a "small amount of time" *(aliquantulum temporis)*.

205.2   *Merlin had predicted*: Most manuscripts of the Vulgate contain the incongruous statement that Merlin made his prophecy "to Arthur," even though Merlin disappears from the narrative long before Arthur's birth. The statement does not appear in the *tres filios* group. The reading *antea* (previously) in Variant manuscript *a* represents a later revision of this passage by the author of the Second Variant Version (see British Library MS Royal 4.C.xi, fol. 248v).

206.1   *the verses of the Sibyl*: The prophecy of the fourth-century Tiburtine Sibyl was one of medieval Europe's most widely disseminated Latin eschatological prophecies. See Anke Holdenried, *The Sibyl and Her Scribes: Manuscripts and Interpretation of the Latin* Sibylla Tiburtina *c. 1050–1500* (Aldershot, 2006). An Anglo-Norman verse translation was composed by Phillipe de Thaon for Henry I's second wife, Adeliza of Louvain.

206.2   *his son Ivor or his nephew*: Unlike the Vulgate, which refers here and in 207 to both a son named Ivor and a nephew named Ini, Variant manuscripts *DES* mention only Ivor. Manuscripts *aR* are corrupt at this point and probably influenced by the Vulgate. Wright emends the text to read *filium . . . suum Ivor ac Yni nepotem suum* (his son Ivor and his nephew Ini), in conformity with the Vulgate. In both versions the syntax is ambiguous: since the subject of the sentence is Alan, the reflexive possessive adjective *suum* could make Ivor (and Ini) his son (and nephew) rather than Cadwallader's. The two are treated as the son and nephew of Alan in the *Brenhinedd y Saesson* and some versions of the *Brut y Brenhinedd.* Other versions of the *Brut* make them the son and nephew of Cadwallader. The *Annales Cambriae* (*C*-text) records the death of "Ivor, son of Cadwallader" under the year 734. See Bartrum, *WCD* 437.

207.1   *forty-eight years*: All manuscripts of the Variant agree that Ivor fought the Saxons for forty-eight years. Manuscripts of the Vulgate have sixty-nine, forty-eight, seventy-one, sixty-four, or sixty-eight years.

207.2   *having degenerated from the British tongue*: The Vulgate says that the Welsh have degenerated from the "nobility" of the Britons. The Variant says that they have degenerated only in terms of their language. In his *Description of Wales* 1.7, Gerald of Wales observed that the language used in Cornwall and Brittany was closer than Welsh to the ancient speech of the Britons.

Bibliography

Editions and Translations

Faral, Edmond, ed. *La légende arthurienne, études et documents: Des origines à Geoffroy de Monmouth.* Paris, 1929.

Griscom, Acton, ed. *The Historia Regum Britanniae of Geoffrey of Monmouth.* New York, 1929.

Hammer, Jacob, ed. *Geoffrey of Monmouth, Historia Regum Britanniae: A Variant Version Edited from Manuscripts.* Cambridge, Mass., 1951.

Reeve, Michael, ed., and Neil Wright, trans. *The History of the Kings of Britain: An Edition and Translation of De Gestis Britonum [Historia Regum Britanniae].* Woodbridge, 2007.

Thorpe, Lewis, trans. *The History of the Kings of Britain.* Harmondsworth, 1966.

Wright, Neil, ed. *The Historia Regum Britannie of Geoffrey of Monmouth I: Bern, Burgerbibliothek MS. 568.* Cambridge, 1984.

———. *The Historia Regum Britannie of Geoffrey of Monmouth II: The First Variant Version: A Critical Edition.* Cambridge, 1988.

Secondary Sources

Arnold, Ivor, ed. *Le Roman de Brut de Wace.* Paris, 1938–1940.

Brooke, Christopher. "The Archbishops of St David's, Llandaff and Caerleon-on-Usk." In *Studies in the Early British Church,* edited by N. K. Chadwick et al., 201–42. Cambridge, 1958.

———. "Geoffrey of Monmouth as a Historian." In *Church and Government in the Middle Ages: Essays Presented to C. R. Cheney on His 70th Birthday,* edited by C. Brooke et al., 77–92. Cambridge, 1976.

Caldwell, Robert A. "Geoffrey of Monmouth, Prince of Liars." *North Dakota Quarterly* (Winter–Spring 1963): 46–51.

——. "The Order of the Variant and Vulgate Versions of the *Historia Regum Britanniae*." *Proceedings of the Linguistic Circle of Manitoba and North Dakota* 1, no. 2 (November 1959): 15–16.

——. "The Use of Sources in the *Variant* and Vulgate Versions of the *Historia Regum Britanniae* and the Question of the Order of the Versions." *Bulletin Bibliographique de la Société Internationale Arthurienne* 9 (1957): 123–24.

——. "Wace's *Roman de Brut* and the Variant Version of Geoffrey of Monmouth's *Historia Regum Britanniae*." *Speculum* 31 (1956): 675–82.

Crick, Julia C. *The Historia Regum Britannie of Geoffrey of Monmouth III: A Summary Catalogue of the Manuscripts*. Cambridge, 1989.

——. *The Historia Regum Britannie of Geoffrey of Monmouth IV: Dissemination and Reception in the Later Middle Ages*. Cambridge, 1991.

Curley, Michael J. *Geoffrey of Monmouth*. New York, 1994.

Davies, Rees. *The Matter of Britain and the Matter of England*. Oxford, 1996.

——. "The Peoples of Britain and Ireland, 1100–1400: IV Language and Historical Mythology." *Transactions of the Royal Historical Society* 7 (1997): 1–24

Fletcher, Robert Huntington. *The Arthurian Material in the Chronicles, Especially Those of Great Britain and France*. Harvard Studies and Notes in Language and Literature 10. Boston, 1906.

Flint, Valerie J. "The *Historia Regum Britanniae* of Geoffrey of Monmouth: A Parody and Its Purpose. A Suggestion." *Speculum* 54 (1979): 447–68.

Gallais, Pierre. "La *Variant Version* de l'*Historia Regum Britanniae* et le *Brut* de Wace." *Romania* 87 (1966): 1–32.

Gillingham, John. "The Context and Purposes of Geoffrey of Monmouth's History of the Kings of Britain." *Anglo-Norman Studies* 13 (1990): 99–118.

Hammer, Jacob. "Geoffrey of Monmouth's Use of the Bible in the *Historia Regum Britanniae*." *Bulletin of the John Rylands Library* 30 (1946/47): 293–311.

——. "Remarks on the Sources and Textual History of Geoffrey of Monmouth's *Historia Regum Britanniae* with an Excursus on the *Chronica Polonorum* of Wincenty Kadłubek (Magister Vincentius)." *Quarterly Bulletin of the Polish Institute of Arts and Sciences in America* 3 (1944): 501–64.

Houck, Margaret. *Sources of the Roman de Brut of Wace*. Berkeley, 1941.

Keeler, Laura. *Geoffrey of Monmouth and the Late Latin Chroniclers, 1300–1500*. University of California Publications in English 17. Berkeley, 1946.

Keller, Hans-Erich. "Wace et Geoffrey de Monmouth: Problème de la chronologie des sources." *Romania* 98 (1977): 1–14.

Leckie, R. William, Jr. *The Passage of Dominion: Geoffrey of Monmouth and the Periodization of Insular History in the Twelfth Century*. Toronto, 1981.

Parry, John J. "A Variant Version of Geoffrey of Monmouth's *Historia*." In *A Miscellany of Studies in Romance Languages and Literatures Presented to Leon E. Kastner*, edited by M. Williams and J. de Rothschild, 364–69. Cambridge, 1932.

Parry, John J., and Robert A. Caldwell. "Geoffrey of Monmouth." In *Arthurian Literature in the Middle Ages: A Collaborative History*, edited by R. S. Loomis, 72–93. Oxford, 1959.

Reeve, Michael D. "The Transmission of the *Historia Regum Britanniae*." *Journal of Medieval Latin* 1 (1991): 73–117.

Roberts, Brynley F. "Geoffrey of Monmouth and the Welsh Historical Tradition." *Nottingham Medieval Studies* 20 (1976): 29–40.

Short, Ian. "Gaimar's Epilogue and Geoffrey of Monmouth's *Liber vetustissimus*." *Speculum* 69 (1994): 323–43.

———, ed. and trans. *Geffrei Gaimar: Estoire des Engleis / History of the English*. Oxford, 2009.

Weiss, Judith, trans. *Wace's Roman de Brut: A History of the British*. Exeter, 2002.

Wright, Neil. "Geoffrey of Monmouth and Bede." *Arthurian Literature* 6 (1986): 27–59.

———. "Geoffrey of Monmouth and Gildas." *Arthurian Literature* 2 (1982): 1–40.

Index

References are to Faral/Wright chapter divisions.